Final OFFER

DREAMLAND BILLIONAIRES

LAUREN ASHER

Published by Bloom Books, an imprint of Sourcebooks
P.O. Box 4410, Naperville, Illinois 60567-4410
(630) 961-3900
sourcebooks.com

Cataloging-in-Publication Data is on file with the Library of Congress.

Printed and bound in the United States of America.
PAH 12

Playlist

in my head – Ariana Grande ♥

Hate Myself – NF ♥

Forever Winter (Taylor's Version) – Taylor Swift ♥

Bad Habits (Acoustic Version) – Ed Sheeran ♥

justified – Kacey Musgraves ♥

If I Ever Feel Better – Phoenix ♥

Unmiss You – Clara Mae ♥

Broken (Acoustic) – Jonah Kagen ♥

Wishful Thinking – Gracie Abrams ♥

Brown Eyes Baby – Keith Urban ♥

favorite crime – Olivia Rodrigo ♥

Clarity – Vance Joy ♥

Break My Heart Again – Danielle Bradbery ♥

This Time Is Right – CVBZ & American Authors ♥

Labyrinth – Taylor Swift ♥

One Life – James Bay ♥

You Let Me Down – Alessia Cara ♥

No Se Va – Morat ♥

Goodbye – Mimi Webb ♥

Time – NF ♥

When We Were Young – Adele ♥

I Won't Give Up – Jason Mraz ♥

ADMV – Maluma ♥

To everyone who has been underestimated.
I hope you prove everyone wrong, including yourself.

CHAPTER ONE
Alana

I f I had known I was going to die tonight, I would have worn sexier underwear. Or at the very least, I would have dressed in something far nicer than mismatched pajamas riddled with holes and bleach stains.

My mother is probably lecturing me from heaven right now, wondering where she went wrong with raising me.

Perdona me, Mami. Debería haberle escuchado.

I do a quick sign of the cross before I aim my handgun at the shadow standing in the open doorway. My heart pounds furiously in my chest, the duration between beats growing smaller by the second. "I'm giving you until the count of five to get out of my house before I shoot. One…two…"

"Fuck." Something heavy smacks against the wall before a switch flips, flooding the entryway of the house with light.

My hold on the gun tightens as I come face-to-face with the one person I never thought I'd see again. Our gazes collide. His blue eyes trace the shape of my face like an invisible caress, sending a rush of warmth through my body.

Despite the blaring alarm in my head warning me to run far away from him, I can't resist taking in all six-foot-four-inches of Callahan Kane. Everything about him feels familiar, all the way down to the ache in my chest that never left, even after he did.

His easygoing smile.

His unruly dirty blond hair, always unkept and begging to be tamed.

His blue eyes the color of the clearest sky, sparkling like the surface of the lake under the noon sun.

It's been over six years since I last saw him. Six long years that have hardened me enough to spot his allure for exactly what it is.

A trap.

If I look carefully, I can spot the cracks in his façade that he tries to hide behind his beauty and charm. He was always careful about letting people look too closely at the broken person beneath his mask. It was what captured my attention in the first place and what resulted in my downfall.

I was twenty-three when he broke my heart, yet the pain feels like it happened just yesterday. Rather than ignore it, I lean into the hurt and use it to fuel my rage.

"What the hell are you doing here?" I snap.

His smile falters before sliding back into place. "Excited to see me?"

I motion him forward with my free hand. "Thrilled. Why don't you come a little closer so I can get a better shot? I'd hate to miss an important organ."

His eyes flicker from my face to the gun in my hand. "Do you even know how to shoot that thing?"

My eyes narrow. "Want to find out?"

"Where did you get that?"

"A gift from my mom." My chest swells.

His brows raise toward his hairline. "Señora Castillo bought you a gun? Why?"

I lower the gun and flip the safety. "She always said a woman should be two things—armed and dangerous."

His mouth drops open. "I thought she was joking about having a gun to keep us in line."

"Not everyone grew up in a safe little Chicago suburb with a rotation of nannies and a full waitstaff."

"The same can be said about those who grew up in a happy little summer vacation town where the local cop can be bought with booze and a crisp Benjamin."

I scowl. "For your information, Sheriff Hank officially retired last year."

"A pity for delinquent teens everywhere." His bright grin widens.

Butterflies take flight in my belly. With the way my stomach dips and dives, it feels like thousands of them awoke after spending the last six years trapped in their cocoons.

He broke your heart. Start acting like it.

The muscles in my shoulders tense. "Do you plan on explaining what you're doing breaking into my house, or are we just going to stand around here all night?"

"Your house?" His forehead creases. "I think you're mistaken. My grandfather might have let your family stay here because your mother looks after the property, but you don't own it."

My mom didn't *just* look after the Kane house, but she loved it like her own ever since she was hired by Brady Kane to manage the property and help watch after his grandchildren.

Yet he left you *the property, not her.*

My chest throbs. "According to your grandfather's deed of the house, I do."

His body stiffens. "What do you mean?"

"That's between me and him."

"Seeing as I can't exactly go ask him to explain since he's six feet under and all, I'm going to need you to elaborate."

The pain above my heart intensifies. "He said this is my property, and I have a right to shoot anyone who questions otherwise."

He crosses his arms against his chest, drawing my eyes toward the muscles straining beneath his shirt. "Now I know you're lying. My grandfather always hated guns."

"Then how do you explain his little collection in the attic?"

He rubs his chin. "What collection?"

My head tilts. "Maybe you didn't know your grandfather as well as you think you did."

"Oh, and you did?" His chuckle comes off condescending.

I raise my chin. "He spent every single summer here until his accident, so yeah, I think I might know him better than the person who couldn't even bother to call for his birthday."

His eyes dart away. "He and I weren't exactly on speaking terms before his coma."

"I wonder why." Sarcasm seeps into my voice.

He rubs the back of his neck. "I made a lot of mistakes the last time I was here."

"Like getting together with me?"

The muscle in his jaw flexes. "I shouldn't have pursued you the way I did."

My chest might feel as if Cal plunged a serrated knife through it, but my face remains devoid of emotion—a skill perfected over the years.

"No, you really shouldn't have." My fingers tighten around the handle of the gun.

"I regret ruining our friendship."

The invisible knife twists, sinking deeper into my flesh. "Dating didn't ruin our friendship. Your addictions did."

Painkillers. Alcohol. *Sex*. Cal used all of them to escape the demons in his head, and I was too stupidly in love to see otherwise.

You can't blame yourself when he was a master at hiding it.

Yet I still struggle with believing the words I tell myself. My throat tightens from years' worth of repressed emotions, making swallowing difficult.

His jaw clenches, and his sharp bone structure stands out even more. "Believe it or not, I didn't drive all the way out here to fight with you about our past."

"Then why exactly did you come here?" Out of the hundred questions I want to ask him, that feels like the safest one.

"I came to check out the house."

"After six years? Why?"

"Because I plan on selling it."

I blink twice. "No. Absolutely not happening."

"Lana—" His use of the old nickname has my dead heart sparking with recognition.

No wonder he thought you were so easy last time. All it takes is one silly nickname for you to let your guard down.

"Don't call me that." My lips pull back.

"*Alana,*" he corrects himself with a small frown. "I don't know what my grandpa told you, but you must have misunderstood him."

"Right. Of course, you assume *I* must have misunderstood him."

His eyes narrow. "Now you're just being difficult."

"As opposed to what? Naïve and stupid like the last time?"

He ignores my outburst and carries on. "We can clear this up easily. Where's the deed?"

I pause and consider the cons of giving in to his request.

The sooner you show him the deed, the sooner he'll leave.

"I'll go get it." I move toward the stairs before throwing him a look over my shoulder. "Don't leave that spot."

"And risk giving you a reason to shoot me? I'm good."

My reply hangs on the tip of my tongue, but I bite down on it. That's the thing about Cal. He can make anyone forget that they're angry with him solely by cracking a joke and flashing a smile. It is his greatest superpower and my personal kryptonite.

You're more prepared now.

Or at least I *hope* I am.

I run upstairs and put my handgun away in the safe before searching my documents for the deed. It only takes me a minute to find it stuck between a few other important legal papers.

Cal checks my hands as I walk down the stairs. "No firearm this time?"

I shrug. "I know five different ways to kill a man with my bare hands, so it's not like I really need it."

His golden skin turns pale. "Please tell me you're joking."

I wish I was. My mom sent me to Colombia to visit my uncle one summer, and he had no idea how to entertain me other than to have me work at his farm and teach me mixed martial arts. I came back a month later with a black belt in kicking people's asses and enough survival skills to compete on one of those outdoor reality shows.

I place the deed on the entry table and point at Brady's signature. "There. Just like I said."

Cal stands beside me while he checks out the deed. He is careful to keep his distance as he reads, but when he shifts his weight, our arms accidentally brush. A current of energy rolls through my body. He's quick to tuck his arms behind his back, although the lingering effect of his touch remains. It's been six years, yet my body reacts as if he only left yesterday.

My frown deepens.

Cal's head shakes after he reads the entire page. "I'm sorry, but whatever deed he gave you is outdated." He points at the date written beside Brady's signature. "This was signed before his updated will."

"What will?"

"The one he rewrote before his accident."

My throat feels as if Cal wrapped his hands around it and squeezed.

No. That's not possible. "I'm calling his lawyer right now so we can clear this all up." I move toward the stairs, desperate to go upstairs and grab my phone.

Cal checks his fancy watch. "It's almost midnight. I doubt Leo would answer a call at this time."

I curse underneath my breath.

He tucks his hands into his pockets. "I'll contact him in the morning so we can sort this out before the realtor stops by."

"What realtor?"

"The one I hired to help me sell the house."

"Exactly what part of 'I'm not selling my house' are you not understanding?"

"The fact that you're referring to the house as yours to begin with."

My fingers curl into themselves, forming two tight fists to prevent myself from wrapping them around his thick neck.

His eyes drop to my clenched hands before returning to my face. "I think until we get a valid explanation from the lawyer, we should table this. It's late and we're getting nowhere." The front door creaks as he opens it.

"Wait." I hold out my hand. "Give me your key."

He ignores me as he drags his luggage inside. "I'm not going anywhere."

"Well, you're sure as hell not staying here," I sputter.

"Where do you expect me to go?"

"The motel off Main Street probably has a vacant room, plus they have Wi-Fi and colored TV now."

His lips part. "You can't be serious. They caught a serial killer there once."

My eyes roll. "He didn't actually commit any murders on the property."

"Oh, that makes it all better then."

"Mommy, who's that?" Camila calls from the top of the stairs. Her wide blue eyes check Cal out before her gaze swings back to mine.

I wave her off without thinking anything of it. "Nobody important. Go back to bed, please."

Cal's wide eyes shift from Cami to me. "Who the fuck is that, and why is she calling you *Mommy*?"

"Don't curse in front of my kid." My whisper comes out more like a hiss.

"Kid? How old is she?" Cal trips over his feet in an attempt to get away from me, although he is quick to regain his balance.

"Five!" Cami holds up her hand like she is waiting for someone to high-five her.

All the color drains from his face as he reaches for the wall. "Five. That's— She's— We—"

"It's not—" My response is cut off as his eyes roll to the back of his head.

His legs give out from underneath him, and his body falls forward.

"Shit!" I reach for him.

Our limbs tangle as we both go down. My breath is knocked out of me as I slam into the worn hardwood floor. Cal's head smashes against my stomach, which hurts more than expected but softens his fall. I'm not able to catch his head in time before it rolls off my lap and smacks against the floor. Cal doesn't wince as he lies on the floor, completely unconscious.

"Fuck. That's going to hurt." I roll his limp body back toward me before lifting his head onto my lap.

"Oooh. Mommy's got to put money in the swear jar."

I have a feeling a swear jar is the least of my worries now that Callahan Kane stormed back into my life with a deadly smile and a big problem.

CHAPTER TWO

Cal

I blink up at the ceiling and wait for the blurry chandelier to come into focus. It takes a minute for my vision to clear, although my brain remains a fuzzy mess.

Why am I on the floor?

"Oh, thank God you're awake. Are you okay?" Lana leans forward. Her dark waves brush against my face, tickling my skin. She smells like snickerdoodle cookies, reminding me of late nights staying up past curfew together, eating raw cookie dough while hanging out on the dock. My attempt to hold back from taking another deep breath fails, and I'm hit with a second inhale of her cinnamon scent.

I can't remember the last time I dreamed of Lana. Months? *Years?* This one is more vivid than my others, nailing the smallest details like the tiny birthmark on her neck in the shape of a heart and the scar above her cupid's bow.

I reach out to brush the faint white mark above her lips, making the tips of my fingers tingle. The world ceases to exist around me as her gaze crashes into mine.

God. Those eyes.

Her brown eyes remind me of the soil right after it rains—with them being so dark, they look black in certain kinds of light. It's an underrated color that rivals all others, although Lana always used to disagree.

My thumb accidentally grazes her bottom lip, drawing a sharp breath from her.

"What are you doing?" She pulls away.

I wince at the sharp pain drilling a hole through the back of my skull.

You're not dreaming, dumbass.

"Sorry about that. I didn't mean to make it hurt worse." She lifts my head off her lap. "How many fingers am I holding up?"

"Three," I grunt.

"What day is it?"

"May third."

"Where are we right now?" Her nails graze my scalp, sending sparks shooting down my spine.

"Hell," I hiss.

"Did that hurt?" She repeats the same move. My skin burns from her touch, and heat spreads throughout my veins like wildfire.

"Stop. I'm fine." I pull away and slide across the floor until my back hits the wall opposite her. Despite the distance I gain, the spicy cinnamon smell of her bodywash sticks to my clothes.

It's the same addictive one she has been using for years.

I take another deep inhale because clearly I must enjoy torturing myself.

God. You're pathetic. I smack my head against the wall, and it throbs with retaliation.

"Here, mister. For your boo-boo."

Oh, shit.

Alana has a daughter. A five-year-old daughter with dirty blond hair and big blue eyes eerily like mine. With me sitting down, we're nearly the same height, although she has a couple of extra inches on me from this angle.

Alana's child—possibly *my* child—stares down at me with round eyes and pajamas that are buttoned incorrectly. Her hair color borders on light brown, with most of the wavy strands falling out of her poorly constructed ponytail.

Is she mine?

God, I hope not.

The thought is shitty but true. I'm not ready to be a father yet. Hell, I'm not sure if I'll ever be ready. Until this point, I was satisfied with becoming the cool uncle who never really got his life together in time to have any kids. How could I when I'm only able to do the bare minimum for myself?

The kid shakes an ice pack in front of my face while she bounces on the tips of her toes. I reach out mindlessly and grab it from her.

"Are you okay?"

I wince at the sound of the child's voice. It reminds me of Lana's, right down to the slight rasp she has. Another dizzy spell hits me.

Lana rises and kisses the top of her daughter's head. "Thank you, baby. That's sweet of you to help him."

"Do we need a doctor?"

"No. He just needs to get some rest."

"And a strong drink," I grumble.

Lana turns toward her daughter. "See? He's good enough to make bad decisions again. All is well in the world."

Her nose twitches. "That don't make sense."

Lana sighs. "I'll explain in the morning, mi amor."

"But—"

Lana points toward the stairs. "Vete a dormir ahora mismo."

God. She looks and sounds just like her mother.

Maybe because she *is* a mother.

My body goes numb.

Are you having a heart attack?

From the way my left arm tingles and my heart feels like it might launch itself out of my chest, I wouldn't rule it out.

The kid points at me with a chubby finger. "He don't look so good."

"He'll be fine. He's just got a headache."

"Maybe your kiss will make it all better like my boo-boos."

"No," Lana and I both say at the same time.

"Okay. No kisses." The child crosses her arms with a pout.

Lana's eyes dip toward my mouth. Her tongue darts out to trace her bottom lip, turning the tips of my ears pink.

You're hopeless. Completely and utterly hopeless.

"Will you read me a story?" The kid interrupts us, her voice having the same effect as an ice bucket on my mood.

Could she really be mine? Would Lana hide a kid from me for years solely because she hates me?

The room spins around me. I shut my eyes to avoid looking at my mini-me and Alana.

"*Camila*," Lana warns.

"You still both owe the swear jar," her daughter reminds her.

I can picture Lana rolling her eyes as she says, "Remind me in the morning."

"Okay!" The sound of feet slapping against the wood stairs echoes off the tall ceilings.

Lana doesn't speak until a door clicks closed in the distance. "She's gone now, so you can stop pretending to be asleep."

I stare up at the chandelier. "Is she—" No matter how hard I try, I can't finish the sentence. Lana never seemed like the type to hide a secret like this, but people do crazy things to protect the ones they love, especially from those that will hurt them.

Maybe that's why Grandpa gave Lana the deed to the house. He could have thought I was doing a shitty job supporting my kid, so he took charge.

Assuming he left her the house in the first place.

"Is she what?" Lana presses.

"Mine?"

She blinks. "Did you seriously just ask me that?"

"Just answer me." My fear morphs into agitation. I'm not quick to give in to my anger, but between the early signs of a headache and learning about a child who I didn't know existed, my patience is running thin.

"Would it matter if she is?"

Lana's question feels like a trap, yet I willingly fall into it anyway. "Yes. No. Maybe. Fuck! I don't know. Is she?" I run my hands through my hair and tug at the strands, making the tender skin throb.

"If you're actually asking me that, then you must not know me at all."

I scramble to my feet, ignoring the unsteadiness as I rise to my full height. "What do you expect me to think? It's not like we left things on good terms the last time we saw each other."

"So you assume I'd keep your child away from you because of my personal feelings?"

"Either that or you moved on pretty damn fast from the sound of it." It's an awful thing to say. An angry, judgmental, stupid-as-fuck statement that I regret the moment it comes out. I can't even blame alcohol this time, which only makes my outburst that much worse.

The temperature in the room drops.

"Get out," she whispers.

I remain frozen in place. "Shit. I'm sorry. I don't know why I said that. I mean, I know why I said it, but I shouldn't have—"

"Get the hell out of my house before I call the cops to escort you out themselves." She turns away from me. The way her shoulders shake with each deep exhale adds to the churning sensation in my stomach.

"Alana—"

She turns on her heels and points at the door. "¡Lárgate!"

I don't need Google Translate to help me out with that one.

I hold my hands up in submission. "Okay. I'm leaving now."

You're just going to go without getting any answers?

As opposed to what? The Lana I knew needed to calm down before she came around to talking. I learned a long time ago that if I pushed her too hard too soon, she would only shove me further away.

I grab the handle of my suitcase and walk out the front door. "Wait."

I pause on the doormat, my feet pressing into the faded *sin postre no entran* letters.

"Give me the spare key." She steps forward and holds out her hand.

Her *ringless* left hand.

What does it matter? It's not like you're here to get her back.

I hold on to that thought, replaying it twice before sliding my usual smile into place.

Her nostrils flare. "The key, Callahan."

I take a second to retrieve the silver key from my pocket. When Lana reaches for it, her fingers brush against my skin, sending a jolt of electricity straight through my body. She snatches her hand back and guards it against her chest.

She must have felt the same thing.

Great. At least I can go to sleep tonight knowing that although she might hate me, her body isn't on the same page.

You're ridiculous for believing that's some kind of accomplishment.

She slams the door shut. I jump backward to avoid a potential broken nose and tip my luggage over.

I bang my head against the wood door with a groan. "What were you thinking by sending me here, Grandpa?"

The deadbolt slides into place before the light above me shuts off.

"You couldn't bother waiting until I got into the car?" I don't expect a response, but I say the words aloud anyway.

Final Offer

One by one, the lights surrounding the wraparound porch turn off, further emphasizing Lana's point.

Get lost.

I release a heavy sigh as I return to my Aston Martin DBS. The engine rumbles to life, and I hold my breath for a few seconds, half expecting Lana to come out wielding her gun and threatening to call the cops again. A whole minute passes without the front door opening, so I consider it safe to turn on the overhead light and search my glove compartment for Grandpa's letter.

The envelope is hidden at the very bottom, right where I left it almost two years ago when he passed. While my brothers rushed to complete my grandfather's tasks to receive their inheritance and Kane Company shares, including Rowan working at my family's fairytale theme park and Declan getting married, I did what I do best.

Avoid what scares me.

Procrastinating never gets you anything but trouble.

I trace over the broken wax seal of the Dreamland castle before I pluck the letter out from inside. My eyes shut, and I take a few deep inhales before unfolding the piece of paper.

Callahan,

If you're reading this version of my final letter, that means I must have passed before we talked out our differences and forgave one another for what we said. While I'm devastated that this is the case, I want to make things right between us with my last will and testament. They say money can't solve everything, but I'm sure it can motivate you and your brothers to step outside of your comfort zones and embrace something new. Out of my three grandchildren, you were always the risk-taker, so I hope you rise to one more challenge for me.

Between us, I tried not to play favorites, but you made it nearly impossible. There is something special about you—something that your brothers and father lack—that draws people in. You always had this light within you that couldn't be snuffed out.

At least not by anyone but you.

It hurt me to watch what made you unique disappear as alcohol and drugs became your crutch. At first, I excused it because you were young and immature. I thought maybe you'd outgrow it. After rehab, you seemed better. It wasn't until I really spent time with you at the lake a few years later that I realized you just got better at hiding it.

I will always regret the things I said to you during our last talk. Back then, I was angry at myself for not stepping in sooner—for not at least checking in on you once you were permanently benched from hockey—and doing the bare minimum because I was too consumed by my job to take the time. You were suffering after your injury in a way none of us could understand, although I should have made an effort to try.

I wish I had swallowed my pride and apologized sooner, so you didn't have to read it in this letter. Better yet, I wish I had never used your addiction against you and said all those hurtful things I did in the first place, thinking it would be a push in the right direction.

You were never a failure, kid.

I was.

Invisible claws sink into my chest, digging their way through years' worth of scar tissue to take a stab at my heart. Grandpa might regret what he said, but he was right. I *am* a failure. What else would you call someone who tried to get sober on two separate occasions, only to relapse not too long after? Weak. Pathetic. Miserable. The options are endless, but I think failure sums it up perfectly.

I take a cleansing breath and continue reading.

Getting sober isn't a goal, it's a journey. YOUR journey. And as much as I wanted you to get healthy, I went about it all the wrong way. There isn't a day that goes by when I don't wonder what might have happened if I supported you rather than turned my back on you. Would you have been interested in finding your place within the company because you no longer resented its connection to me? Or would you have been excited to marry Alana and work on giving Señora Castillo all those grandkids she wanted?

There are a hundred different ways I want to show how I'm sorry, but my options are limited from the afterlife. Hopefully one day—if you pull yourself together and all—we can be reunited. But until then, my will is the best I can do.

So, to my little risk-taker, I have one thing to ask of you in exchange for 18% of the company shares and a twenty-five-billion-dollar inheritance:

Spend one last summer at the Lake Wisteria house before selling it by the second anniversary of my death.

I reread the sentence twice until everything clicks into place.
Oh, shit.

He wants me to live here *with* Lana.

Of course. And to make matters worse, as if they weren't already, my grandpa puts the final nail in my coffin with a single request.

I ask that no one outside of your brothers and my lawyer knows the true reason behind selling the house until it is sold.

Fantastic. Whatever chance I had at appealing to Lana's humanity or pocketbook is stolen away from me with one last wish from my grandfather. I swear he is probably sipping a strawberry margarita from the afterlife, gleefully watching my life implode.

Looks like all I need to do to earn my shares of the company and twenty-five billion dollars is convince Lana—the only woman in the world who would rather shoot my ass than save it—to let me sell the house.

Time to invest in a bulletproof vest.

CHAPTER THREE
Alana

I slide the curtain back into place with a shaky hand as Cal's taillights disappear down the driveway. Whatever semblance of control I had over my emotions breaks, reality punching me in the face with a set of brass knuckles.

Cal is back.

I want to cry. I want to yell. I want to send him running all the way back to Chicago.

Everything about seeing him again hurts. Like someone pulverized my heart until it is unrecognizable.

I hate how he still makes my chest ache from a simple smile, almost as much as I hate the way I wanted to pull him into my arms and beg him to never leave again.

Have you learned nothing after the last time?

I cut myself a little slack. Cal turned my life upside down again, and my mind is still trying to catch up. To ease the sick feeling building in my stomach that hasn't gone away since he showed up at my doorstep, I swallow a few lungfuls of air.

He was never supposed to come back. The last time I saw him, he promised me as much.

Are you really surprised? Since when is he a man of his word?

I thought he would respect me and our past enough to honor his vow.

You were a fool.

No. I was desperate enough to believe him, even when he was in the middle of breaking my heart.

"Cal?"

He ignores me as he continues throwing clothes into the open suitcase on top of his bed.

I step inside his room and shut the door behind me. "Where are you going?"

He doesn't so much as acknowledge me.

"What's wrong?" I place my hand on his shoulder and give it a squeeze.

He tenses, choking the shirt caught within his clenched fist. "Not now, Alana."

Alana? Since when does he call me by my full name?

I walk around him and drop onto the bed. "Why are you packing?"

"I'm leaving." His voice comes out flat.

My brows tug together. "Did something come up in Chicago?"

"No."

Something about the tension in his body and the way he avoids eye contact has my heart racing in my chest. "Okay…" I tuck my legs underneath me. "How long are you going to be gone for?"

He pauses his erratic packing. "I'm not coming back."

My laugh quickly fades at the pinched expression on his face.

I rise onto my knees so we can be eye level with each other. "What's going on? Did something happen at dinner with your grandpa?"

His fist tightens around a shirt. "I can't do this anymore."

"You can't do *what* anymore?"

His gaze slides from his suitcase to my face. "Us."

My chest feels like a lightning bolt split it in half. "What?" *The broken whisper barely makes it past my lips.*

God. It's the same speech my dad gave my mom the day he abandoned our family. Except instead of watching my father pack his bags, it's Cal.

I shake my head.

No. Cal isn't your father. He would never abandon you like that, especially after he promised to love you forever.

"We should have never gotten together," *he says softly.*

My eyes burn as if I kept them open while submerged in salt water. "What did you just say?"

"You and I… It was stupid of me to think we would be a good match."

I suck in a breath. He grabs a bottle of vodka off the nightstand and chugs until the clear liquid dribbles down his chin. My stomach churns at his drinking, but I ignore the acid crawling up my throat.

He is suffering, *I rationalize.*

This is only temporary while he copes with the end of his career, *I repeat the excuse for the millionth time this summer.*

I cradle his head between my hands, ignoring the way they tremble against his cheeks. "You don't mean that."

"I do."

My fingers press into the sides of his face. "Just talk to me and tell me what's happening."

29

His red eyes dart away. "I don't have anything else to say."

"I thought you were...happy."

"No, Alana. I was high." His upper lip curls.

I rear back. "What?"

That's not possible. Cal knows how I feel about drugs. I've had the same negative stance on them ever since my sister overdosed the first time.

"How else do you think I made it through this miserable summer recovering from my injury while my team was out celebrating their big championship?"

Miserable summer?

I ignore the sharp pain reverberating through my body, knowing he can't possibly mean that after everything we have shared together. "You seemed okay whenever I asked about it."

"Because I took enough Oxy to make me feel that way."

I take a deep breath. "Okay. Well, now that I know, I can make sure you get help. You're not the first person to struggle with an opioid addiction after an injury." My voice remains light despite the heaviness weighing me down.

"I don't want help." He pulls away before pressing the vodka bottle against his lips and drinking some more.

I snatch it away from him. "You're better than this."

The muscle in his jaw ticks. "Am I? Or are you too blinded by your love to see the real me?"

My vision blurs. "I'm not blind." Hopeful, sure, but not oblivious to the issues happening here. I just thought we could work on one problem at a time, starting with his depression.

"Please don't make this harder than it needs to be, Alana."

The hole in my chest widens at his use of my full name, the single

letter adding distance between us. "No. Don't Alana me. I'm not going
to give up because you're afraid. We can get through this together."

He shakes his head. "You're not understanding me. This is over."

"What is over?"

"Us."

I lift my trembling chin. "No."

He releases a heavy breath. "What we did this summer...all of it
was a mistake. A huge one I made because I was too drunk and high
to know better."

The crack in my heart widens until I'm afraid it might break in
half. "You don't mean that." My voice quakes.

"I do." He zips up his suitcase and places it on the wood floor,
leaving a few pieces of clothing scattered across his bed.

"I refuse to believe that." I jump off the bed and step between him
and the door.

"Ignoring the truth won't make it any less real."

"Then say the truth! Stop with this bullshit about us being a
mistake! I know how you feel about me. About us."

He might have been high for some of it, but I know he meant all
the things he confessed. The future he painted of our lives together. The
promises he made to me about his love. The wishes he had about us and
the family he wanted to have one day.

His eyes shut. "I wish I had never come back here. It was selfish of
me when you're the last person I ever wanted to hurt," he whispers as
he clutches onto the handle of his luggage.

"You told me you wouldn't ever leave me." He promised. It's the
only reason I let him shatter our friendship with a single kiss. Because
I was just as invested in our future as a couple as he seemed to be.

He looks up at me with cloudy eyes. "I'm sorry."

The fight leaves me along with any hope of him staying. "You want to leave?"

Say no.

He nods. This time, the throbbing sensation in my chest is numbed by something far stronger.

Anger.

My hands curl into fists. "Fine. Then don't ever bother coming back." I'm not sure what would happen to me if he did, so I would rather not find out.

His jaw ticks again. "Is that what you want?"

"Yes." The twinge in my chest doesn't agree.

"Anything for you." He sighs.

"Swear it," I state in a flat voice despite the way my vision blurs from unshed tears.

"I promise not to come back here." He rolls his luggage toward the door. His hand hesitates around the knob before he looks back. "I'm sorry for hurting you. I wish I was different. Stronger. Sober.*"*

I wrap my arms around myself and turn away, hiding the tears streaming down my cheeks. With one last sigh, Cal shuts the door to his room, leaving me alone to crumble. I pull my legs up against my chest and cry until my eyes swell and my head feels like it might explode.

I'm not sure how long I stay in his bedroom, crying myself hoarse, all while wishing for Cal to come back and claim that this all was some sick joke.

Brady Kane comes into the room with furrowed white brows. "Where did Cal go?"

I look up at him with tear-stained cheeks. "He left."

The wrinkled skin around his blue eyes softens as he takes me in. "Oh, Alana." He pulls me into his arms. "I'm so sorry. I thought something like this might happen."

"How?"

His lips press together.

More tears leak from my eyes. "Why wasn't I good enough?" For my dad. For Antonella. For Cal. It always feels as if I'm fighting everyone to stay when all they want to do is leave.

He rubs my back. "This has nothing to do with you."

"Doesn't it? If Cal loved me, he would have stayed. He would have fought for us."

"He can't even fight for himself right now, let alone you."

I shake my head. "I didn't want him to go."

"Anyone who has spent time around you two would know that."

The ache in my chest intensifies. "But I made him promise to never come back."

His hand moves in small, soothing circles. "Is that what you want?"

I sob against Brady's chest. "Yes? No? I don't know."

"Things will be okay. I'll make sure of it."

Except here I am, six years later and still feeling everything but okay.

Things are different now. You're not the same broken-hearted girl anymore.

Aren't I, though? Because all it takes is one interaction with Cal for me to remember everything I spent the last six years trying to forget.

The curve of his lips as he flashes me a smile.

The tug in my chest that always draws me back to him despite all the years of hurt.

The warmth that spreads through my body whenever he cracks a joke, threatening to melt the ice wrapped around my heart.

A part of you still loves him.

I bolt from the couch and escape to my bedroom, although the unwelcome thought follows after me like a dark, threatening storm cloud.

Just because you love him doesn't mean you're in love *with him,* the reasonable voice speaks up.

Truth is, a part of me will always love Cal. It's impossible not to with over two decades of shared history, but I will never be *in love* with him—at least not again. I made that mistake once and I lost my heart in the process.

But unlike the last time Cal showed up at Lake Wisteria, this time is different.

I'm different.

And nothing he says or does will change that.

CHAPTER FOUR

Cal

During my drive to the motel, I take in the sleepy town. The brick buildings along Main Street are the same ones from my childhood, although they have had their paint, awnings, and decor updated over the years. From the general store that opened during the height of prohibition to the pharmacy that hasn't been renovated since the fifties, everything about Lake Wisteria is familiar. Quaint. *Happy.*

I didn't think I would see the town again. When I swore not to return, I made my peace with never coming back to the one place that always felt like home.

It wasn't the place itself, but a special person who made it feel that way.

While Lake Wisteria and its three hundred residents were warm and welcoming, Lana Castillo was the one reason I returned to the lakeside town every single summer.

At least until she had me promise to never come back.

For a good reason.

My chest tightens. I speed past the stores at the end of the road and take a hard left toward the motel inspired by those along Route 66, with a lit-up sign advertising telephones, colored TV, and air-conditioning. It's as if I were transported to a time when women didn't have the right to vote.

Fabulous.

The buzz from the vintage neon light fills the silence as I step out of my car and walk toward the office at the bottom corner of the motel.

A woman I don't think I've met before gives me the worst stink-eye and a metal key to the grimiest room in the place, both of which I'm pretty sure were on purpose. If it weren't for the stocked mini fridge filled with a decent selection of alcohol, I would have passed on this traumatic experience altogether. I drain the last bit of vodka from my flask before plucking the best mini bottle of vodka from the fridge.

I tend to make poor decisions when under duress. Choices that usually lead to me getting so drunk, I forget the reason for why I started drinking in the first place. It's a shitty coping mechanism, but I usually only have two modes: taking small sips from my flask throughout the day to take the edge off my anxiety or getting hammered because I can't stop drinking. The latter usually happens only once or twice a week depending on the stressors, but when it does, I'm out of commission.

I can feel it in my bones that this evening will be one of those kinds of nights. In a last-ditch effort to stop a panic attack, I call Iris.

"Hey. What's up?" Iris's yawn makes the speaker crackle. I can always count on my sister-in-law to answer the phone at any time of the day or night. It might drive my older brother crazy, but Iris was my best friend long before she ever became Declan's wife less than a year ago, so I get exclusive privileges.

"I'm currently staying at a motel straight out of a true crime episode. Literally." I shut my eyes as if that could erase the memory of the stains on the carpet.

"What happened to sleeping at the lake house tonight?"

"Turns out Grandpa forgot to mention that Lana still lives there."

"Are you talking about *the* Lana?"

"The one and only. Plot twist: She has a child I had no idea about." I chug the remaining bit of vodka from the mini bottle.

Since when has drinking solved any of your problems?

I'm not looking to solve them. I'm trying to *numb* them.

Iris sucks in a breath. "When was the last time you had sex with her?"

"Around when she got pregnant—give or take a month, I guess. I didn't pull out a calendar and ask for the kid's birthday before Lana kicked me out."

"Wait. You don't know if the kid is yours or not?"

I rub the sleep from my eyes. "When I tried to clarify, she wasn't exactly open to speaking about it."

Iris curses under her breath. "Does the kid look like you?"

"Her hair is a bit darker, but her eyes are a near perfect match to mine."

She gasps. "It's a girl?"

"Surprise." I toss the bottle in the direction of the trash can, but thanks to my sucky aim, it lands a whole foot away. There's a reason I played hockey over basketball, and that right there proves it.

"No need to freak out just yet. You don't even know if the kid is yours."

"Lana didn't take too kindly to me when I insinuated she might be." Suggesting such a thing wasn't my finest moment. Neither was my comment about her sleeping with someone so soon after we broke up, but I let my emotions get the best of me.

You have no right to be angry at her for what she did after you ended things.

Easier said than done. I'm not the kind of person who usually gets jealous, but I sense it festering inside of me, searching for an outlet.

"Please tell me you didn't ask her like that."

"Okay. I won't." I search the mini fridge for another bottle. Since I already cleared the fridge of all the vodka, I'm stuck choosing between tequila and Fireball.

And here you thought your night couldn't get any worse.

I grab the plastic bottle of Fireball and shut the door with my foot.

Iris groans. "Sometimes I question whether or not you truly are a genius."

"You and I both." If it weren't for my parents forcing me into gifted classes all throughout my life, I'd think they lied to me solely so I was challenged enough in school to avoid getting in trouble.

"There has to be an explanation for this. Based on the stories you shared about Lana, I doubt she would keep a child from you—no matter how much she dislikes you."

"Well, I plan on getting an answer from her tomorrow morning if it's the last thing I do."

"What are you going to do if the kid is yours?"

"Besides drink myself into an alcohol-induced coma?" I twist off the red cap and take a whiff of the cinnamon-scented liquor. Unlike Lana's warm scent, this one makes my stomach churn. I ignore the nausea as I chug, craving the relief only alcohol can provide.

Iris huffs. "That's not even remotely funny."

I stop drinking to answer her. "*If* she's mine, then I'll bring it up with Grandpa's lawyer when I call him tomorrow."

"Why do you need to speak with Leo?"

"There's a...complication."

"What kind of complication?" Worry seeps into her voice, making me feel shitty for calling her in the first place, only to stress her out.

"Don't worry about it." I slur toward the end of my sentence.

"Are you drunk?"

"Nope." Okay, I'm a little drunk, but I don't want to worry Iris with my issues.

Her deep sigh echoes through the speaker. "I thought you were doing better."

If by doing better, she means doing better at hiding my issues from everyone, then yes, I am.

"Turns out I'm in a celebrating mood."

"Cal." It's amazing how a single word can hold so much disappointment.

I pick at the label on the bottle. "What do you expect? I'm in the middle of a crisis right now."

"Is it really considered a crisis if it's a constant state of being for you?" Declan grumbles on the other side of the line.

"Dammit, Iris. Was he listening to us this whole time?"

"It's not like I have much of a choice when you're the one calling at two a.m.," Declan replies for her.

"I need the moral support."

"Or a congratulations based on the news."

"Did you just crack a joke about me possibly being a father?" Horror creeps into my voice.

"It's either that or yell at you about having unprotected sex."

"I'd really rather that." I'm honestly up for anything *but* my brother making jokes about me becoming a dad. I don't know what called for such a change in his character, but I can only imagine it has to do with Iris.

Declan whispers something I don't quite catch. Iris giggles before the line goes dead.

"Iris?" I check the screen for a dropped call. It still looks like she is connected, but no sounds come from her end of the line.

She put you on mute. "Don't mind me. I'm just on the verge of having a mental breakdown."

"Sorry! Declan needed to ask me something." Her breathy voice sends a full-body shudder through me.

"I'll just call you tomorrow morning when my brother isn't busy doing whatever makes you sound like *that*."

"Wait!" She must mute the call again before coming back thirty seconds later. "I told Declan to give me ten minutes."

I drop face-first onto the bed, wishing the fall would knock me out. "I'm not sure why I thought calling you was a good idea, but I regret it immensely."

"Because I'm your best friend and you needed me." She actually coos.

"Debatable after the last few minutes of this conversation."

She huffs. "I don't like it when you're all grumpy. It reminds me of your brothers."

"Sorry, I'm all out of rainbows and unicorns today. Check back in tomorrow to see if I'm in a *stop and smell the roses* kind of mood again."

"How can I help you out?"

"I'm not sure there is much you can do. This is all turning out to be a big pain in my ass." After watching my brothers struggle with their tasks, I knew mine wouldn't be easy, but I didn't think my grandfather would force Lana and me to live together again after the last time he and I spoke.

I'm pissed I didn't connect the dots sooner. Instead, I prolonged the inevitable and made the process harder given my limited timeframe.

And this is why you shouldn't procrastinate.

"If selling the house was really that simple, then you would've cleared out the place and sold it a long time ago. We both know you put off completing your grandfather's request because something was holding you back."

Not something, but *someone*.

A phone alarm I forgot to shut off has me groaning into my pillow. The taste of poor decisions and cheap alcohol lingers on my tongue, making my already queasy stomach churn.

You shouldn't have drunk so much last night.

It's the same thing I say almost every morning when I wake up, although the selection from the mini fridge doesn't help matters.

Rather than obsess over my bad choices, I ditch the motel room and escape into town. Since I don't want to draw any unnecessary attention to myself this morning by stopping at the busy diner, I pull into the small coffee shop near Town Hall. The Angry Rooster has a single barista hustling behind the counter, taking orders and making drinks without breaking a sweat.

All it takes is one sip from my cup of coffee to have me dropping a twenty in the jar labeled, *On a scale of $1 to $10, how big is your…?* Whoever wrote the sign covered up the bad word with an emoji of a rooster. It makes me laugh, which in turn makes my head throb.

The barista chokes on her sudden inhale, so I drop another twenty in the jar solely to entertain myself with how red her face turns.

"Gotta own it." I wink.

"Thank you!" she huffs.

I salute her before taking off out the door. My phone vibrates in my pocket from a new message in my family group chat. With a groan, I unlock my phone and read a new message from my youngest brother.

Rowan

So did you find out if the kid is yours?

Iris would never tell Rowan about my issue, so that only

42

leaves one person.

Declan is officially dead to me. The asshole.

> Who said anything about a kid?

Rowan

> Declan spilled the news when he called me this morning and gave a speech about condoms and safe sex.

Does anything remain a secret in this family anymore? Ever since my brothers met the loves of their lives, it's like everyone knows everything about my business.

Dick-lan

> I didn't give you a speech.

Iris

> It sounded like one to me.

Rowan

> I agree. Rowan was so moved, he ran out to Costco to panic-buy a pack of 1,000 condoms. —Zahra

> 1,000? You'll be dead by the time you finish the box.

Rowan sends a middle finger emoji.

Iris

> AH! Why isn't Zahra in this chat yet?

Dick-lan

> Because it's for Kanes only.

> Look at Declan acting like a dick again. *pretends to be shocked*

Rowan

A notification pops up letting us all know Zahra, Rowan's girlfriend and Dreamland-obsessed adult, has been added to the conversation by Iris. If I didn't feel chronically single before, fifth wheeling in a goddamn group chat would have pushed me over the edge.

Zahra
Hi everyone!!!

She sends another message with a variation of hearts and smiling faces.

Zahra
Cal, when are you bringing your kid to Dreamland?

Zahra
We would love to have her!!!

No wonder Declan didn't want her in the chat. If there is one thing he hates more than texting, it's people who text multiple messages at a time.

I shut my eyes and take a deep breath before replying.

> I gotta go.

I put my phone on silent and ignore the rest of their messages. I've gotten better at avoiding the two couples over the last few months, especially since Rowan and Zahra have been busy working at Dreamland while Declan and Iris are overwhelmed with their house renovation and focused on getting pregnant.

If someone asked me years ago if I would be the last one out of my brothers to be single, I would have laughed in their face. My brothers have the emotional intelligence of toddlers and personalities equivalent to beige paint, yet they both achieved something I never could.

They found happiness and love with someone else.

For a time, I thought I had that too. Or at least I did until I screwed it all up, ruining any chance at having the same thing.

You sound jealous.

Probably because I *am*.

CHAPTER FIVE

Alana

skip my usual morning tinto and have a double shot of espresso, hoping a good hit of caffeine will save me from the utter exhaustion I wake up with. After spending the entire night tossing and turning from Cal's surprise midnight appearance, I'm tempted to crawl back into bed and sleep for the rest of my Saturday. I totally would if I wasn't expected to be in full mom mode all day.

Cami loves constant attention and affection, and I'm happy to spoil her with it. After growing up with a father who abandoned me and a sister who doesn't give a crap about me, there is nothing I want more than for Cami to always feel loved.

Usually, I can whip up arepas con queso from scratch with no problem, but today, my feet drag as I head on over to the pantry. It's days like today that make me wish I bought sugary colorful cereal from the grocery store like most families and called it a meal.

I'm just barely able to make it through preparing breakfast.

By the time I'm done cutting up some fruit and serving Cami a small cup of juice, I'm nearly ready to topple over.

"Are you feeling okay, Mommy?"

"Just tired." I lean against the counter.

Her forehead creases. "Do you still want to watch the game?"

I gesture to our matching yellow soccer jerseys. "Of course. Your grandma would expect nothing less." My mom's love for our national team never faded even after we moved to America from Barranquilla when I was seven. Cami and I honor her memory by continuing the tradition of watching the games together while eating one of her favorites, pandebonos.

"Yay!" Cami's bright grin with her missing front tooth warms my heart.

"It's settled then. Now eat while I fix your hair." Braiding Cami's hair is a soothing task to keep my mind occupied. Throughout the day, I probably fix her hair at least three different times. No matter what kind of hairstyles I try or what products I use, it only takes an hour for her hair to turn into a mess of knots and flyaways.

She stuffs pieces of food into her mouth as I brush her hair. In the middle of me finishing her french braid, my stomach growls, so I reach over to steal a piece of her fruit.

She slaps my hand away. "Hey! Get your own."

I tickle her until she gives up on hoarding her strawberries. Her sassy little sigh makes me smile as she stabs a piece of a cut-up strawberry and offers her fork to me. I'm about to take a bite, but the doorbell chimes, interrupting me.

"I got it!" Cami hops off her stool.

"Not so fast there." I snag her before she runs out of the

kitchen and place her back on the seat. "What did I say about answering the door?"

"Don't open the door to strangers." Her legs swing back and forth underneath her, still too short to reach the floor.

I tap her nose. "Exactly. Why don't you finish up while I go see who is there?" I point at her plate before exiting the kitchen.

On my way to the front door, I check the doorbell app on my phone. Cal paces the front porch. He switches from stuffing his hands into his front pockets to running them through his messy hair to assessing the wood planks on the porch—all in a single minute. I'm not sure whether his ADHD or anxiety is to blame for all the sudden movements, but damn, he can't stand still to save his life.

As much as I resent the idea of speaking to Cal after yesterday, I have to give him credit for showing up this morning bright and early, seeking answers. He gains an ounce of respect from me.

Maybe he cares after all.

I'm quick to shove the thought out of my mind. Him showing up today has nothing to do with me and everything to do with finding out who Cami's father is. He probably wouldn't even be here if I hadn't left things the way I did last night. Since I chose to avoid dealing with Cal and the emotions he stirred up, this is my consequence. It wasn't my most mature moment, but I had no idea how to handle him thinking I would have sex with someone so soon after we broke up.

I know we only dated for a few months, but they meant everything to me. And for a time, I thought he felt the same way.

Should have known better.

Although I'm tempted to leave him out there for a few more

minutes so he can stew in his thoughts, I might as well put us both out of our misery.

His lips moving soundlessly catches my attention, and I raise the volume on the app loud enough that I can hear him.

"What if I suck at being a parent?" he asks himself.

"Well, it's not like you can be any worse than your father," he replies to himself.

"He's a narcissistic psychopath. The bar wasn't set very high to begin with."

I don't want to find him endearing—not even in the slightest—yet I find my lips curving upward at the sight of him having a full-blown conversation with himself.

Why are you smiling at him of all people?

The thought is sobering, and I lock my phone to avoid stealing another glance at him.

I roll my shoulders back before opening the door. Cal looks up at the sound of the creaking hinges, revealing his red-rimmed eyes and haggard appearance. I'd put money on the fact that he is most likely hungover rather than sleep-deprived like me. It's obvious in the way he winces at the bright light hanging above me, illuminating the entryway.

My nails bite into my palms at the evidence of his addiction.

Not your problem.

Then why does the piercing pain in my chest intensify at the thought of him continuing to suffer through his life?

"We need to talk," he blurts out.

I check to make sure Cami isn't sneaking around the corner before shutting the door behind me. "Right now?"

"Yes, right now. I would've wanted to have this conversation last night, but someone kicked me out before we had a chance to clear something up."

A sigh slips out of me before I have a chance to squash it. "All right." I crack the door open. "Cami! I'm going to grab the mail, so I'll be back in a few minutes!" My voice echoes off the high ceilings.

She shouts her reply, but it comes out muffled, most likely due to her stuffing her mouth full of pancakes.

"Do I really only get a few minutes for a conversation like this?"

"I can't leave her alone for long. Last time when I was working outside, she stole my mascara and ended up with an infection after stabbing her eye."

"Okay." He doesn't so much as crack a smile, which is unusual for him.

He's nervous. Without him having a drink to ease his anxiety, the truth is glaringly obvious as we walk to the mailbox in silence. The mansion looms behind us, casting a massive shadow over the overgrown front lawn, making the estate look even larger than its fourteen-thousand square feet.

Part of me wishes he would take over the conversation and force the answer out of me, but his lips remain tightly pressed together while I grab the mail.

What are you waiting for? Just tell him the truth.

That's the thing. I'm not sure how to go about doing that without having a breakdown about my sister. No matter how much time has passed, I still can't speak about Antonella without getting teary-eyed or spitting mad. I hope there is a day when I can think back on our memories and smile.

Except today isn't that day.

Instead, I'm flooded with a wave of negative emotions. Pain. Worry. *Heartache.* Each one hits stronger than the last. Usually, I have a good grasp on them, but I've always been weak when it comes to my older sister and her challenges.

Struggling with drugs isn't a challenge, Alana. It's an addiction.

My hand clutching the mail trembles, making the envelopes shake.

Cal places a hand over mine to halt my task. "Hey."

I find the idea of staring into his eyes impossible, so I keep my gaze focused on the open mailbox. Any reply gets trapped in my throat.

"Is Camila mine?" The way he asks it—soft and nonjudgmental—nearly breaks me.

I wonder for the smallest second what he would do if she was. Is he the kind of man who would step up and offer to help, or would he walk away like always, proving yet again how much of a disappointment he is?

None of this matters.

I steel my spine and look straight into his eyes. "No. She's not."

He releases my hand like his skin might catch on fire if he touches me for a second longer. A dark look passes over his face, completely uncharacteristic. "Who is the guy you slept with?" His question has a sharp edge to it.

I suck in a breath. "Are you seriously accusing me of this *again*?"

"I know how babies are made, and if I'm not the dad, someone sure has to be. So I'm curious who caught your attention not even a month after I left."

My mind goes blank as I charge forward and stab him in the middle of his chest with my pointer finger. "You're right. Someone has to be Cami's father, although I'm not sure who since my sister was high for most of her pregnancy." The words come out loud and clear despite the ringing in my ears.

His thinly pressed lips part, and the creases in his forehead soften until they disappear. "I'm sorry, Alana. I was stupid to assume you slept with—"

Whatever look is on my face has him scrambling back a few steps.

"Sorry? You thought I slept with someone right after you left and then had their child?" My voice booms.

He holds up his hands in submission. "If you did, it's not my place to judge."

"Do you really think that little of what we had together?" I think taking a thousand needles to the heart would feel less painful than this conversation. I'm careful not to let my emotions show on my face, but inside, I allow myself to feel every single stab of hurt. If I cling to the pain, then I won't run the risk of falling for his usual bullshit—the kind that makes my heart soft and my knees weak from a single smile.

He takes a step forward. "Fuck no. But you had every right to do whatever you wanted after I left."

"Which includes hooking up with someone only a month later? Are you serious right now?"

His eyes widen. "I told you to move on."

"The more you say that, the more I wonder if maybe that's what *you* wanted."

He takes a big step back. "What? No. I mean—" He releases a frustrated exhale. "It wasn't like that for me."

"Then what *was* it like?" My heart pounds against my chest.

His brows scrunch with confusion. "What was *what* like?"

My voice drops, barely stronger than a whisper. "Moving on from me." The regret hits me instantly, making me wish I never opened my mouth and asked my question in the first place.

He avoids looking at me as he focuses on something over my shoulder. "I can't answer that."

My heart stutters in my chest. "Why not?"

He did move on, right?

Of course he did. He was the one who broke up with you, not the other way around. While you waited around for him to come back, he was hooking up with every person in all of Chicago.

"You know what? Forget I asked." The thought of him being with someone else makes me sick to my stomach, and I'm suddenly desperate to get away from this conversation. "I've been gone for longer than five minutes, so I should head back."

He grasps on to my elbow while his pained eyes flicker over my face. "You always deserved better than me."

I rip my arm free of his hold. "No. I deserved better *from* you."

CHAPTER SIX

Cal

Lana stuns me into silence. She doesn't stick around for a reply that probably won't come. Whatever relief I gained from finding out neither Lana nor myself are Cami's parents seems short-lived, easily replaced by the ache in my chest as I watch her walk away from me yet again.

I deserved better from *you.*

Of course she did. She deserved the whole damn world, but I was—am—too sick to give her anything but heartache.

And whose fault is that?

I'm not sure how long I stand there mulling over the conversation I had with Lana, but I don't move until my skin prickles from the rising sun. I take a step toward my car and nearly trip over a small person standing in front of me.

"Hi!" Cami smiles up at me and waves.

My heart rate picks up. "Hi?"

"You're the mister from last night." The tan skin around her blue eyes crinkles as her grin widens. Her dad must have some strong genes because Cami barely resembles Lana's sister except for the color of her skin and the shape of her lips.

"Yes?"

"I'm Cami." She holds out her hand for me to shake.

"Cal." I'm on autopilot as I clutch her small palm. The size difference between us is comical, but her grip is strong as she shakes my arm like a pool noodle.

"Hi, Cow-l."

"*Cal,*" I repeat slower this time, emphasizing the *ah* sound.

"*Cam-eee.*" She drags out her name while pointing at her chest, instantly making me feel like an idiot for trying to teach her how to properly say my name.

Who cares how she says it? Just get out of here.

"Well, it's been great talking to you…" I take a step around her.

"Wait."

Jesus, take the wheel and drive me off the nearest cliff please.

She runs ahead and stops in front of me, blocking my path toward the car. "You owe me a dollar."

I blink down at her. "For what?"

"The swear jar." She holds out her hand. "Dinero, por favor."

"The swear jar? What the hell is that?"

Her big eyes stretch wide. "Uh-oh. Now you owe me two dollars."

"I see they're teaching extortion from a young age."

"What's extorshee-on?"

I give my head a good shake. "Forget about it." I sidestep her and put five feet between us before she is chasing after me.

"Hey! What about my money?"

I shut my eyes and count to five. Sweat begins to slide down my neck from my internal temperature spiking. I have absolutely no experience with children besides encountering and avoiding the occasional kid in public. Until Declan and Iris have one of their own, I'm grossly underprepared to deal with any of this.

Just give her the money and go. I check my wallet for singles but come up empty. "Sorry, kiddo, but I don't have any dollars."

"How about that?" She points at the stack of hundred-dollar bills with big eyes.

"Do you even know how much these are worth?"

Her blank stare doesn't give me much to go off.

"Fine. Whatever. Here you go." I give her one of the bills.

"But you said two bad words."

"These are worth more than a dollar." I tap the numbers to emphasize. "That's a hundred. See?"

Are you really trying to reason with a kid?

Her brows scrunch together as she stares at the bill. "Hold on. Let me count to make sure… One…two…three…" She traces each number in the air like she is writing on an invisible sheet of paper.

For fuck's sake. At the rate of her counting, I'll spend the whole morning here.

I grab another hundred and pass it to her. "There."

She pokes her tongue through the gap where one of her front teeth should be. "Oooh."

"Bye." I give her a half-assed salute and resume my walk

toward my car.

"Will you play with me?" She follows behind me like a shadow.

"I can't."

Almost there. The blurry numbers on my license plate get clearer with each step closer to my car.

She runs to keep up with my long strides. "Why not?"

"I've got somewhere to be." *You're so close.* I dig my keys out of my pocket and unlock the door.

Maybe if you throw another hundred on the ground, it will distract her long enough for you to get away.

"Where are you going?"

Anywhere but here is preferable at the moment. "A meeting."

"Oh." Her smile falls. "Will you be back?"

"Uhm…maybe?" My skin itches.

"Yay! Next time you will play with me." Her hands clap.

The kid needs meds or a muzzle. That much is obvious. She reminds me a lot of myself at that age, bouncing with energy and endless rambling. It's a mystery how my brothers didn't try to suffocate me in my sleep.

"Sorry, kid. I'm not here to play with you."

"Oh. But Wyatt plays with me."

Gravel kicks up underneath my shoes from my sudden stop. "Who?"

"Wyatt? It's a spelled like Y-A-T."

"What's his last name?"

Her shrugs. "Umm…deputy?"

That's his damn job, not his name, but it's all the confirmation I need. Lana and he used to bicker like siblings whenever they were in the same room, and for the longest time I thought they hated each other.

To think you once considered him a friend.

My ears pounds from the blood rushing through my body, bubbling beneath the surface of my skin. Of all the people I thought I could trust, Wyatt was pretty high up on that list. We spent most summers together, and he even visited me twice in Denver while I was attending university. When Lana and I were together, whether we were just friends avoiding the inevitable or officially starting to date, he never seemed the least bit interested in her.

Probably because he was biding his time until you fucked everything up indefinitely.

My muscles strain underneath my shirt as I allow myself to acknowledge the emotion I have no right to feel.

Jealousy. It has a mind of its own, devouring all rational thoughts. Deep down, I know that I have no right to be jealous when I'm the one who left. Except I trusted Wyatt to watch after her for me.

Sounds like he did a lot more than that.

I'm glad Wyatt and I aren't friends anymore. It'll make it all the easier for me to kick his ass once I get a hold of him again.

What if he is the man who you saw kissing Lana outside of Last Call Bar two years ago?

"The fucking snake," I blurt out.

Cami gasps.

I flinch. "Shit."

Her mouth drops open.

"Damn?" My voice cracks.

She shakes her head back and forth. I sigh as I pull out my wallet yet again and hand her three more hundred-dollar bills. The way her eyes light up as she squeezes the money is kind of endearing.

You're into kids now?

No, but their fascination with money is pretty funny.

"Are you okay, Cow-l?"

Get a hold of yourself.

I unclench my fists. "I better get going."

She follows behind me like a shadow.

"Camila!" Lana shouts.

We both look up to find Lana stomping down the front steps.

"Busted," Cami mumbles under her breath. She looks identical to Lana with how she averts everyone's gaze when in trouble.

Lana rushes over to us and props her hand on her hip like her mother did whenever she got caught doing something she wasn't supposed to. Which, no thanks to me, was a lot.

"Why do you insist on talking to strangers after everything we have talked about?"

Being referred to as a stranger shouldn't sting, but it does, especially after learning that Wyatt is involved in Lana's daughter's life now that I'm out of the picture. It proves that no matter what history Lana and I have, it's just that.

History.

"I'm sorry, Mommy." Cami rocks back on her heels.

Lana squats down and looks Cami in the eyes. "You can't go talking to everyone you meet—even if they look nice or answer your questions."

"You think I look nice?" I plaster on my usual grin, hoping if I fake being happy for long enough, I can erase the uncomfortable feelings swirling inside of my chest.

That's what you always hope.

Lana's eyes narrow as she gives me a quick once-over. My skin heats when her gaze lingers on my arms, causing warmth to pool in my belly.

"I've seen better." The skin on her nose scrunches.

"You've always been a shitty liar, Alana." I tap the tip of mine to emphasize my point.

Lana and Cami's eyes both widen at the same time. I pull out my wallet with a sigh and pass Cami another crisp bill.

Six hundred dollars poorer and you still haven't learned your lesson.

"Are you in the habit of handing out hundred-dollar bills?" A single one of Lana's brows rises.

"Only to persistent five-year-olds who don't know how to count to a hundred."

Lana shoots her daughter an indiscernible look. "What's five times a hundred?"

"Five hundred!" Cami raises her fist full of money in the air.

That little shit…

"You were saying?" The corners of Lana's lips lift into the smallest smile as she looks up at me. It's the first one I've seen on her face since I showed up here, and it makes my stomach feel all light and bubbly, kind of like I just chugged a vodka seltzer in ten seconds or less.

I recognize the sensation instantly.

Hell no. Not going there. "I better get going."

I don't dare sneak one last peek at the two of them, although I sense Lana's eyes burning a hole into my back as I get inside my car.

It's not until I leave the lake house in my rearview mirror that I can finally breathe again.

The three-hour car ride back to Chicago was a blur. I called Leo's assistant ahead of time to request an emergency meeting, and he was able to squeeze me into his schedule before lunch.

I fiddle with the top of my flask for the third time in the last twenty minutes. I'm about ready to call his assistant when the doors behind me open and the older lawyer strolls inside. Leo looks like he was stolen from the 1920s with his three-piece suit, feather fedora, and golden pocket watch. All the man needs is a cigar to complete his look.

"Callahan!" He pulls me into a bone-crushing hug. "What a nice surprise!"

"Really?" My hands stick out at my sides.

He takes a seat behind his desk. "Yes. I've been meaning to check in on you for some time now. How have you been?"

I consider giving a basic, nondescript answer but choose to be honest. "I've seen better days."

His smile falls a fraction of an inch. "That's a shame. I'm sorry to hear that. Is there anything I can do to help make it a little better?"

I sit up taller in the chair. "As a matter of fact, there is."

"What do you need?"

"I have a couple questions about my grandfather's will, and I'm hoping you can clear them up."

He places his fedora on his desk and leans back in his chair. "Like what?"

"I need to know who owns the lake house."

"Sure. I can answer that for you. Just give me a second to find the file." Leo walks over to the wall of filing cabinets and opens a top drawer. My heart rate speeds up as he flips through various files of information before making a confirmatory noise.

He returns to his desk holding on to a file with my name on it.

"According to the deed, you do."

My lungs deflate from my heavy exhale. "That's a relief because the person currently living there believes my grandfather left the house to her."

Leo clasps his hands in front of him. "Well, that's the tricky thing."

My stomach drops.

No. Tell me he didn't.

Leo continues with a smile, as if he isn't about to shatter my world and any chance I have at selling the place. "Based on the most recent deed, you're listed as a co-owner of the house along with a Miss Alana Castillo."

Fucking hell. "You've got to be kidding me. I'm never going to be able to sell that house so long as Lana owns part of it."

"About that…"

I hold my hand up. "Let me guess. I can't buy her out of her percentage."

His grin doesn't falter. "Correct."

"Of course."

"Your grandfather was very specific about how both you and Ms. Castillo must agree on all legal matters regarding the property."

"What if she doesn't want to sell?"

"Then I would recommend both of you obtain legal counsel."

I don't have time to spare on speaking with Declan's legal team, let alone waiting for Lana to find some representation.

Great.

My molars grind together. "Any other surprises I should be aware of before I head back to Lake Wisteria?"

He flips through the file, scanning pages of legal documents. "I think you're all set. Just remember that any interference from your brothers regarding the sale of the property could have serious repercussions."

Every one of my muscles turns rigid beneath my shirt. "What kind of repercussions?"

He shuts the file with a tight smile. "I think you have enough to worry about given your task. No need to add to that by discussing worst-case situations."

"Could I lose my shares?" I blurt out.

"Let's not let it come to that, shall we?"

Fuck.

I take one last sip from my flask before tucking it inside the inner pocket of my suit and opening the door to Declan's office. His panoramic view of the city is unmatched with floor-to-ceiling windows allowing for ample sunlight. As much as I hate the Kane Company building, the views of Chicago are unparalleled.

My brother sits behind his desk, smashing away at his keyboard with enough force to make it slide forward. "Go away, Todd. I'm busy."

"Seriously? Tim has been working here for months already, and you still don't know his name?"

My brother's head snaps in my direction. "What are you doing here?"

"I came back to clear a few things up with the will."

His dark brows inch closer together. "And?"

I take the seat opposite him, across from his desk. With a quick flick, I undo the button of my suit to give myself some breathing room. Every time I visit the Kane corporate office, it's always the same. An oppressive pressure builds in my chest, forcing me to sip more from my flask than usual. The office reminds me of my failure to live up to my last name and the expectations set forth because of who my family is.

It doesn't matter.

I tap my fingers against my thighs. "You and Rowan need to stay far away from my task."

"What do you mean?" He leans back in his chair.

"When I stopped by Leo's office for the updated deed, he dropped a cryptic comment."

"What did he say exactly?"

I repeat my conversation with Leo.

Declan rises and begins pacing, wearing a hole in the carpet. "What could he mean by interference?"

"I don't know. When I tried to ask if it had anything to do

with my shares, he shut down."

"Shit."

"My thought exactly." The only reason I'm not panicking is because of the steady stream of vodka pumping throughout my system, giving me a false sense of calm.

He runs his hands through his dark hair, mussing the perfectly slicked-back strands. "Grandpa knew I would step in to help you."

Probably because Declan has always cleaned up my messes ever since I was born. He couldn't help suffering from an older sibling savior complex, nearly suffocating Rowan and me with his overprotectiveness.

"Whatever you do, don't help."

His brown eyes drop to the floor.

"Declan…"

He pulls out his phone, looking paler than usual. "I need to make a few calls."

Declan's footsteps quicken as he walks the length of his office.

"You had a buyer lined up already, didn't you?" My teeth grind together.

"Yes." His hand holding the phone tightens.

"Why?"

Why couldn't you trust me to do one thing on my own? The real question lingers on the tip of my tongue.

His jaw clenches, making the vein near his temple throb. "Why else? It's not like I was going to leave anything up to chance."

"More like you didn't want to leave anything up to *me*."

He throws his free hand in the air. "Why would I? It's not as if you've made any effort to complete your part of the will. Do you even care about fucking Rowan and me over?"

I bolt out of my chair. "With how little you think of me, maybe I should give up my shares and walk away from this whole damn thing with my dignity intact."

He releases a bitter laugh. "Of course, that's your first solution. I don't know why I expected anything different from the guy who excels at failing."

"Great dig, asshole. Did you pick that one up from Dad?"

Do you have an interest in being anything but a family failure? The memory of my dad laughing his drunk ass off takes center stage in my head; him shunning my need for a calculus tutor is quickly replaced by a darker memory.

Why am I not surprised that you couldn't even succeed at hitting a block of rubber around—the harsh words my father shared during my post-op after I tore my ACL.

The only reason you're on this company board is because your grandpa knew you wouldn't amount to anything on your own. My father's red-rimmed eyes flick over my seat in the conference room.

The one thing my father succeeded at was finding a hundred different ways to make me feel like a pathetic failure.

And now Declan…

Fuck him.

"Shit. Cal…" Declan's glare softens.

Screw Declan for using my one weakness against me. It's not like I don't want to be better. To *do* better.

I just don't know how.

I shoot him my fakest smile that makes his eye twitch. "No need to apologize, brother. It's not like I didn't spend my entire life hearing those same words time and time again."

Declan's words follow me long after I leave the Kane Company building, feeding off my insecurities like a parasite that can only be cured with a bottle of vodka.

You could get help again. My hand trembles as I pour myself a drink. Some of it spills from my jerky movement, soaking my hand and the surrounding area around the glass.

I shake my head, ignoring the voice in my head beckoning me to stop before I take the first sip.

Always a disappointment.

I pause as my lips touch the rim of the glass.

You're better than this.

No. I'm really not.

I knock back the first drink with a few swallows before pouring myself a second glass. Declan tries to call me twice throughout the night. He even leaves a voicemail, which I delete right away because I'm too drunk to care.

Just how I like it.

CHAPTER SEVEN
Alana

'm sorry, Ms. Castillo." Brady Kane's lawyer apologizes for the second time today, although it does little to ease the burn in my throat.

This can't be happening. I reach out for the kitchen counter to stabilize my wobbly legs.

Leo clears his throat, making the speaker beside my ear crackle. "I understand all of this must come as quite a shock, but I'm sure that Brady had your best intentions at heart. He spoke fondly of you during all of our discussions."

The pressure building behind my temples intensifies despite me rubbing my temples. "It doesn't feel that way."

"If it's any consolation, Callahan expressed a similar frustration during our conversation earlier."

"Did he also mention how he wants to sell the house?"

"He did."

My fingers clutching the counter turn white from the pressure. "What happens if I don't want to sell it?"

"All decisions regarding the property must be mutually made. The only way Callahan can sell the property is if you agree and vice versa."

I release a heavy breath. "Finally, some good news."

Leo pauses for a moment before speaking up. "That being said…"

Oh no.

"If you insist on keeping the house despite Callahan's interest in selling the property, then you will have to buy him out of his percentage of the house."

Hijueputa.

After my phone call with the lawyer, I sent Delilah and Violet a message requesting an emergency girls' night. Both of them arrive at my house that evening armed with snacks and skincare supplies like a little food and self-care can solve all my woes. Violet even went out of her way to get some Bon Bon Bums, my dentist's archenemy and my favorite candy.

I run upstairs to check on Cami and make sure she is asleep. My heart squeezes at the sight of her sleeping soundly, her favorite stuffed lamb crushed beneath both of her arms. I still remember the social worker who gave it to her. Cami was only an infant, so she doesn't remember, but I do. It was the same day I returned to Michigan with a baby in my arms and a new purpose in my life.

Before shutting off Cami's light, I brush the hair out of her eyes and kiss her forehead. "Buenas noches, mi amorcito."

I return to the living room, finding Violet and Delilah already settled into their usual sides of the huge sectional.

Violet plucks my favorite lollipop from the bag and throws it at me. "Here. To take the edge off."

I rip off the wrapper and pop it into my mouth. "Thanks. I needed this."

"Are you sure you don't want any alcohol? I can make a liquor store run and be back in ten minutes." Violet sifts through the bag of Bon Bons for her favorite flavor.

Delilah launches a pillow directly at Violet's face, messing up her blond curls. "You know she doesn't drink."

I haven't had a drop of alcohol in over ten years, ever since Cal went to rehab right before I turned eighteen. At first, it was to support him and his promise to remain sober. I never cared about drinking, and if not doing so helped him, I was all for it.

When he left six years ago, I tried to drink. I even went out and bought a bottle of the most expensive white wine I could find with every intention to break my pledge. To betray him like he did me. The plan seemed solid at the time, given the state of my emotions. Turns out I was so distraught, I didn't even think about buying a corkscrew. My one and only attempt to drink was squashed quickly, and I vowed to never try again.

Violet huffs. "I was joking!"

Delilah's brown eyes roll. "No wonder your stand-up comedy career tanked."

"It's not my fault no one in this town appreciated my brand of humor. The median age around here dates back to the Jurassic period."

Delilah and I both break out into laughter. Lake Wisteria

might lean more toward an older crowd, but there are plenty of young people living here now that the town has gained popularity amongst people from Chicago who are searching for an easier pace of life.

Delilah places a dark piece of hair behind her ear. "So, what's the emergency meeting about?"

I give Delilah and Violet a basic rundown of the situation. They remain quiet, although there are different times when Violet's hazel eyes widen or Delilah's frown becomes more pronounced on her face.

Violet plucks the lollipop from her mouth to say, "Holy shit."

"I know."

"What are you going to do?" Delilah tucks her long tan legs underneath her.

"Isn't that the million-dollar question?"

"Or two million, given how much this house is probably worth." Violet gestures around the room with her half-eaten lollipop.

"You're really thinking about selling it?" Delilah's dark brows rise.

I drop on to the couch with a heavy sigh. "I don't think I have much of a choice."

Violet snorts. "Why? Because Malibu Ken said so?"

I shoot her a look. "He owns half the house, whether I like it or not."

"But so do you."

"That's true, but Brady's lawyer told me if I don't want to sell, then I need to buy Cal out of his percentage."

"That's…" Delilah's tan face pales.

"A million dollars?" My shoulders slump. "Even if I picked up a second job waiting tables or something, I would never be able to afford it."

Violet snaps her fingers. "I'm sure Mitchell down at the bank would be willing to give you a loan."

"After I turned him down for a date? No way."

"What if the town pitched in—"

I stop her with a wave of my hand. "Absolutely not."

The skin between Delilah's eyebrows creases. "There's got to be another way. Maybe some legal loophole that lets you keep the place regardless of who owns it."

My chest aches. "There is none. I checked with the lawyer, and whether I like it or not, Cal is within his rights to sell the property." No matter how much I love the house and the memories I've made here, there is nothing I can do to save it from being listed for sale.

A hint of a smile crosses Violet's lips. "What if—"

"Oh, boy. Here we go." Delilah grimaces.

Violet is known for her crazy plans and being the mastermind behind schemes that ended up with us in handcuffs once or twice. Sheriff Hank could never actually go through with arresting us because he felt the justice system was a slap on the wrist compared to our angry parents.

Violet clears her throat while throwing a pointed glare in Delilah's direction. "What if you don't end up selling the house?"

My brows furrow. "What do you mean?"

"You could set the list price so unreasonably high that no one in their right mind would be willing to buy it." Violet's hazel eyes glint, shining bright from the countless plans bouncing around her head. With her dirty blond curls and rounded, angelic features, no one would think twice about the little devil that lingers beneath her porcelain skin.

"That's…" Delilah's voice drifts off.

"Actually genius," I finish for her.

Violet perks up.

Delilah looks over at me. "You know, Violet's plan might actually work."

Could it really? Part of me is afraid to hope it might, just in case Cal ruins the possibility of me keeping the house.

Better to try and fail than not to try at all.

I throw my hands in the air with defeat. "Screw it. It's not like I have much else to lose."

C al didn't give me more than a weekend to process the news about the lake house before he texted me bright and early Monday morning asking to meet up at Early Bird Diner for lunch. For both our sakes, I decided to comply.

Because Mondays aren't bad enough, my entire morning before our lunch meeting is a complete and utter disaster. Normally my job as a Spanish teacher at Cami's school follows a predictable routine. But naturally, given my luck today, everything has gone wrong, from a broken fire alarm interrupting my tenth graders' final presentations to a first grader throwing up in the back of my class right before lunch. The only thing motivating me to make it through today is the fact that I only have two weeks left before the summer break.

I'm already late by the time I arrive at the diner, so the parking lot is full. I circle around Main Street twice to find a spot with no success. The town is beginning to advertise for the mid-June Strawberry Festival, Lake Wisteria's biggest event of the year, so a majority of the parking spots are taken up by the mayor and his helpers hanging up promotional signs to entice tourists.

It takes me five minutes to find a place to park. It's fitting, with how sucky my day has been, that I would find one right next to my failed dream.

The store has sat empty for years, the landlord unable to permanently fill the space for longer than a few years at a time. Business after business have tried to make it, but they have never been successful. Even a bakery opened here once, which was a whole new level of torture given my dream to open my own shop in the space. They shut down not even a year later.

What makes you think you would be successful then?

My throat thickens, and I turn my back on the storefront.

You have bigger issues to deal with right now.

I hold my head high as I walk toward the diner.

"Hey," Cal calls, startling me.

I turn toward the direction of his voice. He leans against the brick wall outside of the front entrance, appearing completely out of place with his perfectly pressed white linen shirt and his custom-tailored pants. His outfit reminds me of the other rich tourists who visit, looking like they belong yachting in Ibiza rather than on our lake.

He slides his sunglasses down the bridge of his nose to get a better look at me. "Cute dress. Did your mom make it?"

The mention of my mom has my throat closing up. Grief is a strange thing. It comes and goes, usually at the most inconvenient time, turning our lives upside down while we process the loss yet again.

I instinctively reach for the gold necklace she gave me for

my quinceañera, rubbing the cool metal between my fingers back and forth. "Yeah." My voice cracks.

"How is your mom doing by the way? I didn't see her car at the house. Is she visiting your family in Colombia for the summer or something?"

My heart pounds hard against my rib cage as I halt midstride. "You really don't know."

His head tilts. "Don't know what?"

My gaze darts toward the entrance of the diner. "She passed away a couple of years ago while your grandpa was still in a coma. Stage-four pancreatic cancer." I'm surprised I can get the words out without my voice catching.

It only took you two years to get there.

For the first year after my mom passed, it was hard to talk about her without crying. Every memory felt painful—both physically and mentally. It took Cami asking a lot of questions about her grandma for me to get used to speaking about her again with a smile rather than tears.

"Shit, Alana. I had no idea about your mom." Cal places his hand against my shoulder and gives it a squeeze. The warmth of his palm works like a balm, warding off the chill seeping into my bones.

"I thought you knew." *And chose not to show up for her funeral anyway.*

His head shakes hard enough to ruffle his hair. "Of course, I didn't. If I had— Fuck. I forbade my brothers from mentioning… this place."

My breathing becomes increasingly difficult with every inhale.

"I'm so sorry." His grip tightens. "I wish…" He pauses, as if considering whether he should speak or not. "I should have been there for you." The way he says it with absolute certainty makes me believe him.

Our gazes connect. Something unspoken passes between us before he wraps his arms around me and tucks me against his chest. My body relaxes instantly in his hold, and a feeling of rightness consumes me. Any anger, frustration, and heartache from the last few days melts away like it never existed in the first place.

I know the relief is only temporary. That the moment he lets go, reality will come crashing down around me.

Just a few more seconds, I promise myself as I press my cheek against his chest. I forgot how *right* it felt to be held in his arms. Or the comfort that overwhelms me as I listen to the beat of his heart, pumping rapidly in his chest.

I ignore the voice in the back of my head nagging at me and allow myself to enjoy being taken care of.

Why do the things that feel the best always hurt us the most?

"What about your sister?" He runs his hand through my hair, making my spine tingle from the intimate gesture.

"What about her?"

"Is she…" His voice trails off.

"Dead? God no, although sometimes I go to bed worried that she might be."

"But Cami—"

I don't let him finish his train of thought. "Is mine in every way that counts. Anto signed the paperwork and made it official soon after she was born."

His hold tightens, as if he senses me gearing up to pull away. "You never cease to amaze me."

I burry my face into his chest. "I didn't have a choice."

"Of course, you did. You just happened to make the most selfless one because that's the kind of person you are." He chips at whatever control I have left over my emotions as he holds me in his arms.

A car honks nearby. His grip slips as I jump backward, ending the embrace. My cheeks flood with color as I take a second step away from him.

His hands fall to his side before forming fists. Frustration pours from him in waves, hitting me in the face with the power of a blowtorch.

"Let's go inside." I turn toward the entrance.

Cal follows behind me in silence as we walk into the diner.

"Look who finally decided to stop by." Isabelle grabs two menus from the hostess stand.

Cal's cheeks turn pink. "It's nice seeing you again, Isa—"

Isabelle completely ignores him as she throws her arms around me. Her salt-and-pepper hair brushes against my cheek, giving me a fresh inhale of hairspray and pancake batter. "I missed you last week when the girls stopped by for brunch."

"Cami caught a bug, so I had to skip out."

"Oh, no. How's she doing?"

"Better and back in school. She didn't want to miss any more days before the summer break."

Isabelle's brows pull together. "But it's only the second week of May."

"Every day matters according to Cami."

She laughs. "That girl adores school more than anyone else I know."

Cal clears his throat, and Isabelle looks over at him.

"Who's this?" She gives him a once-over.

Cal's brows rise toward his hairline. "Come on, Isabelle. You've known me since I was a little kid."

"Oh." She strains her eyes. "What's your name again? Mal?"

"*Cal.*" He smiles wide despite his right eye twitching.

A few people look up from their tables. Whispers spread through the diner, making my skin flush. Isabelle saves me from any more embarrassment as she leads us to a corner booth far from the gossiping geriatrics on the other side of the diner. They might be far away, but that doesn't stop them from looking over at us and whispering behind their menus.

"Could you all be any more obvious?" I call out.

Beth, the head of bridge club, looks like her head might snap off from how fast she turns in her seat.

"Say the word and we'll kick him out for you," Cindy, the reigning shuffleboard champ and Cami's previous pre-k teacher, offers.

I throw her a thumbs-up.

Isabelle pulls out her notepad before reaching for the pen behind her ear. "What can I get you both started with to drink?"

"Chocolate milkshake," Cal and I say at the same time.

"Glad to see some things haven't changed." His smile returns at full blast, and I look away to prevent myself from struggling with temporary blindness.

Isabelle scribbles on her notepad. "Two chocolate milkshakes coming right up. Do you know what you want to order, or would you rather I come back in a few?"

"Will you give us another couple of minutes?" Cal asks.

"No problem, Al." She gives my shoulder a squeeze before disappearing into the kitchen.

"She hates me, doesn't she?"

I only offer a noncommittal shrug.

"Why?" he asks.

Because you broke my heart.

Silence settles over our table again as we both pretend to assess the menus in front of us. I've been visiting Early Bird Diner since I was a kid, so I can recite the whole thing from front to back without looking. There was once a time Cal could do the same thing, although it doesn't seem to be the case anymore.

My heart squeezes at the reminder.

Cal fidgets in his seat for a whole minute before gaining the nerve to speak again. "Do you know what you're going to order?"

"I'm good with a milkshake." I slap my menu shut.

"I thought you would at least order the most expensive thing on the menu just to spite me."

"If I wanted to spite you, I'd aim for something a little better than your wallet."

"Like where?"

"A kick to the balls is always a good place to start."

His head drops back as he laughs. The sound is hearty and loud, drawing everyone's eyes toward our table. Even I find myself staring at him. I blame Cal's ability to draw everyone in like he is the center of our solar system. Because if Cal is the sun, then the rest of us are aimless planets revolving around him, tragically trapped in his orbit.

Isabelle must sense my desperation as she interrupts us with our milkshakes and taking Cal's order.

I clasp my hands in front of me. "Let's get to the real reason why you asked for this meeting."

He fidgets with his hands. "We need to sell the place by the end of the summer."

My heart rate picks up at the very idea. "But I don't want to sell it."

"Do you have the money to buy me out of my half?" The way he asks the question without a hint of condescension makes me wonder if he actually thinks I can.

A metallic taste fills my mouth from biting down on my tongue. "No, but if you give me a year or two, I'm sure I could figure it out."

His head shakes. "I don't have that kind of time."

"What's the rush?"

He swallows hard. "I need to move on with my life, and I can't do that if I have this house hanging over my head like a ghost of summers past."

My chest feels as if it might split in half from his words. "So, you just expect me to uproot mine instead?"

"I know it's not ideal, but I'm hoping that the money will at least partially make up for it. For what that place is probably worth, you could get a new house and set up a decent savings account."

"And you care about that because…"

His gaze cuts into mine. "I want what's best for you, and no amount of time or distance will change that."

I make a noise in the back of my throat because I don't trust my voice. His words have the unique power to thaw some of the ice around my heart. Bits and pieces of ice break off, melting from the way he looks at me like I might still mean something to him.

If you did, he would have gotten sober and come back to fight for you.

He taps his fingers against the table in a mindless pattern. "I'm not asking you to move out tomorrow. You can spend one last summer there with Cami before we close on the house."

"How thoughtful of you."

"Do we have a deal then?"

"Stop making it sound like I actually have a choice," I lash out.

He raises his hands in front of him. "I'm not here to cause problems."

"Except you *are* the problem, Cal. Always have been and always will be."

"At least I'm consistent at something." He dares to smile.

My fingernails embed themselves into my thighs. "Have you changed at all in the last six years?"

"Of course." He raises his chin.

"But you're still drinking." And using God knows what else.

There is no point in pretending Cal doesn't have a problem. I already did that once, and it only caused me heartache in the end. It took me a long time to realize loving someone didn't mean accepting them for all their faults, but to call them out on their issues because you care enough to not want them to suffer.

I was just too young when Cal and I first got together to understand that concept.

"Contrary to popular belief, my addiction doesn't make up

my entire personality, although my brothers and the media sure like to make it seem that way." He keeps his voice light despite the tightness in his jaw.

"I know that." Which is exactly why having a front-row seat to him spiraling was that much more painful. I knew the person he was while on opioids and alcohol didn't hold a candle to the man I knew he could be.

He sighs. "I don't expect us to pick up where we left off given our past and the fact that you're in a relationship."

In a relationship? What the…

Before I can ask, he continues, "But I hope we can at least be civil with each other."

"Why bother? It's not like you plan on sticking around for long." I keep my face expressionless despite the sting of pain over my heart.

"About that…"

No.

"Since I plan on being very involved in the house sale from start to finish, and all the rentals around the lake are already booked solid from May to September, I'm going to need to stay at the house until it's sold."

Hijo de puta. "No."

"You can't keep me out of my own house."

My fingers itch to wrap themselves around his neck. "What's wrong with the motel?"

"Do you want the short or the long list? Choose wisely because we might be here all day."

Deep breath, Alana. "You can't seriously expect us to live together."

He shakes his head hard enough to make some of his hair fall in front of his eyes. "Of course not. I plan on staying at the guesthouse. That way I can have access to the main house whenever I need it while still giving you privacy."

In theory, Cal's idea isn't terrible. The guesthouse is located at the back of the property with its own private entrance to the main road. I could easily pretend Cal isn't there, so long as we don't run into each other by the lake.

You can't seriously be considering this.

What choice do I have? Cal is right. I can't keep him out of the house with him being a co-owner, and his idea to stay at the guesthouse is far better than him asking to live at the main house.

"Why do you need access to the house?"

"Because I need to pack up whatever stuff was left behind by my family, including that special little collection you mentioned in the attic."

I almost feel bad for him. The attic is a hoarder's dream, packed to the rafters with stuff Brady collected over the decades. It would take anyone at least two weeks to work their way through all those belongings.

But if he packs it all, then you won't have to.

The deal is tempting. I never had the willpower to even try, so I might as well take advantage of Cal being here to free up some space and clear out the last bit of clutter left behind from the Kanes. Then, I can erase any reminders of the Kanes and make the house completely mine.

With the plan I have set in place, it might as well be. Even if Cal owns half of it, he will never sell with the price I have in mind.

I lift my chin. "Fine. But I don't want you inside the house unless I'm there."

"Why? So you can keep an eye on me?"

My eyes narrow. "Like I'd ever trust you around my stuff."

"Probably for the best after that incident with your vibrator." He flashes me a knowing smile.

My cheeks burn, the heat quickly spreading to the rest of my face.

You set yourself up for that one.

I slide out of the booth.

"Running away already? Things were just starting to get interesting." His bright grin is full of promise.

"Bye."

"Are you sure you want to go? I didn't even get around to mentioning the time I found those h—"

I slap my hand over his mouth. Cal's speech comes out muffled as he looks up at me with wide eyes.

I lean in and whisper, "Let's get one thing clear right now. No matter what, we don't speak about what happened the last summer you were here." I'm not sure I would survive him being here if we do.

His eyes narrow.

I press harder against his mouth. "Do you understand?"

He nips at the soft skin of my palm, and I fight a full-on body shudder as I release him.

"Not speaking about it doesn't change what we did."

"I'm not trying to change it. I'm trying to *forget* it." I walk away with an extra sway to my hips, earning a soft groan from the man behind me.

Cal: 0. Alana: 1.

CHAPTER NINE

Cal

I f it weren't for me needing to return to Chicago for my cat, Merlin, and a few more pieces of clothing, I wouldn't have bothered attending the Kane Company board meeting. My presence isn't required unless there is a vote since I don't have an active position within the company.

The only reason I've bothered sitting through the boring meetings in the first place is to fuck with my father. He has always hated me being on the board ever since my grandfather appointed me six years ago after I tore my ACL, so I've made it a point to sit through each miserable meeting solely to spite him.

To think people accuse me of not having a life's purpose.

Every time I step into the Kane Company's corporate office for a meeting, I'm hit with the same urge to run straight out the front door. It's like my senses go haywire due to environmental overstimulation. Despite all the years dealing with sensory processing issues, I still struggle with not hyper-fixating on how my tie feels too tight and my suit too scratchy.

This right here is why I'm not cut out for corporate life. My brothers are the complete opposite, oozing confidence as they speak up throughout the board meeting. Both of them look like corporate clones with their dark, slicked-back hair, pristine pinstripe suits, and perfectly groomed stubble. It's obvious they have always been suited for company politics and dreadful desk jobs while I attempt to beat the all-time high score on Candy Crush underneath the table.

The Head of Acquisitions and Sales for a division of our streaming service, DreamStream, rises from his chair and stands at the front of the room. He fumbles through his first few slides, which catches my attention. I might not be business savvy like my brothers, but I'm a people person who notices everything. There is a slight sheen to his skin that only seems to get worse the longer my father stares at him with piercing dark eyes and a constant scowl.

The presenter uses his laser pointer to highlight a graph. "Monthly subscriptions for our DreamStream platform have decreased by twelve percent over the last quarter."

"Twelve percent? On top of the previous quarter's six percent loss?" I speak out for possibly the first time this year.

Every single person sitting in the conference room looks over at me, including my brothers. Declan's dark brows raise while Rowan's brown eyes go wide. My father faces forward with a clenched jaw, a permanent expression he has worn ever since I took my first breath.

The older man at the front of the room giving the presentation fiddles with his clicker before progressing to the next slide. "Right. Carrying on… Our research shows that families are cutting back on monthly subscription services due to increased competition and oversaturation of the market. Based on our polls, we were voted the second most likely subscription service to be cut from families' budgets."

"Did you ask them why that was?" I press.

"Well…yes. It comes down to two main things: affordability and content."

"But if it was truly an issue of affordability, then other streaming services would be struggling just as much."

Rowan turns toward me, pinning me with his dark gaze. "What's gotten into you?"

I give him a nonchalant shrug. "My interest is piqued."

"Then we better take advantage before you lose it again." His brown eyes light up.

I know my brother means well, but all he does is discourage me from continuing my line of questions. The last thing I want is to give people a reason to want more from me. Being the family reject is an easy gig, and Rowan's comment reminds me of that.

No expectations. No disappointments.

My life motto.

After the board meeting, Declan waves me down to talk but someone distracts him, giving me time to escape. I'm not in the mood to deal with him after our fight last week. My walk to the elevators is a quick one, with no one bothering to stop me to chat.

The doors begin to shut, but a hand shoots out, causing them to reopen. They part to reveal the one person I wouldn't want to share a single second with, let alone the minute trip it takes to get to the lobby.

You knew there was a risk of this happening.

My father's usual scowl only deepens as he takes a look at me with his dark, beady eyes. "Leaving already?"

"Now that I crossed off *annoying you* from today's to-do list, I'm all done." I readjust my suit for the umpteenth time.

"Do you have any intention of doing something useful with your life?"

"I'm not sure. I considered learning to juggle, but then I saw a video about ukuleles, so I started getting into that during my spare time."

He scoffs. "Your entire life is considered spare time. You have no job, no purpose, no *anything* but a loaded trust fund that shouldn't even be yours."

"I see you're still bitter about Mom setting up that trust fund for me without your knowledge, but you should really let it go. My therapist says it isn't good to keep all that inside."

"The only bitterness I have toward your mother is her soft spot for *you*."

I give his shoulder a squeeze, matching the way my chest feels from his words. "Aw, Pops. Don't hold it against her. She believed in you too after all, and we know what a monster you turned out to be."

His nostrils flare. "You're such a disappointment."

"At least I'm doing one thing right."

"You think this is funny? That being the family joke is an accomplishment? Wake up. You're a pathetic waste of space who shouldn't even be allowed in this building given how you're a stain to our last name."

My chest throbs, but I hide my pain with a smile. "This might be the most you've talked to me in an entire year."

My father makes a noise in the back of his throat. Disdain rolls off him in waves, but I ignore it. I learned long ago that getting angry and showing his words matter means he wins.

I can't wait to earn my shares and ruin my father's chance at ever controlling the company again. Whatever letter and inheritance my grandfather left him will never add up to the percentage of shares my brothers and I will have combined. Even if he inherits the 6 percent of shares that are still unaccounted for, he will never have enough power to overturn us again.

Tension builds between us, with neither of us saying a single word. He stares at me like I'm the bane of his existence, and I do everything to keep my smile in place.

Kill them with kindness, Mom used to say.

I hope my father chokes on it.

The elevator dings, and the doors open to the busy tenth floor. A group of people shuffle into the elevator, ending our toxic exchange. My father moves to one corner while I situate myself near the doors for my great escape.

Although I let a majority of my father's comments bounce off of me, sometimes I struggle. I'm only human after all. My father has always been good with picking at my weaknesses. It isn't hard for him, especially once I got injured playing hockey and lost the one thing that made me feel special.

He poked and prodded until I spiraled, turning myself into a copy of the person I resent most.

Him.

"I'm going to miss you, little guy." Iris tucks Merlin against her chest. It only took my cat two years to warm up to her, and now they're the best of friends. His black fur contrasts against her brown skin, bringing out the deep shades in both.

"He'll be back in a few months." I zip up my luggage before placing it upright on the floor.

Her smile drops. "Months? I don't think I can make it that long without you here."

"And they call *me* overly dependent..."

She smacks me in the arm. "Shut up. What if Declan and I come to visit you? I've always wanted to see the lake after all your stories, and you're the one who said the summers were always the best."

"Uhh..."

"Try to look a little less horrified, will ya?" She pinches the skin between my ribs.

"Let me get settled first and then we can talk about you visiting. Okay?"

"Fine." She lets Merlin go before dropping on to my couch. "What was it like being back?"

"I'm still processing all of it."

The gold beads at the ends of her braids clink together as she tilts her head. "That bad?"

"I knew Lana was angry at me…"

"But you ran before you had to deal with it."

I tip my chin. "Exactly."

"Well, you have to face your past eventually."

"It feels like I'm being slapped across the face with it repeatedly."

She laughs. "Maybe all of this will be good for you. It could help you get some closure."

I fall on to the leather chair across from her. "Who says I need closure?"

"The fact that you haven't been in a romantic relationship for six years."

A rare frown crosses my face. "I haven't been interested." The lie slips out easily, perfected after mastering the art of pretending not to give a fuck.

Of course, I am interested, but that doesn't make it possible. At least not when I'm still a screwed-up mess.

Iris stares at me with narrowed eyes. "Are you sure about that?"

"Yes."

"Could have fooled me with the way you asked me out on a date."

I launch a pillow directly at her face. "That was a joke."

"Says the man who kissed me."

"And then proceeded to throw up afterward."

She shivers. "Don't remind me."

I'm not sure whose drunken idea it was, but our kiss was a mistake the moment it happened. Our lack of romantic chemistry was a dead giveaway that Iris and I would never be more than friends.

She shakes her head. "Putting me aside, you'll never be able to move on to someone new if you're still holding on to the memory of someone else."

My stomach churns. "I'm not holding on to the memory of someone else."

"Really? Then give me your wallet." She holds out her hand. "No."

She crosses her arms against her pink T-shirt. "Exactly like I thought."

My eyes narrow. "Holding on to a photo isn't a crime."

"It's not the photo but what it symbolizes that matters."

"And what's that?"

"That a part of you will always love a part of her, no matter how hard you try to deny it."

"It's impossible not to love her."

Iris leans forward. "So you admit that you love her."

"I never denied it in the first place. Those kinds of feelings don't just go away, as much as I wish they did."

"I don't have a good feeling about this." She rubs her temple.

"No need to worry. I know that there is no chance in hell that we are ever getting back together."

I made sure of that the moment I walked away from her, turning her fear of abandonment into a reality.

And I've never forgiven myself.

It's not until Iris leaves for the night that I pull out my wallet and search for the picture she spoke about. The edges of the small photo are worn from years of wear-and-tear and countless wallet transfers.

It's been over a decade since the photo was taken, but I remember the day like it was yesterday. Lana's mom took it of us the summer after I came back from rehab. Both of us are on the dock, drinking cholados Colombianos to celebrate my twenty-first birthday. Lana stares into the camera lens, eyes bright and face beaming, while my focus is solely on her.

It's obvious I loved her, even back then, although I never acted on my feelings. I was happy to stay friends while we were both figuring out our lives. Lana had just turned eighteen, and I was fresh out of rehab and still struggling with the stressors of my life. And then I got drafted into the National Hockey League when Lana wasn't even twenty yet. Neither one of us were ready for the sacrifices we needed to make to be together, so instead, we kept things platonic. It nearly killed me inside, but I knew she was worth the wait.

At least until you fucked things up for good.

I flip the picture over and trace the words she wrote on the back.

Get drunk on life, not alcohol.
Love,
Lana

She gave it to me as a parting gift that summer, and I have kept it ever since.

At first, it was the push I needed to stay sober. Any time I was tempted to drink, I'd pull out her message and stare at it until the demons left me alone. It helped me stay on track for a few years despite all the temptations surrounding me. But then I tore my ACL and lost my hockey career, making it easy to slip back into destructive habits.

Truth is, I lost more than my job that year. I lost *myself*. My life became a series of bad decisions as I tried to fix the gaping hole in my chest.

It took Grandpa's accident to get me on the straight and narrow. But by the time I got on the right path, it was too late. The girl who promised me forever had her arms wrapped around someone else, and I...

I was too late.

CHAPTER TEN

Cal

My neck cranes as I take in all three stories of the lake house. In broad daylight, there is no way to hide the imperfections plaguing the home. The chipped paint and rotting wood siding doesn't bode well, especially when paired with the tarp covering a majority of the roof. Most of the windows look outdated and their wood frames decrepit from old age. Vines crawl up the exterior walls, completely out of control as if they want to swallow the house whole.

Maybe that's for the best.

The house is a wreck. In its current state, I'll be lucky if I find a buyer willing to purchase the place.

All you need to do is find one person willing to take a chance. That's all.

I release a tense breath before ringing the doorbell. It takes

Lana a whole minute to answer the door, her eyes barely open and her hair a wreck as she steps out on to the porch wearing nothing but an oversized T-shirt that barely reaches her mid-thigh. The material falls loosely over her curves, accentuating the shape of her breasts.

Blood rushes through my body, directly toward the source of my newest problem. I wipe my face with my palm. "Please tell me you don't make it a habit of opening doors dressed like that."

"What's wrong with my clothes?" She looks down.

"The fact that you're barely wearing any."

She crosses her arms, which only pushes her boobs up. "You're the one showing up on a Saturday morning without an invitation."

"I need the keys to the guesthouse." My molars smash together.

"Oh." Her lips press together. "Give me a second." She disappears into the house before coming back a minute later with a key ring.

I reach to grab it, but she clutches it against her chest.

"Hold on."

"What?"

"How long do you plan on staying?"

I grin. "Trying to get rid of me already?"

"No, although I'm sure the mice staying in the guesthouse will do that for me."

"Mice?" My eyes widen.

"A whole family of them." She has an extra special glint in her eyes.

I shrug like the idea of mice doesn't repulse me. "No problem.

Merlin will love the challenge."

"Who's Merlin?"

"My cat."

Her head tips to the side. "You have a cat?"

"Surprised?"

"That you can take care of a living, breathing organism? Absolutely." She delivers her venom-coated words with a vicious smile that does wonders for my dick. Blood flows directly to the source, making the front of my pants uncomfortably tight.

I reach for the keys again, but she clutches them in a tight fist.

"Wait."

"Why? So you can insult me some more?"

She takes a deep breath. "I have one thing to ask of you."

"What?" I quit tapping my foot.

"Don't talk about selling the house when Cami is here."

My forehead scrunches. "She doesn't know?"

"Nope, and I plan on keeping it that way." Her gaze drops toward her glossy red toenails.

What are you hiding, Lana?

"She's going to find out eventually, especially when I'm packing stuff into boxes," I press.

Her jaw ticks. "How I handle things with my daughter is none of your business."

"Fine. I won't tell Cami about the house. But if she asks me questions—"

She doesn't bother letting me finish my sentence. "Deflect like you always do. It's one of the few things you're actually good at."

"I seem to remember you thinking I was good at more than just that." I fight my frown with a smile, although her words pierce at what little confidence I have left.

Her nostrils flare as her cheeks turn pink. She all but launches the keys directly at my face before slamming the door shut.

Totally worth it.

Lana is a filthy liar. I checked the guesthouse twice for any mice and didn't find a single critter. The house is in far better condition than I thought it would be in after being abandoned for a few years. My grandfather built it for any visitors long after he moved in, so the modest 1,100-square-foot floor plan is more modern compared to the main house. With three bedrooms and its own private dock, it's the perfect hideaway.

I let Merlin out of his crate and set up his litter box and water bowl before spending the entire day cleaning the house from top to bottom. Although I considered hiring a crew to help me, I decided to do it myself to keep my mind busy. It's not like I have a job or any real responsibilities besides completing my part of the will.

I lose track of time. It's not until my stomach growls that I finally stop cleaning and drive into town for dinner. Most of the restaurants are closed already, so I'm left with only one option.

The diner.

The bell above me rings as I open the door.

"You again?" Isabelle sighs from behind the counter. A couple of people turn in their barstools to search for whom she is talking to, only to glare once their eyes land on me.

"Nice to see you too, Isabelle."

"The feeling isn't mutual." She walks toward the hostess stand at the front of the diner.

"You know, I'm starting to think small towns aren't as sweet and charming as people make them out to be."

"Oh, we are…to anyone but you."

"You wound me." I rub at the spot above my heart with a pout.

She smacks my head with one of the menus before showing me to a corner booth toward the back. There are only a few people seated throughout the place, all of whom watch me take my seat.

"What can I get you to drink, Hal?" She taps her notepad with the tip of her pen.

"It's *Cal*."

"Stick around for long enough this time and maybe eventually I'll get it right."

"Is that the reason why you hate me now?"

Her lips turn down. "I don't hate you."

"Are you sure?"

"My momma raised me better than to hate anyone, including trust fund babies like you."

My head tilts. "Then why do you dislike me?"

"For the same reason a majority of the town does."

Well, at least she's honest. "Is it because of my drinking?"

She scoffs. "No, although that doesn't help matters."

"Then what?"

"It's because you broke Alana's heart."

My smile slips.

"We're a small town here. When one of us hurts, we all do." She tilts her head in the direction of a man gliding into the diner on an electric wheelchair. "When Fred struggled to afford a new wheelchair, we all chipped in to buy him a fancy electric one." She points her pen at a woman wiping the countertop with a rag. "Betsy there married a rich out-of-towner with a heavy fist and the inability to understand the word *no*. And do you know what we did to him?"

"Chopped him up into little pieces and spread his remains across the forest?"

Her lips twitch. "We wish. Wyatt and the new sheriff keep us in line, so we were forced to go about things the legal way. Drove him out of town by hiring a fancy lawyer from the big city. Everyone pitched in to pay the fee, and it was worth every penny because now Betsy and her kids are free to live their lives."

I swallow hard. "That's good."

"Bottom line is that we look after our own here. If Alana doesn't want you around, then who are we to make you feel comfortable?"

My lips press together.

"It's no sweat off our backs after we saw what happened to Alana the last time you left."

Fuck.

My stomach rolls, the acid climbing up my throat.

You need to get out of here.

My eyes flicker to the door.

Isabelle steps into my eye line, forcing me to look up at her.

"We're the ones who had to watch Alana struggle with heartbreak the last time you left. She stopped going out, lost weight, and barely spent time around anyone besides her mama and two best friends. It was like she was fading away before our very eyes. Not that she would ever tell you that because that girl is too sweet for someone like you."

Desperation to escape claws at my throat. I reach for the flask in my pocket, only to pause when Isabelle catches the movement.

Her brow arches. "I'm not sure why you're back or what you want with our girl, but the whole town will be watching closely. One slipup and you will wish you never returned."

My tongue feels heavy against the roof of my mouth. "I'm not here to hurt her."

"For your sake, you better hope not. I'll be back with a water." She turns away, leaving me to process everything she said.

My eyes screw shut as I fight the urge to take a sip from my flask.

You don't need to drink every time someone says something you don't like.

My hands tremble against my lap.

Alcohol won't change your reality.

I'm not looking to change it, but rather cope with it. Yet no matter how many deep breaths I take or what I tell myself, Isabelle's words poison my chances of making it through my meal without drinking.

She was fading away before our very eyes.

The acid in my belly bubbles with each reminder of how much Lana struggled after I left. How she struggled to live because of me.

Did you really expect her to move on from one day to the next?

No, but I wanted more for her than me and my issues.

I pull the flask out and take a swig before tucking it back into my pocket.

My phone vibrates.

Iris

Hey! How was your day?

About as good as I expected. What are you up to?

Her text comes back a minute later after Isabelle stops by to take my order.

Iris

Watching Declan cook dinner.

At least one of us is having a home-cooked meal tonight.

You sound jealous.

Maybe because I am. Not of Iris and Declan per se, but of how my situation compares to theirs. I know it's not right. It makes me feel sick to be anything but happy for them. But there is this part of me—one I rarely like to acknowledge—that wishes I had what they had.

I want to be happy. I try so damn hard, yet no matter how big I smile or how loud I laugh, I always feel empty. It's a cold, creeping feeling that consumes me late into the night, until I'm forced to welcome my old frenemy.

Addiction.

My phone buzzes from an incoming text.

Iris

He just burned himself taking the bread out of the oven and then proceeded to curse in five different languages.

My sadness dissipates with a laugh.

> Shouldn't you be helping him?

Iris

We're a modern couple, Cal. He cooks. I watch. He cleans. I also watch.

> Is that the key to a successful marriage?

Iris:

That and a big dick.

I choke on my sudden inhale of air.

"I thought it was you sitting here but I wanted to make sure."

I look up at Wyatt, whose body casts a shadow over my phone. His dark hair peeks out from underneath his deputy hat, teasing the edge of his uniform collar.

"Wyatt." My teeth grind together.

He tips his hat like a gentleman, tempting me to knock it off his head. "I heard you were back."

"Alana told you?"

He shakes his head. "Cami."

Of course she did. "What do you want?"

"Just thought I would stop by and give you a warm Lake Wisteria welcome."

I cock a brow. "Is there such a thing?"

"Everyone here is good people."

"So long as you don't piss them off," I grumble.

The crackle of Wyatt's cop radio interrupts us, and he adjusts the volume with a quick turn of the knob. "Speaking about that…I wanted to warn you to stay away from Alana and Cami."

"A warning? How utterly unoriginal."

He leans forward while holding on to his holster with a tight grip. "Do you have a death wish?"

"No, although I'm sure you would be more than willing to put a bullet in my head. After all, you didn't mind stabbing me in the back as soon as I left."

His eyes narrow. "What do you mean?"

"You and Alana."

"What about us?" He doesn't even blink.

"How long did it take you to go after my girl?"

"She's not *your* anything."

My fingers dig into the soft flesh of my palms. "Alana might be yours now, but I'll always be her first in every way that counts." First kiss. First love. First heartbreak. No matter how hard Wyatt tries, he will never be able to erase our history, even long after I leave this godforsaken town for the final time.

With the way he stares at me, it feels as if he is reading my soul. "Are you…jealous?"

"Jealous of you? What for?" I give him an unimpressed once-over.

"My question exactly." His lips curve upward, only stoking my irritation like one would fan a flame.

Isabelle arrives with my burger, saving me from Wyatt and his perceptive stare.

I gesture toward my plate. "If you don't mind, I'd rather eat my dinner in peace without your toxic masculinity stinking up the place."

"Of course. Nice seeing you, Percival." He tips his hat.

Him calling me by my middle name reminds me of too much, all at once. My stomach churns, and the food in front of me becomes inedible.

I flip him off. "Fuck you, Eugene."

"I think I'll fuck Alana instead, but thanks for the offer." He winks.

The bastard. My right eye twitches.

"Maybe I'll even go there tonight." His eyes brighten. "It's not like you could hear us all the way from the guesthouse, right?"

I always kept my aggression on the ice and away from others, but all it takes is Wyatt grinning at me, talking about fucking Lana, to tip me over the edge.

I bolt from my seat and reach for him. Either I'm out of practice or he learned some new moves because I end up slammed against a table, my hands cuffed behind my back within five seconds flat. It's embarrassing how quickly he takes me down, so I'm grateful only five people bear witness.

As if she read my mind, Isabelle holds up her cellphone and snaps a photo. If that ends up on the internet, Declan will hang me by the Dreamland flagpole for all the park visitors to see.

Wyatt pulls me up and shoves me toward the diner entrance. "Welcome back, asshole."

CHAPTER ELEVEN
Alana

You what?!" I reach out for the doorframe to hold me up. The flashing blue and red lights on top of Wyatt's cruiser light up the house. Even though I took my contacts out before bed, I can make out Cal's silhouette in the back of Wyatt's police car, glaring a hole into his back.

"I just wanted to get under his skin." Wyatt's gaze drops to his boots.

"Wyatt Eugene Williams the third. What were you thinking?"

His weight shifts. "I'm sorry."

I smack his hat right off his head since I can't slap his face around. "Delilah is going to be so pissed at you for insinuating you were going to fuck me."

"I already got an earful from Dee when I called to let her know I would be late tonight. She told me to go sleep out on the porch like a dog if I was hell-bent on acting like one."

"I don't blame her. You said you were going to…" *Nope. Can't even finish that sentence.*

My stomach rolls in protest. There is no way I would ever touch Wyatt, let alone screw around with him since he is not only a good friend, but my best friend's husband.

Wyatt crosses his arms against his uniform. "I think he's jealous."

I let out a loud laugh. "No way."

"He tried to choke me, Alana."

"Cal?"

"Yes, Cal! I don't think I've ever seen him that pissed before. It caught me off guard."

I try to wrap my head around Cal attacking anyone. The only time I saw him unhinged was while playing hockey, and it never went past the arena. *Ever.*

I shake my head. "He's got the personality of a golden retriever."

"Yeah, a rabid one. I panicked for a moment before my training kicked in."

I rub my eyes. "Is he under arrest?"

"Hell no. There is no way I would risk losing my job for that."

Of course not. Arresting a Kane on anything less than tax fraud or a murder charge would be cause for immediate dismissal.

I sigh. "Why did you bring him here instead of the guesthouse?"

Wyatt grabs the handcuff keys from his belt. "Since I can't arrest him, I thought it would be a fun way to torture him." He leans forward and places both his hands on the doorframe. From Cal's vantage point, it probably looks like he might even be kissing me.

"You're asking for it." I give his shoulder a shove.

"I'm doing it to save you from him sniffing around."

I peek over Wyatt's shoulder to find Cal throwing daggers with his eyes. "Be careful uncuffing him. He looks pretty pissed off."

Wyatt laughs as he jogs back to his car and opens the back door. He is quick to unlock the handcuffs and send Cal on his merry way with another tip of his hat.

"See you tomorrow, Alana!" Wyatt shouts at the top of his lungs.

Cal looks over his shoulder. I can't make out the expression on his face since he is turned in the opposite direction, but I get a good look at his curled fists. He keeps his eyes on Wyatt until his taillights disappear down the driveway.

Cal walks slowly toward the house, drawing out the process. He still hasn't looked directly at me, so the closer he gets, the harder my heart pounds.

"So, first night here and you're already getting arrested." I lean against the doorframe and cross my legs at the ankles.

He looks up with narrowed eyes. "Technically, I was detained." He rubs at his wrists.

I shake my head. "What were you thinking, trying to assault an officer?"

"Are you fucking him?" he asks through gritted teeth.

My heart rate spikes. It's one thing to accuse me of sleeping with someone else, but it's a completely different issue for him to think I would sleep with his old best friend. Instead of allowing my irritation to guide my reply, I choose a different tactic.

"Would it matter if I am?"

Oh, Alana. You know better than to taunt him.

His nostrils flare. "Hell yeah, it matters. You should hear the way he speaks about you."

Wyatt, I hope Delilah gives you hell when you get home. "It's none of your business who I hook up with."

He rubs his clenched jaw, as if it can erase the tic. "You can do better than him."

"He's not *that* bad."

"What a glowing review for a guy who probably couldn't find your clit even if it was labeled with a neon sign."

I choke on my laughter, killing it before he has a chance to hear it. *"Cal."*

His nostrils flare. "What?"

"Wyatt was right. You *are* jealous."

He scoffs. "I'm not jealous."

"Good, because if you plan on staying here, you're going to be seeing Wyatt a lot. I'd hate for things to be…uncomfortable."

Stop baiting him.

It's hard not to when he is clearly jealous yet won't admit it.

So, what if he is? It's not like it matters.

Each of his fingers flex before curling back into themselves. "That's fine."

"Are you sure? You did try to choke him less than twenty minutes ago."

"And I'd do it all over again if I heard someone talking about you the way he did."

My heart beats harder against my rib cage. "Like what?"

"Like you didn't matter to them."

My control over the situation slips, along with the protective shell I keep around my heart. "Cal…"

This is exactly what I was afraid of if he came back. It was always easy to pick back up where we left off every summer, like no time was lost between us.

But we lost more than time over the last six years since he left.

We lost out on whatever future we might have had together.

He breaks eye contact first. "Whatever. It was stupid of me to get pissed. So long as he makes you happy, that's what matters."

This is the Cal I fell in love with. The selfless man who would stop at nothing to make me happy, even if it meant sacrificing his own happiness in the process. It reminds me so much of how he was before the pills, alcohol, and lies.

Before the *betrayal*.

"I'm not dating Wyatt." My confession rushes out of me.

His brows shoot up. "What?"

"He married Delilah almost a year ago. They're celebrating their first wedding anniversary in September."

"Wyatt got married to *Delilah?*"

I cross my arms against my chest. "Yup. I guess you were too busy trying to choke him out to notice the shiny wedding band on his finger."

"Shit. You're right." His cheeks flush. "But if you aren't with Wyatt…" His voice trails off.

"If I'm not with Wyatt *what?*"

He clears his throat. "Nothing."

"You sure about that?"

He tips his chin up at me. "I'm sure. Night."

"Good night."

He stomps off the porch steps and disappears down the path toward the guesthouse.

What the hell was all that about?

I shut the door behind me and lean against it. My legs tremble beneath me, the weight of our conversation making me unsteady on my feet. If this is day one of Cal living here, I can't imagine what's to come.

I'm busy folding laundry upstairs in my bedroom when something heavy thuds above me, right where the attic is located. Cami knows better than to go up there, so that only leaves one person who could have caused such a loud noise. The same person who has spent the last three hours upstairs doing who knows what.

I haven't seen Cal since he went up there with a single cardboard box. He only spoke five words to me, most likely because he was still upset after everything that happened with Wyatt yesterday.

A second crash, this time much louder, has me running for the stairs at the end of the hall. My lungs burn from exertion as I bolt up the steps two at a time.

I storm into the attic. It's impossible to see much past the stacks of boxes nearly reaching the support beams.

"Cal?" I call out.

A groan from somewhere to my left has me working my way in that direction. The attic is a maze of boxes, chests, and containers, so it takes me longer than I'd like to find Cal laid out on the floor like a starfish.

He doesn't move at the sound of my footsteps, although his fingers twitch at his sides. His eyes remain screwed shut as I kneel beside him and scan his body for any injuries.

"What happened?" I ask.

He doesn't sit up. "I fell."

"And you didn't think to get up?"

"The room keeps spinning," he slurs.

Concern has me jumping into action. Is he having a stroke? Or maybe something with his brain? "What—" My question is cut off at the sight of the half-filled bottle of premium vodka spilling out beside him.

Of course.

I shouldn't be surprised. I've seen this story play out time and time again with Cal, yet the sick feeling weaving its way through my stomach has me curling my hands into tight fists. Years' worth of anger rises to the surface at the sight of him plastered on the floor, unable to sit up from how much alcohol he consumed.

Once an addict, always an addict.

I slide my mask into place, keeping my voice detached as I ask, "Are you hurt?"

"Only here." He taps his chest, right over his heart.

God. It's so sad to see a grown man like him suffer the way he does. During our childhood and early adulthood, he was always so full of life. To see him reduced to this broken version of himself only draws out the protector in me.

Cal has so much to offer the world, but his self-loathing and destructive patterns get in his way every single time. A part of me hoped that he found happiness in the six years we spent apart.

Not with someone else, but with *himself.*

He is no better than the day he left.

I pick up the vodka bottle so it doesn't spill any more before taking in our surroundings. A few of Cal's old hockey trophies are scattered around the floor, along with an old NHL jersey of his and a few opened boxes.

No wonder he was drinking. Going through those kinds of memories—the ones that represent the highest highs and the lowest lows—would upset anyone. It's just that Cal's way of coping is the worst.

"What happened?" My voice is much softer this time.

He blinks up at the ceiling. "I fell."

"So you said. But how?"

"Lost my balance when trying to pick up the bottle." He stumbles over the sentence. Despite the puddle on the floor, Cal must have drunk a decent amount if he is falling over himself and tripping over his words.

I help prop him up against one of the travel trunks, grunting from how much he weighs. "What happened before that?"

Stop asking him questions and go.

Except when I think about leaving, the image of Cal tapping his chest and saying it hurts replays in my head.

I don't stick around for the drunk man in front of me. I stay for the man I once loved more than anything.

He steals the vodka bottle back and tips it over an open box beside him.

"Stop!" I steal the bottle from his hands and put it out of reach before assessing the damage.

"Oh, no." I press my hand against my mouth. "What did you do?"

Vodka soaks through hundreds of photos of the Kane family.

The one on top features Cal's mother, who beams at the camera. Her blond hair looks like spun gold and is slightly lighter than Cal's. His father has an arm wrapped around her. He looks just like I remember, stern with a hint of something lurking behind his dark, beady eyes. The three Kane brothers smile up at the camera, with Cal just barely standing taller than Declan. Rowan is the smallest, although he was probably barely ten years old here.

"Who cares? It's all ruined anyway."

I try to salvage some of the photos, wiping off the vodka with the bottom of my shirt. "These are memories."

"Memories of what? A family that doesn't exist anymore?" he snaps.

I keep at my task with every intention to save as many photos as I can. "I understand you're upset."

"What do you know?" He scowls.

"You're not the only one whose mother died. Our situations might not have been the same, but I understand what it feels like to lose someone you love to something you can't control."

His glassy eyes track my movements. "She would be ashamed of me."

I rear back. "What? Why do you say that?"

"Because look at me." He grabs a trophy and launches it in the opposite direction. It slams into a tower of boxes before clattering against the floor.

"Stop it!"

"Why? It's not like any of them mean anything." He repeats the same thing with another trophy, but this time, it smashes into a wall before snapping in half.

"Enough!" I shove the other two trophies away before he destroys those too. "Get angry. Get loud, but don't get violent. You're better than that."

He throws his hands in the air. "Am I? Or am I just biding my time until I turn into him?"

He doesn't need to clarify which *him* he is speaking about because I already know. It's written all over his face.

My chest pinches, the tight sensation making each breath I draw painful. "The only thing you two have in common is an addiction issue."

"You're right. Because unlike me, my father is successful. He has a legacy. What do I have?"

"For starters, a heart."

He frowns. "Who cares? What has that gotten me in the long run? Pain? Misery? Disappointment?" He looks up at the ceiling with a sigh. "I can't get a single thing right. My whole entire life has been one failure after another, and I'm so fucking tired of pretending it doesn't bother me."

Cal steals a fragmented piece of my heart in that moment as a single tear slides down his cheek. A tear that wrecks whatever last bit of anger I have toward him today.

Tomorrow, I'll be angry about him being drunk in the house.

But today…

Today he needs a friend.

I pull him into my arms and wipe away the tear, banishing it from existence like it never happened. "You haven't failed at everything."

"Name one thing."

I don't miss a beat. "You made it into the NHL."

He scoffs. "Only to lose my spot a few years later."

"So what? Not many people can say they even got that far in the first place."

"I didn't even win a championship." His voice sounds so small. So unsure. *So broken.*

It tears me up inside, knowing someone as vibrant and lively as him can be riddled with this many insecurities.

Sometimes it is those with the loudest voices who struggle the hardest.

"Life is about perspective. Until you change yours, you'll always be tied to this." I hand him the vodka bottle.

He clutches the bottle with a death grip.

I lock the image away in my head, reminding myself that no good can come of Cal and me being around each other. Even after all these years apart, he still hasn't put in the work to change himself.

No matter how much I love him, it was and never will be enough so long as he doesn't love himself.

That much I know to be true.

Cal must have gone on a drunken shopping spree yesterday because there is no explanation for the ten packages that show up on my doorstep the next afternoon. The labels on the boxes range from the most expensive luxury department store in America to some French names I can't pronounce, let alone recognize.

"Please sign here." The delivery man hands me a clipboard.

I text Cal once he leaves.

> You have a delivery.

His reply is instantaneous.

> Be right there.

Perfect. At least this way, we can talk about what happened yesterday and get something straight.

I had planned on speaking to Cal once he came over this afternoon to work on the attic, but he never showed after I came home from work.

It doesn't take him long to pull into the driveway with his fancy car. Not sure how he plans on fitting all those boxes inside his trunk, but I wish him the best of luck regardless.

"Hey." He doesn't remove his sunglasses.

I cross my arms. "Hi."

He rubs the back of his neck. "About yesterday... Thanks for checking on me."

My lips tug down into a frown. "I don't want you getting drunk inside of my house again."

"Okay."

"I mean it. If I find you like that again, then I'm calling a moving company to bag your stuff for you."

His head hangs and his sunglasses slide down the bridge of his nose, revealing his bloodshot eyes. "I'm sorry."

"Apologizing doesn't mean anything when you have no intention of fixing the problem in the first place."

His hands clench by his sides. "You're right."

"I am?"

He looks up, and the tick in his jaw has my heart sinking in my chest.

I don't want to hurt him, but I have a kid to think about. There is no way I want Cami to find Cal stumbling about the house, drunk and incapable of controlling his emotions.

She deserves better than that.

"I have a problem. An *addiction*."

My mouth opens only to shut a second later.

"I know I'm powerless over alcohol. They taught me as much in rehab and AA. But I can't ignore how ashamed I am, knowing I'm only slightly better off than I was six years ago."

My eyes burn.

He takes a deep breath. "I can't quit drinking completely yet, but I'll limit myself for you. I don't want to hurt you any more than I already have, and what happened in the attic was unacceptable and pathetic."

Oh, God. My whole chest aches.

"Okay?" he asks.

"Okay," I rasp.

He releases a heavy exhale before grabbing the largest box from the pile and turning toward his car. With the size of his trunk and back seat, he only manages three boxes before he runs out of room.

Rather than stick around, I slip back inside, leaving him to sort out the rest of his packages, along with how the hell he plans on tackling the attic without drinking again.

CHAPTER TWELVE
Alana

I t only took Cal two days after the attic incident to schedule a
meeting with the appraiser. I didn't have an option to say no,
especially when Cal went out of his way to plan it around my
school schedule.

Cami promised to stay upstairs in her room and play with
her toys, so long as I order pizza for dinner tonight. It's a fair
price to pay for her cooperation. I'm not ready for her to ask me
questions about the house, especially when there is a risk my plan
might fail.

Doubts about Violet's idea sink in, eating away at my
confidence as I near the front door.

All you need to do is make it impossible for Cal to sell the house.

Easier said than done, the antagonistic voice that always
speaks up at the most inconvenient times replies.

I roll my shoulders back and open the door. "Hello."

"Hi there. I'm Mr. Thomas," the older man introduces
himself. From the horn-rimmed glasses to the suspenders, I'm

not sure where Cal found this man. Based on the pinstripe suit and his black-and-white wingtip shoes, I suspect the 1920s.

Mr. Thomas shoves his glasses up the bridge of his nose. "Are you Ms. Castillo?"

"That's me."

He looks down at his clipboard with an arched brow. "Is Mr. Kane here?"

I haven't seen him since he disappeared inside of the attic an hour ago.

An idea dawns on me.

I pout. "Actually Cal isn't able to make it today, so it might be best if we reschedule."

"Oh. Okay then. When are you thinking?"

"Does December work for you?"

He looks down at the calendar on his phone. "Of this year?"

I shake my head. "The next."

One of Mr. Thomas's brows raises in question. "I'm not booking that far out yet."

"A pity then. I'll be sure to have Cal give you a call in a year then."

Speaking of the devil, his steps echo off the vaulted ceiling as he runs down the stairs two at a time. "Ignore her. She's just joking." He stops in front of Mr. Thomas and offers his hand. "Please call me Cal."

"Nice to finally meet you." Mr. Thomas gives Cal's hand a good shake. "Now if you don't mind, I'd like to get started. Given the size of the property and my tight schedule, I'd like to not rush before my next appointment."

"No problem." Cal shuts the door behind him and gestures

toward the double staircase. "Would you like to start upstairs or down?"

"Downstairs works for me." Mr. Thomas grabs a pen from the inside pocket of his suit.

While he scribbles something on his clipboard, Cal makes it a point to lean in and whisper in my ear, "Behave or else." His sultry voice makes my heart jolt.

I turn to glare at him. "Or else *what*?"

"Don't taunt me." He tries his damnedest to look intimidating and fails. One would think after growing up with a brother like Declan, Cal would have mastered the art of looking unapproachable by now.

I chuckle to myself, which earns another glare from Cal.

"If you don't mind, I'm going to have a quick look around by myself." Mr. Thomas looks over at us with a quirked brow.

"By all means." I shoot him a tight smile.

Mr. Thomas disappears down a hallway, leaving Cal and me to our stare down.

He crosses his arms, drawing my eyes to his rolled-up sleeves. His golden forearms have always been a weakness of mine. "What's your issue?"

"Isn't it obvious? I told you I don't want to sell the house."

"And *I* told you it's happening whether you want it or not."

"We'll see about that." I smirk.

His eyes drop to my lips, making them tingle with a single glance. "What are you planning?"

"Why ruin all the fun by spoiling the surprise?"

"You know how I feel about those."

"About the same as you do clowns. *Thrilled.*"

I have never been able to throw out the photo I have of Cal crying at the circus. It's one of the few things that brings me joy on a shitty day, right after Cami's hugs and fresh baked goods.

"You know me so well," he replies dryly.

"Now if you'll excuse me, I better go check on dear Mr. Thomas. I'd hate for him to get lost somewhere between the conservatory and the parlor."

I swivel on my heels, only to be stopped by Cal grabbing on to my elbow. His hold is soft, although his words come out sharp. "Whatever you're doing needs to stop now. It's only going to prolong the process."

Now that's an idea…

His head tilts as his eyes scan my face. "Don't even try it."

I rock back on my heels. "I don't know what you're talking about."

He steps closer. The smell of him wraps around me like an aromatic hug, making my head swim from the pheromones. "You're scheming. I can tell by the little sparkle in your eye. It's the same one you always got right before you goaded me into doing something I knew I'd regret."

"It's not my fault that you couldn't turn down a dare."

"That's what I made you think. I was just miserably trying to impress you, even if it meant risking a few broken bones and a criminal record to do so."

My mouth drops open. "You…" Any reply gets lost in the mess of my mind as I try to process Cal's admission.

Cal curses under his breath. "Forget I said anything."

Right. Like I stand a chance of erasing the imprint his words leave behind on my scarred heart.

This is exactly how you got into trouble the first time.

He disappears down the hallway Mr. Thomas went without sparing me another glance.

I take a moment to recover before joining Cal and Mr. Thomas on the property walkthrough. Rather than focus on my conversation with Cal, I spend the entire meeting asking the appraiser questions about the house and surrounding land. I try to keep my face neutral and avoid any shady eyes or sneaky smirks. Cal throws strange glances my way through the whole exchange, most likely because he suspects something is amiss with my interest.

You should have kept your mouth shut.

No going back now.

Based on the appraiser's notes, the house has many issues. From the leaking roof to some termite damage in the basement, the property needs a serious overhaul. The only place that seems somewhat decent is the guesthouse, but mainly because it was built only ten years ago.

I always knew the house needed work, but I didn't realize just *how* much until now. It might take my whole life to get to all the problems.

The appraiser scribbles a few more notes on his clipboard before looking up at us. "Bottom line is I doubt you'd get more than a million for the house."

Cal shrugs. "That's more than my grandfather paid for the place back when he bought it."

I glare at him. "There's no way we are only getting a million for it."

"You have some serious termite damage, a roof that needs

to be completely redone, windows that are fifty years old and desperately in need of being replaced, and enough small renovation jobs to keep a general contractor busy for a whole year."

"How much would that all cost to fix?" I ask.

"I'm guessing two hundred thousand dollars, give or take on the finishes. Prices can vary if you know some people in contracting that can give you a good deal."

"That shouldn't be a problem. I know some people who would do the job for the cost of supplies if I asked them." And they would be willing to draw out the entire process for as long as I wanted, which is a win in my playbook.

Cal's gaze burns into the side of my face. "We're not going to remodel the house."

I turn to face him. "Well, we're not going to put it on the market for a million when most houses around the lake are selling for triple that."

"Those look like the Ritz compared to this."

"Then we give this one a little bit of a facelift."

"With what money?"

I shoot him a look. "Are you pressed for cash all of a sudden?"

He barks out a laugh. "So you expect me to front the money? Of course."

The appraiser's eyes bounce between the two of us like he is following a tennis match.

"We can split the costs," I offer.

"Where will you get those kinds of funds?"

"You can deduct it from my earnings once we sell the place."
Which is never.

If it were anyone else, I'd feel guilty for talking them into this crazy plan, but this is Callahan Kane. His trust fund is padded with enough money to make his great-great-grandkids little baby billionaires one day. Two hundred thousand dollars is nothing for him.

The appraiser shifts his weight from foot to foot. "In theory, she's right." *Don't we love to hear it.* "The more you invest into a property, the more justified a higher listing price is. Remodeling a unique house like this would increase the profit margin significantly. Especially since there are lots of people searching for turn-key vacation homes in the surrounding towns."

I gesture toward the appraiser. "See?"

Cal rubs his stubbled jaw. "Since when do you care about profits? I thought you didn't want to even sell the place."

"I'm thinking about the future, Callahan. I know it's hard but try to keep up with me."

His nostrils flare. "I *am* thinking about the future. It's just that my version happens to be a realistic one."

"Can we sell the house for more than suggested?" I ask.

Mr. Thomas's gaze swings between the two of us. "Technically speaking, yes. Since the house is paid off and doesn't carry a mortgage, you can sell it for any price."

"That's not a real answer," Cal grumbles.

"Just because it isn't the answer you want to hear doesn't make it any less real." I place my hands on my hips and stare him down.

Cal ignores me as he turns back toward the appraiser. "How much increase are we talking?"

The man flips through the pages attached to his clipboard.

"If you fix the glaringly obvious issues I found with the place, then you can possibly get an extra million out of it."

I shake my head. "I want to sell for three."

The appraiser's face pales. "Million?"

"Sure. If the neighbor down the road who had less land could sell their property for that price, why couldn't we?"

"Because their house was brand new and had state-of-the-art everything," Cal answers for the man standing across from me, staring at me like I've lost it.

Maybe I have.

I look out the window that faces the serene lake. "We have more land and a better view of the lake. I'm sure someone will be willing to pay three million for it."

The appraiser tugs at his tie, loosening the knot as if it was choking him. "Well…it's your choice to sell the place for whatever price you think is best."

I raise my chin. "Perfect."

Cal's eyes narrow. "You can't seriously think we will find someone who will buy this place for that much money."

"Of course we can. All it takes is finding the right buyer. Isn't that right?" I face the appraiser again.

"Technically yes. Although setting the price too high might turn some buyers—"

I cut him off. "Great. That's all I needed to hear."

He readjusts his glasses with a huff. In any other scenario, I wouldn't be so forward and rude, but letting him speak out of turn might backfire on me.

Cal rubs his chin. "Now it all makes sense."

I peek over at him. "What?"

"All your questions to the appraiser, your insistence on giving the place a facelift, and the reason why you want to set such a high price."

Well, damn. He figured me out sooner than I anticipated.

CHAPTER THIRTEEN

Cal

I leave Lana in the kitchen while I walk the appraiser out. When I come back, I find she hasn't moved from her spot by the window that overlooks the lake. Her fingers tap against the counter to the beat of her hum.

I seize the opportunity to take her in without being judged for it. She looks heaven-sent, with the golden glow of the sun surrounding her like a halo, highlighting the warm tones of her hair and the edges of her curves.

Those fucking curves.

Lana is soft in all the right places. Her love of baking and all things culinary has turned her body into a work of art, with hips meant for gripping and an ass meant for worshipping.

Don't think about her ass.

Too late. My eyes drop, burning a hole into her leggings.

"As much as my ass appreciates the attention, I'd like to get along with my day. I have a ton of work to grade before tomorrow."

My mouth dries up along with any type of rebuttal as my gaze swings from Lana's legs to her face. Her brow lifts. She was always a straight shooter—a fact I appreciated until now.

How long has she been watching me stare at her?

Given your luck lately, maybe a whole minute. There's a reason my brothers used to tease me for being Space Cadet Cal. I have a propensity to drift off and forget where I am until someone tugs me back to reality, usually by calling me out.

I clear my throat, forcing some oxygen into my airway. "We're selling this house in three months for a million dollars whether you like it or not."

She steps closer, encroaching on my space. "Oh, why? Because you said so?"

"*Because* that's the only option. The sooner you accept it, the easier this process will be."

"Or I could hire a lawyer." She bats her lashes.

The hairs on the back of my neck rise. *Fuck.* "Except you're not going to do that."

Her scoff comes off as condescending as the rise of her chin. "I don't take orders from you."

"Pity. I remember there was once a time you would beg for them." My thumb traces the bottom of her lip, earning a sweet inhale from her.

She leans into my touch before shaking her head and giving my chest a shove. "You're just trying to distract me."

"From what? Stabbing me in the back?"

Her eyes *sparkle*. "Only cowards go for the back."

If I didn't already know I was a bit unhinged, my dick getting hard at the way she threatens me with a vicious smirk would motivate me to get my head checked.

I pin her in place with my stare. "You want to list the house for more money than it's worth so no one buys it, don't you?"

"What? Why would I want to do that?" The glint in her eyes and the small hitch of her lips kill her attempt at feigning innocence.

"Beats me. I'm not sure why you're trying so damn hard to save this place. It's a complete dump."

She rears back. Whatever playfulness was in her eyes dies, replaced by a burning gaze and one end goal.

Shit.

Her nostrils flare. "You might see this place as a dump, but I see it as a home—*my* home—and there is no way I'm giving it up without a fight. So, you better lawyer up and take me to court, asshole." She storms out of the kitchen, leaving me to stew in how our conversation went wrong.

Fuck.

I place one of my grandfather's Victorian era revolvers in a box marked for the Smithsonian. It's the third weapon I've found in the godforsaken attic. The longer I spend in here, the more I question who my grandfather really was.

Maybe Lana was right when she said I didn't know my grandfather as well as I thought I did.

I keep to his side of the attic and avoid the corner that houses all my old belongings and hockey memorabilia since I told Lana I wouldn't get drunk up here again. Besides taking a few breaks at the guesthouse so I can have a few sips of vodka without breaking my word, I keep true to my promise about not drinking *in* the house.

My phone vibrates in my back pocket, so I pull it out and take a seat on one of my grandfather's trunks. I texted Iris an hour ago, only for her not to answer until now. She is slowly getting busier, which only makes it harder for us to talk as often as we used to before she got married.

Iris

> Hey. How's it going?

> I hit a minor snag.

Iris surpasses texting and calls me instead.

"What's going on?" she asks. A car horn honks in the background, making her dog, Ollie, bark.

"Lana threatened to lawyer up, so either I agree to sell the house for three million or I'm screwed."

Silence.

"Are you there?" I check my phone for a dropped call.

She coughs. "Yeah, just trying to wrap my head around that one based on the photos you sent me of the place. The view might be nice, but it's not *that* nice."

"The bones are decent."

"That's exactly what Declan said about our new house right before he took a wrecking ball to the place."

"Only because he was impatient and didn't feel like dealing

with old construction issues."

Iris shouts at Ollie to stop chasing squirrels before remembering I'm on the line. "Why does Alana want to sell it for that price?"

A small smile breaks through my annoyance. "Because she thinks if she sets the price unreasonably high, then no one will buy it." I explain the rest of Lana's plan, including how she wants to remodel the property to justify a high list price.

Iris whistles. "Damn. I respect her efforts."

"Whose side are you on?"

She chuckles under her breath. "Yours always, although I gotta give it to her. She must really want that house if she is willing to fight you this hard on it."

"I wish I could just tell her about the stupid will." I rub my temple.

"Except you can't, so we need a better plan."

"Like what?"

She clears her throat. "If she wants to sell it for a higher price, then do it."

"Are you for real?"

Iris cackles. "Just think about it. What's the worst that can happen if you remodel the house?"

"Based on watching you and Declan argue for hours over paint swatches and tile samples, a lot." The two of them have mulled over every single detail, down to what color the grout should be.

"It's actually kind of fun, although if he had things his way, the entire house would be black."

I'm not looking for fun. I want easy. Simple. *Safe.* Because the longer I stick around Lake Wisteria, the more I put myself at risk for remembering all that I left behind.

The life I could have had.

The only woman I ever loved.

The future I threw away because of an addiction.

If I want to get out of this town unscathed, then I need to sell the house sooner rather than later.

Before I make a decision about the house price, I want to be well-informed about the other houses in the area. I spend the next two days researching every single surrounding lakefront property that has sold in the last five years. Out of those seventy homes put on the market, ten were purchased for over three million dollars. The other sixty properties were bought for half the price, which was still more than the quote we received from the appraiser.

Basically, my shot at hitting gold with Lana's list price will come down to two things: a kick-ass renovation job and enough money to make it happen within three months.

I call the one construction company in all of Lake Wisteria, only to be given the brush-off once I give them my full name. They weren't even willing to add me to their waitlist, which apparently is five years long.

Did you expect anything less from a town full of people who hate you?

The next town isn't much better. Although they have a shorter waitlist, the six-month wait time can't be changed regardless of how much money I am willing to pay.

Frustrated and about ready to pull my hair out, I decide to take a walk to clear my head. I pass the main house on my way to the road. The driveway is empty, so Lana must still be at work.

I keep to the sidewalk during my walk. Each house is acres apart, with their own private driveways leading up to their houses. The houses I used to recognize as a kid are all gone, replaced by mega modern mansions on massive plots of land overlooking the glittering lake.

With each step I take, the truth becomes more obvious. While my grandfather's estate has stayed the same, a majority of the houses have been bought out and completely rebuilt.

Lana might have been on to something when she mentioned remodeling.

Fifteen minutes into my walk, I come across a construction site that is completely blocked off from the public by a perimeter fence. Pinned to the fence is a large sign promoting Lopez Luxury.

A quick search on Google tells me they're a rather new company—less than ten years old—and based out of Michigan.

Just what I need.

I dial the number and ask to speak with someone who can help me get a renovation done in three months. This time, when I give my full name, I'm transferred directly to Julian Lopez, the head of the company, no questions asked.

"Mr. Kane." The low rumble of Mr. Lopez's voice fills my ear.

"Mr. Lopez."

"Please call me Julian. So, I hear you need a renovation job done in three months."

"Can you help me?"

He doesn't miss a beat. "Depends on if you're willing to do the same."

Of course, there is a catch. "What do you want?"

"To have my company chosen for one Kane Company project."

"Are you looking to expand your services to the hospitality industry?"

"Something like that." His deep chuckle lacks any kind of warmth—just like his personality.

Brady's lawyer said my brothers couldn't get involved with the house sale, but he never mentioned anything about offering someone a job in the company in exchange for services.

Look at you finding legal loopholes.

I know my brothers will find Mr. Lopez something to do, however small. "If your team can remodel my house in three months, then—"

"Done. My assistant will be in contact with you to schedule a meeting with one of my best contractors."

The line goes dead without him bothering to say goodbye. Mr. Lopez reminds me of Declan, with his sharp tone and no-bullshit attitude.

Another piece of my plan slides into place, slowly building my confidence. Declan might think I'm good at failing, but I plan on proving him and everyone else who doubted me wrong.

Mommy! Look!" Cami runs into the kitchen, dropping envelopes of mail behind her like a breadcrumb trail. "¡Cuidado!" I grab her before she runs straight into an open cabinet.

She holds her envelope high in the air. "I got mail!"

I recognize the logo instantly. It's been a few months since Cami took the entrance exam for Wisteria Prep, an exclusive private school that only opened a few years ago to cater to the families moving here from Chicago. Cami begged me to apply since a few of her friends were transferring there, so I let her even though the principal warned me they only had two seats available for the incoming first-grade class.

My girl is the smartest kid I know, but those kinds of places are all about politics and who you know. Her chances of getting in were always slim.

Which is why you have to face the consequences of your actions.

She bounces up and down, waving the envelope in the air.

"Can we open it now? Please?"

"Let me do it." At least that way I can have a second to mentally prepare for how I'll break the news to her.

My hands shake as I wipe them across my apron, prolonging the inevitable by cleaning the flour off my fingers.

"Mommy! Hurry up!" She waves the envelope in front of my face.

"All right. Let me have it."

Cami slaps it into my waiting hand. I open the envelope with a butterknife before pulling out the thick piece of paper.

"What does it say?" She shifts her weight from foot to foot, making her sneakers light up.

"I'm going." I unfold the paper and read the first line.

Congratulations, Camila Theresa Castillo…

"You got in." The words come out in a hoarse whisper.

"What?! Ah!" She takes off running and screaming at the top of her lungs. "I get to go to school with all my friends!" She disappears into the hallway, her voice echoing off the twelve-foot ceilings.

I continue reading the letter, my heart tripping over the tuition price at the bottom.

"Thirty-five thousand dollars? For first grade?"

Somehow it continues to get worse. Prices only go up from there, with twelfth grade costing almost fifty grand. The letter also emphasizes how Wisteria Prep encourages the arts and requires students to participate in at least one afterschool activity. They can range from a thousand dollars a month to five, depending on what activity the child chooses.

The room spins around me. When Cami applied, it was only

a pipe dream meant to make her happy temporarily, but now that it is a reality, I feel sick to my stomach. Even after accounting for the financial aid Cami was offered, there is still no way I could afford the school on my kind of salary.

I reach out for the countertop, afraid my knees might buckle.

"Hey, what's all the yelling— Whoa. Are you okay?"

Of all the people to be present during my little breakdown…

I've been lucky enough to avoid him since our fight about the house, but I knew it would only last so long.

Just keep it short and sweet.

I take a deep breath and look up at Cal. His usual casual outfit of a button-down and pants is replaced by athletic pants and a workout T-shirt that is drenched around the collar with sweat.

"What are you wearing?" I try my hardest to keep my eyes focused on his face, but they drift toward the abs pressing against the tight fabric of his T-shirt.

"I was working in the attic when I heard screaming."

"Oh." I speak to his stomach muscles.

His low chuckle snaps me out of my embarrassing display of desperation.

He reaches for a glass in the cabinet and fills it up with water. My skin warms, my heart beating harder at the way his tongue darts out to lick a stray droplet from his lips.

What I would offer to do the same…

"What's going on?" His Adam's apple bobs with each swallow of water.

Fuck.

Is it hot in here or am I just having a meltdown? I fan my

face with Cami's letter, trying to cool my hot cheeks.

Cal catches me staring and winks.

Ugh. Even a simple wink has my body vibrating with excitement.

"What's that?" He points at the paper in my hand.

"Cami's acceptance letter."

"For what?"

"A private school that just opened recently off Main. It's pretty tough to get into, so she's a bit excited about getting to stay with her best friends. I spent half the year preparing her for a rejection letter, but now that she got in…"

"You're worried," he says in a matter-of-fact tone. For someone who has spent the last six years away, he sure hasn't lost the ability to read me well.

My head drops. "Yeah."

"Why?"

"Because not all of us are billionaires." I do my best to support Cami. Whatever my girl wants, my girl gets. Dance lessons, gymnastics classes, afterschool art programs. Keeping her happy and busy comes with personal sacrifices, but I'm happy to provide for her in a way my sister never could. Yet, I still feel like I could do more. That I could work harder. Pick up a side hustle. Find a way to make more money.

There is one option.

A piercing hot sensation shoots through my chest.

Cal's forehead creases with confusion. "Didn't my grandfather leave you some money after he passed?"

My body temperature spikes, and I try to take a deep breath to regulate myself. I'm not even sure who I'm most angry at—Cal for bring up the inheritance or my sister for wasting a majority of it.

Cal's gaze hardens. "He *did* leave you some money, right?"

My jaw hurts from how hard I clamp down on my molars.

"What happened—"

I speak up before he can finish his sentence. "It's gone."

"How much did he give you?"

My nails bite into the flesh of my palms. "Why does it matter?"

His face softens. "Because you're not the kind of person to blow through money like that unless something happened."

"You know what? Forget I said anything." I swipe the rest of my mail off the counter and leave the kitchen before he has a chance to ask me where the money went.

Cal warned me years ago about my sister, but I didn't listen. If he found out about all the mistakes I made, he would be furious.

Not at me.

But *for* me.

And I know with all my heart that I can't risk what a reaction like that might do to me, so I do what Cal has always done best.

I run.

"What's up with you tonight?" Violet nudges me in the shoulder. "You didn't even comment on Mr. Jeffries hitting on Ms. Reyes at the bar."

"Mr. Jeffries likes Ms. Reyes? Since when?" I have worked with both of them at the school for years and never would have guessed either one liked the other based on their STEM rivalry.

"Apparently! Although the feeling is not mutual based on how quickly she shut him down."

"It was pretty sad to watch." Delilah clasps her hands over her heart. "But also weirdly entertaining. Kind of like one of those reality TV dating shows."

"It's a mystery how some people find their future spouses here." I look around Last Call. The bar is old and run-down, but all the locals love it since the tourists don't know about it. There is even a jukebox that still works if hit in the right spot.

"There's always that tourist trap bar off Dale Mayberry Road if you're in the mood for egotistical, stock market assholes who are obsessed with anal because regular sex is 'too intimate.'" Violet throws up a pair of air quotes.

Delilah chokes on her seltzer. "I'm so glad I'm taken."

"Not all of us were lucky enough to find the love of our life in high school." Violet sticks out her tongue.

Delilah looks down at her ring with a smile. My chest tightens, the sensation screwing with my head. I'm not jealous of Delilah. I feel nothing but happiness for her and her husband, yet something in me feels off-kilter.

Maybe you are *jealous.*

The thought makes the acid in my stomach roll.

"I'm going to use the restroom." I slide out of the booth and bolt toward the bathrooms.

A few people stop me along the way to say hello, but I keep the small talk to a minimum as I travel to the back of the bar.

The noise around me disappears as I shut the door and flip the lock. The sick churning sensation in my stomach remains, and I take a few deep breaths to ground myself.

Guilt always hits me first. It tramples all sensible thoughts, making me feel like a shitty person for being jealous of Delilah and Wyatt. Of wanting what they have and wishing it were me who was able to find someone special.

As quickly as the guilt arose, it fades away, leaving me with a hollow feeling in my chest—the same feeling I always get when I think about going home tonight and crawling into bed alone.

Better to be alone yet secure than in a relationship and worried.

It takes me a few minutes to gather myself and let the overwhelming nausea pass. By the time I return, Delilah and Violet have moved on to safer conversations and the empty feeling in my chest is no longer present.

It only took five minutes of deep breathing in a public bathroom to get there.

My mind drifts throughout the next hour. At one point, I go back to drawing mindless patterns through the condensation building on my glass of water.

"What do you think, Alana?" Delilah asks.

"What?" I blink.

"Did you hear a word of what I just said?"

I wince. "Sorry."

"Seriously, what's gotten into you?" Violet turns to look at me.

"I think I'm going to have to sell the house." Even though I spent the last two days processing the news, it still doesn't feel real.

"What? Why?" Delilah gasps.

"Cami got into Wisteria Prep."

"I knew she would! They'd be stupid not to pick her." Delilah claps her hands together. Her enthusiasm quickly dies as she checks out the look on my face. "Wait. Are you going to sell the house to help pay for the school?"

I swallow past the thick lump in my throat. "I don't have any other choice."

"What about financial aid?" Violet frowns.

"They offered me a good amount, but even with the scholarship, it's not enough to cover everything."

"But you love the house." Her scowl deepens.

"And I love Cami more." My voice cracks. "You should have seen the look on her face when she got in." My smile wobbles. "She spent the whole morning working on her dance moves because she wants to be ready for ballet with the big girls. There is no way I can say no."

Delilah clasps on to my hand and gives it a squeeze. "Are you sure about this?"

No, I'm not, but hopefully by the time we are prepped to sell the house, I will be ready to come to terms with leaving it, even if it means breaking a piece of my heart in the process.

I stop in front of the empty store window and stare at my reflection in the glass.

My two best friends keep walking down the sidewalk, unaware of my absence as Violet continues talking to Delilah about her neighbor from hell. "Can you believe he actually told me to go buy earplugs? Like I'm the abnormal one because I don't want to hear him fucking like a porn star at three a.m. I swear, one of these days I'm going to bring someone home just so he can see how it feels… What do you think—hey!" Violet backtracks.

Delilah follows behind, using her cane to prop herself up. Today is a sucky arthritis day for her, but she doesn't let that stop her from chasing after Violet.

"Sorry." I look over at them with a wobbly smile. "I got distracted."

Delilah gives my shoulder a nudge. "What are you dreaming about this time?"

I shut my eyes and imagine the windowfront full of decor and glass pastry stands. "Summer-themed display. Bright colors that pop and treats featuring the fruits of the season."

Violet sighs. "Sounds like a dream."

That's because it is.

"What do you think would be your bestseller?" Delilah points her cane at the window.

I look away from our reflections in the window. "Dee—"

She wags her finger in front of me. "Uh-uh-uh. You know how we play the game."

The three of us have been doing the dream game ever since Violet learned about manifestation. It hasn't worked out for us yet, but that doesn't stop my friends from trying.

She pokes me in the side. "Stop thinking so much and just tell me the first thing that comes to mind."

I bite down on my lip and consider my answer. "Well…you know how crazy everyone gets for my blueberry crumb cake."

Violet grins. "I've never seen so many people fight over a bunch of leftover crumbs. Even Sheriff Hank was ready to throw hands during last year's Fourth of July barbeque, and he is practically medically sedated nowadays."

My lungs burn from how hard I laugh.

Delilah, the softer one of my two best friends, shifts her cane to her left hand so she can wrap her other arm around my shoulder. "You know, if you sold the house, you would have the money to buy this place and turn it into the best bakery in Michigan."

I shake my head so hard, my vision blurs. "Not happening."

Violet pipes up. "Just think about it. You're the one who said you wouldn't risk giving up a steady paying job and health insurance for a dream. But once you sell the lake house, you'll have the money to cover all the startup costs of opening a new business."

I shake my head. "No way. That money isn't for me."

Violet tilts her head. "Even with Wisteria Prep's tuition, you wouldn't spend more than a quarter of it."

"I should be saving, not spending."

Delilah's hold around my shoulders tightens. "It's okay to be a little selfish and think about yourself every now and then. Cami would want you to be happy."

"What if I'm not good enough?" I voice my fear aloud. It's the same one that has kept me up many nights, rooted deep in years of questioning my self-worth. I've spent most of my life running from that worry ever since my father packed his bags and said he wasn't coming back.

"What if you end up spending the rest of your life regretting not taking a chance when you had it?" Violet wraps her arm around me, right above Delilah's.

"Or what if Missy opens a shop here instead and ends up becoming the town's favorite baker?" Delilah teases.

I gasp. "Take that back."

"I don't know. It could be possible that someone comes for your crown. I heard Missy was trying to master a tres leches recipe before the Fourth of July bake-off."

I fold my arms across my chest. "I should have suspected something when she was following me around the grocery store last month, asking me all kinds of questions about what brand of condensed milk I like most."

Violet pinches me in the side, making me laugh. "The point is, you'll miss out on all the things you could have done if you just asked yourself *why not* instead of *what if*."

"Who knew you could be so deep?"

She taps her temple. "Tequila makes me thoughtful."

"And horny," Delilah finishes for her, earning a jab to the ribs.

I wrap my arms around both of my friends and pull them in for a big hug. "You'll be my first two customers?"

Delilah smiles. "Like we ever had a choice."

CHAPTER FIFTEEN

Cal

Lana plucks a page from the tall stack of papers on the kitchen table and reads to herself while using her red pen to mark the page. Without any alcohol to artificially inflate my self-esteem, I'm left with a racing heart and an urge to escape before Lana notices me.

Not relying on vodka to numb your problems is a positive thing.

Yeah, except reducing my consumption always seems like a good idea until I'm faced with any kind of adversity.

Just go on and get this over with.

I tuck my thumbs into my front pockets. "Do you have a second?"

She looks up at me. "I'm a bit busy here grading papers."

"On a Friday night? Riveting stuff."

She shoots me a look. "Unless you're here to admit defeat

about the house, don't bother."

"I prefer the term *compromise*."

"I'm sure that's what all the losers say to make themselves feel better." The shimmer in her eyes fucks with me. Or to be more specific, my dick.

You're fucked in the head.

Of course I am. At this point in my life, I've had more therapists than friends, and neither stick around for long given my issues.

I pull out a chair across from her and take a seat. "I'm going to make you an offer."

"Oh, this ought to be good." She places her pen to the side before giving me her full attention.

"I want you to listen to me completely before you say no or threaten me with taking legal action."

She motions for me to continue.

Time to bring out the big guns. "Let me sell the house for two and a half million dollars and you can keep all the profits."

Her face pales. "*All* the profits?"

"Down to the very last penny. I'll even cover all the remodeling costs myself, which means you will walk away with everything at the end of closing day regardless of how much money we pump into this place."

She blinks twice. "But why would you do that?"

"Selling the house has never been about making money for me. I want to be done with this place as quickly as possible, so if it means losing a few million along the way, then so be it."

Her withering glare doesn't bode well for me. "Oh, yes. I'm sure that's such a sacrifice for a billionaire like yourself."

My clenched fists press into my thighs. "I'm trying to help both of us out while giving you a nice deal."

"I don't *need* your help," she snaps.

"No, but it would be nice to send Cami to that fancy school she got into with the funds."

Her eyes narrow. "Now you're just playing dirty."

I wink. "My favorite kind of strategy. Is it working?"

"Marginally, although your cocky grin isn't doing it for me at the moment."

I wipe the smile off my face. "Work with me." I'm not above begging on my knees to get her to see reason. "This kind of money can change anyone's life."

"How would you know? You made your first billion the moment you took your first breath."

"I'm not completely detached from reality. I understand the value of money."

"Knowing how to spend it isn't the same thing as valuing it."

My teeth grind together. "Valuing your money means knowing *where* to spend it, not how."

"Look at you being all wise."

"I'm more than just a pretty face, Lana. I have a brain too."

"Who lied to you and called you pretty?" She bats her lashes.

"You did…while I was between your legs with my tongue deep inside your needy cunt."

Take that, you little witch.

She chokes on her breath. "God."

"Please, no need to call me God outside of the bedroom. It gives me a complex."

She swipes the swear jar off the top of the fridge and slams it on the table in front of me. "Pay up."

I grab a hundred dollars and drop it in the jar. "Worth every penny."

"Cami's college fund appreciates the donation."

I clasp onto her wrist, and the warmth of her skin bleeds into mine. "You wouldn't need a swear jar anymore if you agree to sell the house."

She stares off into the distance.

I can practically taste victory, so I pull out my wild card. "You could open that bakery you've always dreamed about."

She releases a shuddery breath as she looks away, and I think for the first time since I came to Lake Wisteria, I'm finally winning.

Only because you're using her dreams against her.

Is that what I'm doing? Or am I simply reminding her what she must have forgotten over the years?

She shakes her head, her vision turning clearer as she comes back to reality. "No. I'd rather play it safe and save the money for a house and whatever Cami might need over the years."

"Play it safe? What happened to the girl who would act first and think later?"

"I grew up, Cal." She grabs the swear jar and places it back on top of the fridge.

"So what? Growing up doesn't mean giving up on all your dreams."

"I didn't give up. I just realized I'd rather make someone else's dreams come true a lot more than my own."

"What does that even mean?"

She pulls her stack of papers into her arms and retrieves her red pen. "I don't expect someone like you to understand."

My heart threatens to shrivel up. "Someone like me?"

"Someone who always chooses himself."

As if her words didn't do enough damage, the look on her face lands a killer blow.

She takes a deep breath. "I accept your offer on one condition."

"Name it."

"I want to have the final say in whoever buys the house."

I scoff. "Why? So you can make it impossible for anyone to buy it?"

She can't even look me in the eyes, which only adds to the hollowness in my chest.

"Because I want to make sure whoever owns it next loves my home as much as I do."

I instantly feel like a dick for thinking the worst about her. "Lana—"

Her nostrils flare. "Yes or no, Callahan?"

And now we're back to Callahan.

Lovely.

I nod. "You get the final say, so long as you're not vetoing potential buyers for no good reason."

Hopefully I don't end up regretting my choice.

Lana

I'm starting to wonder if you have a shopping addiction.

She sends me a photo of a box waiting on the porch. I bolt

off the couch, scaring Merlin, who wiggles his way underneath the TV stand.

> Be there in a few.

My excitement grows with each step I take across the property toward the main house.

Lana stands on the porch, waving at the red-headed mailman as he drives off.

I walk up the steps. "Do you know him?"

"Ernie? Yeah. He's Isabelle's son."

My brows rise. "I'm surprised my packages have arrive undamaged then."

"Me too. He's not too happy with you given the thirty packages delivered here in the last few days alone."

"This is the best one yet." I lift the heavy box into my arms.

She peeks at the cardboard box. "What is it?"

"A Kees van der Westen Speedster."

Her brows pull together.

"It's an espresso machine," I clarify. Caffeine, Adderall, and I don't usually mix well. But now that I'm working until late, long after my medicine wears off, I need a little pick-me-up in the afternoons.

She snorts. "Sounds like the name of a car."

"And costs about the same as a cheap one too." I give the box a loving pat.

Her eyes widen. "How much did you pay for it?"

"I don't remember. Twenty thousand, give or take with tax? Why? Do you want one?"

The color drains from her face. "You spent twenty thousand

bucks on an *espresso machine*?"

"I have needs, Lana."

"So do I, but that's worth more than half of my yearly salary!"

I rock back on my sneakers. "I know it sounds excessive…"

"That's because it *is*."

"Forgive me for enjoying the finer things in life."

"It's your money, so do what you want with it. I'm just surprised anyone would spend that kind of cash on coffee." Then let us hope she never finds out how much I spent on the new mattress, bed linens, and couch in the guesthouse.

"Please. This is nothing. Wait until you see the state-of-the-art grill I bought."

She blinks. "You bought a grill knowing you're only going to be here temporarily?"

"Of course. I thought maybe I could tempt you into making some of your mom's carne asada one of these days."

Her mouth drops open.

"It's a really fancy grill with all the bells and whistles and stuff most chefs drool over. I swear you'll love it."

She opens her mouth, only for it to slam shut.

I rub at the back of my neck. "I can cook for you too, although I can't promise it will be half as good."

"You would cook for me?"

"You and Cami," I correct.

Something flashes in her eyes before disappearing.

"You— We…" She rubs her temple in small circles. "You know what? I'm going to wipe this entire conversation from my brain."

"What did I say?" I reach out for her hand, only to have her step away before I have a chance.

"Nothing. I've got to go get Cami ready for her dance class." Lana disappears back into the house, leaving me to wonder what I said wrong this time.

Story of your life.

> I'm bored.

I bounce the tennis ball against the ceiling while I wait for Iris to reply to my message. With the contractor and his team already fixing up the exterior of the house, including replacing the roof, vinyl siding, and old windows, I have nothing else to occupy my time.

Lake Wisteria doesn't have many options for entertainment. Unless I want to drive thirty minutes away to go see a movie, I am stuck with either bowling by myself, hanging out at the park on the other side of the lake, or spending the rest of my day online shopping.

My phone vibrates against the couch.

Iris
> Have you tried picking up a new hobby?

> You mean one besides staring at myself in the mirror?

Iris
> I can't tell if you're being serious or not.

> Let's keep it a mystery.

Iris
> What about knitting?

> Hell no.

Iris
> Crocheting?

> ...

Iris
> Reading a book?

Hmm. I haven't read much since I was a kid, but that seems like a better option than attempting to create something with a ball of yarn.

> Any recommendations?

Iris
> Let's ask Zahra.

Iris follows up with a message in the group chat I share with the two of them.

Iris
> Do you have any book recommendations for Cal?

I throw my ball against the ceiling as I wait for Zahra to answer.

Zahra
> What do you like?

> The opposite of whatever you read.

Zahra

No romance. Got it.

My phone starts pinging from her texts of recommendations. I pull up my notes app and type out her suggestions before leaving the guesthouse.

By the time I park outside One More Chapter Bookstore, Zahra sent an encouraging message about how happy she is about me getting into reading.

The tiny store hasn't changed one bit since Lana and I used to visit. Tall wooden shelves line the walls, packed to the very top with books waiting to be purchased.

"Hi. How can I help you?" Meg, the older woman who has owned the shop since my mom used to take my brothers and I here, pops up behind me.

"I'm looking for a book." I turn to face her.

The smile on her face dims. *Typical.* "Oh. Which one?"

I pull out my phone and rattle off the three Zahra recommended. Meg quickly finds the books for me and rings up my purchase.

"There you go." She hands me the bag full of books.

The bell above the door rings. I look over my shoulder to find Violet strolling inside with Delilah.

Fucking small towns.

I haven't seen them in six years. While Violet's hair color has changed back to her natural blond color, Delilah still looks the same, although the ring on her left hand and the cane she leans against are new to me.

Violet's eyes connect with mine first. "What the hell are you doing here?"

"Isn't it obvious?" I hold up my bag.

Her nose wrinkles. "Since when do you read?"

"It took me a few decades, but I finally got the hang of it."

"You think this is all some kind of joke?" Violet charges toward me.

Meg disappears behind a stack of books, leaving me to deal with the red-faced woman who used to be one of my friends.

"I'm not here to cause problems." I keep my voice neutral, repeating the mantra that seems to follow me everywhere.

"So Alana says, but I have a hard time believing that." Violet stabs me in the chest with her finger.

Delilah frowns as she tugs on her friend's arm. "Come on, Violet. Just leave him alone."

She glances over at her friend. "One second." Her head slowly swivels back toward me like something out of a horror movie. "If you're here to screw with Alana again—"

I stop her. "I'm not."

"You're still drinking," she states.

"Is that considered a crime?"

"It's pathetic," she hisses. It's nothing I haven't heard before, yet having the words slung at me from someone who was once a friend cuts deeper than I care to admit.

You are *pathetic.*

A heavy weight presses against my chest, making breathing an impossible task.

Her upper lip peels back. "You're no better than her sister, making all these promises and never following through."

My hand holding onto the bag tightens until my nails bite

into my skin. "I know. Why do you think I left in the first place?"

Her eyes bulge.

"If you don't mind, I'm going to go now." My feet feel like someone attached two anvils to them, making every step exponentially more difficult than the last.

I bypass my car and head directly toward Last Call at the end of Main Street. It is a locals' spot, so my entrance stirs up whispers and glares from everyone gathered around the bar.

I stick to the unoccupied stool at the end of the counter, right across from a few people I recognize from around town.

The dark-haired bartender walks over to me with a frown. I remember him from one of Lana's birthday parties, although his face has filled out and his muscles have muscles.

Henry shakes his head. "You shouldn't be here."

"Vodka tonic, please." I ignore him as I smack a fifty-dollar bill against the counter.

His scowl only deepens. "No."

"Seriously?"

He crosses his bulging arms against his chest. "Isabelle warned us about you."

For fuck's sake. Did they have a town hall meeting about me?

"What did she say?"

The veins in his arms jump. "We're not allowed to serve you."

"Of course you're not. That's fine. I'll just take my money elsewhere." I snatch the bill and pocket it. I'm sure a nearby town will be more than happy to take my money and help me avoid an exchange like this again.

"Go to hell!" someone shouts from across the bar.

Little do they know, I'm already there.

CHAPTER SIXTEEN

Cal

Things finally feel like they're falling into place for me. Lana has even trusted me with a key to the house again after I needed access to it and she had plans for the weekend.

Even packing has gone smoothly over the last week. Most of my grandpa's items are cleared out of the attic, and the only thing left is to pack up is my old bedroom. It's located at the farthest corner of the house, a long way away from the childish giggling happening on the other side of the second floor.

Walking into my childhood room feels like I've been launched directly into the past. Besides a few taped boxes stacked in a corner, the place looks untouched. Even the glow-in-the-dark stars Lana and I superglued to the ceiling over two decades ago remain, although a few are missing or hanging by a single point. The window overlooking the lake snags my attention in the same way it did years ago when I picked this room as mine.

My brothers never understood why I wanted the smallest room located in a cramped corner of the house, but I thought the answer would be obvious if they took a moment to look out the bay window.

It feels strange to return here after six years away. I'm not sure why my grandpa and Señora Castillo kept the room the same, but it feels like it's been trapped in time.

The floor-to-ceiling shelves covering each of the three other walls feature the model boats I built during my summers here. From my first sailboat to a mini version of the *Titanic*, each boat holds a fond memory of a summer spent at Lake Wisteria. Of Lana and me staying up far too late working on them in the study.

My throat tightens as I stare at the last ship we started building the summer of my accident. The *USS Constitution* Lana bought me for my birthday sits unfinished on the lowest shelf, looking abandoned with its incomplete hull facing toward the ceiling.

You never had a chance to finish it together.

My chest throbs.

"Whoa."

I turn on my heels to find Cami staring up at the shelves with wide eyes. "Did you make that?" She points at a replica of *La Candelaria* sitting on the highest shelf, far away from anyone who could accidentally knock it over.

My throat tightens. "Yeah."

"Really?" She looks over at me with a strange expression.

I nod.

"What about that one?" She directs my attention toward the shelf above the window, where an Elizabethan Navy Rowan warship model sits, the wood dulled from the amount of dust and cobwebs covering the hull.

"Yup."

"And that one too?" There is a special sparkle in her eyes as she checks out the Viking ship.

"I made all of these with your mom." Hopefully that will answer any lingering questions she might have.

She gasps. "My mom? How?" Her forehead wrinkles from her pinched expression.

You spoke too soon.

I run a hand over my stubble, considering the best way to explain the process. "Have you played with Legos?"

"Yes!" She nods her head with a smile.

"It's like that but harder."

"Why?"

Instead of explaining the process, I pull out my phone and show her a time-lapse video of someone building a model sailboat. It's the first time I've been able to keep her quiet for a solid five minutes, so I count my idea as a win. Even I find myself getting swept up in the familiarity of the process and the therapeutic aspect of boatbuilding.

And that right there is why your brothers teased you endlessly about being a nerd.

Once the video ends, she looks up at me with a big smile. "Cool!"

I rear back. "Really?"

Her head bobs up and down. "I want to try."

She might not look like Lana, but she is 100 percent her through and through.

"You do?"

"Yes! Can we make one together?"

I blink twice, focusing on how she grouped us together. "What?"

"Please can we do one, Cow-l? Pretty, pretty please." Her bright eyes pierce through my resolve, tempting me to say yes.

"Ummm…"

She bats her lashes. "I'll be your bestest friend ever."

Don't you dare fall for that.

Except it's pretty hard not to with the way she looks up at me with a beaming smile full of hope. The idea of killing her budding interest makes the acid in my stomach bubble.

Stay strong.

"They're pretty hard." My excuse might be weak, but it's an honest one. I didn't start my first kit until I was double her age, and even then, I struggled until my grandpa stepped in to help.

"I'm no quitter." She lifts her chin.

I can tell based on the way she pushes me to say yes. I'm tempted to, solely because of her tenacity, but one thing holds me back.

"You need to ask your mom if it's okay."

"So, we can build one?" She bounces on the balls of her feet.

"*If* your mom says yes—" Lana will for sure say no, and I wouldn't blame her one bit. It was kind of our thing before it wasn't anymore. There is no chance in hell I expect her to want Cami and me to build one.

Cami cuts me off with a squeal before running out of my room, leaving me to question if I made the right decision.

No turning back now.

I spend the rest of my day packing away each of my model ships carefully into individual moving boxes. The last one I have left to pack, which I debated between dumping or saving all afternoon, is the boat Lana and I never finished.

Before I reconsider my answer, I pack it away with the box of unfinished parts.

My phone goes off a few times, mostly from my family group chat which I've ignored ever since my fight with Declan. I know I'll have to deal with him eventually, but I would rather face him once I'm officially done with my task.

I don't check my phone until I tape up the last box.

> **Lana**
> Care to explain why Cami has spent the last two hours watching boatbuilding videos on YouTube?

> **Lana**
> Never mind. I finally got the answer out of her.

It takes me a whole pathetic minute to come up with a reply.

> And?

Her reply comes through a second later.

> **Lana**
> Is it true that you offered to build a boat with her?

My fingers fly across the screen before I hit send.

> More like I was bribed.

Lana
> Then don't worry about it...

Shit. As nervous as I got from Cami's request earlier, I'd hate to disappoint her after how excited she looked.

In an act of desperation, I send a rapid-fire text without thinking twice about it.

> She offered to be my bestest friend ever if I agreed. I would be stupid to say no, especially with how many enemies I have in this town.

The bubbles pop up before disappearing, only to appear again. It happens twice before a new message appears on my phone.

Lana
> Don't make me regret this.

> What's the worst that can happen?

Lana
> The options are endless whenever you're concerned.

> I can always count on you to knock me down.

Lana
> At least I'm consistent.

She also sends an upside-down smiley face and a shrugging woman emoji. With a smile, I reply with a middle finger emoji.

I spend the rest of my afternoon with a stupid smile on my face, long after our conversation ended. The pressure in my chest is replaced by a lightness I haven't felt in a while, and my usual urge to drink while sorting through my personal items is absent.

It's a small win for an addict like me, but a win nonetheless, so I'll take it.

On my way to drop off the final box in the garage, I pass by the living room. Cami is sprawled out on the couch, fast asleep while wearing a sailor costume. An adult-sized captain's hat is thrown on the floor beside her right next to an empty juice box.

The kid is stupidly cute. No wonder Lana never stood a chance at saying no to her about building a boat with me. Who would?

"Oh, no. She fell asleep before dinner."

I turn to find Lana standing beside me.

"Are you going to wake her up?" I ask.

"Heck no."

I chuckle low. "Do you plan on having her sleep down here?"

"Nope."

"What are you waiting for?"

She presses her palm against the small of her back. "I'm mentally preparing my back for the pain I'm going to feel tomorrow once I carry her up the stairs."

"I can carry her," I offer before thinking.

Surprise. Surprise.

Her brows shoot up. "You can?"

I place the box on the floor. "She probably weighs what… forty-five pounds soaking wet?"

"A little less but yeah."

"No worries. I got her." I walk up to Cami and tuck my arms beneath her head and legs. Cami's head rolls, but Lana is quick to readjust her so her cheek is pressed against my chest. Cami grumbles something under her breath before snuggling deeper into my shirt.

A strange tugging in my chest has me looking away from Cami's face and directly toward Lana's. Her gaze travels from Cami to me, the skin around her eyes softening.

She is quick to break eye contact first. "I'll show you to her room."

I'm mindful not waking Cami as I follow Lana up the stairs and toward Rowan's old room. The dark wood furniture and navy blue paint is gone, replaced by lavender walls and a white canopy bed shaped like a princess carriage.

The Dreamland-themed comforter makes me smile. "Cute—"

"Don't." Her edgy tone matches her eye roll. A few of the princesses from our most famous movies are plastered across the fabric, all grinning up at the ceiling. Lana throws it back before giving me room.

I'm careful to not wake Cami as I place her on the bed. She doesn't stir, so I take a step back and let Lana do her thing. My feet remain glued to the floor while Lana tucks Cami in and whispers something against her forehead before kissing it.

The tugging sensation comes back stronger this time and wraps around my heart like a lasso, tempting me to escape.

So I do just that.

Since I'm in the mood to run away, I throw on my workout gear and take advantage of the breezy evening. I don't stop running until I end up heading down Main Street in search of food and something to occupy my mind.

Warm light pouring out of One More Chapter's windows has me taking off in the direction of the bookshop.

"Back so soon?" Meg shuts her book with a sigh.

"I need a new book." I wipe my damp face with the bottom of my shirt.

"Already? You just bought three a few days ago."

I run my hands through my slick strands of hair. "Not like I have much else to do around here besides read."

"What are you looking for this time?"

I pull out my phone to check Zahra's list, only to remember I already bought all the books she recommended. "Huh." My brows pinch together. "Do you have any recommendations?"

Her brows furrow. "For you?"

I look around the empty shop.

"Are you looking for something similar to what you read last time?" she asks.

"Or whatever you recommend."

Her eyes brighten for the first time ever. "Really?"

"Sure? Just don't set me up with something shitty because

you don't like me."

Her cackle doesn't exactly make me feel warm and fuzzy, but my uneasiness fades away as she bounces around the store with a smile while throwing books at me until the stack surpasses the top of my head.

She motions me toward the counter. "That should keep you busy for some time."

"Or a week," I mutter underneath my breath.

"You know if you have a lot of time on your hands, I heard the team in charge of the Strawberry Festival is still searching for volunteers."

"To do what?"

She shrugs. "I don't know, but if you're interested, you can stop by Town Hall and sign up."

"I'm not sure that's a good idea." I tuck my hands into my pockets.

She raises a brow. "What's the worst that can happen? The town actually has a reason to start liking you again?"

Well, when she puts it that way…

I would rather spend the rest of my weeks at Lake Wisteria without the town going out of their way to make my stay miserable, so if it means volunteering for a weekend, then so be it. What could possibly go wrong?

should have known today was going to be a bad day when one of my kids' parents nearly brought me to tears after ripping into me during a meeting to discuss their child failing my class. Then two of my students got caught skipping school during my period.

All it takes is a certain number calling me to push me straight over the edge and directly into meltdown territory. I consider ignoring my sister's call, but my guilty conscience doesn't let me.

I'm great at establishing boundaries for everyone in my life *but* my sister. It's a massive issue she exploits, and the reason I spent a large chunk of the inheritance Brady left me trying to save her from self-destructing.

The phone vibrates in my hand.

Just get it over with.

I lock the door to my classroom before answering the phone. "Hello."

"Alana!" My sister's overly excited voice makes my speaker crackle.

"Antonella." I keep my tone flat despite my escalating pulse.

"I've missed you. How are you?"

"Working."

She laughs. "Of course. How's your job going at the school?"

"Same old, same old."

"And Cami?"

My spine straightens. Unless my sister needs something from me, she never cares to ask about Cami.

"What do you want?"

She huffs. "Do most people need a reason to call their baby sister?"

"People? No. You? Absolutely." Antonella usually calls for two things: money or housing—neither of which I can provide her with anymore. I made that mistake right after Mom died, and the result nearly broke Cami's heart. Although my little superstar didn't know Anto was her mom, she grew attached to my sister hanging around, only to be broken-hearted when she disappeared.

It was my fault for being stupid and hopeful.

Not anymore though.

"I didn't like how we left things last time," she says like it hasn't been over two years since we have talked.

"It's been two years already and you decide to call *now*?" My hand clutching on to the phone tightens.

"I'm in a bit of a pinch and I was hoping you could help me out."

"No."

"But—"

"I'm not helping you anymore." Pure intentions haven't worked for me in the past, so maybe a little tough love will work better. And even if I wanted to help my sister, I can't. Between paying off my mom's medical bills, supporting Cami, and then saving Antonella from herself, I'm out of funds.

"But I'm sober for real this time. All thanks to you."

More like thanks to the cash you stole from my safe.

I shut my eyes. "That's good."

Assuming she is even telling the truth, the skeptical voice in my head says. I learned a long time ago not to trust my sister. It only took a hundred different disappointments to get there.

"Does that mean you'll let me crash at your place?"

"No, but I'm happy for you."

She makes an indiscernible noise. "Come on, Alana. Just give me a couple of weeks to get things sorted out. I'm struggling to pay my rent and bills since Trent moved out. He covered his half until the end of June to give me some time, but after that, I'm all on my own."

I'm not sure who Trent is or what his connection is to my sister, but at least he paid his part of the rent. I can't say the same about most of the men my sister has hung around with.

She keeps going. "I can't stay here past June, and I don't have anywhere else to go. It's not like I want to head back to Lake Hysteria, but what other choice do I have? I won't be there for long. I promise."

My chest pinches.

Don't you dare fall for her usual shit. Think about Cami.

"I'm sorry, Anto. That's a sucky situation to be in—"

"But you won't help me." Her voice is sharper this time. My sister has always acted the same way, being sweet as flan de coco until she doesn't get what she wants.

I shake my head. "It's not fair to Cami."

"Really? Or is it not fair to *you*?"

I suck in a breath. "What's that supposed to mean?"

"It's obvious you're intimidated that Cami might not want you anymore if I come back around."

I bite back a bitter laugh. "I'm not intimidated by you. Nothing you can do or say will change the fact that I'm her mother." Anto made sure of that the day she signed away her parental rights and made me a mother of a premature baby who was saved from neonatal abstinence syndrome due to her preterm birth.

"You wouldn't even *be* her mother if it weren't for me, so how about you show a little gratitude?"

Anto's harsh comment shouldn't come as a shock, but the heavy disappointment that hits me does. I thought I was used to this kind of treatment. Yet despite all the pep talks I have given myself over the years, my sister's words still have the ability to cut through me quicker than any blade.

It's the people we love most who always hurt us the hardest.

It is hard for me to accept that this version of Anto is the same person who would wipe my tears whenever I cried, and hug me through entire thunderstorms because I was afraid of them. The sister I grew up with would never speak to me like this, which can only mean one thing.

She isn't sober. She's strung out.

The pain blooming over my heart pushes me to end this

conversation before it gets worse. "I've got to get back to work. I'm sorry I can't help you."

"God, I forgot what a coldhearted bitch you can be. No wonder men are always running far away from you." Her words penetrate with the power of a missile, blowing through my last bit of restraint.

"Bye, Anto." I end the call and tuck my phone into the bottom drawer of my desk. My eyes prick, and I do everything in my power to hold the tears back. Rapid blinking. Not blinking at all. Fanning my eyes with my hands and then holding my head back to prevent them from falling.

Despite all my attempts, a single tear escapes in an act of betrayal. I swipe it away with angry fingers.

You will not shed another tear for her.

The chant seems to center me. I take a few deep breaths, lessening some of the weight pressing against my chest.

You made the right choice.

Yet no matter how many times I tell myself, it never feels like I did. And that's what hurts me the most.

On sucky days like today, once Cami falls asleep, I hang out on the dock by myself. Ever since I was a kid, I found something calming about lying out on the planks and listening to the water slapping against the wood poles.

One of the wood planks underneath my sandals creaks, and a large shadow the size of a black bear moves at the end of the dock, striking the fear of God into me. I stumble, and the tip of my shoe catches on a half-exposed nail.

I go down *hard*. The baby monitor flies out of my hand and lands with a *plop* somewhere in the water. My palms slam into the wood, saving my fall, although the momentum from my landing pushes them forward. A piercing sensation of splinters breaking through my skin makes my eyes water.

"Ow." *Just when you thought today couldn't get any worse.*

"Shit! Are you okay?" Cal bolts from his spot, and I internally groan.

"What the hell are you doing out here?" I remain in the same position, too afraid to check out the damage on my palms. Thankfully, the leggings I chose prevent my knees from suffering a similar fate, although they ache from the blow.

The old planks creak under his heavy footsteps. He stops in front of me, and I look up at him from my position on my hands and knees.

Well, of all the positions to be caught in, this might be the worst.

The flush of my cheeks is hidden by the limited lighting.

"Do you plan on getting up or…?" Humor seeps into his voice. Shadows cling to the sharp edges of his jaw, drawing my eyes toward them.

"I think I'm good here. Feel free to head back to the guesthouse after giving me a heart attack."

His raspy chuckle makes my stomach flutter.

You're hopeless, Alana. Absolutely hopeless.

"Sorry for scaring you."

"I thought you were a bear," I hiss through clenched teeth as I sit back on my heels. I'm not sure how many splinters I have pressing into my palms, but it feels like hundreds.

"What's wrong with your hands?"

Damn Cal and his ability to notice everything about me.

"Nothing. Just a couple of splinters."

"A couple?" He grabs my hand and flips it palm side up.

I snatch it back. "Stop!"

"I'm just trying to check out the damage."

I can either choose to be difficult or allow him to help me, solely because I have no chance of pulling the splinters out without any assistance.

"Fine." I hold out my hand for him to assess the splinters.

He pulls out his phone and turns on the flashlight. "Hmm." He delicately traces over the soft skin of my palm, sending a wave of goose bumps across my arms. At least ten splinters are poking through my skin at different angles.

He accidentally brushes over a splinter, and I suck in a breath.

"Sorry. What did your mom used to say? Sana, sana, colita de rana?"

"Si no sanas hoy, sanarás mañana," I finish for him with a small smile.

My mom always made any injury feel ten times better with a single little song. Cal remembering that…

It makes my chest feel all warm and tingly.

He looks up from my hand. "Do you have tweezers and a needle inside?"

I do not like the sound of that whatsoever. "Nope."

He grins as his hand reaches out to trace the slope of my scrunched nose, drawing a sharp breath from me. "Liar," he whispers close enough for me to smell his aftershave. His proximity sends my every cell into hyperdrive, making me feel as if my body was plugged into an electric socket.

He gives his head a shake and pulls away. "Let's get those splinters out before you chicken out and end up with an infection."

I cross my arms and lift my chin. "I'm not a chicken."

"You cried once because of a *papercut*."

The tips of my ears heat. "To be fair, it was a really deep cut."

"You're right. It was nearly fatal, if my memory serves me right. I'm almost positive if it weren't for that Hello Kitty Band-Aid, you might have not made it."

I flip him off, although my lower belly warms at him remembering the tiniest details like what kind of Band-Aid I had on.

"Does that count for the swear jar?" His wide grin makes my heart jolt in my chest.

"Jerk," I mutter under my breath as I walk around Cal and into the house.

"I'll be waiting in the kitchen." He disappears around the corner, leaving me to gather the supplies. I find everything I need in my bathroom. My mom took enough splinters out of my hands for me to know the drill.

I return to the kitchen to find Cal sitting at the island, completely unaware of my presence as he watches a YouTube video describing how to remove splinters as painlessly as possible. He pauses and replays a specific part twice before moving on with a satisfied nod.

My chest clenches at the intense look of concentration on his face. *This* is the reason why I want to create distance between us. Because it's the little things Cal does—the things that most people might not even notice or care much about—that get me every single time.

Sober Cal is a dream. He is witty, charming, and nearly impossible to resist. It's the drunk version of himself that I have a hard time accepting. That version is depressing, angry, and extremely difficult to love.

And it's the version of him that I still resent years later.

I drop all the supplies on the counter.

"Ready?" He looks up with a smile.

I frown. "Please try to look a little less excited about torturing me."

"There are plenty of ways I'd enjoy torturing you—all of which you would be excited for."

My head empties of any coherent thoughts.

Are you surprised? You always knew he was a flirt.

Knowing and experiencing are two very different situations. My heart rate skyrockets as he taps the barstool next to him, and I fall into it with the grace of a newborn foal.

Cal gets up and washes his hands like a doctor prepping for surgery before returning to clean the tweezers and needle with rubbing alcohol. I shut my eyes as I place my hands palms-up on the counter.

The first prick of the tweezers picking at my skin makes me wince.

"You still like sitting out on the dock at night?" Cal asks.

I appreciate the distraction. "Yeah."

"What about Cami?"

"I have—had—a baby monitor before I tripped."

His lips turn down into a frown. "That thing is a death trap."

Another pinch against my skin has me grinding my teeth

together. "Then why were *you* out there?"

"Because one of us was blessed with a gift called balance."

I pop one eye open to give him the stink-eye. "You scared me, and I ended up tripping over a nail that was sticking out."

"This place is a lawsuit waiting to happen." He shakes his head with a sigh before returning to prodding and poking at my hands.

"It's not that bad."

"You have about twenty splinters embedded in your skin that say differently."

I can't tell if his annoyed tone is due to the splinters in my hand or the fact that he is the only one available to take them all out.

"One down. Nineteen more to go."

Motherfucker.

"There. All done." Cal solidifies his place in hell as he wipes my hands with rubbing alcohol.

"It feels wrong saying thank you after you tortured me for an hour, but thank you."

"It was twenty minutes tops, you big baby." He doesn't make an effort to let go of my hands yet.

"You smiled when I screamed, you psychopath."

"It brought back good memories."

I smack him in the chest, only to wince when my sore skin makes contact. "Ouch."

"Let that be a lesson that physical violence is never the answer." He flicks my nose.

"Says the man who tried to choke a police officer."

His nostrils widen. "We're back to this again?"

"I'm not sure I'll ever let that go so long as I live." I pull out my phone and show him the photo Isabelle sent me.

His mouth drops open. "She sent it to you?"

"Yup. Right before she promised to delete it off her phone."

"So, you're the only one with a copy?" He takes a step forward.

"No." I'm concentrating so much on him encroaching in my space that I don't notice my nose twitching until after it happens.

Goddammit.

He holds out his hand. "Let me see your phone."

"Not happening." I press the lock button on the side as I take another step back.

"Alana."

"Callahan."

"Give me the phone."

"No." My ass hits the counter.

Cal's smile widens. "Gotcha."

I fake left, but he anticipates the move and easily swipes the phone out of my hand.

"Cal!" I jump for the phone.

He raises it high above my head. "Just one moment."

I'm no match for his height, so I pathetically bounce up and down. He gets distracted by my boobs at one point, staring at them like he hasn't seen a pair in forever.

"Seriously?" I cross my arms.

He winks before unlocking my phone within three tries.

My mouth falls open. "Are you kidding me?"

"It's cute your passcode is my birthday."

"I didn't—" *0720.*

Oh, shit. I totally did.

"I haven't changed it since I was sixteen." I offer a logical explanation.

"Sure, you haven't."

"It's easy to remember." At this point, I'm grasping for straws.

He opens the photo and deletes it before handing my phone back with a smile. "Here you go."

"I knew I should have submitted it to a gossip magazine like Violet suggested," I mutter under my breath.

"A pity indeed." He walks away with the biggest smile on his face.

CHAPTER EIGHTEEN

Alana

The next morning, I wake up to a crew of men from Lopez Luxury fixing the old dock. Hammers pound against the new planks of wood, the old ones nowhere to be seen.

How did you sleep through all that noise?

Cami calls out my name, but I'm too focused on my mission to give her anything more than a quick morning kiss before running out the back door. I rush across the grassy law, my lungs heaving with each ragged breath.

"Wait!" I wave my hands in the air.

One of the workers looks up before signaling to the others. A few stop pounding their hammers while others start talking amongst themselves.

"Where is the old dock?" I press a hand against my chest as I try to regulate my breathing.

"We were told to get rid of it."

Dammit, Cal. "Where did it go?"

"Our guy just drove off with the dump truck thirty minutes ago."

My stomach dips. "He left?"

The man nods.

Oh, no.

"Get inside now," Cal orders from behind me, sending a shiver up my back.

I spin around. "You destroyed my dock."

"I'm about to destroy a lot more if you don't get your ass in the house." His voice is a deep rumble I feel in my gut.

Goose bumps break out across my skin when I glance back at him. "What's wrong?"

"What isn't?" His gaze flickers over my body, driving his point home.

I look down and register my PJs for the first time this morning.

No wonder my chest hurt while running. It's not like I bothered to throw on a bra before sprinting across the lawn like a crazy woman. "Oh, shit."

"Oh, shit is right. Let's go." He motions for me to lead the way.

We only make it a few steps before someone whistles behind us. I look over my shoulder to see who it is. Even without contacts, I can make out Ernie Henderson, the town's resident redhead and nosy mailman, walking toward me with a box in his hands.

He stops to wave at me. "Lookin' good, Castillo! Wanna run around a little more for me?"

That little…

Ernie isn't even interested in women, but if it means getting a rise out of Cal, he will tease me in a heartbeat. He is just like his mother.

Freaking Isabelle.

I lift my middle finger in the air, which makes my shirt rise up. A fresh breeze hits my now-exposed butt. Cal grunts as he yanks his hoodie off before shoving it over my body, making a mess of my hair in the process.

The smell of him surrounds me like a cloak. I sneak in a second sniff, only to be met with Cal's narrowed eyes.

"What?"

"Get inside. *Now.*"

I must not move fast enough for Cal because he smacks my ass, making the skin sting with the imprint of his palm.

I pause my ascent up the small hill. "What the hell was that for?"

"I just felt like it."

"You just *felt like* smacking my ass?" I lift the hoodie to assess a red outline of Cal's palm on my left butt cheek.

His eyes darken. "Want me to match the other one?"

"No!" My heart calls me out on the lie, the beats growing fast at the idea of Cal following through on his offer. We never explored anything like that in the past, but the idea excites me.

Would he be the type to smack my ass until I can't sit right for a week or would he be the kind to take his time—

Alana Valentina Castillo!

The fantasy shimmers away, although the lingering effects of arousal remain.

I don't even notice Cal dragging me inside until I'm standing in front of him, with my back pressed against the door and his arms caging me. He leans in closer, making my heart go wild in my chest.

If I stood on the tips of my toes, our lips would touch. They part at the idea.

His gaze drops to my mouth before snapping back to my eyes. "What were you thinking going out dressed like that?"

"I needed to save the dock."

"Save the dock? It was falling apart."

"But…" My shoulders slump. "There was a special plank."

His eyes turn big and round as he processes what I said. "You went out for that?"

So, he *does* remember.

How could he not? It was the start of everything.

Cal and I were having a good day hanging out by the lake until I ruined it by opening my big mouth about the date I have tonight with Johnny Westbrook, Wisteria High's star running back.

Cal's sharp jaw tenses. Ever since he came back to the lake for the summer before his sophomore year of college, things have been different. He is different. I'm not sure what happened during his freshman year, but he no longer looks like the kid I grew up with. The bones of his face are more defined, and his muscles are larger than before, making his T-shirt look too small.

This is Cal. Your best friend. *I repeat the same mantra as always, yet it doesn't hit the same today. Maybe it has something to do with the way the lake reflects off his eyes or how he smiles whenever I laugh at something he says.*

"You're really going to let him kiss you tonight?" His question comes out accusatory.

"So what if I am? I'm almost seventeen years old." Everyone else in my grade has been kissed while I'm just biding my time until I

collect a herd of cats and call it a life.

"Wasn't he the same kid who used to shove straws up his nose and pretend to be a walrus?"

I glare at him. "He was six." And now the memory will live on in my brain forever.

Dammit, Cal. I bet he did that on purpose.

His hands clench by his sides. "Cancel your plans and let's hang out instead."

"What? No!"

"Why not? We can order pizza too. I'm even willing to get all those gross toppings you like."

I consider it for two seconds before shaking my head. "Tempting but no."

"You're really that interested in going on a date with him?"

"I am now that you're so against it." I cross my arms against my chest, which only makes my boobs pop out even more. His gaze flicks quickly over my body.

All it takes is one single glance for my stomach muscles to tighten.

He looks away when our eyes connect. "Real mature."

"If you have something to say, then spit it out."

He doesn't even pause before saying, "I dare you to kiss me."

I blink twice before my lips start working. "What?"

"You heard me. I dare you to kiss me." He pulls out his Swiss Army knife from his back pocket and draws a single strike diagonally across the four other vertical lines beneath the letter L that he carved into the plank years ago. Compared to the now five strikes underneath the L, his side has at least ten more, each carrying a fond memory of something I dared him to do.

My hands tremble against my lap. "Are you serious?"

"As serious as you are about going on this date."

"But—"

"Don't tell me you're scared," he taunts with a smirk.

"I'm not scared." I'm just…shocked. Cal has always kept things platonic between us.

It's a kiss, not a proposal. Stop making such a big deal out of it.

"Fine." I close my eyes and lean forward. My mouth softly brushes against his before I pull away. The kiss ended as quickly as it started, but my lips still tingle from the press of his against mine.

His eyes narrow. "Is that how you plan on kissing him?"

My cheeks heat, embarrassment quickly burning into anger. "What's wrong with how—"

I'm cut off by his lips slamming against mine. The air between us crackles, sparks flying as our mouths mold together.

Everything about my first kiss is amazing. The buzz building in my lower belly. The slight shift in his breathing as my arms wrap around the back of his neck so I can pull him in closer. His fingers digging into my hair, trapping me as he kisses me like he spent his whole life dreaming about it.

Cal kisses like he is afraid that I might disappear at any second, so he wants to prolong it.

My fingers brush against the patch of skin between his hair and his shirt. He sucks in a breath, pausing our kiss to press his forehead against mine. "Lana."

"Lana." Cal's voice sounds completely different.

Deeper. Rougher. Sexier.

"Hello, Lana," he says, sharper.

Shit.

The memory disappears in a blink of an eye. I press a hand against my lips as I look up at Cal.

"Why did you want to save the plank?" His question comes out soft.

My gaze drops along with my self-esteem. "It was stupid."

"Tell me," he pushes.

My mouth opens, the truth lying on the tip of my tongue.

Because no matter what has changed between us, the memories tied to that piece of wood will always hold a special place in my heart.

Sharing what the plank meant to me feels like betraying myself and the anger I've spent years holding on to.

It doesn't matter anymore. It's gone now.

I clear my throat. "Whatever. It's not like it matters anyway. It was just a stupid piece of wood."

His face crumples. I slide out from underneath his arms, leaving him staring at the space I once occupied.

I type out a new message to Cal, jabbing my screen like it personally offended me.

> You have another package.

Cal's reply is instant.

> That one's for you.

My mouth drops open.

> You ordered something for me?

> I owed you after scaring you last night.

I battle between opening the package and leaving the cardboard box to rot in the garage. Curiosity wins over common sense, so I grab a pair of scissors from the kitchen and open the box.

My hands tremble as I pull out a new baby monitor.

Oh my God.

My heart betrays me in that moment, throbbing painfully in my chest.

It's just a baby monitor, I try to rationalize with myself. Except it has nothing to do with the baby monitor and everything to do with the fact that Cal cares enough about me to replace the one that fell into the water.

Honestly, I'm not sure he ever stopped caring.

How am I supposed to hate the man when he does thoughtful shit like this?

You'll never be able to hate him and you know it.

No, but at least the *idea* of hating him makes me feel in control.

This feeling though? The one that makes my heart beat wildly in my chest and my head spin with ideas about him?

I need to shut that shit down *fast*.

CHAPTER NINETEEN
Alana

"Por Dios, no empieces conmigo." I smash the side of my hand mixer for the fifth time tonight. Between it overheating from too much use and its old age, I'm lucky the motor still runs.

I haven't been able to part with the baking tool, especially since my mom got it for me, but I'd kill for one of those fancy mixers right about now. Once upon a time I had one, but it broke and I never got around to buying a new one because a majority of my money went into making sure Cami had everything she needed.

If only they didn't cost more than half a paycheck.

"Esta vaina." I continue banging the side of the mixer.

Someone chuckles.

I look up to find Cal standing in the doorway of the kitchen with a smile. "All good?"

"Having the time of my life, thanks for asking."

He motions toward the mixer in my hand. "Need any help?"

"I've got it." In a final act of betrayal, the metal flat beaters spin twice before halting altogether. I place it on the other side of the counter to prevent myself from doing something I might regret.

"I could take a look at it if you want." He reaches for the mixer.

"Don't worry about it. I have enough buttercream to finish up the last few cupcakes."

"Is that guava frosting?" Cal's voice hits a rare high pitch. He reaches for the mixing bowl beside me with bright eyes, but I slap his hand away.

He pouts, reminding me so much of Cami. "Come on. Just let me have a little taste."

"No. That's unsanitary."

His eyes roll. "No one will know."

"My students might not, but I will."

"So? Aren't these the same kids who eat dirt on a daily basis?"

"That only happened one time while I was subbing."

He leans against the counter with a smile. "What do you teach now?"

"Spanish." I refocus my attention on icing the cupcake in front of me. Maybe if I act like I'm not interested in talking to him, then Cal will go away.

"Do you like it?"

"It pays well." Being the only Spanish teacher in all of Lake Wisteria has its perks, especially when kids need private tutoring for advanced placement exams and finals.

"You didn't really answer my question."

Damn him.

"I don't mind it." Sure, it's not my dream job per se, but the kids are cute and I'm able to go home by three in the afternoon, which is a major plus.

He scans the kitchen counters, taking in the hundred cupcakes. "So what's the special occasion?"

So much for him leaving.

My hand clutching the piping bag tightens. A blob of icing drops on to the half-finished cupcake, ruining my design.

"We're celebrating the last week of school." I swipe the botched icing off the cupcake with my index finger and walk over to the sink to rinse it off.

Cal snatches on to my hand and tugs me away from the sink. My chest smacks into his, stealing my breath away.

I attempt to push him away. "What are you doing?"

"Something I can't resist." The glint in his eyes should come with a warning label.

No.

"Cal…" The breathy way I say his name only seems to encourage him.

Cal *tsks* me like a child. "Your mom taught us better than to waste any food." He lifts my hand to his mouth. His eyes hold mine hostage, casting a spell on me while his lips close around my icing-covered finger. Every single cell in my body explodes when his tongue brushes against my skin.

Cal makes sure to take his time, dragging his tongue back and forth across my finger, cleaning off all traces of the icing. Each swipe of his tongue acts like a shock to my body.

The whole thing is both the longest and shortest five seconds of my life.

I attempt to pull my wrist free of his grasp and fail. His fingers on my wrist tighten before he releases me, and my hand drops by my side like a pendulum.

"What the hell?" I shove him in the chest.

He doesn't move an inch, although he makes it a point to obnoxiously lick his lips. "You taste better than I remember."

You. Not the icing. You.

I choke on his words, my sharp inhale causing me to cough.

"You good?"

I take a step back, adding some distance between us. "No, I'm not *good.*"

"You're upset."

I throw my hands in the air. "Of course, I'm upset! You just…"

"What?" He actually *smirks.*

The jerk.

"Sucked on my finger!"

Cal explodes from laughter, his neck knocking backward from the intensity of his amusement.

Sucked on my finger?!

Of all the stupid ways you could have phrased that… My cheeks turn pink. Cal's laughter doesn't help matters, only making my flush worse.

"I'd happily suck on your finger again if you let me," he teases, waggling his brows.

One second, I'm glaring at him. The next, I'm launching one of my cupcakes directly at his stupid mouth. It misses entirely as it smacks against his cheek.

His laughter stops as his eyes go wide. "Did you just throw a cupcake at me?"

My answer dies in my throat as the cupcake slides down his cheek, leaving a buttercream trail across his stubble before falling against the floor.

I break out into a fit of laughter that makes my lungs burn and my eyes water.

He wipes his cheek with his thumb. "I'd run if I were you."

"Why would I run?"

He devours me with his eyes as he sticks his thumb into his mouth. "One…"

My eyes roll. "Seriously, cut it out. I need to get back to work." I motion toward all the cupcakes that still need to be iced.

"Two…" He grabs a finished cupcake from the Tupperware and spins it in his hand.

"You wouldn't dare."

The smile on his face makes my body quiver from excitement. "You know what happens when you dare me to do something."

Hell no.

He takes advantage and lunges while I'm distracted. I jump out of the way and bolt from the kitchen before he can get his hands on me.

Cal and I spent years perfecting our game of tag, so I'm an expert by now at how to evade him. The mansion is like a maze of long hallways and rooms. My lungs heave as I take off down the main hall before making a left, my heart rate skyrocketing as I run across the house.

My socks don't give me the best grip, and I slide across the hardwood as I turn a corner.

I might be smarter, but Cal is faster, making it easy for him to catch up to me despite my efforts to lose him.

His arm wraps around my waist. Next thing I know, I'm being lifted and pressed against a wall.

"Didn't your mom teach us that it isn't nice to play with our food?" His grin makes my heart trip in my chest.

My eyes narrow into two slits. "You started it."

"Then it's only right I end it." He lifts the cupcake toward my face.

"Callahan Percival Kane, I swear to God if you—"

He proceeds to press the cupcake into my cheek with a sinister grin.

"I hate you!" I shriek as he drags it down my skin, wiping the entire cupcake clean of buttercream.

"To think they say revenge isn't sweet."

"I'm going to kill you," I seethe.

"Then I might as well make this worth losing my life over." Cal's eyes darken at my challenge, the blue color slowly being consumed by black.

"What—" My sentence is cut off as he leans forward and runs his tongue through the icing covering my cheek.

I might need someone to bring me back to life because there is no way I'm walking away from this alive. My knees buckle, but Cal's arm acts like a band around my waist, preventing me from falling over.

He stops to lick his lips, wiping the light pink icing away. His eyes shut for a second, and I take advantage. I collect the huge lump of icing from my cheek and swipe it across his stupid smirk.

His eyes snap open.

"You're right. Revenge *is* sweet." I grin so wide, my cheeks hurt.

His eyes drop to my lips. It's the only warning I get before his mouth slams into mine.

Holy shit.

Everything about our kiss is desperate. Passionate. *Familiar.*

His lips are a fuse, making my entire body light up like the midnight sky on New Year's Eve. Our bodies mold together, and I wrap my arms around his neck. He grips my hips with enough pressure to leave marks on my skin.

I dig my hands into his hair and tug hard enough to make him gasp. My tongue darts out to trace the icing off his lips, and Cal grinds into me with a groan. My stomach muscles tighten from the press of his arousal. I sigh, and he takes advantage. His tongue plunges inside my mouth, teasing me until I'm nothing but a whimpering mess.

The sweetest thing about our kiss is the icing lingering on his tongue. His last bit of restraint snaps, and the real Cal comes out. His fingers dig into my scalp as he kisses me like he fucks—a savage with only one mission in mind.

Making me come.

As if he read my mind, his hand trails toward the hem of my shirt. His fingers graze over my stomach, drawing a sharp breath from me that he swallows with his lips.

The tips of his fingers tease the goose bumps spreading across my skin—

"Mommy?" Cami's voice echoes off the tall ceilings before a nearby door slams.

My eyes fly open. Cal flies backward, squishing the abandoned cupcake beneath his shoe. He turns toward the empty hallway before releasing a heavy exhale.

"Mommy, where are you?" Cami's voice sounds closer this time.

Something switches inside of him, the heat in his gaze quickly morphing into something else.

Regret.

I've seen all the signs before. The clenched fists. The avoidance of eye contact. The way he brushes a hand over his mouth, as if he can erase the taste of me from his lips.

My heart sinks.

What did you think would happen if you kissed him?

Except *I* didn't kiss him.

Well, you sure didn't not *kiss him.*

He runs a hand through his hair. "Alana…"

I'm not sure what triggers me more: the way he uses my full name to add some distance or how he can't look me in the eyes while saying it. I save myself the trouble of having to hear him come up with some kind of excuse, mostly because I'm not sure my heart can survive it. "Let's pretend that never happened."

"But—"

"We both got lost in the moment. It's no big deal."

"Right." His heavy exhale of relief drills a hole straight through my heart.

"Can I have a cupcake?" Cami's voice sounds closer this time.

I look down at the smashed one on the floor with a sigh. "I better go…"

I pathetically linger, hoping he might say *something*.

He doesn't.

Instead of standing around, waiting for a possibility that won't ever happen, I turn and walk away. The emptiness in my chest grows with each step away from him.

I spent years trying to fill the void Cal left me with when he abandoned me the first time, and I'm not about to let one kiss ruin all my hard work.

No matter how amazing that kiss was.

Cal disappears back to the guesthouse, leaving me alone to replay our kiss in a hundred different ways. I somehow finish up the rest of the cupcakes, although the task becomes far less enjoyable now that I can't separate Cal from the taste of guava icing.

Shame clings to my every thought, making me question if I was the only one truly affected by the kiss.

Of course he was affected.

He just didn't *want* to be.

I try to distract myself from my thoughts by watching a new episode of one of my favorite shows. It works for about ten minutes. Once the couple begins kissing, I lose all interest in continuing. Instead, I quickly switch to watching a procedural crime drama I have been following for the last few years.

Nothing screams comfort television quite like unhinged serial killers.

My phone vibrates against the coffee table, so I unlock it and read the text Delilah sent in our group chat with Violet.

Delilah

Check out who is watching the latest episode of The Last Rose with me.

She attaches a photo of her and Wyatt wearing face masks

with the TV in the background. I'm not into that kind of reality TV, but the thought of having someone like that who wants to watch a favorite show with me makes my chest twinge. Delilah's life is a far cry from my lonely night watching TV by myself.

Then do something about it.

The thought of dating scares me almost as much as the idea of ending up alone. But if I continue to live in fear of what could go wrong, I'll spend the rest of my life by myself, reciting lines from a TV show by heart.

I deserve more than that for myself, and I plan on getting back out there.

I just don't know when.

CHAPTER TWENTY

Cal

I slam the sealed bottle of vodka against the counter and stare
at it with shaky hands. On the one hand, I want to drink until
I no longer can taste Lana on my tongue. But on the other, it
feels like I'm letting her down in some way.

Blacking out won't solve anything.

Neither will sitting around, reading a book to escape my
reality. We all have coping strategies, and mine just happen to be
found at the bottom of a bottle.

I hesitate while pouring myself a drink.

You told Lana you would limit your drinking for her.

Yeah, well, these are desperate times and all.

I forgo the glass and drink straight from the bottle instead.
The first sip was meant to erase the taste of Lana's guava icing
from my tongue. Alcohol is a poor substitute, but the taste wiped

away any traces of sweetness from my mouth. The second chug was to try—and fail—to forget the way Lana's lips felt pressed against mine. The rightness of it all. The memories that were stirred up by her lips brushing against mine. The craving I have to repeat the kiss all over again, this time without any kid to interrupt us.

The rest of my night is a bit hazy. Next thing I know, a large amount of vodka is missing and the sun is already starting to rise.

This is the feeling I crave. The numbness. The stillness of my thoughts. The ability to disappear into the darkness for a little while and escape my problems.

It's not until I wake up the next day at two p.m. with a pounding headache that I realize just how much I drank.

"Fuck." I squeeze my eyes shut.

I'm only able to get another hour of sleep in before my empty stomach declares war. I climb out of bed and take a quick shower to wipe away the alcohol seeping out of my every pore.

Although I had plans to finish up working on the attic, I think it's best that I stay away from the lake house today.

Only because you're afraid.

Hell yeah, I'm afraid. The last thing I want to do is confront Lana after last night, especially when I look as hungover as I feel.

So, instead of heading in the direction of the house, I get in my car and drive to Main Street in search of food. My options are limited to the coffee shop and Early Bird Diner since most of the nicer places are packed with summer tourists who just arrived.

As tempted as I am to avoid Isabelle after the incident with Wyatt, I need to face her eventually. It's only right after the whole scene I caused in her restaurant. Plus, I really don't want to spend the rest of my summer cooking for myself every single day.

I walk into the diner with my head held high and a smile on my face.

Isabelle turns toward the bell chiming above me and frowns. "You're brave to show your face around here after the last time."

I hold my hands up in surrender. "I come in peace."

Her right brow arches. "I'm not sure you know the meaning of the word after you tried to choke our town hero."

It takes everything in me to not roll my eyes at the way she moons over Wyatt. "I'm sorry for causing a scene the last time I was here. It was wrong of me to stir up trouble like that in your place of business, and I swear not to do it again. Scout's honor." I hold up three fingers.

She remains quiet while pinning me in place with her glare.

"Please take pity on me and my empty stomach." I press the palms of my hands together.

She rolls her eyes. "Quit your moping and take a seat before you make me look bad." With a flick of her hand, I step toward the booth beside the window overlooking Main Street. Lamppost banners hang from each streetlight to remind everyone of the fast-approaching Strawberry Festival I stupidly decided to volunteer for.

Isabelle slaps a menu on my table and leaves to go grab my orange juice.

I flip through the menu and decide on a turkey club before pulling out my phone to text Iris.

> What are you up to?

Iris
> Get a life.

My eyes roll.

> Cute, Declan. Do you always invade Iris's privacy like this?

Iris
> Only when you're texting her while she is napping.

> Since when does she nap?

Iris
> She wasn't feeling well.

> I'll call her later.

Without Iris to entertain me, I'm left to play Candy Crush until Isabelle deems me worthy enough to have my order taken.

"What do you want?" She props her hand on her hip.

I pass her my menu. "A turkey club and a side of french fries, please."

She scribbles the order on her tiny pad before leaving.

A white-haired man with a set of crutches struggles to open the front door, so I jump out of my seat to help him.

"You." He sneers.

My smile widens. "Sheriff Hank. What a nice surprise."

"Can't say the same about you." His eyes narrow.

"Don't tell me you're still holding a grudge against me after the incident Alana and I had with your police cruiser." I only nicked his car with my side mirror, but he never forgave me.

I keep the door open while he hobbles into the diner with his crutches.

He shakes his head. "You should have stayed away. That girl

has been through enough as it is between you and Victor."

My smile falls. "Victor?"

Hank's brows furrow as his mouth clamps shut.

"Who the hell is Victor?" I ask with a low voice.

Is that who you saw kissing Lana near Last Call?

Hank tries to circle around me, but I step in his path.

He looks up with a pinched expression. "Get out of my way."

"Not until you tell me who Victor is and what he has to do with Alana."

You already know who he is.

My fingers curl into themselves. Hank huffs and puffs his way around me, only to be blocked every time.

His gaze cuts into me. "Cut it out or I'll call someone down at the station to come arrest you for being a public nuisance."

"Make sure they're gentle with the cuffs this time." I hold my hands up in front of his face.

"You really want to know?"

The hairs on my arms rise. "Yes."

"Fine. Victor was a guy Alana dated for a few months after her mom passed away."

There's your answer.

My stomach sinks. *Fuck.* "And what was wrong with him?"

"What wasn't? The man was a walking red flag, although none of us paid much attention until it was too late."

Acid crawls up my throat. "How so?"

"That's not my story to tell." His lips thin.

"Then why mention him in the first place?"

"Because if you screw around with Alana, we will run you out of this town just like Victor."

I swallow past the thick lump in my throat. "I'm not here to mess around with her."

"You better not or else."

"Or else what?"

"Pray you never have to find out."

CHAPTER TWENTY-ONE
Alana

I kick the flat tire before teetering on my heels. My arms flail, but I catch my balance before I fall flat on my ass and drop the Tupperware of cocadas I spent a majority of last night making for Cami's graduation event.

"Is everything okay, Mommy?"

I take a deep breath through my nose before turning around and facing Cami. She looks adorable with her tilted graduation cap and miniature gown that drags across the floor behind her like a wedding dress. If I had paid attention to my mom's sewing lessons, maybe I would have been able to adjust the hem for her.

The same heaviness that has been present since this morning grows stronger at the reminder of my mom.

Te extraño muchísimo, Mami.

"I need to ask for someone to pick us up." No way will I be able to change a tire by myself.

The smile on her face dims. "Will we be late?"

I check the time on my phone. "Not if I can help it." Since

I always like arriving early to everything, I made sure to have enough time for any last-minute emergencies. I've come to learn with Cami, anything is possible. Juice spills. Missing favorite sock. A trip to the bathroom.

I choose to call Delilah first. The call goes directly to voicemail, so I dial her again, hoping it was an issue with my service. The voicemail picks up right away.

"Shit," I hiss.

Cami gasps.

I open my purse with shaky fingers and hand her a dollar. "Why don't you go put that in the jar for me?"

"Okay!" She grabs the dollar from my hand and runs inside the house, nearly tripping over the hem of her gown in the process.

Wyatt, the next person on my emergency list, goes straight to voicemail as well. I call Violet next in a last act of desperation, hoping she answers. Except like Delilah and Wyatt, she doesn't pick up.

"Why is no one answering?" I let out a curse as I kick the tire again.

I told everyone to get there thirty minutes before the start time—

Wait!

I slap my forehead. Whenever Lake Wisteria has an event with over fifty people, the area becomes a cellular service dead zone, most likely due to overwhelming our one cell tower. It happens every single year before our Strawberry Festival.

"Dammit." I tug at my hair, the sting of pain grounding me. "What am I supposed to do?"

You could start with staying calm.

I pull up my rideshare app and type in the coordinates for Cami's school. The nearest driver is located a town away and will take thirty minutes to get here.

Panic claws at my chest, turning each breath into a challenge.

A sunbeam bouncing off the roof of Cal's shiny car catches my attention.

No. You can't be serious.

I wish I wasn't. If avoiding Cal was an Olympic sport, I would be a gold medalist. Ever since our kiss a few days ago, I have done everything in my power to keep away from him.

Find another way.

There is no other way. He is the last person I want to ask for a favor, but I'm all out of options. If he doesn't drive us, we won't make it to Cami's ceremony in time.

My heels sink into the gravel as I walk up the driveway toward the house. Pinpointing Cal's location doesn't take more than a second, especially when it's paired with Cami's giggle. I follow the sound of their voices all the way back to the living room, where I find him on his knees, readjusting Cami's crooked cap.

"There. All better now." He taps the edge of her hat with a smile.

"Thanks, Cow-l!"

A warmth spreads through my chest as Cami wraps her arms around Cal's shoulders, smacking him in the face with the tassel on her cap.

My low chuckle draws Cal's attention. Our gazes collide, and his eyes widen.

"What?" I tuck a wave behind my ear.

"You're so beautiful." His voice deepens.

"Ooo. You think Mommy is pretty!" Cami's bright gaze swings from me to Cal.

"I think she's the prettiest damn woman in the world."

The butterflies in my stomach return, their endless flapping creating a buzz in my lower half.

"Really?" The ear-splitting pitch of Cami's voice combined with the hearts shooting out of her eyes warns me away.

He doesn't look away from me as he says, "Absolutely."

I break eye contact. "Uh-oh. Cal said a bad word."

Cami squeals with delight as Cal blindly hands her a hundred-dollar bill without so much as breaking eye contact with me. She takes off toward the kitchen, leaving Cal and me alone.

His gaze darkens as it trails down my body, turning the warmth in my chest into a raging inferno. For Cami's special occasion, I decided to wear a floral summer dress that makes my boobs look amazing, and my favorite pair of heels that hurt like hell if I stand for too long. The two thin suede strings wrapped around my calves cut off most of the blood flow to my feet, but beauty is pain.

Totally worth it. With the way Cal looks at me, I'd willingly risk each one of my ten toes turning purple.

His eyes zero in on my shoes. "Fuck."

"What?" I look down but find nothing wrong.

"The things I would do to have your legs wrapped around my waist while wearing those." He looks up.

Oh. My. God.

He closes the gap between us before kneeling in front of my shoes.

"What are you doing?" My heart pounds against my rib cage, the beats filling my ears.

"You're going to pass out if you keep them on this tight." His fingers trace over one of my swollen calves. I teeter from the simplest touch behind my knee, so I reach out to lay a hand on his shoulder.

A simple brush of his fingers up my leg has me biting on the inside of my cheek to keep from groaning. "I'll be fine."

Cal doesn't leave the choice up to me as he carefully unties the first set of strings. They fall, landing in a messy pile beside my feet.

He rubs at the red marks on my legs with furrowed brows. "Doesn't this hurt?"

"Who cares so long as they look good?"

His fingers work in small circles, massaging my calves until he is pleased with the result. Breathing becomes an impossible task, the growing ache between my legs intensifying with each passing second.

By the time he is finished retying the first shoe, I'm clutching on to his shoulder with a steel grip.

"You doing okay?" He smiles up at me.

My eyes narrow. "You know exactly what you're doing."

Only I don't know *why* Cal is doing it. After how quick he was to pull away after our kiss, I thought he would keep to himself and prevent any future mistakes from happening.

So much for that.

His grin widens as he traces a finger over the goose bumps forming on my skin. I shove his stupid smiling face away, only to nearly fall flat on my ass before he stabilizes me.

He repeats the same thing on my other leg until I'm panting. The push and pull between us will drive me crazy if it continues.

This is exactly why you need to avoid him.

He rises to his full height, although the image of him kneeling in front of me will live on forever in my dreams. His mouth opens, but sneakers slapping against the hardwood stop him.

Cami runs back into the living room. "Is someone coming to get us now, Mommy?"

"No."

Her smile drops. "Why?"

"Can I ask you for a huge favor?" I look over at Cal and tuck my hands behind my back to hide the way they shake.

A line appears between his brows. "Tell me what you need."

A sanity check would be a good place to start.

I swallow back the thought. "Do you mind if I borrow your car? I got a flat and no one is answering their phone, and I wanted to get a rideshare but—"

His eyes stretch to their limits. "You want to drive my car?"

"Umm, well…" I motion toward the imprint of a flask in his front pocket, ignoring the painful tightness in my throat.

"It's nine a.m." He speaks low.

Oh God. You insulted him.

"Right, but—"

He holds a hand up. "Fine. Whatever. You can drive."

"Yay!" Cami claps her hands together.

My shoulders drop, the tension bleeding out of them along with all the pent-up adrenaline. "Thank you."

Cal passes me his keys. "Anything for you."

Three words. Five syllables. One punch to the gut.

I don't let the impact of his words show on my face. But he threw me back into the past without a life preserver, leaving me to drown in the memories of him saying those same three words over and over again.

Anything for you, he said when he broke his arm trying to get my kite out of a tree.

Anything for you, he grumbled after picking me up early from my very first date with Pete Darling, a jerk who didn't quite live up to his last name.

Anything for you, he brokenly whispered after I made him promise to never come back to Lake Wisteria, knowing I wouldn't be strong enough to resist him again, drugs and alcohol be damned.

Reality is a bitch, making my eyes prick from unshed tears.

That was then. This is now.

I shove my emotions to the side and rally for my daughter, who needs me to be focused on the present.

Cami waits inside so she doesn't get sweaty while I set up her booster seat. Due to how cramped Cal's back seat is, the lower half of my body remains outside the car while I struggle to get the seat belt through the holes.

"Is everything okay?" The heat of his breath against my neck makes my skin pebble.

"Perfect." I curse as the seat belt buckle smacks me in the knuckles.

"Here. Let me help you." Cal's chest presses against my back as he reaches over my body to help me with the seat belt. Our bodies click together like two magnets, the pull toward each other too great to ignore.

I suck in a breath as goose bumps spread across my skin. He brushes the pad of his thumb across them, drawing another sharp inhale from me.

"Stop doing that." I release the seat belt, leaving him to fix it.

He doesn't give me room to escape, instead choosing to work around me. It doesn't take him long to figure out the process.

"All done."

I jump at the sound of his voice, and my ass bumps into his crotch.

My eyes widen at the same time as his sharp inhale.

Oh, shit.

CHAPTER TWENTY-TWO

Cal

ana tries to push me away, but with how our bodies are lined up, her ass presses against my dick. She freezes underneath me with a barely audible gasp.

My dick, already semi-hard from what happened in the house, reacts to her touch. Blood pumps directly to the source of my latest issue.

"Are you…" She struggles to finish her sentence.

"You wore the same dress from our first date," I reply, like that answers everything. The dress somehow looks even better now than it did back then, and I'm jealous of any fucker who gets to look at her today.

"I didn't—" She glances at me from over her shoulder, her eyebrows scrunching together. "Wait. You remember what I wore that night?" I know what she is probably assuming given how addicted I was to pills.

"I remember *everything*." My gaze drops to her mouth. The memory of hers pressed against mine makes my lips tingle.

Her tongue darts out to trace her bottom lip, and I'm hit with the temptation to replace her tongue with mine.

Our kiss the other night has lived rent-free in my head since it happened. Regardless of how hard I try to distract myself, it always returns to the forefront of my mind.

What would have happened if I had stayed?

What if we had talked out what happened rather than run away?

What if I had kissed her again, regrets be damned?

Instead, I drank until I was physically unable to walk back to the house and kiss her again.

"Mommy! Are you ready?"

I jolt. Lana pushes against me again, forcing me out of the car and away from the temptation of her lips.

Probably for the best.

"Let's get you buckled in." Lana's voice comes out huskier than usual as she motions for Cami to come over. While Lana gets Cami buckled in, I put the Tupperware of cocadas in the trunk.

The awkward tension between Lana and me intensifies as we both get in the car. I don't let anyone drive my car, yet here I am allowing Lana to do the very thing my brothers are prohibited from doing.

Only because she doesn't trust you behind the wheel.

I tap my fingers against my thighs in a poor attempt to distract myself from the unbearable pressure building inside my chest.

I would never put her and Cami's life at risk like that, so for her to think otherwise…

It fucking *hurts*.

My dark thoughts are instantly driven out of my head as Lana peels out of the driveway. The tires squeal, and a car honks as Lana dictates that she had the right of way, although I know for certain she most definitely did not.

I use the safety handlebar for the first time in my life as she navigates through town. There aren't many stop signs or traffic lights, but she manages to hit every single one in the same way— hard enough to make me suffer from whiplash.

My heart pounds against my chest. "You drive like a madman."

She cackles. "It's not my fault the light changed from yellow to red so fast."

"You were going forty when it turned yellow!"

She shrugs.

I wipe the damp skin over my brow. "How do you still have a license?"

"Probably the same way you avoided staying out of jail after choking Wyatt."

My mouth drops open. "You're a menace."

"I haven't gotten in an accident."

"Probably because everyone in town knows to avoid the road whenever you're on it."

She snaps her fingers. "That explains so much. No wonder I never get caught in any rush hour traffic."

"Only because you're the reason people rush in the first place."

She laughs until her cheeks turn pink and her eyes water. I'm enraptured by the sound almost as much as the look on her face as she turns toward me with the brightest smile.

You're absolutely helpless. I bite down on my cheek to stifle my groan.

Lana finally spares me a glance once she parks the car outside of Cami's school. "Thanks for letting me borrow your car."

"Anything for you." I offer her a half-assed salute.

Her back goes rigid.

That's the second time she's done that. What's that about?

Lana doesn't give me time to second-guess what I said as she opens her door and steps out of the car. "Come on, Cami. Say thank you to Cal."

"Thank you!" She claps her hands together in the back seat.

"Let's get you out of there." Lana grabs the treats from the trunk while I help Cami. It takes two failed attempts and nearly getting stabbed in the eye with the corner of her graduation cap for me to realize two-door cars and kids are a no-go.

Cami finally climbs out of the back, her gown a wrinkled mess and her hat completely off-centered again. I'm not sure how she managed to wreck her outfit in the five-minute car ride, but I'm weirdly impressed.

Although her gown is a goner, I do my best to help her with the hat.

"You remind me of your mother," I say absentmindedly.

Cami looks up at me with wide blue eyes. "Really?"

"Oh yeah. She was a wild child just like you." I wink.

Cami giggles, making my chest all warm and tight from the innocent sound. She looks up at me with the goofiest smile, and

I return the gesture.

The side of my face tingles, and I look over to find Lana staring at me with a strange expression on her face.

"Everything okay?"

She clears her throat. "Yeah. Just realized I forgot the camera." She turns toward her daughter. "We better get going before your teacher gets worried."

"Are you coming?" Cami holds out her hand for me to grab.

I stare at it.

"No. Cal is busy," Lana answers before I have a chance to even consider.

I look up at her, finding her working her jaw.

"Right. Do you need me to pick you up once you're done?"

Her head shakes. "Thanks, but no. Wyatt and Delilah can give us a ride back to the house."

"What about the car seat?" I blurt out.

"I'll grab it from you tomorrow if that's okay."

"Of course."

I expect to feel a warm rush of relief as they walk away, but my chest throbs instead. A sense of longing, deep and forbidden, takes over. The kind of longing I haven't allowed myself to feel for *years*.

This is for the best.

Then why does it feel so shitty to watch Cami and Lana disappear into the school while I stand by myself, looking in like an outsider?

Because you are an outsider.

I try to shake off the feeling and get in my car, but I hesitate outside the vehicle.

A part of me wants to go with them. It's a small part, but a part nonetheless, and it freaks me the fuck out. So I do what I do best.

I run.

I try my hardest to stick to sober activities like grabbing an early lunch at the sandwich shop and picking up a new book at the store, but nothing relieves the pressure in my chest.

The drive to one of the tourist bars on the other side of town is a blur—just like all the vodka tonics I drank afterward to numb my emotions.

So much for limiting yourself.

I tried my hardest, but I'm powerless when it comes to alcohol and controlling myself under extreme stress. It's not until my vision is cloudy and my head is quiet that I finally feel at ease.

No more thoughts of Lana.

No more thoughts of Cami.

No more thoughts of what my life could have been like had I not fucked it all up six years ago.

Just me, the steady beat of the music streaming out of the speakers, and alcohol to cure my problems.

My world feels like someone tilted it at a forty-five-degree angle. I stumble out of the rideshare and manage to walk up the driveway of the house without falling on my face. It takes me three tries to get the front door unlocked. The house is pitch-black inside, and I trip over my own feet.

I run into a wall, except the wall is actually a table that teeters from my weight before falling backward. Whatever was on top of the wood surface shatters, the echo amplifying the horrific sound.

I wince. "Shit." I stand there in the darkness, afraid what I might uncover if I turn on a light.

If I could even *find* a light.

As if the house read my mind, one turns on above me. Flowers of all colors, shapes, and sizes are strewn across the hardwood floor, surrounded by a thousand shards of glass.

"Oh my God." Lana stands at the top of the stairs. "No. No. No."

"Lana!" I shout. "I missed you!"

A man of subtlety, I am not.

Her look of shock morphs into one of anger. "Are you drunk?"

I shake my head. "Buzzed."

"What are you even doing here? You're supposed to be staying at the guesthouse."

"I wanted to say hi." I hold up my hand and wave like a complete loser.

She takes a deep breath. "Don't move. Let me go put some shoes on before coming down there."

"You got it, babe." I salute her, which only earns me a death glare.

I'm not sure how long it takes her to get her sneakers on, but I stare at the wall, questioning how I ended up in this mess.

Lana. Cami. Graduation.

I smack my forehead. "Right. That's how."

"I can't believe this right now." Lana scowls as she walks down the stairs. It only deepens as she assesses the mess surrounding me.

I flinch. "I didn't mean to break it."

Her eyes glaze over, looking shiny underneath the chandelier. I hate the look on her face almost as much as the silence building between us as she analyzes the broken shards of glass.

"I'll buy you a new one. I promise."

"I don't want a new one. I want this one," she snaps.

"I'm sorry." My bottom lip juts out. I saw Cami do it once and it automatically worked on Lana, so maybe I will get lucky too. "It was an accident."

"Accidents happen, but getting drunk is a choice."

"You're right. A bad choice."

"Yet you keep making it anyway. God, Cal. You're thirty-three years old. Act like it." She points at the spot I'm standing in. "Stay right there."

She disappears around the corner before returning a minute later with a broom, a dustpan, and a trash bin. Her anger is like a fire, sucking all the oxygen out of the room as I stand there, useless and silent, while she begins sweeping the mess into a corner opposite of me.

"Who got you flowers?" I point at the mix of wildflowers strewn across the floor. "Was it a guy?"

Smooth, Cal. She will never suspect a single thing.

She shakes her head and keeps sweeping. "I'm not getting into this with you right now."

"Why? Because it's true?"

"Because you're drunk and acting like a jealous idiot over someone who doesn't even matter."

"So what if I am jealous?"

"Why would you be?"

"Because…"

"Because what?" She shoots me a pointed look.

I bite down on my cheek to keep my last shred of dignity after throwing away most of it tonight. She gives up waiting and begins sweeping harder this time, making a few pieces of glass fly across the hardwood floor.

"Did you even bother going to rehab again?" she asks after the longest minute of silence. Her question comes off nonchalant, but there is a tightness in her shoulders as she sweeps.

I laugh. "Of course. Want to take a guess on how that turned out?" I try to bow but my coordination is severely lacking, so I nearly topple over. This time I don't have a table to save me, so I flap my arms until I regain my balance.

Pathetic, Cal. Absolutely pathetic.

She stares at me with an expression I can't make sense of given how much alcohol is pumping through my veins.

"I don't want to pity you, but I do."

"Exactly what every man wants to hear from the woman he loves."

She blinks once. Twice. *Three* times before she strings a sentence together. "And that's our cue to get you to bed."

"Are you joining me?"

She grabs my arm and leads me up the stairs and toward my old room while grumbling to herself in Spanish. We walk in tandem to my bed. My center of gravity is thrown off when the tip of my sneaker catches on the floor, throwing Lana off-balance too.

"Whoops. My bad." I laugh it off.

Her heavy sigh makes my chest hurt. She guides me toward

the bed without any other incident. Once my ass safely lands on the foam mattress, she steps away, but not before I latch on to her wrist.

I tease the inside of it, earning the softest gasp. "I'm sorry."

She tries to tug her hand free, but my grip holds. "Stop saying that."

"Why?"

"Because words have meaning, and your actions cheapen them."

My grip on her hand loosens, so she takes advantage and detaches herself from me. The crack in my chest expands, revealing the emptiness within.

"Sleep it off" is the last thing she says before my bedroom door clicks shut, leaving me alone with my demons to keep me company.

CHAPTER TWENTY-THREE

Cal

I wake up the next morning with a pounding headache and the urge to hide from Lana after last night. Unlike my father, I'm not a mean drunk, but I am a stupid one who can't keep his mouth shut.

To make matters worse, I broke Lana's vase and then made her clean it up afterward.

I throw a pillow over my head to muffle my frustrated groan. *You have no one to blame for your behavior but yourself.*

The door to my room creaks open. I pop my head out from underneath the pillow, expecting to find Lana in the doorway.

"Hi!" Cami shouts.

My head throbs in a silent reply. "Let's use our inside voices."

"Sorry," she whisper-shouts.

Close enough. "Where's your mom?" And how do I avoid her for the rest of the day?

"Making lunch."

Lunch already? How long did I sleep in?

"And what are you doing in here?" I sit up in the bed. I'm still wearing my clothes from last night, which look like they spent a week at the bottom of a laundry hamper.

"Mommy said you're not feeling too good."

My head knocks back. "She did?"

"Yeah. I heard her on the phone telling Aunt Dee you got a hang-ovary."

I bust into laughter, although I regret it instantly with the way my head throbs. "I think you mean *hangover*."

Her goofy, gap-toothed smile is slowly growing on me. "What's a hangover?"

And this right here is the reason why I shouldn't be allowed around kids in the first place.

I clear my throat. "It's when people make bad decisions at night and wake up sick the next day."

Her forehead scrunches. "Like when you eat too much chocolate and get a tummy ache?"

"Sure, kid. Just like that." I wish my problems stemmed from eating too much chocolate. It's far less harmful and way more enjoyable, which are two pluses in my book.

"How do you get better?"

I sigh. "I'm not sure if I ever will get better."

"Why not?"

"Because I get sick a lot." As sad as it is to admit.

Cami's stare doesn't hold an ounce of judgment. "With a hangover?"

"Yes." Just because I have a high tolerance *while* drinking doesn't mean I'm immune to feeling the next-day effects. I've just gotten better at managing them.

And disguising them.

"Oh. Wait! I know what will work! Stay right there, Cow-l."

"It's Cal. Just *Cal*," I emphasize.

"Okay, Cal." But it comes out more like *cow*. Maybe she'll get it eventually, but today isn't that day.

Cami runs out of the room, leaving my door wide open. Her bare feet slap against the wood floor as she rushes down the hall.

I'm tempted to leave just so I can avoid having another conversation with the kid. With the way my head throbs, it might be for the best.

Or you could just play nice and entertain Lana's daughter after everything that happened last night.

Earning a point or two with Lana wouldn't be the worst thing. As much as I'm not a kid person, I'm willing to pretend for a little while if it makes Cami happy, which in turn will make Lana happy.

So, against every cell in my body telling me to run far away from the kid, I stay in my room, waiting for the little wrecking ball to come back with whatever she thinks will make me better. Hopefully it's a bottle of Advil and a glass of water.

A knock on my door has my head whipping in the direction of the sound. The rapid pace of my heart makes my ears pound.

Lana leans against the doorframe. "Do you have a minute?"

I swallow past the thick lump in my throat. "Sure."

She steps inside my room and shuts the door behind her. With the way she stares at me, empty and unflinching, my stomach feels about ready to purge itself of last night's bar food.

"Last night can't ever happen again."

My head drops. "No. It really shouldn't."

"I went ahead and took the key back."

My fists tighten around the comforter. "I understand."

"I don't see how that's even possible." Her tone is sharper than a blade.

I ignore the churning sensation in my abdomen and focus on her. "About the vase…"

"What about it?" The question comes out icy.

"I plan on getting you a new one today."

"Do you really think buying your way out of this will make up for you shattering my mom's vase?"

I blink. "Your mom's?"

Of all the things to break, it had to be something that belonged to her mother…

She releases a shuddery breath. "I knew it was a mistake agreeing to have you live here. I should have just taken my chances with the lawyers and left it up to a judge. I thought maybe you would have some common sense and be on your best behavior, but obviously I was asking for too much. What were you even doing coming inside the house that late?"

I fidget with my hair. "I wasn't exactly thinking straight."

"I should have never given you a key."

"Lana—"

"No. You don't get to *Lana* me and expect all this to go away."

"I'm not trying to make things go away. I'm trying to say sorry."

"Well, you can take your sorry and shove it up your ass along with all the other shit you spew." She slams the door before I have a chance to even apologize.

"I'm back!" Cami barrels inside my bedroom like a torpedo. The door smacks against the wall, and a bit of plaster from the ceiling falls down.

That looks promising.

"Remember your inside voice." I wince.

"Right. Sorry." She bounces from one foot to another.

"What's up?"

"I made you something to feel better." She presses a folded sheet of paper against her chest.

"What is it?"

She beckons me closer with her finger. I consider leaning forward but think better of it, instead choosing to kneel down.

Cami's face lights up as she unfolds the piece of paper. "Ta-da!"

I flinch at the stabbing pain in my skull.

"Do you not like it?" Cami's smile falters, threatening to drop altogether.

"My head just hurts."

"Oh, sorry." Her bottom lip trembles.

A quick scan of the paper makes my heart catapult in my chest. It's the simplest of drawings, with a big, wonky heart taking up a majority of the page. Within the red shape, she drew two blond stick figures. One has large squiggles on their arms while the shorter one has a triangle-shaped body to represent a dress. Below the heart, Cami wrote me a message.

Feel better, Cow-L.

Laughter explodes out of me at I trace over my name. Can't say I've seen someone spell it like that before. "I love it."

Cami's entire face lights up like a firework, bright and impossible to ignore. "Really?"

"Best card ever." My lips pull into a sincere grin.

Someone sucks in a breath. I look up from Cami's face to find Lana staring at us with wide eyes.

"Hey." I offer her a small smile.

"What's going on?" She takes a step inside the room.

"I made Cow-l a card so he feels better." Cami turns to show her mother the sheet of paper.

"Did you?" The tightness in Lana's voice matches her rigid posture. "What's wrong with him?"

Cami's cheeks turn pink. "He's gots a hangover."

Lana glares at me like I'm the one at fault for teaching her daughter the word.

I raise my hands in submission. "She overheard you talking on the phone first about a hang-ovary, so don't go pointing fingers at me."

Lana turns to Cami. "That's sweet of you." She pats her daughter's head, ruffling the tangled strands even more.

"Do you feel better?" Cami's big blue eyes look up at me.

"Absolutely. I'm starting to feel better already." Although the headache and nausea might take some time to wear off, the heaviness pressing against my chest since I woke up feels less intense.

Cami squeals as she clutches the card to her chest, crinkling the paper in the process. "I knew it would work!"

My eye twitches from the high-pitched tone. I discreetly rub my temple, trying to make the pressure go away.

"Why don't we go swimming and leave Cal alone?"

Cami runs out of my room, squealing with excitement.

"Thanks." I stand.

"I didn't do it for you," Lana spits out before following Cami, leaving me to stew in the silence. I try to busy myself with organizing the rest of the stuff in the attic. It's a failed attempt, with me easily becoming distracted by all the noise happening outside the window.

The tightness in my chest intensifies at Cami and Lana hanging out by the lake. I'm hit with a hundred memories of Lana and me doing the same thing, although Lana actually spent time inside the water rather than out of it.

The sun beats down on her, casting a warm glow over her tan skin from where she sits on the dock. She shields her eyes as she looks over at Cami with a big, beaming smile I haven't seen in years.

The feeling of longing from yesterday returns, this time much more intense than the last. I *want* to be down there with them.

Look what happened the last time you wanted something you shouldn't have.

The thought sobers me, and I escape, choosing to return to the guesthouse. Except as soon as I walk outside, I find Lana's car still in the driveway, the tire flatter than a pancake. Before I decide against it, I swipe Lana's keys off the counter and get to changing her flat tire. It's a bold idea, especially given that my experience with tires is limited to spending Sundays watching Formula 1 with Declan and Iris.

It only takes me five minutes in the baking sun to realize the mechanics on TV have it easy with their power drills and quick lift jacks. Unlike the guys on the live camera, the real deal is far less sexy and fast.

My start was shaky, but thanks to YouTube, Adderall, and my inability to be bested by a shitty tire, I replace the flat with the dummy tire I found in Lana's trunk.

Although my head pounds and my stomach is feeling extra queasy after spending the last hour in the sun, I decide to take Lana's car to the mechanic. Since I don't want to leave her without a working vehicle for safety reasons, I take a rideshare back into town to grab my DBS before returning to the lake house. I leave her a note, my keys, and Cami's booster seat just in case she needs a car before driving off into town.

I walk into the car shop. "Hi. I'm looking to get a tire changed."

The mechanic takes one look at me before returning to the episode of a Korean drama playing on the TV in the corner.

"Do you think you can help me?" I stop in front of the counter.

"Sure. We're all booked today but if you want, come in tomorrow morning. *Early*." His eyes don't stray from the TV this time.

One glance at the store hours printed on a paper behind him makes my eyes narrow. "Are you even open tomorrow?"

"Yup."

I point to the sign behind him. He has the audacity to rip it down and crumple it in a ball before chucking it in the trash.

My molars grind together. "I'm willing to pay whatever you want to get it done today."

He glances at me, the wheels obviously turning in his head before he shakes it. "Sorry, Sal. Wish I could help you out."

"But you won't."

I place Lana's keys on the counter. "The car outside that needs fixing is Alana's. Take a look if you don't believe me."

His graying brows pull together. "It is? Why didn't you start with that?"

I roll my eyes and tell him to pick the best tire. He disappears with Lana's keys before coming back ten minutes later to let me know that her other three tires are bald and her oil needs to be changed. I give him the go-ahead to fix whatever he thinks is necessary for her and Cami to be safe. He gives me a weird look before disappearing back into the garage.

Two hours later, I drive away from the shop with a bill that's a mile long and a lightness in my chest that hasn't been present for days. The drive back to the house is quick. I pull into the driveway and park Lana's car in her usual spot before ringing the doorbell.

She steps out, clutching my keys with a tight fist. Based on her clenched jaw and crossed arms, things aren't going well for me, regardless of the fixed car.

She takes a deep breath. "I got your note. You didn't have to do that."

"It was the least I could do after yesterday."

"Well, thank you." She says it low, as if admitting her appreciation aloud would have a greater impact.

"It's fine. I had the mechanic change the other three to match because I didn't want you driving around in the rain with stripped tires."

"You did?" Her eyes flicker from the car to my face.

"Yup. Also, he went ahead and changed your oil and swapped your wipers out for new ones too."

She covers her mouth.

Uncertainty drives me to ask, "Is that fine?"

She nods, her glassy gaze still fixated on the car.

I hand her the keys. "Well, I've taken up enough of your day."

We swap keys. Her fingertips brush across the palm of my hand, and electricity passes over my skin.

"Thanks. That was kind of you to help me with the car." She disappears behind the door before I have a chance to answer her.

I didn't expect much from her after last night's incident, but part of me still wished for more. More what exactly, I'm not too sure. All I know is that my confidence from earlier is replaced by a new wave of emptiness. Except this time, I choose not to drown it with alcohol. It's a self-induced punishment I accept wholeheartedly, knowing it is my fault Lana is upset in the first place.

That night I don't go to bed drunk and numb. Instead, I go to bed alive and angry at my grandfather for putting me in the exact situation I knew would happen if I stuck around the last time.

I can't replace the vase I broke. It's a useless effort to even try, but I head out Sunday morning to the local mall an hour away from the lake with the hope of finding something to make up for my drunken accident.

Finding a vase is easy. The selection is endless, and I choose the nicest, most expensive one. Lana won't care about the price tag, but maybe my effort won't go unnoticed.

While the cashier is carefully wrapping my purchase so it won't break, I walk around the rest of the store. A bright cherry-red standing mixer on a high shelf catches my eye. I think of Lana and her rickety old hand mixer that is on its ninth life before calling over the associate and asking her to charge the item to my card.

I'm not looking to buy Lana's forgiveness.

I'm looking to buy into her dream, even if she doesn't anymore.

Since Lana took my key away when I was drunk, I have to ring the bell and wait for her. At some point, I place the heavy standing mixer on the porch and bounce on the tips of my toes while she takes her sweet time answering the door.

It creaks open, and she blinks up at me. "What do you want?"

"I came to make amends." I hold out the bag with the vase.

"With gifts?" She frowns at the bag.

Safe to say gifts aren't a part of her love language.

My hope dies along with any excitement about the mixer. I step in front of the bag before she can see it while still holding out the other that contains the vase. "I know I can't replace what I broke, but I wanted to get you a new vase anyway."

She doesn't reach for it. "What's the point?"

"I'm trying to fix a problem I caused, not start more of them."

"Then fix what actually matters here, and spoiler warning, it's not the vase."

"I…" I lose the rest of my sentence.

"What was the point of going back to rehab if you were only going to start drinking again?"

My heart feels like someone split it apart with the jaws of life. "I had lost my reason for getting sober in the first place."

Her brows furrow. "What? Money? Hockey? The will to live a normal life?"

"You, Lana. I lost *you*."

CHAPTER TWENTY-FOUR
Alana

I shake my head hard enough to make my vision blurry. "You don't get to stand here and blame me for your addiction."

He clasps on to my chin, forcing me to look him in the eyes. "I'm not blaming you. I'm just being honest about what happened the last time."

"What last time?"

His fingers clutching my chin tighten. "I came back. Even though I swore to you I wouldn't, I did it anyway because I was a stupid, hopeful fool."

I suck in a breath. "When?"

"Right before my grandpa was taken off the ventilators."

"But that was—" *Over two years ago.*

Oh, no.

The look on his face drives an invisible dagger through my heart.

"I didn't believe it at first." His gaze drops. Tension bleeds from his shoulders, each of his muscles rigid underneath the fabric of his shirt. "But then I saw you with my own two eyes, kissing that guy, Victor, right by Last Call."

My eyes narrow. "Who told you about him?"

His upper lip curls from disgust. "Does it matter?"

I look away.

His chest rises and falls from his deep exhale. "You know what? It shouldn't because that's not my point."

My eyes shut. "Then what is?"

"I failed you for the final time that night."

My head shakes hard enough to rattle my brain. "How? I didn't even know you were in town."

"Because instead of fighting for you—for us—I chose the easy way out that night. The familiar one. The *wrong* one. Instead of dealing with my problems, I wanted to drown them in alcohol until I couldn't feel any more pain. Until I numbed the part of my brain that saw you in the arms of another man. It was so fucked up after all that effort to get sober, but I couldn't find it in me to stop. I didn't *want* to. My main reason for getting better was stolen away from me, which was exactly what my grandpa said would happen."

He bares his soul to me, and I find it impossible to tear him down at the moment.

"I know I ruined our chance at something more. It was selfish of me to even try the last time, knowing the kind of mental state I was in and that us getting together could very well ruin our friendship."

"Why take the risk then?" The question I obsessed over flies out of my mouth, along with any sense of self-preservation.

He takes a deep breath. My stomach twists into a knot, the

muscles stretching tight enough to hurt.

His gaze locks on to mine. "I always thought we were meant to be. I might have screwed up the timing a bit, but that doesn't change the fact that there is no one I want more in this world than you."

Breathing becomes exponentially more difficult.

"I was biding my time before because it was never the right moment for us. Three years doesn't sound like a big difference anymore, but back then it felt like a whole other lifetime. By the time you turned eighteen, I was already a twenty-one-year-old loser with one stint in rehab under my belt. I was a fuckup and you were…" He stalls.

"If you say *a virgin*, I'm going to punch you." Cal teased me about it until one night I cracked and hooked up with an out-of-towner. He stayed pissed for an entire week, which was unheard of.

"Perfect. You were *perfect*." He runs his knuckles across my cheek.

Cue the butterflies.

"You had all these dreams and so did I. One of us would have had to settle, and I didn't want that for us. Didn't want to risk you resenting me when we were older." His smile falters. "I guess that was a stupid reason looking back on it."

"I don't *resent* you. I just want to cut off your airflow and watch your face turn purple every now and then."

"Under the right circumstance, I'd love to play out your fantasy." He winks.

"Sure. Our safe word can be *more*."

A laugh explodes from his mouth, pure and light, as he stares at me like…

Like *before*.

"*This* is what I miss." He gestures between us with a grin. "I know I can't go back and change what I did the last time I was here. And as fucked up as it sounds, I don't regret it either, even though I lost you in the process. Because I would have rather known what it felt like to have had you for a summer than to have not had you at all."

My heart feels about ready to implode on itself, especially with what he says next.

"We've had a rocky start this summer, but I just hope we can be friends again. At least while I'm here."

"Friends?" The floor drops out from underneath me.

He reads my face like his favorite book. "I know I screwed up big-time yesterday."

"You did. *Massively.*"

"I'm glad I have you around to keep me humble."

"Consider it my contribution to society. We can't have someone like you running around town with an ego the size of Lake Michigan."

"There must be some hope for me after all when there is still Lake Superior to contend with."

I press my lips together in a poor attempt to conceal my smile.

He sighs. "Look. I know asking to be friends again is a stretch—" *Yeah, because you kissed me senseless only a week ago.* "But I'm hoping we can find some way to get along while I'm here."

I roll my bottom lip between my teeth while I consider his proposal. Being friends would set an expectation. It can give us a few boundaries that will hopefully prevent us from doing something stupid.

Right. Because that worked so well the last time he was here.

I'm smarter now. Back then, the excitement of us becoming a couple trumped my common sense. But now, I'm more prepared. I *evolved*. Letting go of the anger I have toward him would be a sign of maturity.

Not trusting him and his addiction isn't a sign of immaturity, but experience.

Experiences I suffered through not only with him, but my sister, too. The kind that taught me everything I know about living with loved ones who suffer with addictions.

I open my mouth with every intention of rejecting his bid for friendship, only to press my lips together. He isn't the only one who misses our friendship.

I do as well.

I rock back on my heels. "If you want to be friends again, we need to establish some boundaries."

"Like?"

"If you get drunk again like you did on the night of Cami's graduation, we're done. Forever."

He swallows hard. "Fine."

Well, damn. I expected a bit more hesitancy with that one.

"And no more kissing." The words rush out of my mouth.

His lips curve into the sexiest smirk. "It's a hard ask, but I can try."

"You survived a long time without even attempting, so I think you can make it without another slipup." My cheeks warm at the memory of last week.

"That was before." His voice deepens.

"Before what?"

"I knew what you felt like beneath me." He runs his knuckles across the side of my face. The air between us crackles, the goose bumps on my skin rising to the occasion.

It was stupid to ever think we could even attempt to be friends. There is no possible way of that ever happening—not when a simple brush of his hand makes my body react like that.

I hate it. I love it. I shouldn't let it ever happen again.

I clear my head with a quick shake. "You know what? Never mind. I can't be your friend."

He pulls back, stealing his warmth and the tingling feeling running down the length of my spine away from me. "Why not?"

"You can't even last five minutes without flirting with me."

"Well, you're setting me up for failure if you expect me to last five minutes around you."

I give him a once-over. "Disappointed but not surprised."

His face turns red in five seconds flat. "That's not what I meant."

"No need to be embarrassed. You're older now, so I get it. I'm sure with the right pills that problem can get sorted out real quick."

He takes a step closer. "I'm not embarrassed. I'm *enraged*."

I fake a sigh. "Male fragility at its finest."

"Lana."

One word. Four letters. A thousand sparks blasting off my skin as he clasps on to the back of my neck and drags me against his chest. Our lips hover inches apart, the heat of his minty breath hitting my face.

No vodka.

My fingers curl against his chest.

His fingers press into the side of my throat. "I need to defend my honor."

"I'm amazed there is still something left to protect."

His eyes sparkle like a thousand stars exploding at once.

I'm antagonizing him. I know that, yet I can't find it in me to stop, no matter how loud the voice in the back of my head shouts that nothing good can come from this.

Cal shocks me as he wraps his hand around my hair and tugs on it like a rope until my head tilts to the side and my breasts press against his chest. He drags the tip of his nose up the side of my throat. It's erotic, the way a single touch makes my entire body feel like it might be consumed by flames. I shift, wanting to escape the feeling, only to rub against the one part of him I offended.

Fuck.

Every hard inch of him presses into my belly. I suck in a breath, and he chuckles.

"Right. About that." His voice, now rougher than before, causes me to tremble. Tremble with what, I'm not too sure. Arousal. Excitement. *Desperation.* The options are endless, each one more dangerous than the last.

"You're hard."

"Astute as always."

I blink twice. "Why are you hard?"

"Because you exist." His eyes burn a hole directly into my heart, torching his way through the ice surrounding it.

I shake my head, trying to erase the image of his eyes

imprinting on my soul. "We shouldn't be doing this."

His fingers clutching my hair tighten. "I know." He kisses the sensitive spot below my ear with a sigh. A shaky breath escapes me before I have a chance to swallow it.

"It's wrong." My heart pounds harder in my chest, declaring the complete opposite.

His eyes shut, but not before I catch the pain flashing within them. "Is that how you really feel about us?"

"I've never been more certain of anything." I respond automatically, the impact of my answer written clearly across his face.

It makes me physically ill to hurt him, but I don't have any other choice. To risk getting close to him in any way is to risk my heart all over again for someone who doesn't even plan on sticking around.

I don't have it in me to survive another heartbreak. I'm afraid the next one will be the one that finally makes me shatter beyond repair.

His hand releases my hair before dropping by his side like dead weight. "I apologize for crossing a boundary then. I…" He trips over his words. "I got caught up in the moment for a second."

My chest throbs. The churning in my stomach intensifies, acid crawling up my throat, ready to purge itself from my trembling body.

Before I can stop myself, I offer an olive branch. A stupid olive branch I know I'll regret but can't take back.

"If you want to be friends—real friends—you can't manhandle me like that anymore."

His face remains unreadable. "I thought you didn't want to

be my friend."

"Ehh, I changed my mind."

"Why?"

"Because the only other friend you have in town is my five-year-old daughter, and frankly, that's kind of sad."

The look on his face widens the pit in my stomach. "I don't need a pity friend."

"Too bad. It's a bribe-one-get-one Castillo special."

A real smile forms on his face, casting away the shadows in his eyes. "Does that mean you'll help build the boat with us?" His excitement is addictive, and I find myself saying yes. I expect the regret to be imminent, but instead, I only notice a tingly feeling in my chest at the idea of building something special with Cami and Cal.

Maybe an activity like that will be good for us. Maybe we can get closure and move on from all the crap that has been brewing at the surface for the last six years.

He holds my gaze for a moment longer before taking another step back. "I should get going. We have an early morning with the contractor tomorrow."

I blink twice before regaining sensation in my limbs. "Right."

He passes me the bag with the vase before walking back to his car. I'm so distracted by watching him leave that I don't notice the second bag on the porch until he is driving toward the main road.

I walk inside the house and place the first bag on top of the empty table below the stairs before going back out to grab the other.

"What the hell is this?" I grunt from the weight. My arms

tremble as I deposit it on the floor beside the table.

First, I unwrap the vase. It's simple, elegant, and exactly something my mom would have chosen for herself. The second bag surprises me. I kneel on the floor and pull out a wrapped cube. A white envelope is taped to the top of the wrapping paper, and I cut through it with my fingernail before pulling out a card.

> Maybe you were right about wanting to make someone else's dreams come true.
>
> —C

With shaky fingers, I peel apart the wrapping paper to reveal a professional mixer. I recognize the brand as one that belonged in my *never going to happen but might as well torture myself with looking at it* list.

My eyes fill with tears. It's not about the mixer itself, but the meaning behind it that turns me inside out.

I reread the card again, and the butterflies in my stomach rage and riot even harder the second time. The feeling has nothing to do with the urge to bake until two a.m. tonight and everything to do with the man who gave me the rush in the first place.

Before I chicken out, I pull out my phone and shoot Cal a text.

> Thank you for the mixer.

> Thank me by making my favorite.

> Deal.

I go to bed with the stupidest smile on my face that night, feeling better than I have in weeks.

wake up the next morning excited and ready to meet with the contractor. Now that things with Cal seem to be settled, I feel more ready to work with him on the house.

I breeze through the morning routine with enough energy to rival Cami. Her enthusiasm about starting summer camp rubs off on me, and we spend the entire car ride blasting her favorite song from the latest Dreamland princess movie.

I gave up on my battle against the Kanes and their fairytale empire ages ago. It was a pointless fight, especially when all of Cami's friends are obsessed with Dreamland and their princess movies. Even I have to admit the films are pretty cute, although Cami and I both agree it would be nice for them to have a movie about someone from Colombia. Bonus points if they're from Barranquilla like my family.

By the time I arrive back at the house, my mood can't get any better.

"What has you smiling like that?" Cal peeks into the kitchen.

I drop the pan I was cleaning back into the sudsy water and shut off the music streaming from the portable speaker on the counter. "It's the first day of summer."

"Congratulations. What do you plan on doing first?"

I motion toward the dishes. "I need to finish this up before the contractor gets here."

He begins to roll up the sleeves of his linen shirt, revealing his thick forearms. "How about I dry while you wash?"

I look up from his arms. "Why?"

"Because I finished up the attic, and I don't have anything else to do before the contractor gets here."

"You finished that attic already?"

"Yup." He grabs a towel hanging on the oven and throws it over his shoulder before turning toward me.

I can't help smiling at him. "Domesticity looks good on you."

His lips twitch. "Maybe Iris was on to something."

My spine stiffens. *Who the hell is Iris?*

I've never heard that name come out of his mouth before, but he obviously cares a lot about her based on the way his eyes light up at the mere mention of her name.

I grab the Brillo pad and get to scrubbing the leftover eggs off the pan. Cal stands beside me, drying the pot I had washed a minute ago. The scrape of the scouring pad against metal makes my ears ache.

He nudges me with his elbow. "What's wrong?"

"Nothing."

"Iris says the same thing when she's mad." His voice sounds lighter, and I look up to find his eyes sparkling.

What a dick.

I scrub so hard, a piece of the pad breaks off and floats away.

"Are you sure nothing is wrong?" he teases.

"Yup."

"If you insist. I'd hate to put our friendship at risk already."

"Here you go." I rinse the pan off and pass it to him so he can shut up.

He leans forward to whisper in my ear, "It's cute to see you get all jealous over my sister-in-law, but it's really not necessary."

I blink. "Sister-in-law?"

"Iris Elizabeth *Kane*. AKA Declan's wife."

"Declan got married?"

He nods with a smile. "To my best friend."

Well, don't you look like the stupid one now.

"That's nice that you two are close." My nose wrinkles.

He taps it. "Declan doesn't seem to agree either."

A laugh catches in my throat. "How is he?"

"Insufferable as always."

"That's a shame. Hopefully he finally got that surgery to help with his resting dick face."

Cal throws his head back and laughs. The combination of his smile and the light streaming through the window makes him rival the sun. I step closer, desperate for the warmth only he can provide.

"God, I've missed you." He wraps an arm around me and tugs me against him. The gesture is intended to be completely platonic, but the tingling from my head to my toes definitely isn't. Cal doesn't seem any better with the way he leans close and sniffs my hair while he thinks I'm not looking.

My heart thuds loudly, blocking my hearing.

Day one of being just friends is going well. Can't wait for what's in store next.

Ryder Smith, the general contractor from Lopez Luxury, pulls out a tape measure. "Shall we get started with a walkthrough of the house?"

Cal looks over at me with a tight smile that doesn't reach his eyes. "Ready?"

My right eye twitches. "Of course."

Cal and I are careful to keep a wide berth between us while we show Ryder the house. The few times we end up touching, one of us has a knee-jerk reaction. I'm not sure if this is what Cal had in mind when he suggested being friends, but I'm hoping we can snap out of it.

Ryder doesn't seem to notice. He jots down notes on his clipboard while asking us a ton of questions, some of which I don't know the answers to.

Ryder squats down near the entrance to the kitchen where the wood floor switches to vinyl. "Does the wood floor continue under here?"

Cal looks over at me like I should know the answer.

"I remember my mom saying the previous owner covered up the floors in the kitchen, so I think the original flooring runs throughout the house."

"I can have one of my guys take a look and confirm if that's true. If they are original, we only need to refinish them which will save us a lot of time compared to waiting for a new floor."

"With us setting such a high sale price, would buyers expect something more modern? Like marble perhaps?" Cal crosses his arms against his chest, giving me a perfect view of his veiny forearms.

I nearly miss what he says because I'm too distracted from the arm porn happening right now.

"Marble?" I ask.

"What's wrong with marble?" Cal frowns.

"It doesn't fit the style of the house."

"Neither does the price tag, but that didn't bother you before." He grins.

I could strangle him right here, right now with Ryder as my sole witness. Maybe for the right price, he would be willing to supply me with some cement sneakers.

Ryder's dark eyes bounce between the two of us. "If you want marble floors for a house of this size, you're looking at a six-month wait, at the very least, depending on our supplier."

Cal waves his hand in the air. "That won't work then. Let's stick with the original floors."

Ryder moves on to the kitchen while Cal and I follow behind. He pokes around and scribbles notes across his clipboard while making different noises to himself. Some sound confirmatory while others make the hairs on my arms raise.

He seems especially unhappy when he whips out a handy-dandy tool and starts hacking away at a goddamn wall. He mutters a curse under his breath before turning to face us. "So do you want the good news or the bad news first?"

Cal leans against the island with a smile. "You found something good about the place? I'm absolutely shocked."

I pinch him in the side. "I'll take the bad news first please."

"You have asbestos."

Oh, no.

"You're kidding me." Cal frowns.

"It's pretty typical in homes of this age. We need to contact an asbestos abatement contractor who works with us to come out and carefully remove the mineral fiber from the walls, floors, and insulation."

Cal pulls out his phone and gets to researching, completely tuning out my panicked gasp.

"They're going to have to rip out walls?"

"Potentially. I'm not going to open up any more holes without the proper equipment."

"What's the good news?" I rub my temple.

"It shouldn't take longer than three weeks, give or take how soon someone can come out here to clear it out. By the time you come back, all of it should be removed and we can get started on the demo. It will set us behind a bit with our timeline, but you can spend the time picking out the finishes."

My world spins around me like I just stepped off a tilt-a-whirl. "Whoa. Wait. What do you mean come back? Where are we going?"

Ryder frowns. "Now that we found asbestos, I don't recommend you stay here until we have professionals remove it."

"Why not?"

Cal speaks up, his jaw working. "Because there is no way I'm letting you live around something that could cause you cancer."

"Cancer?" My eyes widen.

"Pack your bags because you and Cami are staying with me at the guesthouse."

After Ryder leaves, I do my own thorough search about what kind of health risks asbestos poses while Cal takes the initiative and books an abatement team to get started on Friday once I pack up the rest of the house.

I only have two options for a temporary living situation, one of which is automatically a no-go because Violet has two roommates right now and no guest bedroom for me and a small child. Delilah and Wyatt's two-bedroom starter home is my only other option. I just need to call Delilah once she gets off work and ask her first.

Cal doesn't seem to like me evading his order to stay at the guesthouse. He hasn't stopped following me around all afternoon, which has been both annoying and useful when I need to reach tall items.

I navigate my way through the garage, careful not to run into any of the stacks of boxes Cal lined up for the moving company.

I get distracted by his presence and trip. He catches my elbow before I fall face-first into a row of boxes.

"Will you stop following me around everywhere?" I rip my hand out of his grasp.

"Not until you agree to not staying here tonight."

"Fine!" I throw my hands in the air. "I didn't plan on sleeping here anyway."

His brows pull together. "So, you're staying at the guesthouse?"

"No." I struggle to reach for the luggage on the top shelf despite balancing on the tips of my toes.

Cal reaches around my body and grabs the suitcase off the shelf for me. The brush of his chest against my back has me suppressing a shiver, a fact that doesn't seem to go unnoticed based on the way he trails a single digit down my spine.

"Where are you going to go then?" His question has a certain edge to it.

Oh, that's it.

I turn on my heels, and our chests brush. "I don't know, but there is no way in hell I'm sharing the guesthouse with you."

"Why not?"

I throw my hands in the air. "Because it's a terrible idea!"

"Afraid you can't control yourself around me?" His signature smile comes back at full force, turning my whole world upside down.

My scoff lacks its usual bravado. "I can control myself."

"Is that so?" The pad of his thumb follows the curve of my bottom lip, sending a zip of energy down my spine. My head pathetically tilts closer to him.

Emphasis on pathetic.

I shove him away, although the push is weak at best. My fingers itch to dig themselves into his shirt and pull him back, solely so I can feel the rush his touch provides.

That right there is why you can't live with him.

I slip out of his cage and charge away, dragging the suitcases behind me to the soundtrack of Cal's laugh.

I spend the rest of the day packing up the necessities for Cami and myself, which is an exhausting endeavor in itself. I'm not looking forward to packing everything else away before the asbestos abatement team comes.

I don't have a lot of keepsakes. The most important thing I own happens to be a shoebox crammed full of memories. I climb the ladder in my closet and search for the box. It's kept out of reach, hidden behind an old Santa gift I forgot to put under the tree a couple of years ago.

I brush a shaky hand across the dusty shoebox top before removing it. My hand trembles as I sift through the countless photos, tickets, a few of Cal's hospital bands from all the times he got injured because of me, Cami's favorite pacifier, and other memorabilia from my entire life. It's bittersweet how twenty-nine years of memories can fit in a single shoebox. There was once a time I dreamed of more for myself than this town. I love Lake Wisteria—I really do—but it was never meant to be the adventure.

It was supposed to be the final destination.

Now you will finally have a chance to make your dreams come true.

With the money I'm bound to get from the selling the house, there isn't anything stopping me anymore from traveling around the world and opening my own bakery here.

Well, nothing except for myself. Self-doubt always rears its ugly head at the worst times, making me wonder if I really have what it takes to be successful.

You'll never know if you don't try.

"Mommy!" Cami runs into the closet.

My grip on the shoebox slips and falls against the floor,

bottom side up.

"Oh, no! I'm sorry!" Cami gets on her knees and lifts the box, proceeding to dump all the contents.

"I got it. Don't worry about it." I climb down the ladder.

She holds up a photo with a big smile. "Look! It's you and Cow-l holding hands!"

Of all the photos she found, it had to be the one of him and me at the Strawberry Festival six summers ago.

"Mm-hm." I pluck the photo from her hands and drop it into the box.

Her head tilts. "Do you like him, Mommy?"

"We were friends."

"Like kissing friends or *friends* friends?"

Por el amor de Dios. "Just friends."

A rare frown crosses her face.

"What?"

"Nothing," she replies with a tone that says the opposite.

You need to be more careful with him when you're around her.

Cami is the last person who should be getting her hopes up about us. Whatever happened in the past between Cal and me is just that.

The past.

was wondering how long it would take you to come to the right decision." Cal holds open the door with a grin.

My eyes turn into slits. "I have one condition."

"Name it."

"No drinking in front of Cami."

His smile slips. "Of course not."

I release a breath. "Thank you."

"Hi!" Cami pops out from behind me.

"What's up, kiddo?" He kneels to Cami's eye level. His eyes widen when she throws her arms around his neck and squeezes until his skin turns red.

Damn my heart straight to hell for betraying me with the way it throbs at their embrace.

He stands to his full height. "What happened to staying with Delilah and Wyatt?"

"Her grandmother is visiting from out of town for the month," I grumble.

"And Violet?"

"She lives in a small apartment with two roommates."

"There's nothing I love more than being last choice." He reaches for my luggage and rolls it inside. I follow behind him, taking in the large stacks of books scattered around the living room.

"Since when are you into reading?"

A flush spreads up his neck as he tucks his thumbs into the front pockets of his jeans. "I like to keep my mind busy."

"You read all those in the last few weeks?" There must be at least fifty books spread around the space.

He nods.

"Wow."

His gaze flicks over me. "Do you need any help grabbing the rest of the stuff?"

"Be careful what you volunteer for."

"It's not like I have anything else to do."

Cal spends the next hour helping me carry over boxes and bags full of stuff. By the time we're done, the guesthouse's entire living room floor is covered with toys. The kitchen cabinets spill with groceries and cooking tools, and the bedrooms are crammed with our personal items that we didn't want to risk leaving behind, including my vibrator that I hid in my nightstand. No way was I leaving that around for some random guy to find.

Cal disappears while I do my best to make Cami's new room look homey with her princess comforter, butterfly lamp, and LED lights.

By the time I'm done, I need to pee. I open the bathroom door closest to Cami's room only to get yelled at by my kid, who sits on the toilet claiming she has a tummy ache. Taking her off the toilet after that warning is no longer an option.

Light spills out from underneath the crack of the second bathroom located at the end of the hall. I turn the knob, but the door doesn't open.

"Give me a second." The door muffles Cal's deep voice.

The door opens, and a cloud of steam billows around Cal, who stands in the doorway wearing nothing but a white towel. He is so focused on wrapping it around his waist that he doesn't notice my tongue falling out of my mouth.

I don't know where to look. Although his bulging traps are tempting, I quickly become distracted by his glistening abs that lead straight toward the muscles pointing like an arrow toward his cock. He isn't even hard, but I can make out the shape of him from beneath the terrycloth material.

The man was created by God to fulfill every woman's fantasy.

More like yours.

The faraway sound of Cami's tablet pushes me into action.

"Get in there." I push him back into the bathroom and shut the door behind us.

"What's wrong?" He trips over his feet before catching himself on the counter.

I rip a second towel off the shelf before slapping him in the face with it. "Cover all that up before you go outside again."

"Cover this? What for?" His lips twitch as he runs his hand along the curves and divots of his abdominal muscles.

"There is a child here!" I whisper-shout.

"Relax. I'm just joking with you." He reaches for the towel and covers his upper body until he resembles a mummy. "All better?" He looks ridiculous with the way his wet hair flops in front of his face.

"Not even remotely." I throw a damp hand towel over his face. "There. All better."

He pulls it off with a laugh. "Sorry about that. I forgot about Cami staying here."

"Oh, so if it's just me, then it's okay to walk around in only a towel?"

"If it were just you, I'd lose the towel altogether." He winks.

My mouth waters at the image of him doing just that.

"You'd like that, wouldn't you?" His husky voice makes my belly heat.

"No." I notice my nose twitching too late.

He runs his finger down the slope, eliciting a pleasant shiver. "Are you sure?" His hands reach for the edge of the towel.

My heart thumps harder against my chest, making it impossible to hear as he begins to undo the towel.

"No!" I slap my hands against his waist to stop him, only to brush against his cock in the process.

I blink. He grins.

My pinkie reaches out to tease his length just to confirm what I felt. He shivers, the tiny exhale he releases making me press my legs together.

"Unless you plan on finishing what you started, I wouldn't do that again." He pushes my hand away.

All five of my fingers itch to wrap themselves around his length. It hurts me to deny the instinct, especially with how he looks at me.

"Keep staring at me like that and I might get the wrong

idea." He squeezes his cock through the towel with a smirk.

That fucker…

The pulsing between my legs has nothing to do with needing to use the bathroom. "For the record, you're a terrible friend. No wonder Declan doesn't like you hanging around his wife." I shove him out of the bathroom and lock the door before I do something stupid like kiss the smile off his face.

I give up on trying to blindly plug in my cellphone charger into the outlet behind my bed. It's impossible to reach without getting on my hands and knees, so I kneel and use the flashlight on my cellphone to light up the dark space underneath.

A loud hiss makes me fall back on my ass and release a blood-curdling scream straight out of a movie. Quick, heavy footsteps running down the hall match the erratic beat of my heart. My door swings open before the knob slams into the wall.

"What's wrong?" Cal looks around the room with wild eyes while clutching onto a lamp.

I press a hand against my chest, willing my heart to calm down. "What kind of weapon is that?"

His cheeks turn a light shade of pink. "It was the first thing within grabbing distance."

He thought you were in danger, so he didn't want to waste any time.

My throat swells, stealing my ability to speak.

Cami barrels into the room, her small hands raised in a fighting stance she learned in karate. "I'll save you!" She slices her hands through the air and spin kicks. Her feet slide across the carpet, her arms flailing as she loses her balance.

Cal ditches the lamp to catch her right before she crashes against the floor. He lifts her into the air, making her giggle.

My heart thuds against my chest in betrayal. It's impossible not to have some sort of reaction as Cal throws her in the air again, earning another loud laugh before placing her back on her feet.

Cal looks up at me, catching me staring at him and Cami's interaction. "What happened?"

I point a shaky finger at the dark space under the bed. "There is something underneath the bed."

"What?"

"I don't know. It's not like I got a good look before it hissed at me."

"Oh, that's Merlin." Cal's eyes sparkle as he offers me his hand. I'm a little wobbly on my feet, mainly due to the way Cal scans my body for any injuries.

I look away first. "That thing is your cat?"

Cami gasps. "You have a cat?"

He nods, and Cami instantly abandons us for the bed.

"Cami, no! He's not nice." I swoop and pull her back.

Cal shakes his head. "That's not true. Merlin might sound scary, but he's harmless. I swear. He doesn't even have claws because his last owner was an abusive jerk, so you don't have to worry about him hurting anyone. The worst thing he does is shed, but I have a robot vacuum for that."

My heart aches. "He was declawed?"

"Yes, and that isn't even the worst of it."

Good God. My weakness for strays is starting to show itself at the worst time.

"Can I pet him? Please?" Cami looks up at me while batting her lashes.

I look to Cal for approval.

"It's fine with me."

I sigh with resignation. "All right." I can just tell with the way Cami's eyes light up, she is going to be attached to Merlin by the end of the night.

Cami army crawls toward the bed while cooing and calling Merlin's name. He doesn't come out, which makes her frown.

"He doesn't like me."

Cal shakes his head with a smile and kneels beside her.

For the second time tonight, I bear witness to Cal being sweet to my kid for no other reason than he is just that kind of guy.

"He is a little shy." He holds out his hand beneath the bed.

Cami waits, her body trembling from her growing excitement.

It takes a minute, but thanks to Cal's persistence and Cami's patience, a skinny black cat comes crawling out from underneath the bed. He rubs against Cal's thigh, his tail swishing back and forth as Cal runs his hand down the cat's spine.

"Slowly pet him." Cal shows Cami one more time before letting her try.

Cami reaches out her hand with the intention to brush her fingers across Merlin's fur, but the cat darts outside of the room before she has a chance.

Her smile falls. "He hates me."

"He's just grumpy, but I have a trick." Cal stands before

lifting Cami up and on to her feet.

He shows her his secret stash of catnip and Merlin's favorite toy. Cami watches with fascination as he fills the toy full of the stuff before handing her the pole it is attached to with a string.

With Cal's instruction, Cami dangles the fish in front of the couch where Merlin is hiding underneath. When Merlin's paw darts out to catch the feathered fish, Cami squeals. Cal ends up laughing at her reaction, and I find myself doing the same.

I stick back, both enamored and terrified by their interaction. The more the two of them spend time together, the more I worry that Cami might grow attached to Cal. I know what it feels like to have your heart crushed by none other than Callahan Kane. It leaves a void that can't be filled, no matter how hard one tries.

I've made plenty of mistakes, but I wonder if I made the biggest one yet by allowing my daughter to get caught up in Cal's spell. If she is anything like me, then there is no way she won't end up loving him. But then he will leave, and I'll be stuck picking up the pieces yet again.

Except this time, it won't be my heart he breaks.

It will be my daughter's.

CHAPTER TWENTY-SEVEN

Cal

Living with Lana and Cami is a completely different experience than seeing them every now and then back at the main house while I was cleaning out the attic. For starters, the entire house is filled with toys. Boxes upon boxes of toys. The whole living room is a minefield of Legos, princess dolls, and enough stuffed animals for Cami to play pretend school.

The kid is cute as fuck as she acts out her mother's Spanish class, switching from English to Spanish, with Lana correcting her every now and then while she prepares dinner in the kitchen.

Cami points a paper towel roll at the mini whiteboard she wrote on. "Vamos a apprendo español."

"Vamos a aprender español."

Cami repeats the phrase before earning a flour-covered thumbs-up from her mother.

I chuckle underneath my breath, giving away the fact that I was pretending to read.

"Cal, do you want to play with me?" Cami runs over to me and tugs on my hand.

Lana looks up from her cutting board. "I think Cal is busy."

She's been rather icy the last couple of days, ever since the day after she moved in. I've tried to break through with a few jokes, but nothing seems to get past her. Even my attempts to not drink do nothing to lighten the mood.

She has been careful to not leave me alone with Cami for longer than a minute, which wasn't the case before.

What changed?

Honestly, not knowing is driving me a little crazy. I'm not sure what happened between her offering to be my friend and now. Whatever is going on in her head can't be good, and I'm tempted to corner her and get some answers.

Maybe once Cami falls asleep I can.

"Please?" Cami blinks up at me with her long lashes.

"Sure. I'd love to play with you, kiddo." I stand and follow a beaming Cami, all while Lana glares at me.

I spend the next twenty minutes impersonating a student while Cami attempts to read me a book in Spanish. She trips over the words, and I do my best to help her out, with Lana interjecting every now and then on words I mispronounce.

My neck and spine prickle every now and then. When I look around, I find Lana quickly busying herself with something in the kitchen.

What's going on?

"All right, Camila. Time for dinner." Lana tugs her apron

over her head.

The smells coming from the oven make me wish she extended me the same invitation, although I know that won't happen.

Cami latches on to my hand and tugs. "Vamos a comer."

Lana doesn't say anything, but the silence between us doesn't bode well. As good as a home-cooked Colombian meal sounds right now, I'm not about to give Lana another reason to be annoyed with me.

I shake my head. "I can't."

"Why?"

"I have plans."

"Like what?" The kid lacks any personal boundaries or social skills.

She is five. Give her a break.

"I'm going to eat at the diner."

Her face scrunches in the same way Lana's does. "Booooo."

Just when I thought my life couldn't get any lower, I get heckled by a five-year-old.

Great.

Lana walks up to Cami and gives her shoulders a squeeze. "Maybe next time."

"Right."

"But my mommy's the bestest cook in the whole wide world." Her beaming smile is a force to be reckoned with. I doubt I would stand much of a chance at telling her no if it weren't for Lana glaring a hole into the side of my face as I address her child.

"I know. She learned from the second bestest cook in the whole wide world—her mom."

Cami gasps, and I instantly know I said the wrong thing.

"You had Abuela's food? When?" Cami looks up at me with wide eyes.

I glance toward Lana for approval before I say something I shouldn't. She gives me a small nod, and I let out a breath of relief.

"She worked here while I visited in the summers growing up and cooked the best food I've ever had. After your mom, that is"

Cami's eyes look about ready to pop out of her head from how hard she is straining them. "Really?"

Lana looks away, her chest rising and falling with each deep breath.

"Yup."

Cami's grin widens even more. "Did you like her?"

"It was impossible not to. Every person who met her loved her." I mean every word. Señora Castillo had this energy about her that made everyone want to stick around. She loved to cook, clean, and tell stories while doing both, which was a welcomed change compared to the nannies I spent time around growing up.

It's one of the reasons I loved visiting for the summers, although my brothers didn't share the same feelings.

"Do you miss her?"

Cami's question makes my chest pinch with uncomfortable tightness.

"Yes, I do. I wish I could have said goodbye."

Lana's hands grasping on to Cami's shoulders tighten.

"Where were you?" Cami's brows pull together.

Lana shakes her head. "Por favor, no más preguntas. Me has hecho suficiente por hoy."

"But—"

"Why don't you go set the table while I talk to Cal?"

"Okay!" Cami barrels toward the small kitchen table we pushed into a corner to allow for more space for all the toys.

"If you want to have dinner with us, you can." She brushes some flour off her apron.

"I don't want to impose." *You're such a rotten liar.*

My stomach betrays me as it growls loud enough for Lana to hear it. She cracks a small smile. It's the first one I've seen directed toward me in days, and I soak it up like a plant deprived of sunshine.

"Just go take a seat at the table while I get the arepas."

"Arepas?"

"Y chorizo."

My mouth waters. "Chorizo? Do you need any help?"

"I've been cooking food for years without any help, so I think I can manage just fine on my own, but thanks."

"It wouldn't hurt to make a man feel useful every now and then."

She bats her lashes. "Would you like me to find a lightbulb that needs changing?"

I give her a little shove on the shoulder, and she curls over laughing. The sound feels as if I just injected pure serotonin into my veins.

The timer on the oven beeps, stealing Lana and that rush of happiness with her.

I take a seat next to Cami and give her my attention while ignoring the pull I have toward the woman working around the kitchen.

Lana places my plate in front of me. Before she has a chance to move back, I clasp on to her hand and give it a light squeeze. "Thank you. I'm so happy you invited me."

Lana's cheeks, already pink from exertion, turn red. "You're welcome."

I brush my thumb over her skin. "I missed your food." I missed a hell of a lot more than her food, but it feels like a safe way to express myself. She squeezes my hand back in silent acknowledgment before I release her.

While Lana grabs a juice box from the fridge, Cami leans over the table to whisper in my ear.

"You like my mommy."

My eyes stretch to their limits.

"I can keep a secret." Cami zips her lips and throws an invisible key over her shoulder.

Damn, the kid is smart. Either that or my interest in Lana is so pathetically obvious that even a five-year-old child notices.

Probably a combination of both.

The aroma of arepas tickles my nose and makes my mouth water. Cami digs in, taking bites in between telling us about how she went swimming at the community pool today with her summer camp. Between her storytelling and Lana's questions, the entire meal is filled with laughter, fake gasps, and Lana goading Cami with silly questions meant to stir up controversy.

I love how there isn't a single moment of silence.

I don't remember the last time I felt this content while doing something so simple. Sure, I've had dinner with my family, but something about being surrounded by two couples only amplified the empty feeling in my chest. Tonight, though, that sensation is long gone.

There was a point in my life that I thought it wouldn't be possible to feel this complete. But tonight, I can sense it.

For the first time in a long time, I begin to hope. To believe that there is more for me in this life than chronic loneliness and a desperation to fit in somewhere. That I can be sober *and* happy, so long as I put in the effort.

Or so I wish.

The hum of the dishwashing machine fills the silence as I scrub the counter with a disinfectant wipe.

Lana comes out of Cami's bedroom and shuts the door softly behind her. She has been at the bedtime routine for an hour already, with Cami asking for ten more minutes of her bath, one extra bedtime story, and a special request for Lana to sing her a lullaby before bed. I tried not to eavesdrop much, but it was hard given how small the house is.

She looks over at me with a strange expression. "You did the dishes."

"It's the least I can do after you made dinner."

Her head tilts. "I might have to invite you to eat with us every single night if it means you doing the dishes."

"Deal," I say too fast, my voice reeking of desperation.

She bites down on her bottom lip, rolling it between her front teeth before speaking up. "It was nice."

My heart thuds harder against my chest. "What was?"

"Having you eat with us. It felt like…" Her voice drifts off.

I refuse to let her get away with not explaining. "What?" I

press.

"It felt like you fit in with us." She looks down at her bare feet as she tucks a piece of hair behind her ear.

I swallow past the lump in my throat. As much as I want to vocalize my agreement, I'm afraid what might happen if I do.

She wouldn't have brought it up if she was worried about what you might say.

"For a moment during dinner, I wished I did."

Her brows pull together. "What?"

I shrug, attempting to look like I don't care but probably failing miserably based on how tense my shoulders are. "I like spending time with you and Cami. She reminds me a lot of myself when I was her age."

A ghost of a smile crosses her lips. "For my own mental health and sanity, I'm going to pretend you didn't say that."

"I wasn't *that* bad."

"By ten years old, you already had three broken bones, one concussion, and an inability to sit still for longer than ten minutes."

"That doesn't mean she will."

"I sure hope not. My insurance co-pay is already through the roof." She throws her hands in the air.

I end up laughing, which only makes her lips purse.

"I'm serious!"

"You're about to be a millionaire once we sell the house. I'm sure you can cover a couple of broken bones after that."

"Right." Her elation dies, killed along with the small smile taking form on her face.

"Don't tell me you're second-guessing everything. I thought

we had an agreement with one another."

Her frown deepens. "No."

"Then what's wrong?"

"Nothing. I'm going to bed." She turns toward the hall.

"Why are you leaving?" I follow after her.

"I'm tired." She walks to her bedroom, which is right across from mine.

When Lana goes to reach for the knob, I stop her by grabbing her hand and turning her toward me.

"What did I say?"

She takes a deep breath, making her shoulders rise and fall. "It's not what you said exactly, but what it reminded me of that bothered me."

My hand holding on to hers tightens. "What?"

She lifts her other hand in the air and rotates her finger. "That all this has an expiration date."

My brows scrunch together. "Isn't that what you wanted?"

Her face contorts, confusion etching itself into every wrinkle of her forehead. "I don't know what I want and maybe that's my problem." She releases a heavy breath. "I just forgot what it felt like to—" Her sentence dies as she presses her lips together.

"Forgot what it felt like to *what*?"

She drops her gaze. "Not feel so damn lonely for once."

The pressure in my chest builds. "Lana—"

"It sounded even more pathetic when I said it aloud. Just pretend I didn't say anything." She tugs her hand free and slips inside her room before I can ask her anything else.

I go to my room and climb into bed. Merlin jumps up on to the mattress and cuddles at the foot of the bed, filling the silence with his steady purr.

I consider what Lana said about her not knowing what she wanted. Of how she didn't like being reminded that everything has an expiration date.

If she hadn't rushed off to her room, I would have told her I feel the same. That I also struggle with crippling loneliness and a desire to fill the chronic void in my chest.

I swore to myself that I would only be here until I sold the house. That there was no point to sticking around longer than that, especially when I wasn't wanted here.

But what if…

No. There is no possible way she would give me a chance.

Right?

During all my hypothetical situations about returning back to Lake Wisteria, I didn't even consider the possibility of Lana being interested in me. Wouldn't even entertain it because I couldn't get my hopes up.

But what if she is open to us trying something new together? Something that isn't weighed down by drugs or depression or bad decisions made out of desperation to feel something other than pain?

I could help lessen the loneliness both of us suffer from. It would be easy to become her companion. Friend. *Lover.*

My mind takes off, a plan forming as I mull through all our interactions up until this point. If Lana is confused, it's time I clarified a few things—starting with my feelings toward her. I might not have an answer for everything, but I do know one thing.

Lana is the only woman I ever loved, and it's time I started acting like it.

S econd to Christmas, the Strawberry Festival is my favorite time of the year at Lake Wisteria. Everyone in town goes all out to make it the best event to celebrate the season. People from all over come to visit the park near Town Square and enjoy the carnival rides, pageants, and amazing food inspired by the fruit of the season.

Cami yanks on my arm. "Mommy! Look!"

I turn to where Cami points. "What?"

"It's Cow-l!" She jumps up on her tippy toes to get a better look, making her strawberry print dress flap around her.

"Cal isn't here." At least I don't think he is, since he never mentioned coming during the last few meals we shared together.

"It's him!" She points toward the entrance of the festival.

At first, I think Cami must be imagining things. But then the person wearing a strawberry costume turns and looks at us with wide eyes.

Oh. My. God.

No freaking way.

From the green leafy headpiece and oversized white gloves to the red strawberry-shaped body piece and green pants, Cal looks like something out of a cartoon.

I burst out laughing. My hold on Cami's hand slips, and she takes off toward him.

Usually, the costume is reserved for an angsty teen in need of a punishment from their parents or an adult who lost a bet. I'm not sure how Cal ended up wearing it, but I have to personally thank whoever convinced him to put it on.

I pull out my phone and snap a photo of him. Cal grabs Cami and throws her in the air, turning my already-softening heart into absolute goo as she breaks into a fit of giggles.

So much for trying to avoid the warm fuzzies around him.

I wipe a stray tear that fell as I walk over to them. "How much did they pay you to wear that?"

He places Cami on her feet. "Sadly, I volunteered."

"*Why?*"

A breeze pushes a leaf into his eyes. "I was bored."

"And they set you up with this?" I flick one of the leaves falling over his eyes.

"I guess they wanted to make an ass out of me. Surprise, surprise."

Cami sucks in a breath.

He looks down at her. "Remind me later, okay?"

She tries to wink, only to end up blinking each eye one at a time.

Just another thing she picked up on from Cal.

"What do you mean?" I ask.

"Meg was the one who suggested I go to Town Hall to volunteer for the festival."

My eyes bulge. "Oh, no."

"Yup. And since I have to protect my pride, here I am."

"I'm surprised you have any left after wearing that."

His leaf headband bobs with his shrug. "What can I say? Vodka makes me confident."

My smile slips.

His eyes screw shut. "Wait, Lana. I didn't mean—"

My chest pinches. "It's fine. I get how it is."

"No, you don't." He reaches out to clutch my arm, although the oversized gloves don't allow for much of a grip.

I pull away. "We should get going. Got places to go and people to meet and whatnot."

He huffs. "Just let me explain myself first."

"Don't bother. It's not like it would change anything." I take Cami's hand and walk away before I let him do just that.

Cami and her friends laugh as they jump around the bounce house while I sit at a nearby picnic table with my friends.

Violet zooms in on the photo of Cal dressed in the horrendous costume. "Why didn't you warn us about this, Lana? I almost peed my pants when I saw him out front."

"I had no idea." I sigh.

Her brows rise. "He didn't say anything to you?"

"Nope." I look away, focusing on the crowd of people making their way through the rows of vendors selling strawberry jams, desserts, and deep-fried food.

"Why would he agree to wear that in the first place?" Delilah asks.

"Because he is too buzzed to care otherwise," I grumble.

"He's drinking?" Wyatt's jaw ticks.

"So he says." I look down at my clasped hands.

"Let me go talk to him." Violet rises from the bench, only to be dragged down by Delilah.

"Just leave it."

"Why?" Violet frowns.

I speak up. "Because Dee is right. It's not like he is bothering anyone, so there is no reason to make a show."

Violet looks at something over my shoulder. "Really? Then why is he walking over here right now?"

My eyes widen. "He found us?"

"Yup." Dee slurps on her strawberry smoothie.

My lips purse. "How?"

"Probably because this is always where we hang out every year." Violet knocks back the rest of her drink.

"Hey." Cal's voice makes the hairs on the back of my neck rise.

Violet and Delilah shoot daggers over my head while I remain frozen with my fists clenched in front of me. Wyatt is the only person to acknowledge his presence with a small tip of his chin.

"Lana, can I talk to you for a second?" Cal's soft voice makes me frown.

"She's a bit busy right now." Violet scowls.

"I think she can talk for herself," Cal replies with a light tone.

I rise from my seat. "Will you watch Cami for me?"

"Sure. I'll go let her know now." Wyatt takes off toward the bounce house.

I turn to find Cal no longer dressed in the strawberry costume. I'm unsure if he burned the monstrosity or returned it to Town Hall.

"Thanks." He leads us away from the loud music toward the walkway surrounding the park. A few people I know spare us a pinched look, but I wave away their concern with a small smile.

"So…" I kick a rock.

"Mind if we walk and talk?"

"Okay."

Cal leaves space between us as he walks beside me. "I wanted to talk about what happened earlier and get something off my chest."

"What for?"

"It's not what you think."

"Except isn't it? I've seen the bottle of vodka you keep in the freezer, so it's not like I didn't know you were drinking." Day by day, more of the clear liquid disappears, so I'm well aware of his habits.

He tears his eyes away from me. "I'm not proud of it, you know?"

My stomach drops.

"It makes me feel like a weak piece of shit knowing I need to carry a flask on me at all times, just in case I get anxious or wired. Just the thought of going somewhere without it makes me feel all panicky, especially when I might be forced into a situation that makes me uncomfortable." He tucks his clenched hands behind his back.

My mouth opens, but I struggle to form any words.

"I haven't gotten drunk since I broke your mom's vase." He looks at me out of the corner of his eye.

"So? You're still drinking daily."

"Taking sips throughout the day to cope isn't the same as getting shit-faced. Trust me on that one."

"But they're both part of the same issue regardless."

"True. But can't you see I'm trying to cut back here?" His voice cracks.

My head shakes. "Yes, but who knows what will happen the next time something difficult happens? I've already been through this with you before."

"This isn't like the last time."

"Of course, it isn't." A bitter laugh crawls up my throat.

He stops walking to look me in the eyes. "For starters, I'm not on Oxy anymore."

I break eye contact first. "I know."

"I'm not going to make that mistake again. That much I can promise." His deep sigh makes me tense. "It took me a long time to let go. *Too long*. But I swear I will never ever go back to that shit or else I give you permission to shoot me."

My lips twitch. "Anywhere I want?"

"If you want to aim for the dick, make sure to land a bullet in my skull first." He smiles.

I begin walking again to escape the tingle in my chest. "Do you ever think about getting sober?"

"Lately, all the damn time."

I want to believe him. I really do, but something still holds me back.

You don't trust him.

No, I don't. And I'm unsure if I ever will after everything we have been through together. I've been through enough life lessons to learn that the more someone lets you down, the higher probability there is of it happening again.

I clear my throat. "I'm proud of you for getting off Oxy. I know that must have been hard."

"Not nearly as hard as coming to grips with how badly I hurt you while on it." He reaches for my hand and gives it a squeeze.

My chest aches when he lets go. Cal continues walking, so I fall in step with him as comfortable silence surrounds us.

Cal is the first one to break it when someone glares in his direction. "Do you think people will hate me a little less now that I'm going to be featured on the front page of the paper wearing that costume?"

I bite back my laugh. "Nope, but it was a good try."

"It must be nice to have so many people who care enough about you to give me nonstop hell." His lips twitch.

"You could say that. Although they're a bit overprotective at times."

"Only because they love you." His voice matches the warmth in his eyes.

I look away. "You know, I can spread the word that you're no longer a persona non grata."

"Please don't go out of your way to be so nice to me. I might read too much into it."

I nudge him in the ribs with my elbow. "Jerk."

He laughs. "I'll get them to warm up to me eventually."

"How so?"

"By proving I won't hurt you, no matter how much they expect me to."

And just like that, Cal snatches another piece of my heart to add to his growing collection.

CHAPTER TWENTY-NINE

Cal

The smells and giggles coming from the kitchen wake me up far earlier than I'd like. Merlin seems to agree with the way he darts underneath the bed at the sound of a pot clanging, leaving me alone.

I stumble out of my room while rubbing my eyes. "Hey."

"Morning!" Cami hops off her stool to come give my legs a hug. Her polka dot apron is covered in the same sticky red substance as her fingers, leaving a nice smear on my sweatpants. Red, white, and blue star clips hold back her wild hair from her face.

"What's going on?" I cover my mouth to yawn.

"Mommy is going to beat Missy's butt." Cami holds out her fist for me to pound.

Lana shoots Cami a glare from over her shoulder. *"Camila."*

The kid shrugs. "What did I say?"

"I told you not to repeat that to anyone."

"Oopsy daisy." Cami pokes her tongue out of the gap between her teeth.

"Who's Missy?" I ask.

Lana returns her attention to the stovetop. "My competition."

"Boo!" Cami makes a big show of turning down her thumbs.

I choke on a laugh. "Competition for what?"

"The Fourth of July bake-off," Cami answers for her while stealing a strawberry from a large bowl. "Are you coming?"

Shit. I completely forgot the bake-off was still a thing. It's been a long time since I celebrated Fourth of July the Lake Wisteria way, with the town gathering at the lakeside park for a barbeque and firework show.

I run a hand through my messy hair. "I don't think so." If I learned anything from last week's Strawberry Festival, it's that spending time around the town only amplifies my anxiety. So, the only way I can limit my alcohol intake and keep Lana happy is if I avoid stressors.

"Oh." Cami's shoulders drop.

Sorry, kiddo. This is for the best.

I walk to the stove and peek over Lana's shoulder. "What are you making?"

She drops a single dot of red food coloring into the pot of strawberries. "Something that is going to make Missy regret ever thinking she could copy my strawberry tres leches cake recipe and get away with it."

My mouth drops open. Damn, competitive Lana is hot as hell.

"Do you need any help?" I tuck a strand of her hair behind her ear, making sure to drag my fingers over the curved slope of her neck before retreating.

Her stirring pauses as her breath hitches. "Thanks for the offer, but I'm almost done."

"How long have you been at this?" I fill a glass with water and take a sip.

"Five a.m."

"Seriously? You're going to fall asleep before you ever make it to the bake-off."

She shoots me a pointed look. "I can sleep when I'm dead."

"Would you like to be buried with your trophy?"

She grins. "Absolutely. That and whatever tissue Missy uses to wipe her tears after she loses."

"This side of you is hot yet somewhat terrifying."

Her smile is all teeth.

Although Lana said she didn't need my assistance, I decide to help with the overwhelming number of dishes pouring out of the sink.

Cami keeps the conversation going while stealing strawberries whenever she thinks Lana isn't looking. The red fruit juice around her mouth is a dead giveaway, so I clean her up while her mother has her back turned.

The doorbell ringing has the three of us looking up.

"We have a doorbell?" Lana pauses her mixer.

"That's the first time I've heard it. Are you expecting someone?" I ask.

She shakes her head. "No. Are you?"

"A majority of the town hates me, so I'm going to go with a no."

Lana looks down at her half-mixed whipped cream. "Do you mind checking who it is?"

"I got it!" Cami hops off her stool.

"Camila!" Lana rounds the corner, but I'm closer.

Cami rises on the tips of her toes to reach the deadbolt, only to be swept into my arms.

"I don't think that's such a good idea."

Cami pouts.

I take a peek through the peephole. Lana's sister, Antonella, paces a few feet away. Her tan skin looks paler than usual, and her thin hair hangs limply around her face, accentuating a sharp bone structure that can only be achieved by malnutrition.

"Shit."

Cami sucks in a breath.

I put her down. "My wallet is on my nightstand. If you count all my bills correctly, I'll let you keep them all."

Her eyes widen. "Really?"

"Yup. But you have to stay in my room until I come and get you."

"Okay!" Cami squeals as she takes off for my bedroom.

Lana abandons her whipping cream. "What's wrong?"

"Your sister is outside."

Lana's mouth drops open. "Antonella is here?" Her face pales. "Oh my God."

"You didn't know she was coming."

Her head shakes. "No. I thought I made myself clear during our last phone call."

"Do you want me to see what she wants?"

Her hardened gaze lingers on the door. "I already know what

she came here for."

My brows tug together. "But—"

Her shoulders slump. "Let me go talk to her."

I step in her way. "Lana."

She doesn't look up at me, so I tip her head back.

"Do you want to speak with her?"

Her head shakes ever so slightly. "Not really after she…"

"After she *what?*"

"Took the last bit of inheritance money I had."

Fuck. "She stole from you?"

Her eyes drop. "Yes."

"Is that why she's back? To get more money?"

"Probably."

"Do you want me to give her some?"

Her teeth sink into her bottom lip as she shakes her head again.

"What do you want to do then?"

"I don't know. After the way she talked to me on the phone… I hate seeing her that way. I hate it so damn much, knowing she is struggling and there is nothing I can do to make it better." Her voice cracks.

My heart feels like Lana wrapped her fist around it and squeezed. "You've done everything possible to help her."

"Then why isn't it enough to help her stay clean? I've done everything. Paying, praying, pleading, yet she always goes back." There is a sheen to her eyes that wasn't present before.

"It has nothing to do with you." I wrap my arms around her.

She places her head against my chest with a sniffle. "I'm so freaking tired of people hurting me."

The tightness in my chest becomes unbearable. "I'm sorry." For me. For Anto. And for everyone who has caused her pain in the first place.

The doorbell rings again, followed by hard pounding. Lana flinches against me.

I kiss the top of her head. "Let me go talk to her."

"But—"

"Just allow me to do this for you."

She sighs as I release my hold around her body.

"Stay inside." I reach for the doorknob.

"Cal?"

I glance at her from over my shoulder.

She twists the fabric of her apron. "Thank you."

"I'd do anything for you."

Her bottom lip wobbles. "I know."

I tip my head before walking outside. Antonella tugs at the sleeves of her long-sleeve shirt as if it can hide the track marks speckled across her skin. She looks thinner than ever, with her bones jutting out from underneath her shirt and her brown eyes nearly bugling from their sockets.

"What the hell are you doing here?" she snaps.

"Antonella. It's been a while."

She sneers. "Don't tell me my little sister took you back."

"That's none of your business."

"Like hell it isn't." She tries to walk around me, but I block her path.

"Get out of my way." She speaks through clenched teeth.

"No."

"I need to speak with Alana."

I give my head a hard shake. "I don't think that's a good idea."

"Because you said so?" Her frown deepens.

"Because you're strung out."

Staring into her beady eyes feels like I've been thrown back into the past. If anyone understands Antonella's desperation for her next fix, it's me. Going through my own shit made me aware of the darkness and self-loathing that fester right below the surface, waiting to be unleashed.

"Like you're one to judge. Lana told me all about your issue with Oxy. It nearly broke my sister when she realized the man she loved let her down just like everyone else."

Her blow lands its intended mark right over my heart.

You're not that guy anymore.

I switch tactics before I lose my cool. "I can get you the help you need."

There is a certain spark in her eyes. "Like money?"

"Like rehab, therapy, and whatever you need to have a clean start." I tuck my hands into the pockets of my sweats.

Her head shakes. "I just wanted a place to stay and some money to get back on my feet."

"I can head over to the motel and book you a room or I can fly you out to a facility and cover the cost, but I'm not going to give you cash." Doing so would only enable her addiction and hurt Lana even more, neither of which I find acceptable.

Her head shakes, making her thin hair fly. "I don't want to go to a facility again."

I check out the marks across her arms. "That's the only way you'll be able to manage that."

She pulls at her sleeves again.

I try one last time. "If you decide differently, all you need to do is give me a call and I can take you somewhere where they can help you get better. I haven't changed my number."

Her head shakes. "I'm not ready."

"I understand." Far more than I'm comfortable acknowledging. As much as I hate to admit it, I get Antonella and her decisions in a way Lana never can. Having an addiction isn't easy to accept, let alone treat.

"If you understood me, then you'd help me." Her pitch rises, reminding me so much of Lana when she gets upset.

"I am offering to help. Just not in the way you want."

Her gaze hardens. "Fuck you, Cal."

My lips press together.

She rips at her cuticle, making the skin bleed. "Just let me see my sister. I… Shit." Her head hangs. "The last time I was here, I did some screwed-up things and I want to apologize."

"Not like this, Antonella. You of all people should know how much it hurts her to see you this way."

She looks away. "Fine."

"Do you want me to book you a room at the motel?"

"Hell no. I'm going to crash on a friend's couch who lives a few towns over." Her hair flies from how hard she shakes her head.

"If that's what you want. Just know that I meant what I said. If you need help, all you need to do is call me. But if you come back here again without being clean, I'll make sure you never see your sister again."

She turns toward her rundown car packed to the roof with boxes and personal belongings. It's sad to see the mess her life has become.

I wish I could help her, but I need to protect Lana first and foremost.

I check on Cami before knocking my fist against the locked bathroom door. "Lana?"

"Is she gone?"

"Yeah. I waited until her car drove off before coming back inside."

"Thank you." Her sniffle is soft but audible, making my muscles tighten.

My hand chokes the doorknob. "Open up for me."

"I'd rather not."

"Please."

Her heavy sigh is followed by the flick of the lock. I open the door to find Lana sitting on the floor with her arms wrapped around her legs.

"Hey." I kneel beside her and pull her into my arms. "It's going to be okay."

"I thought I would be used to this by now." Her fingers wrap around the cotton fabric of my shirt.

"Used to what?"

"The disappointment." Her chin trembles.

"I'm sorry." The words leave my mouth in a rush.

She shifts her gaze to the floor. "It's not your fault Antonella is the way she is."

"No, it's not. But I'm sorry for being another person who let you down because I was too selfish to do anything else."

Some of the tension bleeds from her muscles as she releases a heavy sigh.

"Seeing your sister…shit. I understand her and where she is coming from, but I also want to shake her for hurting you and Cami like she has."

Her nails dig into my skin. "Does being grateful that she gave Cami up make me a bad person?"

"No, Lana. It makes you human." My arms around her tighten. "Antonella is in no position to look after a child. And you… You were born to be that little girl's mother."

She looks up at me with tear-soaked lashes and glassy eyes. "You think so?"

"I've never been more certain of anything."

CHAPTER THIRTY

Cal

Fix a house, Iris said.

It'll be fun, she said.

What a load of bullshit.

With the asbestos team hard at work on the main house, Lana and I are forced to make some tough decisions about the remodel.

She pushes aside the fifth cabinet sample. It slides across the coffee table, straight into the other samples she rejected. "No."

"What do you mean no?" My right eye twitches.

Lana and I have been at this since she dropped Cami off at her summer camp two hours ago, and we haven't made much progress. The only thing we have agreed upon is the new shape of the pool.

At this rate, it's going to take us three years to pick out

everything that needs to go into the house. As it is, Ryder is already pressuring me about ordering the supplies if we want to make our deadline.

There is no *want*. I *need* the property to be listed by the end of August if I plan on meeting my grandfather's deadline.

"It looks cheap." Her forehead creases.

"How is that even possible? Each cabinet costs over a thousand dollars."

Her eyes widen. "For one cabinet? But we need like…"

"Just ignore what I said." The last thing I want to do today is argue about money too.

She stares at the cabinet a little longer. "Nope. Still hate it, hefty price tag and all."

"What *do* you like?"

"I don't know." She makes the cutest exasperated sigh as she looks up to the ceiling.

Maybe our issue isn't that the options are bad, but rather Lana doesn't know what she wants.

"Let me grab my laptop. I think I have an idea."

I return to the living room with my laptop open and Pinterest already pulled up. Instead of sitting across from Lana, I take a seat next to her and place the laptop over my thighs so she can see the screen.

The heat coming off her body seeps through my skin. I'm tempted to brush my arm against hers and be rewarded with a gasp, but I hold back.

Business first.

Her brow arches. "Pinterest? Really?"

"Iris swears by it after planning most of her wedding and

honeymoon with it."

She laughs. "Of course. I wish I thought of it first. I like to pin new ideas for teaching, but I didn't think about it for the house."

"Look at me being useful for once." My laugh comes out half-hearted.

She nudges me with her thigh. "You can be useful."

"How? Because I opened a jar of spaghetti sauce for you last night?"

"The lid was stuck pretty tight. I'm not sure I would have gotten it off without you."

I roll my eyes. "I'm glad my life's purpose has been narrowed down to domestic tasks and arm muscle."

"Well, you did always joke around about wanting to be a stay-at-home dad. Maybe it's your calling after all."

"Don't tempt me. You know how I feel about corporate life."

Her head tilts. "You know there are other jobs out there besides a basic nine-to-five desk job."

"I'm aware." Doesn't mean I've found one that works for me. It's not like I need a job, but my brothers make it seem like that's the point of life. Or at least they did until they found something nicer.

Love.

"Have you done anything since hockey?"

My shoulders turn to stone. "Does stepping in as Declan's assistant count?"

Her mouth drops open. "You were Declan's assistant?"

"Don't look so surprised." I flick her nose, earning a breathy chuckle that makes my heart pathetically swell.

"I'm surprised you lived to tell the tale."

"He wasn't *that* bad. Iris was the one who had to put up with him for three years."

Her lips part. "Iris worked for him?"

"Yup."

"And she still fell in love with him? Wow."

Wow is right. If it weren't for my grandfather's will and his marriage-of-convenience clause, I'm not sure the two of them would have ever gotten together in the first place.

"Declan is lucky because Iris is one hell of a woman."

Her face softens. "You really care about her."

"She's always been there for me when I needed someone." I break eye contact and focus on my laptop screen.

Lana reaches out and squeezes my hand. "She sounds like a great friend. I'm glad you found someone who could be that for you."

I nod as I swallow the thick lump in my throat. "I love her like the sister I never had, but she was never you. What she and I had was always different."

"You never tried to…" Her voice drifts off as the question dies on the tip of her tongue.

"We kissed once, but that was all." I clasp her palm and tuck it against my thigh.

"If your friendship is anything like ours, then I'm questioning it." The muscles in her back remain wound tight despite the playfulness of her words.

"Nothing has ever compared to us, and nothing ever will." I lift her hand to my mouth and press my lips against the faded scar on her knuckle. It's small but a constant reminder of her getting hurt after I stupidly dared her to climb a chain-link fence.

She releases a shaky breath. "You need to stop talking and doing things like that."

"Why?"

"Because this isn't the past." She attempts to tug her hand free of my grasp, but my hold is too strong.

"Good, because I'd much rather focus on our future." I pry her fingers apart before kissing the soft flesh of her palm, earning the softest inhale from her.

"We don't have a future."

"Not yet, but give me some time to prove you wrong." A pink flush blooms across her cheeks, so I trace it with the pad of my thumb. "I don't expect you to believe me, but I'm just warning you."

"Warning me about what?"

"I walked away from you before because I thought I was doing the right thing. That you were better off without me. That you would be happier. I don't plan on making that same mistake again, even if you expect me to. While I might mess up—hell, I can practically guarantee it—I'm not going to run away again. I'll fight for us no matter what." I release her hand, although there is nothing I want more than to never let go.

Tension between us grows as I refocus on the laptop screen in front of us. Lana loses herself in her thoughts for a few minutes before resuming as if our conversation didn't happen.

Maybe it's for the best. Speaking about my intentions doesn't matter when I have years of mistakes and mistrust to overcome.

But that starts today.

Lana and I spend the rest of the afternoon searching Pinterest for different ideas. She points out everything she likes, and together we quickly create a few different boards for each of the rooms in the house. It doesn't take us long to determine Lana hates futuristic modern ideas almost as much as I dislike mid-century style. Together, we decide the best option is to go with a transitional modern style.

"I think I'm in love." Lana sighs to herself as she scrolls through the board we made for the bathroom one last time.

"I shared the links with Ryder so he can get to work finding something that matches our vision."

"I'm jealous of whomever gets to buy the place. It's like everything I ever wanted all in one house."

My chest aches at the look of pure longing on her face.

"You can always recreate it."

She snorts. "With what money? The only reason we're even doing this is because of you."

I bite down on my tongue to stop myself from saying anything.

With a sigh, she shuts my laptop. "I better go pick up Cami from summer camp."

"Do you care if I join you?"

Her brows jump. "You want to come?"

"Sure. It's not like I have much else to do." I motion toward the empty house.

"I need to pass by the grocery store on the way home though."

"Okay?" Is that supposed to discourage me or something?

Her eyes flicker over me. "You're serious."

I roll my eyes as I stand. "Do you want to drive my car or yours?"

Her mouth pops open.

"What?"

She shakes her head. "Nothing. Let's take mine."

"What's wrong with my car?"

"Besides the fact that it isn't ideal or probably safe for a kid?" She stands as tall as she can, with the top of her head barely reaching my chin.

"You didn't have a problem with it when you needed a ride to the school."

"Because I was desperate and didn't want to miss Cami's graduation." Her lips thin.

"You're going to drive?"

"Of course. It's the twenty-first century. Women can drive men around now."

God help us all.

She spends the short drive to Cami's summer camp laughing at the expletives that pour out of my mouth. Whatever small bit of restraint she showed while driving my car is gone.

A few people removing the leftover Fourth of July decorations from Main Street wave at her, and she honks before turning the wheel.

My grip on the safety bar slips as she makes a sharp left turn. "No wonder your tires were balding. You drive like you're being chased by the cops."

She laughs herself hoarse. I'm hopeless as I watch in complete fascination, my chest swelling with emotion at the sight of her happiness.

This was all I wanted for her. I just never thought I could be the one to make it happen with all the other stuff bogging me down, getting in the way of our chance at a happy ending.

But the only thing getting in the way was me. Not my addiction. Not my career.

Me.

Because at the end of the day, I'm the one who makes the final decisions over my life.

I chose wrong when I left her the last time. She was supposed to be better off without me, but her obvious loneliness has proved the exact opposite.

Lana was surviving—not thriving—and I have only myself to blame.

And I don't plan on making the same mistake again.

CHAPTER THIRTY-ONE

Cal

ana drives down a few more blocks before pulling into the
parking lot of Cami's summer camp. With the way she
navigates the streets, I'm surprised she hasn't ended up
injured or in far worse condition.

Lana comes out of the building with Cami skipping behind
her. Cami's whole face lights up when she catches me sitting
inside.

"Hi!" she squeals as she drops into the back seat.

I hold out my hand for her to slap. "What's up, kiddo?"

My question turns into a whole story about her day. Cami
spends the short drive to the market talking about her afternoon
at the swimming pool and me following up with questions.

"Come on." Cami bounces out of the car before grabbing
on to Lana's hand. She clutches mine with her other, linking the

three of us together.

I lift her arm up and nudge Lana to do the same. She copies me, causing Cami to swing between us. The giggle she lets out makes my whole heart threaten to burst like a confetti cannon. Lana's eyes flicker from Cami to me. Whatever she finds in my gaze makes her face soften and her lips turn up into a fraction of a smile.

"Again! Again!" Cami tugs on our arms with a surprising amount of strength for someone so tiny. Lana and I oblige, earning another high-pitched squeal from Cami.

I'm not sure who is having more fun: Cami or us. By the time we make it inside the grocery store, Cami's face is red from laughing so hard and Lana is beaming.

Damn. I did that.

I'm quick to shake off the minor win before pulling a cart free from the rest.

"No. I want this one." Cami climbs inside the special kid cart. While the front half of the cart is normal, the back half looks like a kid's car. Her head touches the top of the car, and her legs look cramped in the small space.

"Are you sure? It looks like a tight fit."

She turns the wheel like she is on a Formula 1 track versus in a grocery store.

"I see you inherited your mother's driving skills."

Lana slaps my ass. "Hey."

"You did not just…"

Her eyes shimmer. "But I did." I reach out, but she escapes my grasp with a breathy laugh.

Cami slams her hand on the horn for emphasis. Lana moves

to grab the handle of the cart, but I step in before she has a chance.

I turn the cart slowly, being mindful not to jostle Cami. "This thing is heavier than it looks."

Lana pokes at my straining arms. "Don't tell me those muscles are just for show."

"There's a few ways we can test that theory out." I wink at her.

She walks ahead of us with her list. I'm hypnotized by the sway of her hips, my skin turning hot with each step she takes.

"Go, go, go!" Cami honks her horn again to get my attention.

I take off after Lana, who is already speaking to the butcher. He smiles at her before shooting me a scowl. I'm quick to smile and wave, although my right eye twitches from how hard I fake the grin.

The rest of the shopping trip goes similarly. A few other people I recognize from my summers here give me a range of looks, varying from surprised to downright angry at my existence. By now, I should be used to how people treat me, but I'm not. It's hard knowing everyone had a front-row seat to the lowest moment of my life.

You have no one to blame but yourself.

The only thing that saves me from walking out the door is Cami. I treat every aisle like a racetrack, making zipping and zooming noises as I gain speed and glide. She absolutely loves it. Between her clapping, chanting, and cheering, I completely forget about everyone around us. Even Lana cracks and ends up laughing when I create a driving obstacle course with some of the displays scattered throughout the store.

Maybe small towns aren't the worst. I could never get away with this kind of thing at a busy supermarket in Chicago.

It isn't until we get to the baking supplies aisle that Cami loses interest in me and our game. She climbs out of the cart and abandons me for Lana.

"Hey!" I call out.

Cami pokes her tongue out through the gap of her missing tooth before running off.

I roll the cart toward the two of them.

"What flavor do you want for your birthday cake?" Lana drops a bag of confectioner's sugar into the cart.

"Chocolate!" Cami claps her hands together, making her wonky pigtails shake.

Lana grabs some baker's chocolate chips and dumps them in the cart.

"When is your birthday?" I ask Cami.

She grins. "July 15."

Turns out little Cami is a Cancer just like me.

No wonder you both get along so well.

"That's on Saturday."

"Yup." She points to a set of birthday candles. "I like that one, Mommy!"

"Let's hope I can get decorations delivered by Friday." Lana throws the candles into the cart.

I check out the latest Dreamland princess and laugh. "You like Princess Marianna?"

"Yes! She's my favorite." She spins in a circle while pressing her clasped hands against her heart.

"I like her too. She was nice when I met her." I wink.

Lana's eyes widen and she shakes her head.

Shit. Was that the wrong thing to say?

"You met Princess Marianna? *When?*" Cami nearly rips my arm out of its socket from how hard she tugs.

I kneel in front of her. "When I went to visit my brother at Dreamland."

Lana shuts her eyes with a sigh.

"You went to Dreamland?" Cami's voice hits the highest pitch I've ever heard.

I rub at my eardrum to stop it from ringing. "Yes?"

Her eyes stretch so wide, I'm afraid they might pop out. "When?"

"A few months ago. My brother has a house there."

"At Dreamland?" Her mouth drops open.

"Yes?"

She gasps. Lana groans.

"Can we go?" She looks up at me with the biggest blue eyes. "Please, Cow-l. Pretty, pretty please can we go to Dreamland? It'll be the bestest birthday ever." The way she looks up at me with her gap-toothed smile makes me weak in the knees.

You got yourself into this mess by opening your big mouth. Now fix it.

"You need to ask your mom." I throw the invisible stick of dynamite into Lana's hands.

Lana mouths *I'm going to kill you.*

At least I'll leave this world knowing I gave a five-year-old kid the bestest birthday present.

Cami turns to her mother and latches on to her legs. "Please, Mommy? I will pick up my toys and eat all my vegetables forever.

I swears."

I snicker, earning a death glare from Lana.

She looks up at the ceiling and sighs. "I guess we're going to Dreamland."

I fire off a quick text to Rowan while Cami and Lana debate which ice cream they want to buy. Lana is pushing for the BOGO Ben and Jerry's while Cami moans about popsicles.

> I'm going to need a favor.

I grab the box of colorful Popsicles and drop them in the cart while Lana isn't looking, earning a wide grin from Cami. Having them argue over a budget is pointless when I planned on paying for the whole cart anyway. It's the least I can do if Lana is cooking dinner for me.

My phone buzzes a second later, which is a fast turnaround time for Rowan. He usually only looks at his phone a few times a day now with all the Dreamland meetings he packs into his schedule.

Iris
> What favor?

Shit. I texted the family group chat instead of Rowan individually.

> Ignore that. I meant to text Rowan.

Dick-lan
> At least you're talking to one of us.

> Whose number got added to the group chat and why?

Declan sends a solo middle finger emoji, and I laugh underneath my breath.

Iris
I hate it when you two fight.

Dick-lan
I'm trying to be the mature one here, but Cal keeps running away before I have a chance to say sorry.

> I'm not running away, asshole. I'm just busy.

Dick-lan
Doing what?

> Since when do you care?

Dick-lan
...

Iris
Facepalm.

Rowan sends me a private text after. I explain what I need while Lana double-checks her shopping list.

Rowan
Are you sure this is a good idea?

> Nothing has felt more right in a long time.

I mean it in more ways than one—not that my brother

would understand. Spending time with Cami and Lana makes me feel whole in a way I haven't felt in years, and I'd do just about anything to keep it that way.

Rowan

> Zahra already volunteered to plan the best birthday ever. Her words, not mine.

If there is one person I trust to give Cami the ultimate Dreamland experience, it would be none other than Zahra. She is the biggest Dreamland fan ever and the Top Creator in the park.

> Thanks in advance.

Rowan

> Whatever it takes to keep the smile on your face, pretty boy.

An idea dawns on me, and I shoot him another message.

> Whatever it takes?

Rowan

> I'm going to regret saying that, aren't I?

> I have one more favor to ask.

I follow up with a Hail Mary request, knowing there is a chance he won't be able to pull it off on such short notice.

> I understand if you can't...

Rowan

> Give me forty-eight hours.

CHAPTER THIRTY-TWO
Alana

Cal and Cami are chatting away as I drive down Main Street. Cami hasn't stopped asking him questions about Dreamland ever since I agreed to the trip at the grocery store, and he has been a champ while answering every single one.

The warm feeling in my chest intensifies as Cami breaks out into a fit of giggles at whatever Cal said. He chuckles, and I look over at him.

Except something in the window catches my attention.

My eyes bulge. I brake hard, causing all of us to jolt forward from the momentum.

"What's wrong?" Anxiety bleeds into his voice.

I look out the back window and find the road empty. "One second."

He looks at me like I might be going crazy.

Maybe you are.

I shift the car into reverse before parking in front of the abandoned store.

No.

I nearly crawl on top of Cal's lap to get a better look out his window.

The once-empty shop window now has a giant red *Coming Soon* sign plastered across it, advertising some fast casual dining restaurant opening later this year.

You're too late.

Watching someone else live my dream feels like a punch to the gut. Like I was so close to finally achieving what I had hoped for, only to fall short by a few months.

It's stupid to feel a sense of loss over a shop that wasn't even mine. I have no one to blame but myself in this situation. If I had been selfish, maybe I would have had the money to buy it.

But I couldn't turn my back on those I loved.

I didn't *want* to.

If I was to go back in time knowing everything I know now, I would still make the same choices, even if it meant losing all my money again in the process. Because trying to treat Mom's cancer and not giving up on Anto because Mom never did was worth every penny.

"Is everything okay?" Cal asks.

I nod despite the tightness in my throat. His gaze roams over my face, although I don't dare look him in the eyes.

"You look sad," Cami adds as she peeks over the side of Cal's chair.

My nod is weaker this time, and my chin trembles.

Cal turns my face toward him with a single finger. "How can I fix it?"

How can I fix it?

I bite down on the inside of my cheek, fighting the temptation to vent.

Screw it.

"You can't. I just thought one day maybe I could…" My eyes travel toward the shop.

"Open your bakery there," he finishes for me.

My throat becomes impossibly tight as I nod. "It sounds stupid in theory."

"It's not." He speaks without a single ounce of judgment.

"Isn't it, though? It's not like I have the money or time right now."

"I'm sure when it's the right time, the perfect opportunity will come up."

I take one last look at the shop, knowing that although my dream to open a bakery one day is alive and well, the wish to open my shop on Main Street might not ever happen.

Cal lifts my chin up. "When you're ready one day, I'd love to be there to cheer you on."

Everything in me wants to believe him, yet I can't deny the kernel of doubt growing within my gut.

He may not even be here one day.

I want to ask him more about what he means, but Cami chucks her stuffed animal onto my lap.

"Here, Mommy. Lamby always helps me when I'm sad."

"Thank you, baby." My voice is thick with emotion. I press Lamby against my chest and squeeze him so hard, I'm afraid his stuffing might burst.

Cal continues answering Cami's questions about Dreamland while I drive home. I can feel Cal's eyes occasionally sweeping over me, but I pretend not to notice as I focus on the road.

At some point during the short drive, Cal places his hand on my thigh. The weight of his palm comforts me, and before I have a chance to stop myself, I grasp his hand and interlock our fingers.

For the first time since Cal showed up, I'm not scared, angry, or irritated by his presence.

I'm grateful for it.

After we return from the grocery store, Cal goes out of his way to give me space. It's as if he knows I might break down if he asks a single question about the bakery. He spares me a few glances throughout the night, but I focus on pouring my heart out through baking rather than talking to him about it.

I pull out my shiny new mixer while Cami drags him into a fake tea party with her Dreamland dolls. As much as I wish I could protect Cami from getting attached, I'm unable to pull her away from Cal. The connection they have is special. It might be a lost cause, but I'm hoping once he moves away again that he will be up for visiting Lake Wisteria solely for Cami's sake.

And yours too.

The thought of Cal leaving makes my chest ache, so I push it away and get back to baking. Cal keeps Cami entertained the entire time I make his favorite dessert, as I promised when he bought the mixer.

He is an easy guy to please. His favorite sweet happens to be snickerdoodle cookies, although I haven't figured out why. Out of all the things I can bake, this one seems so simple.

While working on rolling the dough in the cinnamon-sugar mix, I find myself getting lost in Cami and Cal's pretend play. I even laugh a couple of times when Cal slips into a British accent to match the princess from England. For someone who despises Dreamland and everything Kane-related, he sure knows a lot about the characters. He can even sing the songs, which is both hot and oddly impressive.

"Only one or else you'll spoil your appetite before dinner." I give Cami a look as I drop off a plate of fresh cookies for the tea party.

Cal bats his lashes at me. "What about me?"

"What's the point of saying anything? You always were a fan of having dessert before dinner anyway."

"Only because you were on the menu." He winks.

This man is the Devil.

He takes a bite of the cookie and lets out a mix of a groan and moan. It's the hottest sound ever, and heat pools in my belly from it and the way his eyes shut. He was always the type to savor things.

Sweets. Drinks. *Me.*

The last thought triggers a memory of Cal tucked between my legs, his tongue and fingers working in tandem to make me come. My lower half throbs.

You need to get laid.

By what? A vibrator?

Huh. Now that's an idea.

Although I won't be able to make all my problems go away permanently, I wouldn't mind trying to take some of the edge off tonight. At this point, I'll do whatever it takes to keep the fantasy of Cal between my legs from becoming a reality.

I've always loved having dinner with Cami. It's the one part of the day where we can sit down together and enjoy each other's company, and I thought life couldn't get any better than that.

At least I did until Cal joined us.

Having him spend time with us at dinner feels natural. Like we were always meant to be a trio, even if we spent six years apart.

I prolong the dinner for as long as possible, solely because I want to relish in Cami's happiness and Cal's attention for a little longer. Cami gives me a weird look when I offer snickerdoodles for a second time today, but she doesn't call me out on the fact that I already let her have dessert before dinner.

"Can we watch a movie?" Cami asks as Cal chomps on his fifth cookie. Seriously. Where does he pack it all, and how do I get my body to do the same?

"Sure. I'd love to see a movie." I don't think twice before answering. Cami's bedtime is in a couple of hours, so we have enough time.

She clasps her hands together. "And build a fort?"

"That sounds like a fun idea." Cal's eyes lock on to mine as his tongue darts out to lick the crumbs away from his mouth.

That freaking tease.

I'm tempted to take a bite out of his bottom lip just to make a point.

"Who said you were invited?" I shoot him a look.

"Me!" Cami raises her hand.

Cal grins. "It's settled, then."

Asshole.

The only reason I decide to go along with their plan is because Cal hasn't had a single drink all night. I can tell he is trying, so I don't want to squash his efforts.

"Fine," I sigh before turning to Cami. "But you need to wash your hands and brush your teeth first."

"Okay!" Cami bolts for the bathroom.

Cal grabs blankets and a few spare pillows from the linen closet while I turn on the massive TV Cal bought during one of his shopping sprees. I download the KidFlix app and log in using my credentials.

"What's that?" Cal drops the blankets on the couch.

"KidFlix?"

"Yeah." He drags a few of the chairs over from the dining area.

"A streaming service."

"What about DreamStream?"

My head tilts. "What about it?"

He freezes in place. "You don't like it?"

I bite down on my lip. "Umm…"

"What?"

"It's not that I don't like it." DreamStream is a Kane Company baby, so I have to be careful how I phrase my opinion.

"Then what?"

I consider how to mince my words before settling on the truth. "It's just that it's not that good."

His eyes widen. "What do you mean?"

"We liked it at first. Cami really loved having constant access to all the classic Dreamland shows and movies."

"So you had a subscription?" He unfolds one of the blankets. I grab on to one of the sides and hold it out while he ties the end to the back of one of the chairs.

"Yeah. For about a year or so."

"Why did you cancel it?"

"A couple of reasons. First off, they increased the monthly price by double the amount last year. Then, they introduced ads on top of that, which I understand is necessary for making money, but it became too much. If we wanted to skip the ads, then it would increase our subscription cost by double."

"So, quadruple the original price?"

"Exactly. That's ridiculous for the content they were offering. For the price of a DreamStream subscription, I could pay for four other streaming apps."

"Why would they quadruple it?" he asks, more so to himself.

"I'm not sure. It's not like they were producing a lot of new content or anything that could justify the monthly cost. It was just reruns of all their famous shows and movies with a high price tag, and honestly, with a paycheck like mine, it wasn't worth it."

"What would have made the price tag justifiable?"

"I'm not sure. Maybe more new releases and less commercials. Oh, and maybe combining all the Kane Company channels into one place. It's a bit ridiculous to ask people to pay for four different subscriptions all owned by the same media conglomerate."

He rubs his stubble. "I think you're on to something."

"Me?" I laugh. "I don't know anything about those kinds of things."

"I've been wondering why the profits were going down when compared to our competitors."

I laugh. "Oh, I could give you a whole list."

"Would you?" His head tilts with interest.

"Sure. At this rate, I've probably had a subscription for every single streaming app available."

Cami comes running out of the bathroom with toothpaste smeared across her cheek and soap suds stuck between her fingers. I take her back to the bathroom and help her while Cal finishes up the fort.

It's a tight squeeze but somehow the three of us fit under the blanket fort, although the top part of the TV is cut off. Cami doesn't seem to mind, her excitement about watching a movie outweighing the logistics.

I lie beside Cami, who chooses the spot closest to the edge, where Merlin sleeps while curled into a ball. Cal looks torn with what to do before settling on sitting crisscross near the opposite side of the fort. I'm not sure he can even see the TV from his position, let alone feel comfortable with how he needs to hunch his body to fit underneath the blanket.

"You can go next to Mommy." Cami points to the spot on the other side of me.

Lovely. Look at Little Miss Cami playing matchmaker without even knowing it.

Cal glances over at me for approval before I nod slightly.

You're totally going to regret this one.

With a little sigh, he lies down beside me. His proximity, combined with the smell of his bodywash and the rhythm of his deep breathing, makes my brain foggy and my skin tingle.

Cami picks the movie and gets settled beside me. I barely pay attention to what happens on the screen, my mind too attuned to the man next to me. My heart pounds furiously, the blood rushing to my ears as I resist the temptation to turn around and snuggle into his chest.

At some point, Cal locks his pinky finger with mine, linking us together for the rest of the movie. The connection that flares to life from a single touch makes my toes curl.

Yup. Definitely need to get laid.

After I put Cami down to sleep, I lock my bedroom door, shut off the lights, and grab my vibrator from its case in the nightstand. It's been a while since I got off, and although the vibrator doesn't come close to the real thing, it gets the job done.

I light a candle and turn on some acoustic music to drown out any noise before settling in bed. My thoughts wander to all the things I need to do before I remember what I wanted to do in the first place.

I tug my sleep shirt over my head and toss my underwear before getting back into bed. This time, my thoughts drift to something far more dangerous.

Something forbidden for a hundred different reasons.

Callahan Kane.

The man hasn't left my head since he stumbled back into my life, dragging me into the past I've spent years trying to forget.

Might as well take advantage of his proximity and use him to get off.

I shut my eyes and imagine Cal looming above me, his fingers dragging across my chest rather than my own. He takes his time to reacquaint himself with my body. Each gasp, sigh, and moan encourage him, and he teases one breast until I'm breathless and panting beneath him before moving on to the other.

My nail catches on the sharp peak, but I replace the image with Cal's.

He is the one teasing my body with his hands until I'm begging for release.

He is the one angling the vibrator so the G-spot stimulator hits at the perfect angle.

He is the one… *Knocking on the door?!*

My eyes fly open. I sit up and gasp as the vibration intensifies, making my eyes roll.

"Lana? Did you hear me?" Cal knocks harder.

I groan into a pillow as I pull the vibrator free and shut the button off.

"One minute," I rasp, my voice coming out huskier than I would have liked.

His knocking stops.

Thank God.

I slide off the sheets. My legs feel like jelly as I search for my shirt. With a quick run through my hair, I crack the door open.

"What?"

His eyes scan my face. "I wanted to ask you a couple things about DreamStream."

"Now? It's nine p.m."

He looks at me like I'm crazy. "And?"

"It's late. Ask me tomorrow." I push the door closed, but he presses his palm against the wood to block it from shutting.

"It's late? Wait…" He sniffs. "Is that lavender?"

"Yeah. I lit a candle. So what?"

"You lit a candle?" he repeats. "You never light a candle unless—" His eyes widen with recognition. "Of course. The candle. The music. The…" He looks over my head at the panties on the floor. "A nice touch."

My cheeks flush. I reach to shut the door, but his strength prevents it from closing.

"How do I score an invite?" His eyes dip, the heat of his gaze burning a path down my body. With the way he looks at me, I'm afraid I might catch on fire.

The warmth in my belly from earlier comes back with a vengeance. "You don't. Now go away." I push against the door again, but his hold remains strong, preventing it from moving a single centimeter.

"Let me make you feel good. *Please,*" he rasps.

God. No man should look or sound that desperate to pleasure a woman. It can give anyone a complex, especially when paired with Cal licking his lips.

A single plea has my walls crumbling like a poorly constructed gingerbread house.

What's the worst that can happen?

If you're asking yourself that question, then you're further gone than I thought.

I shake my head. "No."

It's for the best. I didn't spend the last two months keeping him at a distance to ruin it because I'm desperate for relief.

You're not desperate for relief.

You're desperate for him.

The truth hits me like a punch to the gut, stealing my breath.

His grip on the doorframe tightens. "I'll beg on my hands and knees if I have to."

"Fine. Go ahead." I release my grip on the door and take a step back.

You're going to regret this tomorrow.

Then I better make the most of tonight.

He doesn't move—doesn't even so much as blink—as I retreat farther into my room, adding enough distance to make his begging worth my while.

"Are you going to get on your knees and beg, or are you going to stand there and watch while I make myself come harder than you ever could?"

His nostrils flare. "Is that a dare?"

A devious grin stretches across my face. "It's a promise."

Something snaps inside of Cal. It's evident in the way his gaze shifts, the wildness he keeps tamped down coming to the forefront. My body vibrates from anticipation as he shuts the door behind him and flips the lock.

"Where do you want me?" He takes a step closer to me.

"Plenty of places, but on your knees is good enough for now."

His Adam's apple bobs as his knees sink into the fabric of the carpet. I feel light-headed from the sight of him ready to follow my every command.

"Perfect. Now just stay there and look pretty for me."

He smirks. "That's all?"

I search the sheets for my vibrator before hopping on the bed and facing him.

"What are you doing?" His brows knit together.

"I said you could beg. Not that you could be the one to make me come."

His mouth drops open, but no words come out.

I turn on the device. The hum, combined with his stare, sends a fresh wave of goose bumps across my skin.

I swallow past the thick lump in my throat. "If you touch me, all of this is over. Got it?"

His fingers dig into his thighs, drawing my eyes toward the growing erection beneath his sweatpants. "Are you trying to avoid any physical contact because you think that will protect you from what's happening between us?"

My eyes narrow. "I didn't say that."

But you sure thought it.

Maldita sea.

"You didn't have to. But that's fine because I'll just have you do my dirty work for me. Now take off your shirt and spread your legs for me."

"You're not the one in control here." The words come out shaky, lacking any confidence from before.

"Oh, babe. I've been in control since the moment you let me inside this room. I just like watching you get high on your power trip."

My breath catches in my throat.

"You want me to beg?" Cal places his hands on the carpet and gets on all fours. "You want me to crawl to you like a man starved for your pussy?" He does just that, the invisible string between us going taut as he gets closer. "Because I want to taste you so damn badly, I might die if I don't get a chance tonight."

He closes the gap between us and stops in front of me, his eyes glittering with mischief as he rises on his knees. With his height and the position of the mattress, he gets a perfect view of the place that throbs for his attention.

His tongue darts out to trace the curve of his bottom lip.

Sparks skate down my spine. My lower half pulses and liquid pools between my legs. "It's your funeral."

"Then I might as well enjoy my last meal." His gaze darkens as it lands on the apex of my thighs.

"And how do you plan on doing that without touching me?"

"Why ruin the surprise?" He flashes me that signature smile of his that gets my heart pumping wildly in my chest.

"But—"

"Shirt off and legs spread apart or else all of this is over. Got it?" He throws my words back at me.

I swear he remembers every single thing I say solely so he can use it against me at the most inconvenient time.

"Got it." I rip the shirt off my head and push my thighs apart, wiping the stupid grin off his face. He groans as his hands grip the mattress on either side of my thighs.

The sensual woman who lay dormant inside of me rises to the surface, fueled by the lust in his gaze and the pulsing sensation at my core. Maybe I am on a power trip because nothing feels better than making a man like him wild with need.

I reach for the silicon tool. One end tilts up, while the other is curved and meant for G-spot stimulation.

"What's that?" Cal's voice trembles, eliciting a shiver from me.

I hold it up for him to see.

He stands to get a better look, encroaching on my space and flooding my nose with his addicting smell. "That one is new."

"The last one broke."

His eyes narrow. "How?"

"It was well-loved." I do a quick sign of the cross in mock remembrance.

"With *him?*" The lethal tone of his voice makes my stomach clench.

"No, you possessive asshole. By myself."

The tightness in his jaw fades away. "Good. Now get in the middle of the bed and show me what you usually do to get off."

I do what he says. He climbs up on to the mattress, making the butterflies in my stomach swarm. My body dips closer to him from his added weight, but he is careful to avoid touching me. Instead, he lies beside me, leaving a small gap between our bodies.

I release a shaky breath. "First, I like to touch myself."

The color of his eyes shifts like the ocean before a storm, the light blue color quickly turning darker from his dilating pupils. "I said to *show* me."

My fingers grip on to the sheets.

Are you really going to do this?

One night won't change things between us. At least not unless I let it, and I don't plan on making that mistake again.

"Lana," he says with a strained voice, attempting to pull me away from my thoughts.

Just let go for a single night.

My eyes shut as I stroke my belly. The tips of my fingers run back and forth across the smooth flesh, tickling the skin until my muscles loosen. It's not until my heart begins to race that I travel past my ribs, straight toward my breasts.

I can feel his eyes *everywhere*. It fuels the fire burning within me, feeding it until I'm squirming on the bed as I tease myself.

"God. The way you look right now makes me wish..." He

bites back a groan before blowing on the nipple closest to him, catching me by surprise.

"Makes you wish what?" I press.

"That you would let me touch you."

I'm careful not to let my hands get too close to my nipples, instead focusing on traveling around the circumference of my breast first. Each pass gets me closer to the peak. "What would you do if you could?"

Cal curses under his breath. "Worship your body with my hands and lips until you're crying for my cock."

I huff. "You always were a tease."

"Says the woman who has her dripping cunt on display for my personal torture."

I spread my legs wider, earning another pained grunt from him. Cal leans forward and blows against the tip of my other nipple in retribution.

My back bows, my chest inching closer to his mouth.

His deep chuckle makes goose bumps explode across my skin. "Just say the words and I'll take over."

"No." I try to sound strong, but my answer comes out like a broken whisper.

"Are you sure?" Cal's breathing grows heavier. "Because I'd love take you into my mouth until you're writhing beneath me, with your back arched and your pussy grinding against my thigh, soaking it with your need."

I can picture it vividly. Cal would press his knee into me, encouraging me to prove how much I want him by seeking my own release on his thigh. He always liked making me work for my pleasure. The gentleness he usually shows me outside of the bedroom would be gone, replaced by a wildness he keeps on a tight leash.

I hope you know what you're doing.

The more I'm reminded of our connection, the stronger my doubt grows.

Regret this later.

My lower half throbs with the need for more. I grab the vibrator only to have it stolen right out of my hands.

"Use your hand first." He slides off the bed, walking around the end before lying between my legs.

Fuck.

I tease my clit and drag my hand back and forth from my entrance, using my arousal to my advantage.

My finger dips inside, pumping slowly.

"Show me how much you want me." He watches with the utmost fascination as I lift my finger. It shines under the moonlight peeking through the blinds. The vibrator slips from his hand, completely abandoned as he focuses on me.

"Another."

I follow his command, my body shaking as I slip a second finger inside, soaking it to the knuckle as I slowly push in and out. I've never been able to turn myself on this much. Cal's presence works like an aphrodisiac, turning me into a whimpering mess at his command.

The muscles in my stomach contract with each thrust of my fingers.

"Let me taste you." His voice cracks, the wildness in his gaze splitting my heart in two.

"No." I state it firmly—for him and for myself.

He drops his head against the mattress and groans.

I grin as I reach for the vibrator again, only to have Cal hold it hostage against his chest.

"Hand it over." I wiggle my fingers.

"You said *I* couldn't touch you, but you never said anything about me using your toy." He presses the button, and the hum fills the room.

"Wha—" My protest is cut off by Cal pressing the warm vibrating end against my clit.

My back arches, pleasure spreading through my body like a tidal wave.

"You're a cheat," I moan as he slides the tip inside of me, soaking it before returning it back to my clit.

He repeats the same motion over and over, collecting my arousal before teasing my clit. "You can tell me to stop at any time."

Like I stand a chance of doing that now that he retook control and turned me into a mindless mess. My frustration grows as I chase my orgasm, only to have it denied every single time.

I clutch on to the sheet beneath me and grunt. My skin has a slight sheen to it from the sweat dampening it.

He *tsks* as I attempt to snag the vibrator away again. "Do you want to come?"

"Yes," I say between gritted teeth.

"Then let me touch you."

"No."

"Pity then. Let me know when you're ready to accept defeat." He shuts off the vibrator before inserting the tip inside me. His thrusts are deliberately shallow, barely scratching the itch. If anything, it makes the pulsing worse.

I moan. *"Please."*

"Please *what?* Use your words, sweetheart. I want to hear how much you need me."

My lips remain clamped together. His condescending chuckle makes me want to rage. He turns the vibrator on to the lowest setting to take the edge off, and I melt further into the mattress.

"All this could be over if you just surrender." He lowers himself until his face is inches away from my pussy and blows against my swollen clit.

For fuck's sake.

"If you don't make me come in the next minute, I'll shove that vibrator straight up your ass and finish this myself."

He winks. "I'm down if you are, so long as you let me come afterward."

"I hate you," I grind out as he shoves the vibrator deeper.

"No. You hate how I make you feel." He removes the vibrator and wipes away my essence with a few strokes of his tongue. The way he shuts his eyes in reverence pushes me over the edge.

"Please touch me." The words come out strained, matching the way my heart feels like it is being pulled apart at the seams.

You're the one who wanted this.

With quick abandon, Cal ditches the vibrator and spreads my legs wider to accommodate his body. He kisses his way up and down each of my thighs, taking his sweet time. The brush of his soft lips against my flesh is too much. I lift my hips to remind him of what I want, only to be met with the scrape of his stubbled cheek against my thigh.

I dig my fingers into his hair and drag his head to my dripping center. "Enough teasing. Either fuck me or fuck off."

"So bossy." His tongue swipes out, darting across my swollen clit. When he tries to retreat, I hold his head against me and force him to stay. "So needy." He drags the tip toward my aching center. "So fucking sexy, my cock feels like it might burst from the sight of you."

His tongue sinks inside me. My back curves, sparks shooting off my skin as he devours me like he hasn't eaten for years. Like I'm the first meal he has had and he wants to savor it. His fingers dig into my ass cheeks as he holds me against his face, his eyes solely focused on me.

The unrelenting torture of his mouth drives me closer to the edge. I want to hold out, but my toes tingle and my breathing quickens as his tongue teases my center before diving inside.

My thighs press into the sides of his head as I come. Spots fill my vision as wave after wave of pleasure rolls through me. Cal doesn't cease his stroking, sucking, and licking until my body stops trembling and my release coats the entire lower half of his face.

"Fuck." My head drops back, and I blink up at the ceiling.

He kisses my center one last time before crawling over my body. His familiar weight presses me deeper into the mattress as he cradles my head and kisses me. The combined taste of his minty breath and my arousal floods my mouth, causing another spike of pleasure. I moan against his lips, and his tongue swoops in, forcing me to taste how much I want him.

He moves to break away, but I grip on to his hair and tug him closer, not able to end our connection just yet. I'm not prepared for the regret I might feel once he walks away. The *fear*.

"Thank you." He presses one last peck against my lips.

Thank you? I should be the one thanking him for making me come harder than I have in *years*.

He kisses the top of my forehead before pulling away from me. Besides his messy hair and the erection threatening to burst the seams of his sweatpants, he looks completely put together.

I rise on my elbows and look over at him. "Where are you going?"

"I'd rather leave before you come to your senses and kick me out."

My heart threatens to explode as he slides off the mattress. It beats hard and fast as he tucks me in, thoroughly destroying any last bit of resistance I had against him.

"I wouldn't have kicked you out if you had asked to stay," I blurt out.

He releases a heavy exhale. "I want to stay because you want me here, not because you feel obligated by a request and an orgasm."

My lips part, but no words come out.

"You know where to find me if you want me." Cal offers me a tight smile before walking out of my bedroom.

I fall back against the bed with a sigh. The empty hole in my chest grows until it consumes all the warmth from before, leaving me feeling cold and alone.

I consider crawling into Cal's bed, but hold back. I'm too overwhelmed to think about the consequences of something like that.

You already let him eat you out. What's the worst that can happen?

Simply put: I fall in love with him all over again.

CHAPTER THIRTY-FOUR

Cal

Walking away from Lana is nearly impossible. I almost caved and stayed, but I couldn't do that to either of us, no matter how much I wanted to hold her tightly against my chest and whisper in her ear until she fell asleep.

Instead, I lie down alone in my bed, sexually and emotionally frustrated.

Are you really surprised?

No. Part of me knew the moment I walked out the door that she wouldn't follow me. It was written all over her face. The indecision. The uncertainty. The fear that whatever we did might lead to more.

Of course, I want it to. I wouldn't have done what I did if I wasn't sure of the fact that I want her any way I can get her, so long as she is open to the same.

Give her time.

I rub my stubbled chin with my hand. The smell of Lana's arousal lingers on my fingers, making my already-stiff cock ache with a need for release. I push the band of my sweatpants down and wrap my hand around my dick, giving it a single tug.

Just a little something to take the edge off, I tell myself as I pump up and down until pre-cum runs down my shaft, helping my hand slide more easily across the soft skin.

It's better than drinking, I repeat twice as my stomach contracts and my toes flex from the building pleasure at the base of my spine. Heat travels toward my cock, making it impossible to think about anything but seeking my own pleasure.

I imagine Lana's fingers replacing mine. The tease of her touch. The tight grip of her hand wrapping around my shaft, pumping until my balls draw tight. The warmth of her mouth replacing her hand, teasing and testing until I'm bucking underneath her, choking her with my cock.

I can picture it all vividly.

Her eyes watering as she takes all of me.

Me shoving my cock as far as it can go before I come down her throat.

The taste of my release on her tongue as I pull her against me and kiss her until we're both ready for me to sink inside of her.

My spine tingles, and my pumping becomes more erratic. With a few more tugs, my cock explodes, covering my shirt.

I screw my eyes shut and curse to myself. Whatever peace I thought I might feel quickly fades away as I picture Lana cleaning off my dick with the flat of her tongue.

"Fuck," I rasp.

So much for taking the edge off.

The next morning, Lana wakes up bright and early to take Cami down to the lake. I consider joining them so I can talk to her about last night but decide it would be better to speak to her once Cami is asleep.

I spend the next hour sifting through the DreamStream app while scrolling through Reddit, gathering information about the app and what people really think of it. Thanks to Lana's insight and the data I collected, I have a good understanding of the app and its competitors.

I shoot Rowan a text before I lose my confidence.

> Want to talk about DreamStream sometime? I've got a couple ideas.

Rowan

> I'm free in thirty. I'll send you a video call link.

My brother and I hop on to the call thirty minutes later. Zahra pops in to say hi. Rowan's eyes brighten as he looks up at her while she speaks to me.

Damn. Love looks good on my brother. I'm happy he found someone who could make him look that happy all the time.

Once Zahra leaves, he and I get down to business.

DreamStream was my brother's baby before he became the director of Dreamland. I'm surprised he hasn't stepped in to help since they're struggling, but given how busy he is with the park and Zahra, it makes sense. He doesn't have time to get involved in other divisions of the company.

So, you're the next best option?

The seed of doubt plants itself in my head, but I do my best to ignore it.

The longer I speak to Rowan about my assessment, the more enthusiastic and confident I become about everything.

"You really thought this out." Rowan stares into the camera.

"It was hard to fall asleep last night." That's an understatement. It took me hours to knock out after everything with Lana, so the best thing I could do was try to distract myself with DreamStream.

"What do you suggest we do?" He leans back in his office chair.

"I think we need a refresh."

"How so?"

"I'm pretty sure the guy you appointed grew up with a black-and-white TV that had five channels, so what does he know about streaming?"

"Enough to have lasted this long on the job." He clasps his hands together underneath his chin.

"He has been floundering and you know it. The numbers aren't in our favor, and the slow decline dates back to a little after you left the position."

"Then what do you think is best?" His lips curve upward.

"Ask the board to appoint someone else who actually knows what they're doing."

"Like you?"

A laugh explodes out of me. I expect Rowan to follow, but

his face remains stone-cold.

"You're serious?" My smile falls.

"Why not?"

"Because I'm grossly underqualified and equally uninterested in a position like that." The thought of spending the rest of my days chained to a desk doesn't spark any joy.

"I'm not suggesting you become a CEO."

"Then what?"

"A director."

I bite back my laugh this time.

His brows furrow. "I'm being serious. I heard that there are some issues with the current director in charge of content strategy and analysis."

"And?"

"You could give it a try."

I shake my head hard enough to make my neck hurt. "Hell no."

"Why not?"

"First off, I have no experience." I tick off a finger.

So much for being a risk-taker.

My teeth grind together as my grandpa's old nickname for me pops into my head. This isn't the time to take a risk.

Rowan readjusts his already-perfect tie. "Then start out as an associate."

"I hate office jobs."

"DreamStream is different."

"Why? Because they have breakout rooms and beanbag chairs? Hard pass."

"I'm talking more about the philosophy."

I give him a blank stare.

He sighs. "Just think about it."

"There is nothing to think about because I'm not looking for a job. I just wanted to share what I found."

"Then be sure to mention it at the next board meeting. I'm sure Mr. Wheeler will be open to suggestions if this month's report is even more grim than the last."

"Rowan…" I warn. The last thing I want to do is draw attention to myself given my lack of experience and the gigantic expectations associated with my last name.

"If you don't want to join a team that can make a difference, then at least bring it up to the person who can." He hangs up before giving me a chance to say anything else.

"Asshole."

Turns out I don't have to seek Lana out. She comes knocking on my bedroom door with a baby monitor in her hand and a closed-off expression on her face.

"Want to go on a little walk by the lake?" she asks in a soft voice like she hasn't spent the better part of today avoiding me.

My heart beats harder against my chest. "Sure. Let me grab a pair of sneakers."

Once I have my shoes tied, I follow Lana out of the house and into the summer night. For the first couple of minutes, neither of us says anything. Crickets fill the silence as we walk toward the dock behind the guesthouse. It's a much smaller version of the one by the main house, mainly meant for a single boat and a couple of chairs at the end.

Both of us take a seat at the end of the dock. Lana shakes off her flip-flops and swings her legs over the edge so the tips of her toes can graze the water.

"So…" I start because she clearly won't.

Her eyes flicker from the lake to my face. "What do you have planned after we sell the house?"

The air in my lungs stalls. "What?"

"Do you think you'll go back to Chicago?"

"Would it matter to you if I go?"

She stares at her toes tracing the water. "It shouldn't."

My eyes narrow. "That's not a real answer."

Her eyes roll. "Neither is answering my question with another question."

My lips curve into a small smile. "True. To be honest, I'm not sure what I have planned after selling the house. I didn't really think that far ahead."

"Of course you didn't. It must be nice to not have a job or any responsibilities outside of living in the moment."

My smile drops. "It's kind of lonely."

She snorts. "What? How is that even possible? You have a bajillion friends."

"I *had* a bajillion friends. Turns out a lot of them were either too toxic to be around or too fed up with my shitty coping mechanisms."

Her brows scrunch together like she can't fathom what I'm telling her. "Iris—"

"Is busy starting her life with my brother."

"So? That doesn't mean she can't spend time with you."

"She does, but we can't hang out nearly as much as we used to. And that's fine. I understand things are different now."

Her head tilts. "Different how?"

I look up at the starlit sky to avoid her perceptive stare. "I don't expect her to stop living her life just because I don't have one."

"You have a life," she counters.

A bitter laugh escapes me. "An empty one."

"What do you mean?"

"I'm a nobody, Lana."

"You're somebody to me." Her hand clasps on to mine.

You're somebody to me.

Her words act like medicine, sinking into my skin and easing the pain of years' worth of damage from feeling inadequate.

"Do you really mean that?" I rasp.

Her head barely moves as she nods.

"Why didn't you ask me to stay last night?" I ask the question I've been beating myself up over since then.

"Because I was scared," she admits, her voice barely audible over the leaves rustling around us from a strong gust of wind.

"Scared of what?" I give her hand a squeeze.

"Plenty of things when it comes to you."

Such a Lana answer. "Pick one."

"I'm afraid what will happen once you leave again."

"What if I stayed?" The question bursts out of me without any hesitancy.

Smooth, Cal.

She blinks. "What?"

"I'm not in a rush to go anywhere, so what if I stuck around

Lake Wisteria for a while?"

Her forehead pinches. "Why would you do that?"

"Isn't the answer obvious?" I tuck the fluttering strand of hair behind her ear before tracing the soft curve. Her breathing shifts as she looks up at me with her large brown eyes that reflect the moon above us.

Her lips part, and I find the idea of kissing her impossible to ignore. I lean forward and capture her mouth with mine, swallowing her gasp.

The kiss ends as quickly as it began, yet she breathes heavy like she just ran a race.

"You want to stay?" The words rush out of her mouth.

"Only if you want me to—"

She initiates the kiss this time, cutting off the last bit of my sentence with her mouth pressing against mine. The buzz starts at my lips and travels down my spine.

Kissing Lana feels like the world started spinning again. Like I've been frozen in place until she reentered my life, tilting it back on its axis.

I'm not sure how long we kiss for. At some point, she breaks away to straddle my lap. We both groan when she grinds down against my cock. Her head drops to the side, so I kiss my way up her neck, teasing her until she ends up rocking back and forth against me.

Everything about our kiss feels different. New. *Hopeful*.

And I want to make sure that hope never dies. No matter what it takes.

Y ou can't seriously be going on a vacation with Cal of all people." Violet launches a dart at the circle she drew directly over Cal's face marked with a *50*. She found the photo of Cal in a suit and tie on the Kane Company's webpage and printed it out for our emergency girls' night.

This time, I wasn't the one who called the meeting. Delilah and Violet did after I told them the news about Dreamland and our vacation next week.

"You try telling Cami no after he offered to take her to *Dreamland*. She has been begging me to go ever since she saw that commercial on the TV two years ago."

"Why would he even offer a trip like that in the first place? What does he get out of it?" Delilah takes a sip of her drink before standing and grabbing a dart from the table. Today is a good day for her and her arthritis, so she wants to take advantage.

"Besides increasing his odds of getting into Alana's pants?" Violet snorts.

A little too late for that.

I shoot her a look. "Say what you want about Cal and me, but I know he is doing this because he likes Cami. I can see it in the way they interact. The thing they have is…special."

He is everything I want in a partner and more.

Delilah's frown deepens. "Oh, no." She and Violet spare a glance at each other.

"What?" I ask.

"You've got that look in your eyes."

"What look?"

"The *I'm falling in love with Callahan Kane* look."

I laugh. "What kind is that?"

Both Delilah and Violet try to imitate it and fail miserably, which causes us all to break out into laughter.

"I'm not falling in love with him." At least I don't *think* I am. We have only just started taking the next step, so there is no possible way I would be falling in love. It's way too soon.

Right? A small swell of panic builds in my chest, right above my heart.

"I don't know…" Delilah rocks back on her shoes.

"Trust me. I would know seeing as I've already done it once before."

"That's the thing about *falling* in love. You don't exactly expect it to happen until you're crash landing into someone else's arms, wondering how the hell you lost the battle against gravity in the first place."

Shit.

Alana Valentina Castillo, you were supposed to be smarter. Wiser. Stronger.

There is no way I would do something as stupid as fall in love with the same man twice, right? My heart throbs at the very idea.

"I know you're both worried…" My voice stays neutral despite the anxiety growing by the second.

"Only because we love you and don't want to see you suffer because of Cal. *Again*," Violet adds.

I shake off the nerves. "This time is different." With him cutting back on drinking and his commitment to trying to secure a place in my life, it would be stupid to ignore his efforts, even if we still have a long way to go.

"How? You don't even trust him," Violet says with a soft voice.

"Violet…" Delilah warns.

I cross my arms. "I trust him enough to live with him."

"But you don't trust him enough to take care of Cami on his own," Violet counters.

"Trust takes time." Delilah gives my hand a squeeze.

My head hangs. Deep down, I know Violet and Delilah are right. Cal and I can play house for as long as we want, but that won't change the fact that I still don't fully trust him.

Trust takes time. Delilah's words replay in my head.

I hope so.

I return from girls' night to find Wyatt and Cal caught in a death stare match. They both sit on opposite sides of the living room, the tension bleeding from both of their hiked shoulders.

"Glad you're back. Can you call off your guard dog now?" Cal doesn't look in my direction.

Wyatt's muscles strain beneath his T-shirt. "I'm a babysitter, not a guard dog."

Cal's eyes narrow. "You wouldn't even let me read Cami a bedtime story."

"Because I'm the one who usually does it when I watch her." Wyatt pokes his chest.

"Well, she didn't ask you, did she?"

Wyatt's jaw ticks.

Good God. Watching the two of them get jealous over who Cami wants to read a bedtime story with is too much, even for me.

My ovaries, on the other hand, are living their best life.

"Thanks for watching Cami. I appreciate it." I pat Wyatt on the back.

Merlin comes out from under the couch to rub his body against my leg. I reach down and run my hand across his silky coat. It only took Merlin a week to warm up to Cami and me, thanks to the fancy cans of tuna I bought him.

"Hey there," I coo.

"You have a cat?" Wyatt's head swings in Cal's direction.

"Yup."

I carry the cat into my arms and wave his paw in the air. "Say hi to Merlin."

And you were worried about Cami getting attached...

Wyatt's eyes right. "Merlin? Wasn't he King Arthur's mentor or something?"

"Yup." Cal's jaw clenches.

"That's cute, Percival. Who knew you had a King Arthur

kink?"

"I called him that because the name reminded me of my mom, asshole."

Wyatt's smile falls. "Sorry."

Cal doesn't bother sticking around. The door to his bedroom clicks shut behind him, leaving me to deal with Wyatt.

"What's gotten into him?" I ask.

Wyatt shrugs. "I'm not sure. He's been pissed since the moment I showed up."

Cal was in a good mood when I left, so I'm not sure what happened within the few seconds it took Wyatt to walk inside the house.

I give him a shove. "Could you at least try to be civil with him?"

"I *am* trying, even if it doesn't seem like it. Most of the town is trying, after seeing him make a damn fool of himself in that strawberry costume."

"Then why did he look like you kicked his cat?"

"Probably because he feels threatened by my relationship with Cami or something."

"Threatened? Why?"

"Most likely because the rich prick didn't have to share a single thing his whole life."

I roll my eyes. "You are both ridiculous."

"Me? The guy made it a point to ice me out the whole time. When I tried to play with them at Cami's request, Cal killed my Barbie before I ever had a chance to join."

My mouth drops open. "How?"

"My doll didn't listen to my mom and got in a stranger's car."

"At least he made it an educational experience." I cover my mouth to muffle my chuckle.

Wyatt glares, and I end up laughing harder.

"Don't call me next time you need someone to babysit."

I wrap my arms around him. "I love you!"

He returns the gesture. "Whatever. Next time I'll be smarter and send his Barbie to jail. Maybe incorporate something about breaking laws."

I laugh and pull away. "You do that."

Wyatt sees himself out, leaving me to pick up the toys left out after Cami went to bed.

"He's gone?" Cal's voice has me jumping in place.

I turn to face him. "You scared me."

"Sorry. I was wondering how long it would take him to leave. I've been at it all night with no success."

"He wasn't going to leave until I got home."

"Seriously? Why? I could have taken care of Cami if you had asked me."

He sounds…hurt?

No. That can't be.

Can it?

I tuck the bin of toys back in its shelf. "I'm sorry."

"Why didn't you ask me?" He steps closer until I can smell his aftershave.

Something in my chest tugs hard.

"Lana."

I look away from his face. "The guy I was with before…"

Cal takes a deep breath as he tucks his hands into his pockets.

"I asked him a few times to watch Cami while I went out

with Violet and Delilah. Wyatt didn't mind taking care of Cami, but I thought it would be a good bonding opportunity for Victor and her, so I let him." I release a laugh that borders on hysterical.

Cal abandons his spot and swoops me into his arms.

"I really want a full name for this asshole."

I clutch the fabric of his shirt, holding on to him like a lifeline. "It's not like anything physically happened to her, but she would ask him a few too many questions and he would lose his cool. Ended up yelling at her and making her cry multiple times. Even sent her to her room once, like he had any right to punish her."

"I know you don't condone physical violence, but for him, I hope you made an exception."

I shake my head against his chest. "I didn't find out what happened until a few months later, once we broke up over something else. Cami kept it a secret the whole time because she was worried I would choose Victor over her. How freaking sad is it that my kid couldn't tell me someone hurt her because she didn't want to lose me? Like I would ever choose a man over her." Tears begin to fall, soaking the material of his shirt.

He runs a hand up and down my back, soothing me through my sobs. I didn't mean to cry, but the tears won't stop flowing now that they have started.

"I'm sorry you and Cami had to go through that together. But I can assure you, I wouldn't dare raise my voice at your kid. That's the last thing I would want after going through something similar myself."

I sniffle, trying to fight back the tears. "I know that—deep down I *know* you wouldn't—but I made myself a promise after I learned about what Victor did."

"What promise?"

"That I wouldn't let anyone who I didn't fully trust take care of Cami."

He winces, although his hand never stops running up and down my spine. "I know you don't have a reason to fully trust me yet, but I know one day you will." He speaks with absolute certainty, as if he won't accept any other option.

Honestly, I'm not sure there is another one for Cal.

"Look! My name!" Cami's arms shake from exertion as she drags a huge box behind her.

Cal hops off the couch and helps her bring the package inside the guesthouse.

"What is that?" I check out the label with Cami's name on it. The box is plain without any kind of branding or clue to tell me where it is from.

Cal kneels on the floor beside her. "Cami's birthday present."

"For me?" She hits a new octave from how excited she is.

I blink a few times to confirm the facts. "You got her a present?"

Cal looks up at me from his spot beside Cami on the floor. "Yeah?"

"But you're already taking us to Dreamland next week."

"And? I told Cami I would build a ship with her."

Cami gasps.

Cal curses under his breath. "Well, there goes that surprise."

"Swears jar!"

Cal sifts through his wallet and hands her a fifty-dollar bill.

Cami's brow rises.

"What? I ran out of hundreds yesterday."

"That's okay. Fifty times two." She holds up her two fingers like a peace sign.

I stifle my laugh with the palm of my hand, earning a glare from Cal.

His lips turn into a smile before he hands her a second bill. "You better invite me to your graduation with how much I'm paying for your education."

"Okay!" Cami takes off for the swear jar. She drags a chair toward the fridge, but Cal swoops in and stops her before she has a chance to climb it.

"I'll help you." He lifts her into the air so she can drop the bills inside the jar. I already had to empty it last week with how often Cal and I slip up around one another.

Someone might need to call the heart doctor because mine is about ready to explode from how full it feels. I never thought watching Cal interact with Cami—watching him care about her—would make my entire body feel warm and tingly.

I take a seat on the couch and watch the two of them rip open the birthday present he got her.

Cami pulls out a second nondescript box that is the size of her entire body.

"Uhhh. What is it?" She stares at the box with scrunched brows.

"Hold on." Cal pulls out his phone and searches for a photo.

He shows it to Cami, and she gasps. "Princess Marianna's ship?"

"Wait. What?" I stand and peek over her shoulder at the phone screen. The picture was taken in a workshop of some sort, with wood shavings everywhere and a bottle of glue on its side. In the center of the photo, there is a replica of Princess Marianna's ship that she went searching for sunken treasure in.

Cal rubs the back of his neck. "I asked Rowan to make us something special. He got his Creators to base it off one of the model ships I recommended after doing some research."

Oh my God. My legs shake from how weak in the knees I feel. "How is that even possible?"

"For once, it pays to have the Kane name."

My heart doesn't stand a chance.

Cami and Cal open the box and pull out the pieces, and I sit next to them while they get started. I keep out of the way while they work together. Sometimes I offer assistance when she can't do what he asks, but for the most part, I'm happy to watch them work with each other. There is something sweet about how patient Cal is with Cami and the way he takes time to answer her every question.

At one point, Cami climbs into Cal's lap so she can get a better look at what he is doing. He freezes for a second before clutching her hands and modeling how to glue a piece together.

I always knew Cal would be an incredible father one day, and how he treats Cami is proof of that, even if he doubts his own skills. It's in the little things he does without even noticing.

The patience. The understanding. The reassuring way he speaks to Cami when she gets frustrated or upset.

The longer I stick around watching them, the more apparent it becomes that I don't want this to end once we sell the house.

Just the idea of Cal leaving makes my chest ache, and I'm not sure what to do with that feeling.

There are so many things standing in our way of ever moving forward together—his drinking being the biggest one. But I can't help but wonder what might happen if he gets that part of his life under control. Would we have a real chance at the life we could have had six years ago? Could we let go of the past and make a family of our own?

I'm tempted to find out.

CHAPTER THIRTY-SIX

Cal

On Saturday, I wake up to chaos. Lana is hunched over the counter, finishing up Cami's birthday cake while the kid runs around the kitchen in circles, trying to steal frosting from the bowl.

"Go get dressed before everyone gets here." Lana points in the direction of Cami's room without glancing up from her task.

Cami takes off, not looking where she is going. I jump out of her way before she can crash against my legs, saving us both from falling over.

"Watch where you're going there."

Her eyes light up. "Sorry!"

"Happy birthday." I rub the top of her head.

She launches herself at my legs, giving them a big squeeze. I never thought I would come to crave hugs from a little kid, but every time Cami does it, I feel like I'm winning at life. Although mine isn't put together like my brothers', Lana and Cami make me feel whole in a way a job or an inheritance could never even attempt.

Maybe Declan and Iris were on to something when they said they wanted a whole brood of kids and a dog. There's something about a family that can't be beat.

Cami breaks away and runs into her room, leaving Lana and me alone.

"It's only nine a.m. and I already have a headache." Lana rubs her face with the back of her hand, effectively smearing chocolate frosting across her cheek.

I can't resist leaning forward and licking it off her skin before she has a chance to wipe it away. Blood begins to flow downward, especially when she looks up at me with hooded eyes.

I'm tempted to recreate our first kiss with chocolate icing this time. Lana seems to have a similar thought with the way her eyes drag from my lips to the bowl beside her.

"Tastes great." I wink.

Her eyes narrow, although the brightness in them doesn't quite fit.

I walk around her and sift through the medicine cabinet. "Here." I pass Lana two Tylenols and a glass of water.

"Thanks." She sighs before knocking back the pills.

I lean against the counter next to her. "Rough morning?"

"I have like, a hundred people coming over in two hours, and I'm not even close to being ready."

"What do you need help with?"

"Everything." She slumps against the counter.

I grab my phone and pull up a notetaking app.

She shoots me a look.

"What?" I ask when she doesn't say anything. "I work best with a list or else I might forget something."

"You're really offering to help?"

"Sure. I don't mind if you put me to work." I smirk.

She rolls her eyes with a smile. "Fine, but don't say I didn't warn you."

Lana rattles off a list of random tasks, most of which require me to drive into town. It's evident that with each task I take on, her tense shoulders drop a little more.

"Be back soon." I give her a quick kiss on the temple before leaving the house.

It takes me over ninety minutes to finish all the tasks. My car is filled to the max with balloons, food, and a few last-minute supplies Lana forgot at the store.

By the time I make it back inside the guesthouse, it's been transformed into a Princess Marianna wonderland, with decorations covering almost every surface, streamers hanging across the ceiling in fun patterns, and a half-complete balloon arch behind the cake table.

"You made it!" Lana rushes out of her room and grabs the balloons from my hand. She ties them to the balloon arch to finish it, although she needs my help reaching the tallest point to secure the Princess Marianna inflatable.

"You really go all out."

She laughs to herself. "Too bad you didn't see last year's theme. Cami wanted a Christmas-themed birthday because she didn't want to wait until December, so I turned the backyard into a winter wonderland. Most of the town donated their Christmas decorations, so it ended up being epic. Blew out the power grid for the night and everything." She laughs to herself, making my chest warm.

I grab her by the hand and pull her against me. "I wish I had been there." I place a soft kiss on the top of her head.

She looks up at me with batted lashes. "I do too," she says and places a quick kiss on my cheek before wiggling out of my embrace, brushing against my cock in the process.

I groan. "Cruel woman."

"Sorry! Gotta get ready!" She darts away toward her room with a laugh, leaving me wondering how the hell I spent six years away from the one person who made me feel whole.

And how do I make sure I don't spend another day without her ever again?

My anxiety about spending time with Delilah, Violet, Wyatt, and the rest of the town who hates me intensifies as the clock gets closer to noon. The more I help Lana carry everything outside, the more real the whole birthday party becomes.

The first shot of vodka was only meant to take the edge off. I wasn't proud of sneaking back inside the guesthouse, but the fear of what might go wrong overrode my pride.

Music playing and people talking outside only makes my anxiety worse, which fuels the vicious cycle.

I'm not happy with my moment of weakness, which drives me to drink some more. It's a pathetic sight. Me sitting on the floor, nursing a bottle of vodka while Merlin stares from the other side of the room, secretly judging me. I don't stop until the burn in my throat rivals the one in my chest.

By the time I pull myself together and go outside, the party is in full swing. I slide my sunglasses into place to hide any signs of my secret.

Wyatt lifts his chin in my direction before resuming his conversation with a couple other men I don't recognize.

"I was wondering where you went. I've been looking all over for you." Lana holds out a plastic inner tube for me. "Cami was hoping you could help her with this one."

I grab the inflatable from her hands without speaking.

"Is everything okay?"

"Yup." I stick the little plastic nozzle in my mouth and start blowing.

Her head tilts. "Are you sure?"

I nod.

She places her hand against my cheek. Her furrowed brows add to the shitty feeling brewing in my chest. "What's wrong?"

The fact that I drank despite knowing how much you hate it.

I lean away from her touch. "Just tired."

"That's a shame then because I had plans for us tonight." A teasing smile tugs at her lips.

"I'm sure I'll get a second wind."

She rises on the tips of her toes and kisses my cheek. "I hope so. After our last time, I owe you."

"I'm going to hold you to that."

"I'd expect no less from you." She flashes me a flirty smile that has my cock rising into action. "But you have to leave before

Cami wakes up. If she catches us together, she will go into wedding-planning mode."

I laugh. "Deal."

Something in Lana shifts at the sound. Her nose twitches and her mouth pulls down into a frown. "Are you…" She steals my sunglasses off my face. "Really? At a kid's party?"

My stomach drops. "I can explain."

"Why bother?" She throws my sunglasses at me before she turns around. Her hips sway as she walks away, tempting me to grab her so she can hear me out.

And say what? You drank because you couldn't handle a six-year-old's birthday party?

Right. Because that doesn't sound pathetic at all.

You're no better than her sister, making her upset with your selfish choices and lack of control.

The thought of relating to someone like Antonella only feeds on my fears, allowing them to grow until I have no choice but to escape.

Did you really expect anything less from someone who is so damn good at fucking up?

Nope. Not at all.

My anxiety and self-loathing fester and grow with each passing hour of Cami's birthday party. For the most part, I keep to myself, mainly because Wyatt, Delilah, and Violet made it obvious from the start that they don't want anything to do with me. I know what my old friends think of me. It's obvious in the way they stare.

I'm the drunk. The washed-up athlete. The man who broke their best friend's heart.

I collected more bad titles than I ever did championships.

Even Lana has done her best to avoid me since she found out about my drinking. She and the other parents keep to the covered seating area that was added to the dock when I had it redone. The boat slip beside it is empty, although the extra room gives the kids a place to practice their jumps into the water.

No one comes to talk to me, minus Cami, who makes an effort to check on me at least once before running back to her friends.

The icy glares and whispers taunt my demons out of hiding, and I'm driven to fill my half-empty cup of soda to the top with vodka.

If Lana is going to be mad at me, I might as well not suffer through the buildup. Slowly, after two trips inside the guesthouse, my muscles loosen and the thick knot in my throat disappears. The warmth spreading through my veins replaces the cold chill, justifying my reason to drink in the first place.

Peace.

I'm not sure how long I sit by myself, swaying to the country music pouring out of Lana's portable speaker, but at some point Wyatt sneaks up on me.

"Here." Wyatt drops a cheeseburger in front of me before taking a seat. "Eat it and sober up."

I'm barely buzzed, yet he speaks to me like I'm a sloppy mess.

"I'm fine." I shove the plate away.

He grabs my cup and sniffs. "Still masking your issues with vodka?"

I steal it back and drain the rest of the drink in spite. "What are you doing here with me?"

"I want to talk."

"What about?"

"You can't keep doing this to Alana. It's not fair."

My nails bite into my skin. "I'm not doing anything."

"You're leading her on and making her believe you two have a chance."

"Because we do," I seethe.

He gives me a bored once-over, being sure to drive home how utterly unimpressed he is of me. "Not if you keep this up, you won't. This is why I knew it was a bad idea for you to come back. You aren't ready."

I'm not ready? Ready for what exactly?

I keep my face calm and collected despite the rage building within. "What do you want?"

"To help you for some goddamn reason."

I laugh. "What do you know about helping someone like me? You've got the perfect life. Happy wife, good job, bright future."

His grip on the picnic table tightens. "Why do you think that is?"

"Because you got lucky?"

"No. Because I put in the work."

My lips press together.

He continues. "If you want to ever get Alana back, then you need to pull yourself together. For real this time. Starting with this." He grabs my cup and tosses it in the trash bin nearby.

My eyes narrow. "Why are you helping me?"

"Because I want what's best for Alana and Cami, even if it's you." He scowls.

"So you think she could do better."

"In the end, it doesn't matter what I think because she loves you, so maybe it's *you* who should do better by her."

My heart stalls in my chest. "She loves me?"

His eyes swing over to the dock, where Lana helps a child with their floatie. "I'm not sure she ever stopped."

I shake my head. "She dated someone else."

"And? I'm sure you did too."

"Dated? Hell no."

"So, you fucked around then."

My teeth grind together. The period of my life when I was still getting high on Oxy was possibly the lowest I've ever stooped. Just thinking about the risks I took and the people I used to get high with makes me sick to my stomach.

On cue like always, the acid in my belly churns.

"Not that it's any of your business, but I haven't been with anyone in over two years."

"Two years? That's…" His voice drops off.

The same time I saw Lana with Victor.

If Lana felt even a fraction of what I experienced when I found her kissing someone else, I can't imagine the kind of pain she went through reading some of the headlines posted about me.

The person I was when high isn't the man I am now. Yet no matter how many times I repeat the same words, I can't erase the disgust I feel toward myself when I think back on my past.

Shame makes my throat close up.

His low whistle grates against my nerves. "Damn." He

actually laughs. "That's rough."

His comment drags me away from the dark thoughts. "Shut up, Eugene."

He flashes me a blinding smile. "Delilah is never going to let that one go."

"Glad my sex life is an amusing topic for all of you." I take a bite out of my burger to stop myself from saying anything else.

He rubs the back of his neck. "Delilah warned me against doing this but…" His voice drifts off.

"What?"

He takes a deep breath. "If you need a sponsor, I'm willing to be yours."

My mouth drops open. "You?"

He nods. "We have an AA group that meets at the chapel every night."

"Since when?" Wyatt was always squeaky clean and willing to do everything to remain in the town's good graces. Violet used to call it the quarterback complex. The biggest scandal of Wyatt's life was his parents getting an amicable divorce where they both stayed friends.

"A little less than a year after you left, I transferred to a Detroit precinct to be closer to my dad after his heart attack, but the things I saw while working there… God. They would haunt me even in my dreams." He looks over at Delilah, who waves at him with her cane. She shoots me a glare while slicing a line across her throat with the handle of the cane.

Glad to know my presence draws such a passion from her.

Wyatt steals my attention back. "The transition from small-town life to the big city was hard. I struggled for a long time with

PTSD and alcoholism before I finally got help."

"Shit. I had no idea, man. I'm sorry." I reach over and clap him on the shoulder.

He offers me a weak smile. "You're not the only one who struggled, you know?"

My head hangs. "I see."

Lana. Wyatt. Señora Castillo. The list goes on and on, making my chest ache.

He rises from the picnic table. "Just think about it. My offer will always stand, even if you decide to move back to Chicago once the house is sold."

"Really?"

"Yeah, *really*. I owe it to the man who used to be my best friend." He takes a few steps away, but I call his name.

He glances over his shoulder. "What?"

"Does this mean we're friends now?"

He scoffs. "Absolutely not."

The small smile on his face makes me believe it might become a possibility one day, though.

"Come on!" Cami grabs my hand and tugs, ineffectively getting me to rise from the picnic table I've spent the last two hours wallowing at.

"What's up?" I look around at the empty lawn.

"We're going to cut the cake!" She yanks harder this time. "You almost missed it."

"Sorry. I was daydreaming."

"Do that later!" She digs her feet into the ground and pulls.

"All right. Let's go." The last thing I want to do is be stuck inside the guesthouse with a bunch of people who don't like me, but if it makes Cami happy, I'm willing to be an adult and suck it up.

After all, who am I to deny the birthday girl?

I rise from the bench, my movements much more fluid after spending the last two hours without touching another drink.

Cami doesn't release my hand as she drags me into the guesthouse and places me behind the cake table. Lana stands beside me, her body as stiff as her smile. Everyone else remains on the other side with their phones in the air. A range of emotions is written across the parents' faces. Surprise. Annoyance. Curiosity.

Delilah and Wyatt share a knowing look while Violet pretends I don't even exist, which is possibly even worse.

I move to take a step around the table, but Lana latches on to my hand.

"Cami wants you here." Her face remains calm, cool, and collected, although her eyes burn with enough anger to make me frown.

Cami looks up at us two with a big smile. "Ready?"

I nod, my throat feeling impossibly tight.

The crowd begins singing the happy birthday song while Cami sways on her feet. Once the singing stops, Cami blows out her candles. Everyone cheers and claps for her.

While Lana is busy cutting the cake, Cami beckons me closer.

I kneel down. "What's up?"

She rises on the tips of her toes and whispers in my ear, "I wished you can be my new daddy."

I wished you can be my new daddy.

God. Somehow eight words make my knees as weak as my heart.

I wrap my arms around her and squeeze. "There is nothing I'd like more than that."

And I mean every single word.

CHAPTER THIRTY-SEVEN

Cal

Once everyone left, I tried to pull Lana aside to talk, but she threw herself into cleaning up the mess left behind after the party. Wyatt, Delilah, and Violet helped her. Instead of sitting around, I joined even though it was obvious no one wanted me to. The mindless task gave me time to sober up and think over everything that happened today.

By the time I threw away the last bag of trash, Lana was already moving on to Cami's bedtime routine.

I hold off on bothering her until an hour later. When I turn the doorknob, it doesn't move.

I press my forehead against the door and sigh. "Lana."

"Go away. I'm tired."

I can only imagine. After spending most of the day hosting Cami's party, I'm surprised she isn't asleep already.

My hand remains glued to the knob. "Can we please talk?"

"No."

"I'm begging you to give me a few minutes of your time."

Her groan comes out muffled due to the door between us. "I have nothing nice to say to you right now."

"Then tell me the not-so-nice things."

"Why?"

"Because I'd rather you get angry at me than shut me out. I don't think I could take that again." It seems impossible to go back to the way things were before. I'm not sure I would be able to live in the same house like that, knowing how good things could be between us if I had my shit together.

"You want to fight? Fine. Let's fight." She drags me inside and shuts the door.

I hold up my hands. "I knew it was wrong."

She crosses her arms. "Then why do it?"

My head drops. "Because I couldn't help it. Being around everyone…knowing what they probably think of me… It was too much all at once."

Her eyes shut as she takes a few deep breaths. "I can't take this up and down again, Cal. I just can't." Her voice cracks, matching the one that forms across my heart. "I can't make you want to get sober. And honestly, I don't want to be your reason for quitting alcohol in the first place. It didn't work the last time, and it's not going to this time because something like that needs to come from deep inside. And until it does, you will never get better. That much I know." She releases a heavy exhale. "I'm willing to support you through your journey to get sober—I always have been and I always will be—but only if you are willing to put in the hard work that it takes to find better ways to manage your feelings."

All the progress I've made with Lana up until this point slips through my fingers.

I swallow past the thick lump in my throat. "I can choose to be sober." I just need time. As much as I want to take Wyatt up on his offer to attend the local AA meetings, I can't do that until I go to rehab first. I've been through the process enough times to know what I need, and daily AA meetings aren't going to cut it right now.

Her lips lift into a small, reassuring smile that cuts me more than any of her words. "I know you can. I never stopped believing in you, even when you gave up on yourself."

I clutch her hands and tuck them against my pounding heart. "Please give me until we sell the house to get help. That's all I ask."

My hope deflates with a single shake of her head.

"Please." I press her palm against my cheek, drawing her eyes toward my pleading ones. "I want to be someone you can count on. I really fucking do, but I can't commit to going back to rehab until the house is sold." Desperation bleeds through my voice.

The process of combing through my past and working through my shit will knock me on my ass for weeks or maybe more, and I'm not ready for that kind of emotional pain until I meet my grandfather's deadline.

You mean the deadline for an inheritance that you haven't even told her about?

My stomach churns, guilt clawing its way up my throat.

You could tell her.

No, the voice of reason speaks up.

Telling Lana about my grandfather's will could risk everything, and I didn't go through all this trouble to prove I'm a failure yet again.

One day, I'll be able to tell her all about the inheritance, but today isn't that day—no matter how sick to my stomach I feel by withholding the truth.

Her gaze pins me in place. "Who cares about selling the house?"

"I do." My voice cracks.

Her lips purse with distaste.

You're losing her all over again.

"Why?" she asks.

"Because I made a commitment to selling it and I can't back down." My throat feels as if someone wrapped their hand around it and squeezed.

"A commitment to who?"

"Myself." I speak with absolute honesty.

"What?"

"You have lots of happy memories in that house, and while I do too, it's not enough to make me want to keep it. Not by a long shot."

She visibly swallows. "Why not?"

"Because it reminds me of some of the worst moments of my life. The mother I lost. The father who no longer exists. A grandfather who abandoned me when I needed him." I take a deep breath. "I don't think I could ever truly move forward with my life with that house still hanging over my head." The words I speak are completely true, yet they still feel like a lie.

You're doing this to protect your brothers and their futures.

If I'm doing the right thing, then why does it feel so shitty?

Her head shakes. "If you're serious about us, then you'd go and get help before this gets worse, regardless of needing to sell a house. I refuse to watch history repeat itself—for me and for my daughter."

"It won't anymore. I can promise you that."

"How am I supposed to trust you?"

As good a question as any, and one that makes my heart pound harder in my chest.

I clasp on to her chin. "Because I can't survive losing you again. Getting a glimpse of the life we could have if I changed is enough to convince me that I will never be happier than I am with you, even if I have a long way to go before we can move forward together. You asked if I'm willing to put in the work? I'm so fucking ready, I would sell the house tomorrow."

Different emotions flicker across her face.

Sadness. Uncertainty. *Resignation.* It's the last one that makes the acid rolling my stomach unbearable.

Lana takes a few deep breaths before peeking up from underneath her lashes. "Then do it."

My eyebrows tug together. "Do what?"

"Put the house on the market tomorrow before we leave for Dreamland."

My mouth drops open. *"Tomorrow?"*

"Is that a problem? You're the one who wants to sell it so you can move on with your life, so here's your chance. Contact the realtor first thing in the morning."

The tightness in my chest makes breathing a nearly impossible task. "I thought we agreed to remodel the house first."

What are you doing questioning her? Just agree and take your win where you can get it.

Her chin quivers. "Plenty of people put houses on the market while they are in the middle of construction. We can just have the realtor share the renovation mock-ups Ryder sent us, along with the blueprints."

Her plan is logical and foolproof, yet the look on her face has me questioning the whole thing.

If you tell her about the inheritance, you're not only letting your brothers down, but yourself too.

It's one thing to fail myself, but to risk everyone else's future, including Iris's, isn't worth it.

I release a pent-up breath. "I'll contact the realtor and the rehab facility early in the morning."

I'm not sure if leaving before the end of the summer is a possibility, but I will call Leo before to find out how or if that could affect the will.

Hopefully not. I've already spent a good portion of my summer here.

She blinks twice. "Are you sure that's what *you* want?"

I've never been more sure of anything. Getting sober was always the end goal, and Lana encouraged me to find a way to get there sooner.

"Yes. There is nothing *I* want more for myself than a future with you."

She bites down on her bottom lip. "It's not just me anymore. Cami and I are a package deal."

I wrap an arm around her waist and pull her flush against me. "You and Cami aren't a deal. You two are a lottery jackpot, and it's time someone treated you both that way."

stare at Cal, processing everything he said. I've never had anyone speak about Cami and me the way he does. His words make my eyes water, the tears from before threatening to come back with a vengeance.

You and Cami aren't a deal. You two are a lottery jackpot, and it's time someone treated you both that way.

My whole heart feels impossibly full and ready to burst. I want to believe what Cal says. That he will get better. But I can't deny the tiny shred of doubt worming its way through my happiness, threatening to poison it with my worries.

As if he senses my thoughts, Cal tucks his fingers under my chin and lifts my head. "I know you don't trust me. Not fully at least, and I don't blame you one bit. So, push me away. Get mad at me for drinking. Ice me out because you're afraid of letting me in again. Do whatever makes you feel safe, happy, and in control.

"But just know that whatever you do won't change the fact that I will keep fighting for us and the future I know we can have.

The one we *deserve* to have. Whatever you do won't stop me from getting help. Just like it won't stop me from wanting to be a part of Cami's life in whatever way I can, even if we aren't together. From—"

That's it.

Watching Cal love my kid to the point of wanting to stay in her life regardless of our relationship status is enough to snap the last bit of restraint I have.

I cut him off with a searing kiss. A kiss I pour all my feelings into. Excitement. Fear. *Adoration.*

Cal matches my desperation, his lips teasing me until I'm wild for more. A tingle spreads down my spine as he slides his fingers through my hair and tugs me closer. His lips press against mine and match my pace, turning my world upside down from all the different sensations overwhelming me.

Everything about our kiss is amplified as we reacquaint ourselves with what we like.

The brush of his tongue against mine, light and teasing.

My lips ripping away from his solely so I can pull his shirt over his head and run my hands down his chest.

His stubble scraping against my neck as he sucks on the sensitive skin below my ear, bruising it with the harsh pull of his mouth.

At one point, he lifts me up and carries me to the bed without breaking our kiss. I straddle his thighs and deepen it. One quick grind of my hips against his straining erection causes him to release the sweetest groan, and I soak it up, drowning the sound with my lips.

He only breaks contact for a moment to remove my sleep

shirt from over my head. His hands never stay in one place for too long. They glide over my body, teasing and touching until I'm grinding against his thick length in a frantic search for release.

Desperation for more of Cal makes me impatient. The combination of my body pressing against his and my random burst of strength throws him off-balance, and he falls backward, taking me with him.

Our lips break apart, and I pepper his jawline with soft, quick kisses.

"Lana," Cal moans.

I shift my attention to his neck. My lips trail down the curve, sucking and nipping at his skin until his fingers dig into my ass. The bite of pain is intoxicating. Thrilling. *Addictive.*

He threads his fingers into my hair and holds me in place.

"What?" I suck harder, marking his neck with the memory of me.

"Hold on a second." He tugs on the strands, pulling me away from his skin.

"Why?" I whine. "Do you want me to stop?"

He shudders beneath me. "Fuck no, but I want to make something clear."

"What?" My eyelids shut with a sigh.

He squeezes the back of my neck. "Are you sure you want to do this?"

I roll my body over his and press down hard against his thick length. "Does that clarify your question?"

"I want to hear it." He presses his hands into my ass, trapping me on top of his erection.

Heat pools in my lower belly. "Yes. We're doing this. But if you screw up—"

One moment, I'm on top, but in a single second, I find myself with my back pressed against the mattress and Cal looming above me, his gaze wild with hunger.

A hunger for me.

"Screwing up is inevitable, but I promise to make it up to you every single time." He tugs my underwear down my legs.

"How so?"

"Like this." He rips my thighs apart before trailing the sensitive flesh with light pecks. Slowly, he kisses his way toward the area begging for his attention, only to retreat. His mouth returns to my other thigh, repeating the same torture all over again.

I shimmy my body closer to his mouth, only to earn a low chuckle.

"I'm not about to rush this when I have six years to make up for, Lana."

"Make up for it later," I groan.

He traces a path from my clit to the place desperate to be filled. His tongue sinks inside, teasing, taunting, and testing how my body responds. Whenever I react a certain way, he repeats the same move before attempting something else.

My entire body feels like it is being engulfed in flames.

The world explodes around me as Cal amplifies the pressure building inside me with a few flicks of his tongue. I reach down, desperate for some kind of release. My attempt is cut off the moment I touch my clit. Cal slaps my pussy.

I gasp.

"What do you think you're doing?" He teases my clit with a quick flick of his tongue. It rolls over the sensitive bump, sending a pulsing wave of pleasure through me.

"Making myself come since you're not up for the task."

"The only one making you come is *me*." His eyes sparkle as he looks up at me, his stubble shining with my arousal. "Touch yourself again and I'll find a better way to keep your hands occupied."

His threat makes my toes curl and my heart pound. My body tightens, the urge to defy him driving me mad.

All it takes is one single pinch of my nipple to send him reeling.

Cal all but drags me off the bed and on to my knees. The carpet burns my skin, but the sting of pain is only temporary compared to the heat rolling through me as Cal pinches the same nipple I touched.

"Hands where I can see them," he orders.

I flip him off with both.

He chuckles. "You want to play?" He gives my other nipple the same attention, teasing the hard peak until my head drops back. "You want to get yourself off?"

"Yes." My fingernails dig into my thighs.

"That's too damn bad. You touch yourself when I say you can." He tugs his shorts down. The moon peeks through the blinds, illuminating every inch of him.

Every. Single. Hard. Inch.

Saliva pools in my mouth, the sheer size of him bringing all kinds of dirty thoughts to mind.

"Just like you come when I say you do." He fists his cock once, drawing a bead of pre-cum from the tip. "Open your mouth."

I do what he says. His cock slides against my tongue, the

taste of him overriding all my other senses. He pushes until my lungs burn and my eyes water.

"Breathe." He doesn't pull out. Doesn't so much as retreat a single inch, forcing me to breathe through my nose and fight the panic clawing at my chest.

He reaches out to cup my chin. "You look so pretty with your lips wrapped around my cock." His gaze slides from me to the antique mirror across from us. Our eyes catch each other's in the reflection, and he holds that connection as he withdraws.

Goose bumps break out across my skin, the sight of him thrusting his cock into my mouth nearly making my eyes roll.

"Look how good you take me." His hands latch on to my scalp as he plunges into my mouth over and over again, all while I watch in the mirror.

Everything about him entrances me.

The rise and fall of his chest with each powerful thrust.

His muscles rippling as he fucks my mouth, using me like his favorite toy.

The way he looks at me with affection despite the way he ravages my throat. Like our very souls are reconnecting again after being apart for years.

He pulls out all too soon, leaving a string of saliva connecting the head of his cock to my lips.

"Fuck. That's hot." He wipes the bead of pre-cum oozing from his tip and swipes it across my lips, branding the swollen flesh with his arousal.

My tongue darts out, teasing the pad of his thumb before swiping away at the salty release.

Cal throws me back on the bed before dragging my legs

toward the edge.

"Are you on the pill?" He dips a finger inside me before releasing a confirmatory noise.

I shake my head. "Shot."

"Condom?" He pumps his cock once, the sight of him seeking his own pleasure making my heart beat harder against my rib cage.

"I'd rather feel you come inside me."

He groans, making me feel like a queen. I wrap my legs around his waist and pull him closer. My heart pounds in my chest as he leans forward and lines himself up, his fingers gripping into my ass as he angles me higher.

There is no warning. No sweet words whispered in my ear. No easing me into the situation as he thrusts inside me in one single stroke, making my eyes water and my legs shake around him as I take all of him.

My back curves up to the ceiling as he seats himself to the hilt inside of me.

He leans forward, pressing his weight into me. "You know what you feel like?" There is a slight tremble to his voice.

I shake my head.

"You feel like home." He retreats, only to slam into me again. "Like I spent the last six years lost with no way of being able to return. As if I was stuck in an endless night with no light to help guide me back to you." He lifts me higher this time, changing his angle as he slides in slower this time, drawing out our pleasure.

My legs tighten around his body, tugging him forward until he hovers over me again.

Whatever control Cal had over the situation snaps as he

throws my legs over his shoulders and drives himself inside me with enough power to push me backward. I grasp the comforter and take his thrusts.

Pleasure builds, my orgasm slowly rising like the beginnings of a wave. I want to give in but the urge to hold out has me fighting back the pressure building in my lower belly. Cal takes my lack of orgasm as a challenge. His thrusts deepen, stealing my breath away with every single push.

When he catches me slipping backward, he pulls me back and wraps his fingers around my throat, holding me in place as he drives into me with abandon.

Shit. He fucks like a man on the brink of madness.

"Cal," I rasp.

"Say my name like that again." His hand around my neck tightens.

"Cal." I gasp as his cock brushes against the sensitive spot inside me. He repeats the same move, and my back arches as if pulled by a string.

My legs hanging over his shoulders tremble as I explode.

Cal doesn't stop thrusting until another orgasm builds inside of me. This time, he follows soon after me, his body shuddering from his release. His pumps become shallower, his movements jerkier as he rides his orgasm until the end.

He collapses against me, driving us both deeper into the mattress. I brush through the slick strands of his hair with my fingers.

He presses a chaste kiss against my skin. "I don't deserve you."

"Then become the man who does."

CHAPTER THIRTY-NINE

Cal

I run my hands through Lana's hair. She always loved when I would play with the strands until she fell asleep. My own eyes begin to droop, post-sex drowsiness trying to pull me under.

Time to go.

I'm not ready to leave, although I know I'm going to have to. It's inevitable with Cami in the house.

"I should go before I fall asleep." My fingers run down her back, tracing the goose bumps breaking out across her skin. She snuggles deeper into my chest and throws her leg over mine.

"I don't want you to leave," she grumbles against my skin.

I chuckle and drop a soft kiss on the top of her head, earning a sweet sigh from her. "I know, but I doubt you want to wake up in the morning to Cami asking you a hundred questions about us."

She flinches against me.

This is exactly why you need to leave.

Because no matter what has changed between us, Lana will always protect her daughter first, even if it means hiding what we are until she trusts me fully.

"It's not that I'm ashamed…" Her voice trails off.

"I get it." And with me leaving to rehab soon, it's probably for the best. I have every intention of coming back, but Cami won't understand.

She releases a heavy sigh. "She was so excited about Victor."

I wince and my hands remain frozen against her back.

Lana traces an invisible pattern against my chest. "I was careful at first and didn't have them meet until I was sure he and I were serious."

The only thing keeping me from slipping away is her soft touch teasing my skin and my growing curiosity at what happened.

"He pressured me into meeting her. That should have been the first sign of many that he wasn't a good match, but I felt so damn lonely and was scared of losing the one person who made me feel a fraction of what we had." Her voice cracks, and my arms tighten around her.

I release a heavy sigh.

It's only right you listen to every word since you're the one who drove her into this situation in the first place.

I'm an expert at self-inflicted torture, so I can handle one uncomfortable conversation.

"In the beginning, things were good. Cami was happy with him. Even asked me a few times if we were going to get married, although she stopped asking after the first time he babysat her." Her voice wavers.

I press her tighter against my chest. "You didn't know."

She peeks up at me with glassy eyes. "Shouldn't I have, though? She's my kid. I'm supposed to know every little thing about her, yet I couldn't even notice that."

"He was an asshole."

"I know that now, but I missed the signs. It wasn't until she timidly asked me if he would become her daddy that I finally started putting things together."

My lungs stall, and a hot spike of pain shoots through my chest. I don't speak in fear of my voice giving me away.

I wished you can be my new daddy.

Did she wish the same about Victor?

Lana continues, unaware of the shift in my mood. "When I questioned her about it, she told me she would rather not have a daddy at all. It was the first warning sign that I actually listened to. Because my girl is a romantic through and through, ever since she watched her first Dreamland princess movie. She even wrote letters to Santa asking for a daddy, only to be disappointed when her search under the tree came up empty."

A laugh explodes out of me, followed by relief.

She didn't want Victor to be her dad.

She wanted you.

It's terrifying yet empowering all at the same time.

A small smile teases Lana's lips. "One year I had to write a fake letter from Santa to let her know that he can only deliver toys, not people."

My chest shakes with silent laughter. "A shame."

"A shame indeed, until she took it up with the next best person."

"Who?"

"The Easter Bunny."

My head shakes. "She is the cutest kid ever."

She sinks into me, her body melting against mine. "I think so, but it's nice to hear it from someone unbiased."

I chuckle. "Oh, I was biased the day she hustled me out of six hundred bucks."

"You didn't stand a chance, did you?"

"Looks like Castillo women are my one weakness."

"Only the one?" She grins.

I kiss the stupid smile off her face. She reciprocates, matching my fire with one of her own. I'm not sure how I survived six years without this. Without *her*. The way I feel around Lana makes the whole world pale in comparison. Like I've been stuck living my life in black-and-white, only to have it switched to color.

I'm not sure I can go back to a life without her.

You won't have to.

So long as I commit to working on myself, I can have Lana forever.

Just like you were meant to.

I pour everything I feel into my kiss. Desire. Love. *Hope.*

Lana wraps her arms around me and tugs me closer. Everything about us feels right. Like two halves of a puzzle finally joined.

I'm desperate to keep the connection going for as long as I can. I tease, suck, and kiss every inch of her body until she is writhing beneath me, chanting my name with desperation.

It doesn't take long before I find my head between her thighs again, worshiping her body like I was always meant to. The combined taste of her and me is addicting, and I can't stop teasing her cunt until she comes on my tongue, rewarding me for my hard work.

Somehow, I end up beneath her with my back pressed against the headboard while she rides my cock.

Every gasp. Every moan. Every little sigh pushes us closer toward the edge.

I drag Lana down with me, teasing her clit until she comes around my dick. She doesn't stop moving until she comes down from her orgasm. Her body goes slack, and she falls against my chest with a content sigh.

My hands grip her hips as I lift her up and down my cock, desperate to find my own release. Her head rolls back, giving me the perfect opportunity to take one of her nipples into my mouth.

She quivers around me, taking every inch of me like she was meant to.

"Cal." She grips my hair and tugs, making my scalp prickle from the sensation.

"You like this?" I slam her against my dick, earning a gasp. "Driving me wild?"

She reaches between us and teases her clit.

Fuck. That's hot.

One of the things I love about Lana is that she has never been shy about seeking her own pleasure. Her finger accidentally grazes against my cock as I slide out of her, making me come so hard I nearly black out. Lana continues riding my cock, playing with her clit until she orgasms again.

Her small smile of triumph draws one of my own. It hits me then that Lana doesn't just feel like home—she feels like my everything.

I stay inside her for as long as I can, settling back into the mattress while holding her to my chest. Her breathing evens out eventually as she slips into unconsciousness, and I'm left grappling with the emotions she stirred up.

At some point, I drift off to the sound of her steady breathing.

I'll get up in a minute, I repeat to myself for the third time.

I lied.

"Mommy! Wake up! We're going to Dreamland today!" Cami bangs against the door.

Lana bolts upright, the sheet falling around her waist. "Oh my God! What are you still doing here?" she whisper-shouts.

"Fuck." I grab a pillow and cover my head. "I fell asleep."

"You need to hide!" She rips the pillow away from my hands and throws it toward the end of the bed.

"Mommy? Did you hear me?" Cami slams her palm a few more times.

"Coming! Why don't you go ahead and pick out your outfit for today."

"Okay!" Cami's voice sounds farther away when she answers.

Lana shoots me a look as she slides out of the bed, distracting me with her naked body as she darts around the room, collecting our clothes. She throws her shirt over her head before brushing her fingers through her wild waves.

"Get dressed." She throws my shorts at my chest.

"I'm going." I reluctantly climb out of bed.

Lana's eyes widen as she presses a hand against her mouth.

"What?" I look down at my erection. "This?" I give it a few pumps, earning a hiss from Lana.

"No. I—" Her eyes widen. "I'm so sorry."

"What's wrong?" I turn and look at my reflection in the mirror.

Damn.

Lana left some souvenirs of our time together. Besides the few hickeys marking my neck and chest, my skin is covered with faint scratches and a couple of bite marks.

I run my hand over one of the marks. "If you wanted to mark your territory, a tattoo might have been more effective in the long run."

"Shut up." She tosses my shirt directly at my smirk.

I pull her in for a quick kiss. Her lips mold to mine, and I run my hands down her body, tracing her curves before giving her ass a squeeze.

I pull away although I'd rather not. "You distract Cami and I'll sneak out."

She places a quick peck on my cheek. "Deal."

Fortunately, the real estate agent is able to drop by early Sunday afternoon. With us leaving to Dreamland tonight for Cami's birthday, I want to make sure everything with the lake house is settled while Wyatt and Delilah take Cami out for lunch.

The meeting with the agent goes smoothly, and he assures me that the house will be put on the market first thing tomorrow morning while we are in Florida.

I should be happy with that kind of news. Thrilled even. The sooner I sell the house, the more liberated I will feel. Hopefully, the heavy weight pressing against my chest that has been present since last night's conversation will lessen before disappearing altogether.

Lana stayed quiet, keeping to herself while we reviewed the logistics of the sale and our price tag. She only spoke up after the agent said goodbye and asked me to do one last walkthrough of the house by ourselves. She saves the kitchen for last, something I know is intentional given how much time she spends inside of it.

She opens the pantry door and frowns. "Hmm."

"What?" I peer over her shoulder.

"Just was wondering if they're going to paint over this or replace the door and the frame altogether."

"Probably replace it."

She makes an indiscernible noise.

"What?" I ask at the sight of her frown.

"It's a shame." She traces the different marks etched into the wooden frame—all written in her mother's handwriting. Five different initials in varying colors mark the entire side: RGK, DLK, CPK, AVC, and CTC. Rowan and Declan's heights were no longer recorded once they stopped visiting the lake house, while mine continues until my final six-four marking.

"You added Cami's height?" I squat down and trace over the first small pink mark at the bottom, which is barely two feet tall.

"Yeah. My mom thought it would be a fun idea." Lana looks

at it with a watery smile. "Cami couldn't even stand yet, but I held her up while my mom used the ruler to mark her spot."

"You miss her," I state.

"All the time." She looks around the kitchen. "Being here… it feels like I'm still connected to her. She spent a majority of her time in the kitchen, cooking, cleaning, *eating*. It was her favorite place in the whole house."

"And yours."

"Most definitely." Lana gives the kitchen counter a loving pat. "It's hard to believe that by tomorrow, all of this will be gone."

"Crazy, huh?" I lean against the counter beside her.

"If my mom were here, she would have been excited to say goodbye to the counters. She probably would have begged Ryder to let her take a sledgehammer to them herself."

I grin. "Really?"

"Oh yeah. She warned your grandpa against picking blue tile as a countertop, but he was very insistent. Mom said it wouldn't age well and she was right. Plus, she hated cleaning the grout all the time, and after being stuck doing the same, I completely agree." Lana's nose twitches with distaste.

"That was Brady for you. Stubborn as a mule and always thinking he knew best, even when he didn't."

She walks toward the window above the sink and looks out at the lake. "I still haven't wrapped my head around the fact that we're selling the house."

Neither have I. "Are you going to talk to Cami?"

Her fingers clutching on to the counter twitch. "After we come back from Dreamland."

"She will understand." I walk up behind her and place my

hands on top of hers.

"I hope so. I just…"

"What?"

"I'm scared to let go." Her voice cracks.

"Lana." I turn her face toward mine. Her gaze remains glued to the lake outside. "Look at me." The glassiness in her eyes guts me, and I'm questioning giving up on my grandfather's task altogether.

"We can call this off," I blurt out.

Are you…

A lovesick idiot? Absolutely. Sue me.

If you don't, your brothers will.

I shove the thoughts of Rowan and Declan out of my head.

Her eyes shut. When they open again, the watery sheen is gone. "No."

"Are you sure?"

Her fingers interlace with mine, banishing the cold dread spreading through my veins. "I want you to be happy."

My lips press together. I feel like the biggest dick on the planet for keeping the truth from her.

You don't have a choice.

Well, I wish I did. My grandpa's will makes me feel helpless. Dirty. *Dishonest.*

"We can start somewhere new." She sighs. Her use of the word *we* draws a sharp breath from me and latches on to my heart, breaking through the scar tissue.

I give her hand a reassuring squeeze. "I'd like that."

While Lana and Cami pack for the trip, I sit inside my car with my phone pressed to my ear.

"Callahan Kane. To what do I owe the pleasure of this call?" The easygoing tone of my grandfather's lawyer's voice draws a small smile from me.

"I have a question for you."

"What is it?"

"When my grandfather asked me to stay the whole summer at Lake Wisteria, was he specific about how long?"

"I don't recall off the top of my head. Would you like me to check the will?"

"Yes, please."

"Give me a moment." Papers rustle and Leo breathes heavily into the microphone, his confirmatory noise only adding to the growing tension in my shoulders.

"One hundred and twenty days."

Shit.

"Is there any way of getting around that?" My molars smash together.

He only grumbles to himself.

That can't be good.

"What's the rush?" he asks. "You only have a month left."

"I need to check myself into rehab next week."

"Rehab?" His voice perks up. It's a strange way to react to someone who clearly has an issue with alcohol, but Leo was always a weird guy. That's why he and my grandfather got along so damn well.

"Yes. I have a place lined up in Arizona, but the will is holding me back from going."

More papers shift in the background. "I see."

"Well, I can't, so do you mind sharing?" I shut my eyes and take a deep breath to calm my fraying nerves. Without any alcohol to take the edge off this conversation, I'm stuck facing my anxiety head-on.

Lovely.

"Your grandfather was willing to adjust the time period on one condition."

"Let me guess: If I go to rehab."

He laughs. "No."

My shoulders slump. "Then what? Does he want me to take a breathalyzer test every day for the next however many days? Or maybe he wants me to be homebound with a babysitter?"

"Nothing quite that severe. All he said was the required four months at Lake Wisteria could be null and void if you earn a green chip."

"A green chip?"

"From AA."

My lips press together as I consider my two other times attending Alcoholics Anonymous. Green was a color I achieved yet lost not long after.

My grip around the phone tightens. "And you didn't think to tell me this before I moved in?"

"I wasn't at liberty to say unless you came to me first regarding sobriety. Your grandfather emphasized the importance of you making this choice on your own, so he didn't want you to feel enticed to get sober for an inheritance."

I close my eyes to stop the world from spinning around me.

Leo clears his throat. "Your grandfather already chose an AA program for you as well."

My laugh comes out forced. "Of course he did."

The motherfucker set me up.

My grandfather had to have known that if I came back here, it would only be a matter of time before I would want to get sober again.

"Will you please send me the information so I can take a look?" I ask.

"Of course. I'll have my assistant send you that and the phone number for the person to contact. From what I've heard, it's a small group for those who require discretion."

Fantastic. Can't wait to spend my AA meetings with a bunch of rich snobs who can't get their shit together despite having access to everything.

"Sell the house and get me that green chip so we can get the rest of the inheritance squared away." He speaks with a light and airy tone, as if getting sober is a simple task.

No big deal. My teeth grind together. "Right. Thanks, Leo." My finger hovers over the red end call button, but Leo's voice stops me.

"Just know that your grandfather would be really proud of you. Every choice he made up until his accident was meticulously thought out."

"Even selling the house?"

"Especially that. For you and Ms. Castillo."

CHAPTER FORTY
Alana

Thanks to the Kane brothers' family jet and Cal's connections, Cami and I are leaving Michigan for the first time since I brought her home with me almost six years ago. The whole adoption process feels like it happened a lifetime ago. When I met Cami for the first time in the NICU while she was being weaned off drugs, I was barely twenty-four years old and was still nursing a huge heartbreak.

The social worker assigned to her case gave me the easiest choice of my life when I arrived in California.

Adopt Cami or let someone else do so.

Best decision ever, I say to myself as I check out Cami. She has her cat-ear headphones on while she watches an episode of her favorite show on the flat screen embedded into the wall of the jet. I tried to sit next to her, but she wanted the couch all to herself because my girl is a cushion hog, so Cal and I settle into the captain's seats diagonal to hers.

The flight attendant passes Cami a juice box before placing

our waters on the table in front of us. I place my wireless earbuds in my ears only to have Cal steal one.

"I forgot mine." His fingers lock with mine, sending a blast of warmth up my arm.

"Are you going to play something or should I?" He motions toward my phone on the table.

I hit play and settle into the chair. Cal flips my hand over and starts to run the tips of his fingers across the inner part of my arm.

"Cosquillas?" I gasp.

His lips form into the sweetest smile. "Some things never change."

My lips purse like I sucked on something sour. "I've changed."

He raises a brow. "How?"

I pause the music to answer him. "Well, for starters, I like country music now."

"Talk about a metamorphosis," he replies dryly.

I give his shoulder a shove.

He only laughs as he latches on to my hand again. "What else?"

"I went full vegetarian for a year after watching a documentary."

His eyes stretch wide. "Was your mother alive at the time?"

"Yes. She was completely horrified by the idea and unofficially revoked my Colombian citizenship."

He chuckles under his breath. "That sounds just like her. That woman loved her churrasco more than anything."

"I know. Why do you think I started eating meat again? She didn't give me much of a choice."

His smile widens.

"Also, I'm now a morning person. No more snoozing and skipping alarms for me."

"Shame. I used to love finding new ways to motivate you to get out of bed." He smirks.

My eyes roll. "More like you found ways to keep me *in* bed for as long as humanly possible."

"It was a noble effort."

"The only thing noble about you was your commitment to making me come first."

"It's an obsession, not a commitment."

We both laugh. I continue telling him about the different things that changed for me, which in reality aren't many once I list them. The most life-altering event was becoming a mother, and Cal already knows all about that.

"What about you? Anything changed?" I nudge him with my shoulder.

"My life is pretty uneventful." He sighs.

"That's not true. You're a cat dad."

"Right. The pinnacle of my life right there."

"No job?"

"Nope." He taps his fingers against his thigh in a random pattern.

"Come on. Something has to have changed in six years."

"I'm no longer afraid of clowns."

"What?" I gasp. "Since when?"

"Since Iris convinced me to go to a haunted Halloween maze. Turns out the theme that year was—"

"Clowns?" My pitch rises.

"I should have known she was setting me up the moment she asked me to go with her. I don't do horror, but for her, I was willing to put on a brave face and try. Plus, Declan seemed pissed when she talked about us going out together."

"Why didn't you turn around and leave when you found out the theme?"

"Because Iris blackmailed me."

"How?"

"She threatened to release this video if I ditched her." Cal pulls out his phone and plays a video of him using an umbrella as a weapon against a creepy clown.

"I think I love her." I wipe the tears from my eyes after the minute-long video finishes with Cal shrieking.

"I'm positive you two will become instant best friends the moment you meet."

My chest warms. "I can't wait to share the photo I have of you at your fifth birthday party."

His eyes bulge. "Tell me you didn't save that."

I grin. "Of course I did. It always makes the bad days better."

His hand holding on to mine tightens. "I have one of those too."

My cheeks heat. "Please don't say it's the one of me trying on makeup for the first time."

His eyes spark. "No, although that one is a classic."

I scratch my head. "I thought I got rid of all my mom's incriminating photos."

He shrugs. "Maybe you didn't."

I shake his shoulders. "You need to tell me which one." I will not rest until I know which embarrassing photo Cal keeps of me for the bad days.

"Relax. I was just joking. I swear it's not bad."

"Like I should believe you," I scoff.

His eyes roll as he pulls a photo out of his wallet and tosses it on my lap. "Consider this our first test in trusting one another."

My hands shake as I lift the photo Cal saved in *his wallet*.

"Is this…" I flip the photo, answering my question for me.

Get drunk on life, not alcohol.

Love,

Lana

"You saved it." I turn it over again and stare at the younger versions of us. The photo has lightened with age and light exposure, and the edges have worn over the years. "This is what you look at on the bad days?"

He swipes the photo from my hands and tucks it back inside his wallet. "Yup."

"Of all the photos, why this one?" My voice shakes.

"Because it reminds me that there was once a time when I was truly happy."

I wrap my arms around his neck and pull him into a hug. "I want you to be truly happy again."

His arms tighten around me. "I'm getting there."

The private car drops us off at the fanciest hotel Dreamland has to offer. Cal takes us up to a penthouse suite with its own private elevator, chef's kitchen, movie theater room, and a perfect view of the lake that makes up a large part of the Kane Company property.

"This is so cool!" Cami gets lost somewhere between the dining area and the chef's kitchen.

Never in my life have I stayed somewhere quite like this.

Rowan, Cal's brother who I haven't seen since he was wearing braces and freaking out over comic books, left a note about the all-access VIP passes.

Food. Drinks. Behind-the-scenes exclusive experiences.

I've spent my whole life around the Kanes' wealth, but this is the first real time I'm able to enjoy it myself. Since Cal said to spare no expense, I call room service and order three expensive steaks and an overly priced bottle of orange juice for Cami.

I have a Michelin star taste on a Betty Crocker budget, so I might as well enjoy the finer things in life while they last.

When in Dreamland…

A loud foghorn snags Cami's attention. She runs back to the sliding door and presses her face against the glass, making it fog from her hot breath.

"Look! A boat!" Cami points at a ferry pulling into the dock to drop off the families.

I kneel beside her. "I see that."

"We can take the ferry tomorrow if you want." Cal kneels on the other side of Cami.

"Really?" Her eyes go big with wonder.

"For sure. Whatever you want." He rubs the top of her already-messy hair.

This is the reason I'm willing to wait for Cal. Because love like that—the unconditional kind that comes straight from the heart—isn't easy to find. I would know after searching for it and failing miserably since he left.

"Thank you!" Cami throws herself into Cal's arms.

Cal blinks twice at my smile before returning my grin with one of his own. Before I know it, he is swooping me into his arms too, smushing me against Cami. The added weight throws him off-balance and the three of us crash against the carpet, with him taking the brunt of the weight. Cami giggling between us makes both Cal and me both laugh too.

Cami wiggles free and takes off to claim her bedroom. Cal's arms remain wrapped around me and adjust my weight so I lie on top of him. I suck in a breath as his hand runs down my spine, leaving sparks behind.

His hand pauses on the small of my back. "I want to make the two of you laugh like that for the rest of our lives."

A tingle spreads through me, starting at my cheeks and heading toward my toes. He cups my cheek and drags me closer to his face.

"Cal…" I warn. "What about Cami?"

The squeak of a mattress and the steady thump of someone jumping makes him smile.

"I think she's a bit busy at the moment." His thumb brushes my bottom lip.

"Still."

He removes his hand, taking his warmth with him. "I dare you to kiss me."

I blink. "What?"

"You heard me. Either kiss me or be forced into giving up a secret." The low rumble of his voice makes my lower belly clench.

"That's not fair." My voice cracks. Dares have always been a weakness of mine, right after the man who instigated them in the first place.

He tugs my chin closer. "Truth or dare? Choose carefully."

I bite down on my lip. "I've got a lot of dares to make up for. Fifteen, to be exact, according to my last tally count." The piece of wood on the dock might be long gone, but the memory lives on in my head.

"At this rate you'll never catch up to me."

"Only because you're a daredevil."

He grins. "And you're a coward."

Coward? I'll show him.

I rise to Cal's challenge and kiss him. Our lips mold together, the zap of energy sparking between us. He sucks in a breath as I trace the curve of his bottom lip with the tip of my tongue. The sound travels straight toward my clit.

My entire body is overwhelmed by the taste and smell of him, turning the experience into sensory overload. I try to place what the feeling in my chest is, but Cal doesn't let me get distracted for long as he cups the back of my neck.

Control slips from my grasp as Cal dominates. The world I know shifts as Cal becomes my center of gravity, grounding me to *him*.

"Mommy and Cal, sitting in a tree. K-I-S-S-I-N-G."

Cal and I break apart. Both our eyes are wide as we take each other in. His lips are as swollen as his dick pressing against my stomach.

"First comes love. Then comes marriage. Then comes Cami in a Dreamland carriage!" She throws herself on top of me, squishing me against Cal's chest.

So much for not getting caught.

"Are you and Cal getting married?"

The comb I was using to brush Cami's wet hair slips out of my hand. "Umm."

"Can I have a sister?" Her smile expands until it takes over half her face.

Shit. Shit. Shit. I knew Cami would have questions, but things are escalating far too fast for me to keep up with.

I reach for the comb and place it on top of Cami's king-sized mattress. "Cal and I aren't getting married." My tongue suddenly feels heavy.

"Why not?"

"Because not everyone who likes each other gets married." And because I have no idea if we will ever get to a place where that is even remotely possible.

Don't be so negative.

Hard not to be when pessimism is practically a default setting for me on some days.

"So, you *do* like him?" She punctuates her question with a few air kisses, making me laugh.

"Of course."

"Me too." She grins.

"You do?" Her answer doesn't surprise me, but it's nice to get confirmation, especially after everything that happened with Victor.

"Yes. He's nicer than Victor. He listens to me and likes to ask me questions and doesn't make me feel like I bother him." The confession rushes out of her.

I try my hardest to keep my emotions in check. It's nearly impossible, especially with Cami bringing up Victor. It's my fault she was ever put in a situation where a man would treat her as anything less than a princess.

Never again.

I tuck a strand of wet hair behind her ear. "I think he's a lot nicer than Victor too."

"*And* he makes you laugh and smile."

My brows rise. "I've always laughed and smiled."

"Yeah, but you do it a lot more now."

I'm at a loss for words. It's such a simple observation on Cami's part, but it is one that makes my entire chest ache.

Cami pops the bubble of emotion building in my chest with a random question, proving that six-year-old kids truly have the attention span of a puppy.

"Can I have a bedtime story now?"

I go along with Cami's request, although her comment sticks with me long after she falls asleep.

Cal found his way into my bed while I was busy with Cami. I crawl under the sheets and snuggle against him, although I'm completely ignored as he continues reading his book. His look of concentration draws a soft chuckle from me.

He makes you laugh and smile.

Cal makes me do a lot more than that. He makes me want to have fun, enjoy life, and dream in a way I have long since forgotten over the years. Even with the odds stacked against us, he makes me want to believe we can work out.

But most of all, he makes me want to trust him. To fall in love once again.

With him.

CHAPTER FORTY-ONE

Cal

Sun rays peek through the sides of the blackout curtains, basking Lana in an early morning glow. If I could, I would spend the whole morning here with her. Sneaking out of the bedroom before Cami wakes up is pure torture. Like every cell in my body is protesting against moving, making each step away from her impossible.

"I should go before Cami wakes up." Even though Cami caught us kissing, we don't want her to assume anything else is going on. I look forward to the day that I don't have to sneak around my own place, hiding my feelings because of a six-year-old kid.

Lana's only reply is to burrow deeper into my chest.

I try to untangle her limbs from mine, but she holds on.

"What if we told her?" she mumbles against my chest.

"Told her what?"

"That we're dating."

I pause. "Is that what you want?"

"She's starting to ask me questions anyway."

"Like what?"

"She wanted to know when she is going to get a baby sister."

I choke on my inhale. "What?"

She peeks up at me. "Do you not want kids?"

"Of course I do." Spending time around Cami made me realize just how fun children can be.

"Are you sure? You're going to have to invest in a lot more swear jars." A smile tugs at her lips.

"I better stock up on some hundreds then."

She smiles in a way that not only reaches her eyes but her *soul*.

I can't resist kissing her in that moment. To steal a little bit of that happiness for myself.

"Mommy!"

One second, I'm lying flat on the bed. The next, Lana shoves me off the mattress with an inhuman amount of strength that I never thought she possessed.

I land on the floor with an oomph. "Fuck."

She peeks over the edge with wide eyes. "Oh my God. Are you okay? I'm so sorry!"

I lift my hand and give her a thumbs-up.

The knob rattles before Cami comes barreling in. "Morning!"

Lana intercepts her before she catches me hiding. "Whoa there. Look at your hair! Let's go do something about it before breakfast."

The door shuts behind them with a soft click, leaving me alone, wondering how the hell I'm going to survive sneaking around for much longer.

Outside of visiting Rowan's house at the back of the Dreamland property for a company Christmas party, I have pretty much avoided the park since my mother passed, so Cami's first experience at the park might as well be mine too.

Our first stop is at the Magic Wand Salon. Beauty chairs and fancy vanity mirrors make up one side of the salon while the other half is an entire store designed like a princess's closet. Hundreds of girls sift through the racks, riffling through ballgown dresses and accessories fit for royalty.

Cami takes off toward the shop, leaving Lana and me behind with Rowan and Zahra. Compared to my brother's plain navy suit, Zahra wears a bright yellow dress that complements the brown tones of her skin and hair.

"Cal!" Zahra throws her arms around me.

Lana looks at the two of us with raised brows.

I clear my throat. "Hey. Long time no see."

"Iris and I have missed you at the last couple of brunches. This one is a complete bore." She nods in Rowan's direction. Rowan glares at her, which only makes Zahra beam.

"Is this Alana?" Zahra's brown eyes glitter as she checks out Lana.

I introduce the two of them.

Zahra pulls Lana into a hug. "I've heard so much about you."

"You have?"

Zahra pulls away. "Oh, yeah. Get a few mimosas in Cal's system and he won't stop talking about you."

My cheeks heat. Lana stiffens, the muscles in her back going rigid.

"Mimosas?" She glances up at me, a storm brewing behind her eyes.

"I'm not sure there will be many more mimosas in my future." I offer Zahra a tight smile.

Rowan, sensing the need for a topic change, thank God, offers his hand to Lana. "Nice to see you again after all this time."

She shakes it with a wrinkled nose. "Ugh. Still stuffy as ever, Galahad."

Zahra's wide eyes bounce between Lana and my brother. "She knows your middle name?"

"Oh, I know a lot more than that." Lana laughs.

Rowan *blushes*, and it's quite the sight. I wish I got it on camera solely for future entertainment purposes.

Zahra leans forward. "I'd love nothing more than to pick your brain and learn all about baby Rowan."

My brother shoots me a look. "Tell your girlfriend I can revoke those VIP passes as quickly as I handed them out."

"I'm standing right here, so feel free to tell me yourself." Lana waves with a small smile.

Damn. Getting turned on by Lana putting my brother in his place is a new level of fucked up, and I'm dying for more of it. Even Rowan's eyes glitter at her comment. If there is anything my brother respects more than submission, it's those willing to stand up to him when he is wrong.

"Iris is totally going to love you." Zahra wags her finger at Lana before breaking out into a laugh.

"Look what I found!" Cami rushes back over to us, balancing two different tiaras on her head, holding three princess dresses in her arms, and wearing two different plastic heels on her feet.

"You can only pick one outfit." Lana plucks the dresses out of her hands and holds them up for her to choose.

I'm quick to steal them out of Lana's hands and pass them over to Zahra, who is going to do Cami's makeover. "We'll take them all. Have the store send everything Cami wants up to our room."

Lana shoots me a look. "You're spoiling her."

"And I'm loving every second of it." My smile widens.

She rolls her eyes. "You can't buy her everything she wants."

"Why not?" Cami grins as she not-so-sneakily adds a third pair of costume heels to the growing pile in Zahra's arm.

"*Camila.*" Lana puts her hands on her hips.

"*Mommy.*" Cami matches her mother's stance, earning laughs from everyone but Lana.

Cami catches something out of the corner of her eye and takes off toward the costume jewelry area, dragging Zahra behind her. Rowan busies himself behind the check-in desk, leaving Lana and me alone.

Lana lets out a long sigh as she watches Cami from across the room.

I wrap my arms around her from behind and tug her body against mine. "I plan on spoiling you just as much later," I whisper in her ear. "All night long if you want me to."

She shivers. "Is that a promise?"

"Depends on if you're going to let me treat Cami to whatever she wants today."

She pouts. "You're not fighting fair."

"I'd rather not fight at all." I tuck her hair behind her ear before brushing my fingers down the slope of her neck. "Especially when I could fuck you instead." I kiss the sensitive spot below her ear before letting her go.

We only have a minute to spare before Cami and Zahra come back to drag Lana away. She gives me one last look over her shoulder before Zahra tugs her in the direction of the beauty salon, leaving me standing all by myself.

Lana lifts Cami into one of the chairs while Zahra holds up the different dresses against Cami's torso. I laugh at the two extra ones the sneaky girl added to the selection.

Rowan walks up next to me. "So, you're dating each other again?"

"Yes."

His cheek hollows from how hard he gnaws on it.

I give him a once-over. "Spit it out."

He releases a heavy breath. "I'm worried about you."

My head tilts. "Why?"

"I know she's the reason you went back to drinking the last time."

My muscles turn to stone beneath my shirt. "I'm not going to fault her for my issues, and you shouldn't either. If I chose to relapse, it's on me, not her."

"I don't fault her, but I can't help being worried either way about the two of you potentially getting back together. You were never the same after you went back to Lake Wisteria two years ago."

My hands tighten into fists. I never spoke about going there in the first place, so Rowan had to find out from someone. "Who told you?"

His eyes dart toward the salon chair where Zahra stands behind Cami, curling her hair. "Declan."

"He knew?"

His Adam's apple bobs from his thick swallow. "You know how he is."

"An overprotective ass with no concept of privacy?"

"It comes from a good place."

"Does it? Because it feels pretty damn invasive and oppressive from my point of view." All my life, Declan has done the same thing.

He sighs. "At the time, Declan was desperate to figure out what was wrong because he wanted to fix it for you."

I scoff.

"Why do you think he had a buyer set up to purchase the house?" Rowan's question comes out of nowhere.

"Because he didn't believe that I could sell the lake house."

"No. He wanted to save you from any pain you would experience by having to go back to Lake Wisteria after the last time. It was his way of trying to *help* you."

My lips part.

"It's the same reason he threatened the trust Mom left you and forced you into rehab the first time." Rowan shakes his head with a sigh. "If you stopped for a second to ask him why he does things, rather than assume the worst about him, you'd both spend a lot less time fighting."

"He's still an asshole who says stupid shit."

"Of course he is. But I also know he is working on apologizing, which he never used to do before he married Iris. So maybe you should give him a chance to learn from his mistakes instead of ignoring him out of spite."

I take a deep breath. "He told you something?"

"Not in so many words. You know Declan isn't the type to open up and gush about his feelings."

Damn. He must be really affected if he talked to Rowan of all people.

I sigh. "Fine. I'll give him a call after this weekend."

Rowan winces. "About that…"

Fuck. Rowan was the suckiest secret keeper, right after Lana.

"You told him I was here, didn't you?"

"Surprise?"

My eyes roll. "When is he coming?"

"Tomorrow night. Zahra and Iris are planning an early birthday dinner for you."

Shit.

Cami walks out of the Magic Wand Salon with a contagious smile on her face. She looks adorable with her glittered-covered blond curls and her purple princess dress, with the shiny material shifting colors depending on how much sunlight peeks through the clouds.

"Thank you from both of us." Lana plants a kiss on my cheek before taking off after Cami, who wobbles toward the castle in her plastic heels.

"Will they be joining us for dinner tomorrow?" Rowan tips his chin in their direction.

The three of us.

I really like the sound of that.

"I need to check with Alana and see how she feels first. She might not be up for something like that." Not that I would blame her. My family is a bit much, especially when we are all together.

"Shoot us a text either way," Rowan says before he and Zahra walk away.

It's easy to find Cami and Lana in the crowd with how the rhinestones on Cami's tiara glitter under the bright sun. Her plastic heels click and clack against the cobbled road leading up to Princess Cara's castle. Lana clutches Cami's sneakers in her other hand, ready to replace the heels once Cami's feet hurt.

I pull out my phone and snap a photo of Cami and Lana holding hands before walking up to them. Cami doesn't hesitate as she grabs on to mine, and the three of us take off to the first activity I have planned.

In the middle of the park, hidden away within the rose bushes and tall hedges, is a small table occupied by none other than Princess Marianna herself. While her dress is the same shade and style as Cami's, her hair is similar to Lana's dark strands.

Even when next to the Dreamland princess herself, my girl looks like a million bucks, especially with the smile on her face.

My girl.

The term never sounded more right than in this moment.

The shriek-squeal combination Cami lets out quickly becomes my new favorite sound.

Lana blinks, rubs her eyes, and then blinks again. "Tell me

you didn't."

"Okay, I won't."

A few servers come out in costumes, carrying trays with teacups and snacks. Cami claps her hands and bounces in her chair while Princess Marianna whispers something in her ear.

Lana shakes her head. "I'm never going to be able to top this birthday."

I grab her hand and spin her in a circle, making her laugh. "Sounds like a fun challenge to me."

"What's next? A trip to Africa to see wild animals?"

"That can be arranged. I helped Iris plan her honeymoon there, so I know all the good spots."

She wipes the disbelief off her face. "This isn't real life."

I tug her against my chest. "It can be if you let me take care of you two."

She shoots me a smile that rivals all the beauty surrounding us. "Get sober and I'll let you."

always knew bringing Cami to Dreamland would be magical, but the reality is so much more than that. Everything about the park excites her. The castle. The food. The characters dressed up in the costumes that used to make me cry as a kid. She soaks up everything, and her happiness is a living, breathing entity that I find extremely contagious.

I couldn't have imagined a better day. At least I hadn't until Cal lifts Cami up on to his shoulders so she can get a better look at the evening show happening in front of the castle.

I never stood a chance at surviving this trip without falling in love with Cal. It was a valiant effort on my part to even think otherwise, but I'm no match for the *girl dad* energy he is giving off. A few women around us seem to take notice, although I shoot daggers in their direction until they turn away, flustered and somewhat disturbed.

I've been perfecting the look since everyone in my age range started lusting after Cal when we were teens. It's not pretty, but it gets the job done.

I smile as I snap a photo of Cami and Cal from behind so I can print it out and store it in my memory box.

Cal glances over his shoulder at me. "What are you doing?"

I motion toward him and Cami. "Saving the memory."

Something flashes in Cal's eyes before he grabs the person next to him.

"Do you mind taking a photo of my girls and me?"

His girls.

They might have to airlift me out of here, because I'm about ready to go into cardiac arrest. With the way my left arm tingles and my heart pounds, I wouldn't doubt it.

Cami remains on Cal's shoulders, her smile bright and ready while I stand, stunned and blinking rapidly. Cal shakes his head with a smile before tugging me against him and wrapping an arm around my front while keeping Cami secured with the other one.

The man holds up the phone and begins his countdown. A firework explodes above us. Cami and I both look up at the same time as the flash goes off, ruining our photo.

The man practically throws Cal's phone at him before returning to his family.

"More!" Cami claps her hands.

"They're coming," Cal says.

Fireworks erupt above us, painting the sky in different colors. Cal keeps his arm wrapped around me during the entire show. At some point during the explosions above, Cami falls asleep.

"How is that even possible?" He removes her from his shoulders before cradling her against his chest.

My legs might give out from how hard I swoon. "I told you

she can sleep through anything."

Another firework explodes above us, proving my point as Cami doesn't even flinch.

"See?"

"Damn. Do you want to head back?" His eyes slide from Cami to me.

I look up at the sky, taking in a few more seconds of the show before nodding. When I turn, Cal's gaze is already fixed on me, although it burns with promise as he follows the curves of my body.

Between Cal showering Cami with love and attention, and his soft whispers when no one is around, I'm more than ready to head back.

Fireworks be damned.

I shut the door to Cami's room behind me before sagging against it. There isn't a single part of my body that doesn't ache from walking around the park all day, and no amount of working out would have prepared me for that kind of soreness.

"She went back to sleep easily?" Cal sits up on the couch.

"Yup. Out like a light." I hated waking Cami up after she knocked out, but I refused to let her go to bed covered in theme park germs and butterfly face paint.

"It's impressive how she can sleep through fireworks, a screaming baby on the ferry, and the entire walk up to the room."

"If only the rest of us could be that lucky." I fall face-first into the cushions of the couch across from the one Cal sits on.

He lets out a low laugh. "Tired?"

"My whole body hurts from head to toe." My voice is muffled by the cushions pressing against my face.

The couch creaks under him. "I think I have an idea."

"If it's not a full-body massage, I don't want it."

"That can easily be arranged, so long as you return the favor." He lowers his voice. "Preferably without clothes on."

I blindly launch a throw pillow in the direction of his laugh.

The door to his room clicks shut soon after. I nod off for a bit before I'm woken by Cal coming back to lift me into his arms like a bride. I'm too tired to object, and honestly, I doubt I would either way. It feels good to be on the receiving end of being spoiled after spending all day on my feet.

He carries me into his bathroom and sets me on my feet. The sound of water rushing out of the tap drags my eyes away from his face.

"A bubble bath?" The deep tub is almost filled to the top with bubbles nearly spilling out of it.

He reaches over to shut off the tap. "I added some bath salts to help with your sore muscles."

I drop my head back with sigh. "I love you." The thought slips out by accident, and my eyes fly open. "I..." I can't finish the rest of my sentence. It's not that I don't love Cal, but I don't want to give that love away so freely again. Not without being able to trust that he won't shatter my heart for a second time around.

"Don't worry about it." He offers me a tight smile.

"But—"

Cal shuts me up with a hard kiss that puts our awkward conversation to an end. I deepen it, earning the sweetest groan against my lips.

My hands find the hem of Cal's shirt, and I lift the material over his head. He breaks apart from our kiss and does the same with my shirt, both of them landing on the floor. The pile quickly grows as we ditch our shorts and underwear.

"I don't know where to start with you." His gaze runs down my naked body.

"I have a few ideas if you need inspiration."

His eyes darken. "Like what?"

"A bath for starters."

His short laugh makes me smile. "Not what I was going for, but fine."

He helps me into the bath first before settling in on the opposite side of me.

"Afraid to sit next to me?" I flick water at him with my toes.

He latches on to my foot and tugs me closer, making me sink deeper into the water. I open my mouth to object, only to be cut off as he begins kneading the sore muscles.

My head drops back against the tub. "Oh, God."

His pressure intensifies. "Feels good?"

"Like heaven." I sigh.

A small smile tugs at his lips. My eyes droop with each minute that goes by, the ache in my muscles easing with every pass and push of Cal's hands. Eventually, the pain morphs into something else altogether.

Pleasure.

Cal must sense the shift in mood because he abandons his massage and stands. Water droplets slide down his muscular body, tempting me to wipe them away with my tongue. His thick erection stands as proud as him when he finds me checking him out.

I give my head a shake. "Where are you going?"

"Nowhere without you. Scoot forward."

I do what he says, and he slides in behind me. His hard length presses against my back as he gets comfortable and places both his legs on the outside of mine.

I sink deeper into the bubble water and place my head in the crook of his neck. "I might never leave."

Cal grabs a wet towel and squeezes a decent amount of bodywash on to the top before swiping it down my body. He takes his time, dragging the washcloth across my skin with soft, teasing strokes. I press my thighs together only to have Cal pry them apart so he can swipe the towel between my legs.

I squeeze his bicep. "Cal."

He teases my clit again, adding more pressure this time. "What?"

"You know what you're doing." The words come out shaky.

He nips at my shoulder, earning a sharp intake of breath from me. "Is it working?"

I turn around and straddle his thighs, trapping him beneath me. His erection presses into me, and I grind against him, sending a zing of pleasure down my spine. "Does that answer your question?"

His fingers dig into my hips as I lean forward and lick a stray water droplet from his neck.

"Lana." The way he whispers my name like a prayer goes straight to my head. His teeth grit together as I rub against his erection, so I wiggle again, earning another grunt.

He grips my thighs hard enough to leave marks. "Unless you want to end up getting fucked against the side of the tub, I'd stop."

"Hmm. A tempting idea." I run the tips of my fingers up his cock before gripping him tightly and giving him a single pump.

He snags my hand and drags it toward his mouth. The kiss he places on the inside of my palm is innocent, although the throbbing between my legs isn't. I push forward and rub my pussy against his cock to relieve the building ache.

I kiss a path from his sharp jawline to the base of his throat. His breathing shallows out with each pass of my lips over his skin, his fingers digging into my skin like a lifeline. My lips suck on the spot beneath his ear that drives him wild while my fingers dance across his chest, carefully brushing down toward his navel without actually touching his nipples.

He moans my name again, sending another wave of pleasure rolling through my body. "What the fuck are you doing to me?"

"Having fun." I tease his chest again. The tip of my fingernail catches on his nipple, and he sucks in a breath.

"This isn't fun. *It's torture.*"

"It's only fair when you do the same thing." I lean forward, my tongue just barely swiping over the hard disk when something breaks inside of him.

"Good idea," he rasps as he grabs my hair and tugs. My back arches, giving him the perfect position to tease the very area I denied him. His tongue swipes over the pointed peak, teasing and torturing me until I force him to give my other breast the same attention.

He sucks hard enough to make me gasp, and I jolt in his lap.

"You want to tease me?" His teeth scrape over the sensitive spot, and black dots fill my vision as a wave of pleasure rushes through me. "You want to fuck with me?"

"I'd rather fuck you. Period. End of story," I hiss between gritted teeth as he tugs on my nipple.

Cal releases me before he climbs out of the tub with my legs still wrapped around his waist. He quickly places me back on my feet before running a dry towel over me, collecting the water dripping down my skin. Goose bumps break out across my body—both from the sudden chill and the anticipation of what is coming next.

When he is all done, I grab a towel from behind him and do the same. I commit to my task, his breathing growing heavier with every pass of the towel over his rippling muscles. When I kneel down to get his legs, I avoid his erection.

The scar on his knee stands out against his skin, representing one of the biggest shifts in his life. In *our* life together.

I trace the scar while Cal breathes heavily above me, his hands fisting by his sides.

"It healed well." The last summer he was here, he avoided wearing clothes that exposed his scar, so I never had much of an opportunity to look.

His chest rises and falls. "I hate it."

"Every part of you is perfect." I lean forward and kiss the scar.

Cal releases a shuddery breath.

Except when I go to swipe away the last bit of water dripping from his cock, he pulls me on to my feet and drags me toward the bedroom.

"But—"

Cal throws the towel in the direction of the bathroom. "I'm done with the games. Kneel," he orders in that gruff voice of his that only comes out during sex. There are two versions of Callahan Kane, and this one happens to be my favorite because no one knows about it but me. It's the one he keeps locked away, begging to be unleashed.

He presses a single finger against my shoulder. A shiver shoots down my spine as I kneel against the tightly woven carpet.

I reach for his cock, only to have him step out of my reach.

"What are you doing?"

"Payback." He pumps once. His tip gleams from a single drop of pre-cum, and I lick my lips.

"Payback for what?" When I reach for him, he takes another step back, making me frown.

"Your stunt with the vibrator." His gaze travels over my body. "You remember what you ordered me to do?"

"Stay there and look pretty for me." I repeat the words. My body temperature spikes, along with my heart rate.

He reaches out to cup my cheek with one hand while pumping his cock with the other. "There truly is nothing prettier than watching you on your knees."

"Nothing at all?"

His chest heaves from his heavy exhale. "Mmm. Actually, there might be one other thing."

I yearn to reach for him, yet my hands remain pressed flat against my thighs. "What's that?"

"This." His fingers dig into my scalp and tug. I gasp, and Cal takes advantage of my surprise to thrust his cock inside my mouth. My lips wrap around him instinctively, and my hands reach out to hold him at the base while I pull him deeper into my mouth.

I drag my tongue across the underside of his silky skin, tracing and teasing my way up and down his length. His fingers thread themselves through my hair and hold me in place.

Like I ever stood a chance of leaving.

Cal's muscles twitch and ripple as I pump, suck, and lick every solid inch of him.

There is nothing sweet and ladylike about sucking his cock. The way I hunger for his release drives my own orgasm to the surface, and my movements become more desperate as the pulsing between my legs intensifies.

"Touch yourself," he rasps.

I follow his command, reaching between my legs.

"Show me how much sucking my cock turns you on."

I lift my hand in the air, and his cock jerks in my mouth, flooding my tongue with his arousal.

"I want you to make yourself come."

I blink in acknowledgment.

Cal's fingers grip my scalp as he fucks my mouth. I tease my clit with the flat of my hand while pumping two fingers inside, sinking them in and out to the rhythm of his thrusts.

He groans at the sight, his eyes devouring me like I'm the last thing he might ever see.

"Fuck, Lana." His movements become jerkier. Less in sync as he pistons his hips with enough power to make me almost gag.

The pressure in my belly builds, growing with each tease of my thumb against my clit.

"That's it, babe." He cups my cheek. "Come for me."

His gaze brands itself into my very soul, with him pouring every ounce of love he feels toward me with a single look.

The world around me fades away as I'm hit with my orgasm. My body shakes, my release turning my muscles to jelly as I ride the wave of pleasure rolling through me.

The affection in his gaze morphs into pure lust, his eyes devouring me whole as his cum shoots down my throat and fills my mouth. I swallow multiple times but that doesn't stop some of it from spilling past my lips.

Cal pulls his shiny cock away. He swipes at the cum dripping down my chin before sticking his thumb back into my mouth. I suck on the pad, cleaning him off before he repeats the same thing again. Once he is satisfied, I reach for his cock and wipe it clean with my tongue. He rubs my cheek with approval, and I lean into his touch.

More blood rushes to his dick, earning a giggle from me.

He actually looks offended as he pulls me up on to my feet. "You think it's funny what you do to me? I'm suffering from constant blue balls around you."

"It's not my fault." I laugh harder.

He smiles as he walks me back toward the bed. With a little shove, I fall against the mattress. Cal follows me, his weight pressing me farther into the bed as he steals a kiss.

I slide my hands up his body and comb my fingers through his hair. The intensity of our kiss increases as his tongue lashes against mine, seeking for me to submit. He bites down on my bottom lip and draws blood. His tongue sweeps in and coaxes a sigh from me as he sucks on the swollen flesh in a silent apology.

He continues teasing me until both of us are panting. The

ache in my core grows with each pass of his tongue and every press of his lips. From my breasts to my pussy, not a single inch of my body goes unappreciated.

Cal denies me another orgasm, which makes me groan with frustration. "God."

"You should know better than to call me another man in bed." He slaps my pussy hard. Once. Twice. Three times until I'm panting and squirming underneath him.

The urgency to come has me digging my fingernails into his skin and grinding my pussy against his cock. He chuckles in my ear before pulling us both under the covers.

This time he takes me from behind, sliding his leg between mine and sinking into me with one drawn-out thrust. The position is intimate, with him holding me between his arms. He kisses my neck and teases my clit as he pistons into me over and over again. Pleasure rolls through me as he whispers the sweetest praises into my ear.

My climax builds with each thrust of his hips and every brush of his fingers against my skin. With a final pinch of my clit, I spasm around him.

His cock drives into me hard with enough force to push me forward as he uses me to find his own pleasure. My body trembles from the aftereffects of my orgasm, and his movements become less coordinated with each pump of his hips.

He reminds me of a man possessed. Of someone on the verge of losing himself to lust, with a wildness in his gaze that I find intoxicating.

Cal grunts as he comes, not ceasing his torture of my body until he is finished. He doesn't pull out right away but instead chooses to wrap his arms around me. My thighs are sticky from our combined releases, yet I can't find it in me to move.

I don't think I even *can* move.

He kisses the top of my head with a sigh. Eventually, my heart rate settles, the steady thump lulling me to sleep.

"I love you," he whispers into the dark.

I've heard the words hundreds of times from his lips, yet they still manage to take my breath away every single time.

I open my mouth to say the same, yet something holds me back.

Fear.

It's not that I don't love him, because I do. Maybe even more than ever before if that is possible.

It's just that the last time I deliberately shared those three little words, he left. My love wasn't enough before, so why would it be this time?

And after Cal left the last time, I'm scared to share that part of myself. At least not until I can fully trust him again.

If I ever can.

Y ou want us to go to dinner with your family?" My fork slips from my hand, and the scrambled eggs splatter against the plate.

Cal rubs the back of his neck. "You don't have to come if you don't want to. It's just that I haven't seen Declan in a while, and Iris flew out all this way since my birthday is next week…"

Shit. His birthday!

I completely forgot about that. It's been so long since I actually acknowledged the day.

"You're having a birthday dinner here? At Dreamland? Why?"

"Because my family is nosy and insufferable."

"So just the usual?"

He chuckles.

"I don't know…" I hesitate, my gaze sliding over to Cami, who raises her fork in the air like an airplane before stabbing a piece of her pancake.

"I understand." The skin surrounding his eyes tightens. "No worries. My family can be a bit overbearing, so I don't blame you."

"It's not that." I stumble over the words.

"Then what?"

Yeah, Alana, then what?

"Isn't having dinner with the family kind of…serious?"

"Only if you want it to be. I'd love for you to come, but I understand if you don't want to."

He took your kid to Dreamland. The least you can do is go to a dinner for him.

I look over at Cami. "I can't leave Cami alone."

"Of course not. Everyone is excited to meet her."

"They are?"

He pulls out his phone and shows me a group chat he shares with Zahra and Iris.

I stifle my laugh. "Bad and Boozie?"

He looks up at the ceiling as if he needs to pray for patience. "I didn't come up with it."

"God, I hope not."

"It's the chat the two of them created to get on Declan and Rowan's nerves after we went to brunch one time."

"And does it?"

"Astronomically, which is the only reason I would willingly stay in a chat with the two of them. I have the notifications silenced most of the time."

I laugh as I check out the chat. The first photo is a selfie that Cal took of the three of us eating funnel cakes in front of the castle. I'm clearly trying to clean Cami's face, which is covered in powdered sugar as she devours the fried dough, while Cal grins at the two of us with an expression that makes my chest pinch. I'm not sure I've ever seen him look that happy before—that at peace.

Not even in the photo of us on the dock sharing cholados Colombianos.

Iris

OMG. Funnel cakes? One-on-one meet-and-greets with princess? A private dinner inside the castle with an exclusive chef? You're completely spoiling them.

As it should be.

Zahra:

Falls over from swooning so hard.

Zahra

I'm jealous I had to work instead of hanging out with them all day.

Iris

Well, I'm jealous that you met them already!

Maybe you can meet them tomorrow.

Iris

Really?!?!

Zahra

Yes!!!

Zahra

Can you imagine me screaming?

I said maybe...

Iris

How can we turn that into a yes?

I haven't even gotten around to asking her yet.

Iris

Tell her that I have been dying to meet her for years ever since you cried about her.

I end up laughing so hard that Cal frowns.

"You cried over me?" I wheeze.

He steals his phone out of my hand. "I had something in my eye."

"What? A reality check?"

He scratches his eyebrow with his middle finger, making me laugh again.

"So, what time is dinner?" I ask.

"Why?"

"Because I'm dying to hear all about you from Iris."

His head drops back with a sigh. "Worst idea ever."

Cal asks the golf cart driver to stop the cart outside of a row of warehouses. Cami looks up from my phone to take in her surroundings before deeming them far less interesting than the video playing on the screen.

"Where are we?" I shield my eyes from the sun as I take in the various warehouses with people coming in and out of the front doors.

"This is where all the magic happens."

My forehead wrinkles with confusion. "What does that even mean?"

"I'd rather show you instead." He jumps off the cart and offers me his hand. Cami follows behind us, her head down as she continues watching the show on my phone.

"But what about going to the waterpark?" I take in my outfit of flip-flops, a one-piece, and a pair of jean shorts.

"As much as I'd love to spend the whole day with you in a swimsuit, that can wait for tomorrow."

"But Cami—"

He cuts me off. "Is fine with what I have planned. She gave me the go-ahead herself yesterday. Right, kiddo?"

Cami throws him a thumbs-up without looking away from her screen.

"See?" Cal raises a brow.

"She was in on this the whole time?" My mouth drops open.

"Surprise." Cami looks up with a wide grin.

"She didn't say a single thing when I got her all dressed up in her swimsuit this morning."

"Because he gave me money!"

I blink up at Cal. "How much?"

"Can you really put a price tag on discretion?"

"One thousand dollars!" Cami squeals, nearly dropping my phone.

"One. Thousand. Dollars?" My pitch rises at the end.

"I hustled him good, Mommy." She holds out her fist for me to pound, something she no doubt learned from the man smiling beside me.

I press my palm against my forehead. "I'm not sure how I'll survive the two of you."

"Come on. We're late." He places his hand on the small of my back.

"Late for what?"

"You'll see." He leads us toward a blue door a little ways off from where the golf cart dropped us. With a tug, it creaks open.

The smell of fresh baked bread and cinnamon rolls hits me all at once.

"Oh my God." I take a second sniff. "That smells amazing."

His grin widens as he grabs my hand and pulls me inside. We walk through a semi-lit hallway before it opens into a massive kitchen with state-of-the-art everything.

"Bonjour!" A man wearing a white chef's outfit waves his knife in the air.

"Tell me that's not who I think it is." I pull Cal back a step.

"Surprise." He grins.

"You're Alana?" Chef Gabriel asks with a hint of a French accent. He wipes the flour off his hand with a towel before offering me it to shake. His smile is even brighter in person than it is on those TV shows he guest stars on, making him look much more approachable than what would be expected of someone who gets paid to yell at bakers and critique their skills.

"Hi," I squeak as I grab on to his hand.

Oh my God. You're shaking hands with the Chocolate King.

My hand trembles in his, which he doesn't comment on. I never thought I would be the kind of girl who would get starstruck, but here I am with my heart pounding in my chest and my palm sweating as I stand before the man whose career I have followed since I was in high school.

Chef lets go of my hand. "Cal has told me all about your love for baking."

"He has?" My voice hits the highest pitch ever.

"Yes. He and I thought it would be fun if we made his birthday cakes together."

I blink twice. "I'm sorry. Did you say cakes? As in plural?"

Cal coughs in a poor attempt to cover up his laugh.

"Yes. Cakes." He emphasizes the *s* sound with a grin. "I was supposed to teach you one of my recipes, but once I spoke to Cal about his favorite sweets of yours, I thought we could swap recipes. I've been told your tres leches cake is to die for."

I shoot Cal a look over my shoulder. "I didn't realize you and Cal knew each other."

Cal shrugs. "We produce his show."

"Of course you do." Is anything in the world safe from the Kane Company and their influence?

Who are you to complain? Now you get to spend the day with the Chocolate King!

Chef Gabriel shoots me a small smile. "Shall we get started? I have a plane to catch this evening and Cal told me you have a dinner to attend."

"Sure. Yes!" I take a few hesitant steps toward the metal counter.

"Cami and I are going to go work on decorating some

sugar cookies and cupcakes for Rowan's buddies' team meeting tomorrow." Cal kisses my cheek.

Cami hands me my phone before reaching up and clasping Cal's hand. The two of them walk to the other side of the warehouse, where a few employees stand by with trays of cookies, cupcakes, and decorating supplies.

"Are you ready to get started?" Chef claps his hands together.

"Yes, Chef."

He chuckles. "Please call me Gabriel."

I spare a glance toward Cal and mouth *oh my God*. His smile widens before he turns back to Cami, who is already dipping her fingers into the frosting bowl. She looks up at him with wide eyes and parted lips, only to break out into a smile when Cal swipes his finger against the side of the bowl too.

Those two are way too similar for my liking.

Liar.

Chef Gabriel starts rattling off steps while speaking about the ingredients he is using. I take in every single thing like a brand new baker who is learning how to properly crack an egg for the first time.

Together, Chef and I get to work on Cal's birthday cake. It's one thing to see Gabriel's techniques on TV, but it is a whole other experience to witness someone as talented as him firsthand. Everything about him is incredible.

The way he turns granules of sugar into decorations that rival the best restaurants in Las Vegas.

His technique for glazing, which makes what happens on TV look amateur.

Him finding the balance between passion and perfectionism

while he turns Cal's birthday cake into a work of art.

"Fini." He spins the cake tray in a circle, showing off his creation.

"Wow." I take in Cal's cake from all angles.

The skills Gabriel picked up during his twenty years of baking speak for themselves, and I itch to have even a fraction of his experience.

You could if you wanted to.

Instead of shoving away the thought like I usually do, I sit with it. A bit of the money from the house could pay for me to receive some formal training. It could help finance a few trips around the world so I can learn from chefs of all backgrounds, although those kinds of vacations would have to wait until Cami is out of school for the summer.

An idea starts forming. I could do anything I want to, so long as I am willing to take the risk.

"What do you think?" he asks, pulling me back from my thoughts.

"That my cake is going to look like it was made by a child compared to yours."

He laughs to himself. "So long as it tastes good, who cares?"

"Says the man who just spent the last hour working on a single sugar art flower."

He laughs to himself. "The chef I worked with in Las Vegas was a bit of a perfectionist."

"You worked in Vegas? When?" I don't remember that being part of his introduction on the show.

"Last year at the Dahlia."

"The Dahlia?" I suck in a breath. That's one of the most

exclusive hotels in all of Vegas.

"Oui."

"Where do you find the time? Don't you have like ten restaurants to run and a million things to do?"

"When I was still a student, I told myself that once I made enough money, I would spend one month in a different city every year, learning about new techniques and skills to improve my craft."

I lean forward on my elbows. "Wow. What inspired that?"

"Working for a stubborn chef who never wanted to branch out and experiment beyond what he was good at."

I busy myself with clearing the counter of the all the dirty bowls and baking tools. "I always wanted to travel and eat my way around the world."

His grin stretches across his face. "You need to. Some of the best experiences I had baking are from my time traveling."

"Really?"

"Oh yes. It brought the food I loved to life and taught me to appreciate the culture and people behind the recipes." He clears the station to prepare for my tres leches layer cake, leaving me to consider what he said.

What would it be like to spend summers traveling the world, learning new recipes while exploring cities and cultures?

You could find out.

Maybe I will.

CHAPTER FORTY-FOUR

Cal

I spend the entire drive to Rowan's house tapping my hand against my thigh to the beat of my racing heart. Lana spares me a few glances through the ride, but I keep my eyes focused elsewhere, not wanting to burden her with my thoughts.

I'm not worried about her.

I'm worried about how I will manage my family around her. My two brothers don't mind embarrassing me and finding a way to mention my flaws on a continuous basis. It's fucked up to think the worst of Rowan and Declan, but I've spent enough of my life dodging their jabs to expect anything less.

The drive to the house ends all too soon, forcing me to push aside my reeling thoughts.

Lana tugs on my elbow and stops me a few feet away from the front door. "Is everything okay?"

"It will be." *Once I have a drink or two.*

Regret hits me instantly, making my stomach churn.

Her eyebrows draw together. "What's wrong?"

"Just nervous about being around everyone."

Lana doesn't hesitate before speaking up. "We don't need to go."

I blink. "What?"

"If you don't want to go, then don't. We can take the cakes and sneak away before they even know we're here."

"Just like that?"

She snaps with a smile. "Yeah, just like that."

"What about all the time you put into getting ready?"

She drags her eyes down my body, making my skin burn beneath my button-down. "I'm sure you'll make it worth my while."

My grin stretches to its limit.

The temptation to ditch my family and spend time with Lana is nearly impossible to dismiss.

Running has never solved any of your problems before.

As if my family sensed my urge to flee, Iris opens the front door and steps out on to the porch with Zahra on her heels.

Iris doesn't even acknowledge me, her eyes immediately landing on Lana. My best friend doesn't hesitate before throwing her arms around her.

"Hi?" Lana's voice tips up.

Iris releases her. "Sorry. I'm just so excited to finally meet you and put a face to the name that Cal has spoken so much about."

Lana's cheeks flush. "Hopefully good things."

"Please. As if Cal would ever say anything but the most

flattering things about his *Lana*."

My face turns red. "Iris."

She tosses her braids over her shoulder with a smile. "I'm just teasing."

"Oh, by all means, keep going. There is nothing I like more than seeing him get all flustered and embarrassed." Lana winks at my best friend.

"Serves him right for what he puts everyone else through," Iris quips.

You knew them getting together would be trouble.

And I love every second of it.

"We can exchange stories over dinner." Iris locks elbows with Lana and drags her into the house. Zahra walks beside them, letting Cami talk her ear off about everything that happened yesterday at Dreamland while I follow behind them.

Something that smells slightly burnt catches my nose, and I trace the scent to the kitchen, where Declan fusses over the cloud of smoke coming out of the oven. He curses as he shuts the door and dumps the burnt lump of what looks to be bread in the trash.

He reaches over the sink and opens the window looking out on to the backyard.

"Need help?"

He jumps in place before turning around to face me. "You didn't see that."

"Not a single thing, although I'm sure everyone in the house can smell it."

He sighs. "I miscalculated the timing on the bread."

"Happens to the best of us."

He checks whatever is simmering on the stove. "So now you

feel like talking to me?"

"You didn't give me much of a choice after deciding to crash my vacation."

He shoots me a look. "You shouldn't even be on a vacation."

"My entire life is a vacation." I grin, although it doesn't reach my eyes.

He shuts his eyes and takes a few deep breaths.

Huh. Is he taking the time to think before he speaks?

That's new.

Consider me intrigued.

Rowan walks into the kitchen sipping on a glass of whiskey. All it takes is one glance in our direction to have him backtracking in the opposite direction, leaving Declan and me alone again.

"How was Dreamland?" He returns to sautéing some vegetables.

I blink. "Since when do you care?"

"Since the day you were born."

"You have a weird way of showing it."

His forehead crinkles from how hard he frowns. "Listen. I'm sorry for what I said back in the office. It was screwed up of me to lose my temper like that and take out my worries about the will on you. I am trying to be better, and I even started seeing a therapist to explore my…issues."

"You?" My lips part.

His gaze drops. "Yup. After everything that happened with Iris, I couldn't count on myself not to screw up again." His Adam's apple bobs. "I'm working on a few things."

"Like your apologies? Because those severely need some work."

His lips quirk up. "That and actually thinking before speaking."

"What a novel concept."

His gaze narrows. "That's rich coming from the man who's suffered from verbal diarrhea all his life."

"At least I have my ADHD diagnosis as an excuse. What's yours?"

"None that are good enough for me to act the way I do." His voice lowers. "I'm not perfect, nor can I make a promise that I will be, but I'm working on it. Just give me a chance."

I clap him on the shoulder. "Fine, but only because Iris doesn't like it when we fight."

His eyes roll. "Good enough for me."

Cami sits at the end of the long dining table beside Zahra and Rowan. My brother wears one of Cami's crowns on his head like royalty while answering her never-ending questions about Dreamland and his job.

Her attachment to Rowan is endearing. Especially when paired with Declan shooting daggers at him because Iris keeps swooning and commenting on how Rowan will make a good father one day.

The typical heaviness that arises whenever I'm with my family settles as I wrap my arm around the back of Lana's chair. She looks up at me with a smile before continuing her conversation with Iris, who spares me a few curious glances throughout dinner.

Once I'm done eating, I fiddle with the ends of Lana's hair, twirling them around my finger over and over again.

"You're quiet tonight," Declan says from across the table.

Because I don't feel the need to disguise my pain and loneliness with endless conversation and fake laughter.

"Just taking it all in," I say instead.

"Taking what in?" Declan asks.

The family I always wanted but never felt like I could have. "Rowan showing you up as the best uncle." I stick to a silly answer, knowing that's what's expected of me. I'm the fun brother. The *happy* one. The guy who can cut tension with a single smile and a self-deprecating comment. No one wants to hear about my demons, depression, and damn insecurities.

I don't even notice what I said until uncomfortable silence settles over the table. Zahra and Iris shoot looks at each other over the rims of their wineglasses while Declan's eyes look ready to bulge. I can't bear looking in Lana's direction, so I face forward like a soldier reporting for duty.

Rowan points at the crown on his head. "Please. Like Declan ever stood a chance at beating me."

Cami presses her hand to her mouth and giggles.

Declan frowns. "I haven't even had a chance to spend time with her, asshole. You've been hovering over her the whole night because she feeds your ego."

"You owe the swear jar!" Cami jumps out of her seat and walks over to Declan with her hand held out. "Billetes, por favor."

"What?" He stares at her fingers like they might carry a flesh-eating bacteria.

Iris nudges him in the ribs with her elbow. "That means you have to pay whenever you curse."

"How much?" His expression is a pleasant mix of panicked and somewhat intrigued.

Cami gives Declan a quick pass-over with her eyes. "One thousand dollars."

Lana chokes while sipping her water. I pat her back as she sucks in huge breaths of air.

"One thousand dollars? What's it for?" Declan doesn't even blink before pulling out his money clip and handing her hundreds.

"Collages." She grins up at him.

"College," I correct for her when Declan's brows tug together with confusion.

Declan shrugs as he drops the last hundred in her palm. "A good cause I can get behind."

Lana finally regains the ability to speak. "Camila Theresa Castillo, give all that back right now. You know we don't ask people to pay a thousand dollars at home."

"But Cal gave me a thousand dollars." Her pinched expression is so damn cute that even Declan smiles.

Iris shoots me a look and mouths *one thousand dollars?*

I shrug. *Totally worth it.*

Lana's brows rise. "Doesn't make it right to ask that of strangers."

Declan's eyes darken. *"Stranger?* I've known you since you were about her age."

Lana gives him a once-over. "So? I haven't seen you since you were stealing my dolls because you wanted to play with them."

Zahra giggles into her wineglass while Iris howls with laughter, her hand slapping the table as she sucks in deep breaths.

Declan frowns, a tinge of pink creeping up his cheeks. "My action figures needed to save the damsel in distress."

Iris pats his shoulder. "No need to be self-conscious. An active imagination is a sign of a healthy childhood."

"Sure, it is." Zahra lifts her wineglass in a mocking cheer.

Declan glares at Lana in a way that makes most grown men piss themselves. Lana laughs, the sound filling all the cracks of my broken heart with her warmth.

The conversation changes, although the steady feeling of contentedness pumping through my veins never wanes. If anything, it only intensifies as the night continues. Iris and Lana break off into a corner, laughing at whatever blackmail they are exchanging at my expense.

Eventually, Zahra and Lana come out carrying the two cakes, both of which are covered in lit candles. Iris begins clapping her hands and singing happy birthday. My brothers begrudgingly chime in, their enthusiasm on par with a funeral march.

"Make a wish, old man," Lana whispers in my ear.

Wax drips down the candles and lands on the icing. Cami comes up to my side and bounces on the balls of her feet with excitement, so I lift her up and place her on my lap.

"Wanna help me out? It's a lot of candles."

"Yes!" She grins, her two eyes bright orbs rivaling the sun.

Together, we blow out every single candle except for one. I take a deep breath and repeat the same wish in my head from before.

I wish to kick my addiction for good.

Getting dry is one thing, but staying sober is a completely different animal. One that I've battled and lost already.

Failing isn't an option this time. I want to triumph. Overcome. *Evolve*.

I want to shed the addiction that feels like an anchor wrapped around my neck, keeping me from rising above the demons holding me down, almost as much as I want to become a man worthy of Lana and Cami.

No matter how long it takes me to get there.

Cami pushes her empty plate in front of her. Usually I don't let her have sweets this late, but tonight is a special occasion.

"Can I go play now?" she asks.

"Sure."

She bolts from the table, her feet slapping against the wood as she escapes with her dolls.

"She's so cute." Iris shoots me a warm smile.

Zahra plucks the crown off Rowan's head and places it on her own. "Seriously. I see a lot of kids every day, and yours makes the top five."

I bite back a smile.

"You made this?" Rowan stabs his spoon through his second piece of the tres leches cake.

"Yup." I swipe at some of the dulce de leche glaze.

"It's good." Declan shuts his eyes as he takes another bite.

To most people, good is a basic compliment, but from

Declan, it's considered high praise.

"*So* good." Iris licks her fork clean.

My cheeks ache from how hard I smile.

"Told you my girl could bake." Cal wraps his arm around the back of my chair.

I swear, every single time he calls me his girl, my heart skips a beat before returning to its normal programming.

"We could definitely have something like this in our shops." Rowan assesses the cake on the stand from all angles.

My breath catches. "Really?"

"How much do you charge?" The change in him is instant as he switches from family man to business entrepreneur.

"Umm…nothing?"

"Hmm." Declan's gaze slides from me to his brother.

"What?" I blurt out.

"Name a price." Rowan neatly places his spoon beside his plate.

"For a cake? Why?" I look over to Cal for help, but he remains aloof. If it weren't for the way his fingers stopped twirling my hair, I wouldn't think he was actively listening.

Rowan's eyes connect with mine. "Because I'm interested in buying your recipe."

"What for?"

"We've been considering expanding our Princess Marianna section in the park, and I want this to be a part of it."

The room spins around me as I take in everything he is saying.

"So, name a price." He folds his hands over his lap.

Cal pulls me closer and whispers in my ear, "Tell him you'll think about it."

My brows furrow. "But—"

"It will only make him want it more. Trust me."

This calculating version of Cal isn't one I'm used to, and it's a major turn-on. Naturally, I listen to him. "I'll need to get back to you."

Rowan's lips press together. "I'll give you a million."

My eyes widen. "For a recipe?"

Cal shakes his head ever so slightly.

Rowan glares at him. "Stop influencing her."

"I will when you stop giving her bad offers. The park makes about twenty million in a single day, and a good chunk of that comes from food and beverages. With how many people come through the golden gates ready to open their wallets and their stomachs, Alana deserves more. And don't think I forgot how much you spent on buying that secret Hawaiian frozen drink recipe."

My mouth drops open.

Damn. Where has this business savvy Cal been hiding my whole life and how soon can I fuck him?

Rowan's eyes sparkle with admiration. "I thought you weren't paying attention in meetings."

"The worst mistake you could have made was underestimating me." Cal winks, making my stomach muscles tighten from the wave of pleasure swirling inside of me.

Iris raises her wineglass. "To the smartest Kane."

Declan shoots her a glare, and Iris ignores him as she sips her drink.

I give Cal's hand a squeeze before looking up at Rowan. "I need to think about it. That recipe has been in my family for years, and I'm not sure how I would feel about giving it up, especially when I wouldn't have control over the final product."

Sharing it with Chef Gabriel was one thing, but handing it over to the Kanes feels like a risk I'm not too sure about.

"What's your number?" Rowan pulls out his phone.

"Why? So you can add her to the group chat too?" Declan's eyes narrow.

Iris swats Declan on the back of his head, making his perfectly styled hair go everywhere.

Zahra snorts into her wineglass. "Serves you right."

I recite my number so Rowan can save it.

"We'll be in touch."

Cal sighs. "Are we done talking business now? I hear Declan got some Cubans to celebrate my thirty-fourth trip around the sun and I'm dying to try them."

And just like that, the conversation is tabled, although the excitement building in my chest at the idea of Rowan buying my recipe doesn't go away.

The boys leave the house to go outside and smoke the cigars Declan bought, leaving us to bond over drinks. Well, Zahra and Iris each nurse a glass of wine while I stick to my water.

"So, how's the house renovation going?" Zahra leans back against the couch and tucks her legs under her. She reminds me of Delilah, always trying to burrow herself deep into the cushions.

"Good. The contractor has been hard at work with his team while we've been enjoying the park."

"When is it going to be finished?" Iris takes a sip of her wine.

"We actually already put it on the market." My hands clutching my glass of water tighten.

"You did?" Iris perks up.

"Cal didn't say anything," Zahra says.

"Yeah. It's time." Yet no matter how many times I tell myself that, I feel like someone grabbed my heart and squeezed hard enough to make the organ pop.

"You're not happy about it." Iris frowns.

"No, but I'll get over it." I sigh.

"Are you sure?" The skin between Zahra's eyebrows creases.

"If it means helping Cal, then so be it."

"What do you mean?" Iris's brows tug together.

"Cal told me he would go to rehab if we put the house up for sale this week, so it was an easy choice. I was already willing to sell it so I could send Cami to a private school, so Cal only sped up the timeline a bit."

Iris's eyes widen. "He promised to go to rehab?"

"He didn't tell you?"

"No." Her brows scrunch together. "When does he leave?"

"Next week."

"Next week?" Zahra squeaks. She and Iris share a look.

The hairs on my arms raise from how strange they're acting. "What?"

"Nothing. It just seems…" Zahra's voice drifts off.

"Sudden," Iris finishes for her.

"I'm not putting up with his drinking anymore. He can either get his life together or see himself out of mine." I lift my water glass in the air.

Whatever nervous energy that was building in the air disappears with everyone breaking out into laughter.

"I like you already." Iris's eyes glitter.

"Same." I grin.

Zahra raises her glass. "Let's toast."

"To what?" I ask.

Zahra taps her glass against mine. "To three strong women who refuse to put up with the Kane brothers' usual bullshit."

"I can cheers to that." Iris does the same.

The three of us share stories about each of the brothers. Between Zahra and Iris, I spend the rest of the next hour laughing and crying until my belly hurts and my voice is hoarse. The two of them remind me of Violet and Delilah, and I just know that the five of us need to get together one day.

Once Cal gets sober, that is.

Iris and Zahra are splayed out on the couch, their wineglasses as empty as the bottle of expensive white wine on the coffee table. Neither one moves to go get another one, although they both expressed wanting another glass, so I volunteer to grab one from the wine fridge in the kitchen.

I use the bathroom before going to retrieve the bottle. As I'm grabbing the corkscrew, Declan's voice catches my attention.

It takes me a moment to realize his voice is coming from outside rather than inside. The kitchen window is open with the faded scent of cigars lingering in the air, making my nose wrinkle.

"I saw you put the lake house on the market," Declan says in that gruff, no-bullshit voice of his.

"Yup. I doubt it will last more than a few weeks before someone buys it." Cal speaks with confidence.

Stop eavesdropping and go.

The corkscrew shakes in my hand. I'm about to start walking away and give them privacy, but something Declan says has my feet staying glued to the floor.

"I'm surprised you got Alana to go along with it."

What. The. Fuck. Go along with what?

"She was the one who suggested we put the house up for sale sooner," Cal says.

"Shouldn't be long now before you receive your part of the inheritance, then."

Inheritance? What inheritance?

"About that…" Cal's voice drifts off.

"Here we go," Rowan grumbles before ice rattles in a glass.

I take a step forward to get a better look at them. The three brothers sit on their respective lounge chairs, blowing smoke rings into the sky. While Declan and Rowan have drinks on a side table, Cal only clutches a cigar in his hand.

"Don't tell me you're backing out of your part of the will." Agitation bleeds through Declan's voice.

The food I ate for dinner sits like a lead block in my stomach and threatens to crawl up my throat.

Cal spares him a look. "I'm not backing out. I'm just… amending it."

"Fuck." Rowan sighs up to the sky.

"Amending *what?*" Declan's jaw clenches so hard, I can make out the slight tic from here.

"I fly out to Arizona on Friday."

"For what?"

"Rehab."

My chest tightens. I'm proud of him for being open and honest about his struggles. It will only help him in the long run if he feels like he can count on those around him to support the process.

"Rehab? Right now? What happened to the plan?" Declan snaps.

What plan?

The one he obviously never told you about. The hairs on my arms rise, pointing straight up.

Alana, eres una tonta.

Rowan curses under his breath.

"I already spoke to Leo. So long as I sell the house by the end of the summer and commit to getting sober, then it won't affect earning my part of the inheritance."

My lungs feel like they might explode from how hard I suck in a breath. The corkscrew falls from my fingers, landing on the wood floor with a soft thud.

Piecing the puzzle together isn't hard. In fact, it's so simple, my eyes water from how stupid I was to not put everything together sooner.

Cal's willingness to come back to Lake Wisteria when he could have left the house alone with me in it.

His insistence on selling the house despite my personal feelings, playing on my dreams and love for Cami to get his way.

The way he made me believe he wanted to go to rehab when, in reality, he was only getting sober for a stupid freaking inheritance.

Oh, Alana. When will you ever learn?

I might not have every single detail, but I have enough

to understand just how easily I was taken advantage of. How desperate I was to believe he wanted to get help after he spent six years doing just fine without me and sobriety. How stupid I must have looked, willing to put the house on the market sooner solely because I wanted him to get help.

Just another person who lied in order to get something out of me.

A single tear slips out of my eye, but I'm quick to swipe away the evidence.

You will not cry over him.

My gut churns, and I cling to the sink, willing myself to keep my dinner down. Acid crawls up my throat regardless, and I breathe through my nose to stop myself from getting sick.

Declan breaks the silence. "What happened to the original plan?"

"It changed."

"Then change it back. There's too much at stake here for you to be betting twenty-five billion dollars and your shares of the company on your sobriety." Declan's voice comes out flat, as if the topic of getting sober is a chore rather than an accomplishment.

Cal's eyes roll. "Thanks for the vote of confidence."

"Hey, is everything okay?"

I jump in place at the sound of Iris's voice. She bends down to pick up the corkscrew I dropped, which gives me enough time to pull myself together and put on a happy face.

"Yup. I just couldn't figure out how to properly uncork the bottle since I don't drink." My nervous laugh borders on hysterical, but Iris doesn't seem to notice since she doesn't know me.

"You should have just brought it to us. We could have done that." She grabs the bottle.

I freeze as a breeze comes through the window, the scent of cigars permeating the air. I'm afraid the rapid beat of my heart will betray me with how hard it pounds against my chest.

Iris's nose twitches. "What's that smell?"

I look around the kitchen, doing my best to try to look confused.

Iris's gaze lands on the curtain swaying in the breeze. "Ahh. Someone left the window open." She reaches over the sink to shut it, only to pause before she drags the pane down.

"Everything okay?" I ask. The blood in my ears makes it impossible to hear much besides my own heartbeat.

Her back freezes. "Yeah. Just thought I overheard one of them trying to talk shit about us."

This time, my fake laughter comes out more genuine. "Like Declan would dare talk bad about you. Safe to say he is obsessed."

At least one Kane brother is loyal.

She turns around with a smile. "The same can be said about you. I don't think I've seen Cal this happy in well…ever."

I try to smile. I try so damn hard, my eye twitches and my cheeks ache.

Her head tilts. "Are you sure everything is okay?"

"Yup. Just fighting the early signs of a migraine."

A small frown makes her forehead wrinkle. "Oh, no. Do you want any medicine?"

"I've got some in my purse. Hence the water." I reach for the glass of water I left abandoned on the counter and lead the way out of the kitchen. I'm careful to keep my head held high despite the unbearable weight pressing down around me, threatening to drown me.

You will not let him break you.

Yet no matter how many times I repeat the phrase, bits and pieces of my heart break off and shatter against the floor, leaving an invisible trail of my despair.

As soon as I put Cami to sleep, I lock my bedroom door and pull out my phone.

> SOS

Texts pop up instantly.

Delilah
> Is everything okay?

Violet
> What did he do?

I can always count on Violet to point fingers first and ask questions later. Tonight, I need to borrow some of her anger. At least that way I can feel something other than numbness.

Ever since I overheard the conversation outside, I've been on autopilot. Just going through the motions until I could crawl into a ball and process the last few months of my life.

My fingers shake as I type.

> I overheard some things...

My phone vibrates in my hand from an incoming video call. "I'm going to kill him," Violet seethes.

"What did you overhear?" Delilah, the voice of reason, asks.

"Hold on." I enter my bathroom and turn on the shower to

drown out any noise. "I'm not entirely sure what I heard."

Oh, you're sure. You just don't want to be.

I slide down the wall and cradle the phone against my chest. Panic builds, so I take a few deep breaths.

"Alana, talk to us."

"I feel so stupid." My voice quivers.

"You're not stupid. He is," Delilah says.

"You don't even know what happened." If Cal kept his secret about his inheritance from me, I doubt anyone else is supposed to know.

Why are you still being loyal to him?

Because I stupidly fell in love with him despite having every reason not to.

God. How did I put myself in this position again?

The skin surrounding Violet's eyes softens. "We don't need all the facts. If it makes you upset, then that's all the information we need."

I prop my head against the wall. "What am I supposed to do? I'm stuck here with him."

"Come home." Violet's lips press together into a thin white line.

I sniffle, fighting the tears threatening to fall. "No. I can't do that to Cami."

"She would understand," Delilah offers.

"No, she won't. You know how much she wanted to go on this trip." I don't have the heart to take it away from her no matter how much I am hurting.

"How can we help?" Delilah's soft voice soothes the throb in my chest.

"I'm not sure if you can. I'm the one who got myself into this mess."

Not just yourself.

Fuck. Cami.

If I hadn't been so naïve, she would have never gotten close to Cal. I could have kept my defenses up instead of letting my heart rule over my brain.

Did you seriously learn nothing from the past?

The realization makes me lose the battle against my tears. A few fall, sliding down my cheeks before landing on my dress.

You let them form a bond together.

"Alana," Violet calls.

I look up at the ceiling. My vision blurs from the tears, dulling the fluorescent lighting.

"Look at me." Violet speaks firmer this time.

My eyes slide to my phone. "What?"

"Whatever happened…none of it is your fault."

My chest pricks. "It sure feels like it."

"We will make him pay for what he did. That much I promise."

My laugh comes out broken and hollow. "I don't want revenge. I just want him gone. *Forever.*"

"Then that's what we will do."

Her use of *we* makes me emotional for a completely different reason.

You're not alone in this.

Violet and Delilah remain on the phone while I cry it out. Come tomorrow, I will need to pretend none of this ever happened, so I allow myself to feel everything tonight. My anger.

My sadness. My *betrayal*.

I might not have everything figured out by the time I stop crying, but I'm sure of one thing: Callahan Kane is going to regret ever thinking he could take advantage of my kindness and get away with it.

CHAPTER FORTY-SIX

Cal

Lana has been acting strange. Ever since we returned from Rowan and Zahra's place, she has kept quiet. Before I had a chance to ask her what she thought about the night, she disappeared into Cami's room, claiming she needed to get her ready for bed.

By the time I come out of the shower, the door to her room is locked with no answer when I knock.

She is probably still in the shower.

I take a seat on the couch and pull up Candy Crush. My highest score was quickly beaten by the same little git across the world who scored the top spot by a measly three points.

I'm not sure how long I play for. Lana doesn't ever open her door, so I lose track of time. I only quit once my eyes start to get heavy.

I rise from my spot on the couch and knock on Lana's door again.

"Lana." My knuckles tap against the wood.

No answer.

I press my ear against the door but still can't hear anything.

Rather than wait around, I go to my room and text her.

> Everything okay? You didn't answer when I knocked.

My text goes unanswered, too. Either Lana fell asleep the moment she put her head on the pillow or she is avoiding me. While the first option is highly plausible, especially after the long day we had, I can't help considering the second.

I sift through the memories of the night. From my point of view, it seemed like she had a great night. Lana got along well with Zahra and Iris, and she held her own when going up against Declan. She even got that special glint in her eyes that I love when Rowan tried to buy out her recipe for a million dollars.

I don't think anything went wrong. Yet I can't seem to shake the nagging sensation in the back of my head.

I text Iris individually.

> Hey.

Time goes by painfully slow as I wait for her to answer.

> Hey. What's up?

> Did anything seem off about Alana after dinner?

The dots appear and disappear twice before a message pops up.

> I'm not sure. Ask me tomorrow when I'm sober.

I throw a pillow over my face and groan. Although Iris won't be much help tonight, I plan on hounding her for answers once she is coherent enough to remember what happened.

Sleep evades me no matter how long I lie on the bed, staring up at the ceiling as I comb through everything that happened tonight for a second time. Despite considering every little detail, I can't think of anything that might have upset Lana. My family was on their best behavior—a shocker in itself—so I'm not sure what could have gone wrong.

Just ask her in the morning.

It's the last thought I have before my eyes slide shut and my breathing evens out.

"Hey." I kiss the top of Lana's head. She doesn't lean in to me like she usually does, which only adds to my growing evidence that something is wrong.

I already texted Iris early this morning, but she hasn't answered yet. Knowing my sister-in-law and the headache she gets after drinking too much wine, it might be a little while.

"Hi." Her gaze flickers from her food to my face before turning back to her plate.

I take a seat next to her and wrap my arm around the back of her chair. Lana is careful to keep from touching me.

"Everything okay?" I twirl a piece of her hair around my finger.

"Just tired." She takes a long sip of her coffee.

"You went to bed early."

"I had a headache." Her lips thin.

"Are you feeling better this morning? We can always skip the waterpark today if you're not."

"I'm not going to let Cami down no matter how shitty I feel." Something passes across her face, but it fades away quickly as she returns to her empty expression that makes the acid roll in my stomach.

"Do you want me to get you some medicine?"

"Sometimes the best cure is time." She looks away in a poor attempt to hide the tic in her jaw.

"Ready!" Cami comes out wearing a bathing suit and a cover-up skirt that resembles a mermaid tail.

Lana places her cup on the table and stands. "Perfect. Let me help you with your hair."

"Can you do a braid crown? Pretty please?"

"Sure." She walks around the table, leaving me behind.

Compared to the icy interaction with me, Lana is nothing but warm to her daughter. The tightness in my chest intensifies until I'm subconsciously rubbing at the spot over my heart with a frown.

The silence surrounding me adds to the weight pressing against my chest. After spending weeks around Cami and Lana, eating meals alone seems unbearable.

I take a deep breath and fight the temptation to drink as I pull out my phone and text Iris again.

> Alana is acting weird and I don't know why.

> I think something happened at dinner. Did Declan pull her aside when I was in the bathroom or something?

I sit with bated breath, waiting for a text that never comes.

She is probably still sleeping.

Instead of stewing in the quiet, obsessing over why Lana is upset, I eat breakfast and get ready for a day at the Dreamland waterpark.

By the time I am tying the string of my swim trunks, Cami bolts into my room.

"Let's go!"

I grab my shirt off the bed and follow her out of the room.

Lana is dressed in a white dress that brings out the warm tones in her tan skin, and her wavy hair is pulled back in an intricate braid.

I pause midstep, with my shirt hanging in my hand as I check her out.

"You look beautiful," I rasp.

Her gaze drops to my body for only a second before she turns away and busies herself with searching for something in her purse.

No response. No acknowledgment. No anything but cold, desolate silence eating away at the calmness I feel in her proximity.

The stomach-churning sensation from earlier returns, accompanied with a sick sense of dread.

Cami grabs my hand with a huge smile. "Ready?"

At least whatever Lana is feeling hasn't affected Cami, which gives me a little hope. Because if I didn't do anything to affect my relationship with the little kid, then whatever happened was specific to Lana.

If only I knew what.

Since my phone is kept away in a locker the whole day, I don't have a chance to check Iris's messages until we are done with the waterpark. While Lana is busy in the bathroom helping Cami change into a dry pair of clothes, I read the text Iris sent.

> Hmm. Everything seemed fine. And no, Declan didn't speak to her, although I'm sure Alana would have been fine with that.

> You don't remember her seeming off?

Her message comes a lot faster this time.

> I'm just getting to know her, so I don't think so. Why?

I wipe my face with frustration, muffling my groan.

> She has barely spoken to me today and locked me out of her room last night.

> Did you do something?

> No.

At least I don't believe so. All I've done is try to make this week special.

> Are you sure?

> Yes. She seemed happy before and even during dinner.

> Let me think...

I take a seat on a bench and drop my head into my hands while I wait for her reply.

> After Alana grabbed the wine bottle out of the fridge, she seemed a little more quiet, but she mentioned having a headache, so I didn't think too much of it.

She mentioned the same thing to me about the headache, but that wouldn't explain her attitude today.

> Anything off about the kitchen?

> Besides a lingering smell of whatever Declan burnt coming from the trash? Nope.

My groan of frustration draws the attention of a few people.

> Why don't you ask her?

> I wanted to have all the facts before I tried again.

> Keep me posted.

She adds a saluting emoji after her message.

> If you don't hear from me in 24 hours, call the cops.

> You got it.

I attempt to speak to Lana privately twice after my text conversation with Iris, but she does an incredible job keeping busy with Cami, the parks, and everything else Dreamland has to offer. If she and Cami aren't in the room, they are out visiting the different resorts and tourist areas. Lana doesn't ice me out completely, but it feels as if she erected an impenetrable wall between us.

I succumb to drinking again to ease the anxious feelings festering inside me like an infection. It makes me feel like shit to depend on alcohol, but I don't know how else to cope with the stress. It's either that or corner her. And knowing Lana, she won't respond well to that kind of confrontation.

By the time we are boarding the private jet, I still haven't had a single opportunity to speak with her. My texts are ignored and my knocks on her door go unanswered, which only fuels my growing anxiety, and with it, more drinking.

My shoulders slump as I drop into the large seat across from the couch Cami loves. Unlike the last time, Cami leaves room for Lana to sit. The two of them spend the entire flight back to Michigan watching Dreamland movies and laughing together, although Lana's smiles never quite reach her eyes. It's the same smile she had plastered on her face the entire week. The one that makes my chest ache, knowing it is a watered-down version of her real smiles.

I vow in that moment to speak to Lana tonight, even if it means having to tie her down to get some answers.

CHAPTER FORTY-SEVEN

Alana

I tried my absolute hardest to make the rest of the week go by smoothly. It nearly killed me to put on a brave face and charge forward, knowing that everything coming out of Cal's mouth was a lie, but I did so for Cami. She always wanted to go to Dreamland, and I was not going to ruin her experience by letting my personal feelings about a man get in the way.

If anyone is to blame for believing Cal, it's me, so it's only right I suffer through the rest of the week. And suffer I did. Every interaction with Cal felt like someone was piercing my chest with a thousand needles.

Cal knows something is up. I haven't done a great job at hiding it, but Cal reads me like his favorite book—every single highlight memorized and every other page tabbed.

His ability to recognize my tells is what makes him perfect at playing me like a fool. He knows which buttons to push and what magic words to say, leaving me vulnerable to his manipulations.

Not anymore.

I stare up at the night sky. Water slaps against the dock, filling the silence. Besides the quick rustle of Cami's sheets making the baby monitor crackle, I'm left alone with my thoughts.

What a miserable place to be.

I'm not sure how long I sit under the stars, watching the moon's reflection dance across the water. Coming out here was a risk, but one I found worth taking.

I knew it was only a matter of time before Cal cornered me on the dock. After all, it's where our story began.

"You're going to fall in if you're not careful."

I look away from the glittering water. My neck cranes as I take in the tall kid with hair that matches the sun shining above us and blue eyes that rival the water in front of us, clearer than a cloudless day.

Everything about him screams money. Boat shoes. Pastel shorts. Striped T-shirt.

I haven't seen him before, but that isn't saying much. My family only just moved here from Colombia.

My nose wrinkles. "No hablo inglés."

His eyes sparkle. "Que raro. Te he escuchado hablar con tu mamá en inglés antes."

Damn. Busted.

"My name is Cal." He smiles.

"Cal?" My accent peeks through, accentuating the ah *sound.*

He laughs as he drops on to the dock and crisscrosses his legs next to me.

"What are you doing?" I try my best to annunciate my words like how I learned from watching too much American TV after school.

"Grandpa told me you moved here from Colombia a few weeks ago."

My chest tightens as I think about home. Mami wanted a fresh start after Papi left us, so she called a cousin who moved to the States and bought three one-way plane tickets. Anto has spent most of her days locked in her room, while I've hung out by the lake by myself, ignoring my mom. If I'm going to protest living here, I might as well enjoy the view.

"Yup." *Maybe if I keep my answers short, he will go away.*

"Do you miss it?"

"Yes."

"Do you have any friends here?"

I release a heavy breath. "Why are you asking?"

"You looked lonely."

Because I am. *"So?"*

"So, I thought we could be friends."

"I don't want any." *Making friends with anyone might make Mami believe I'm happy about living here. And if she thinks I like it here, then we will never move back to Colombia.*

His smile widens, taking up the lower half of his face. "Okay. No friends."

He doesn't leave, which only annoys me more. Instead, he stares out at the lake and taps his fingers against the wood plank in a mindless patter.

I clamp my hand over his to stop the tapping sound. "Will you stop?"

"Sorry." *His cheeks turn pink.* "I can't help it sometimes."

"Why?"

He looks away from me. "Because I've got issues."

"Says who?"

"My dad."

My lips purse. "Sounds like a pendejo."

A small smile tugs at his lips. "What does that mean?"

I shrug. "I don't know, but I think it's a bad word. My mom said it to my dad when he made her cry." My chest aches at the memory, but I do my best to push the thought away.

"Pendejo. I like it. What other bad words do you know?"

I spend the rest of the afternoon teaching Cal a bunch of bad words I have overheard, and he teaches me the English equivalent. By the time my mom is calling us in for dinner, I realize the sun has already set and my cheeks hurt from smiling so much.

"Are you eating with us tonight?" Cal offers me his hand.

I take it and gasp at the little tingle in my fingers. "You shocked me!"

He laughs, which makes me laugh.

For the first time since I moved to America, I wonder if it isn't the worst thing in the world to make a friend…

"Lana."

The memory shimmers away, and the younger version of Cal is replaced by the man. The same man who broke my heart again, although this time feels even worse than the last. Before, I had hope he could get better. That he would snap out of his selfish behavior and choose to be a bigger, better version of himself.

That hope was nothing but a lie I told myself to feel good about our situation.

"Mind if I take a seat?" he asks.

I stare out at the lake without replying.

He leaves room between us as he sits down next to me. My pinky finger yearns to interlock with his, but I repress any urge to touch him by holding on to my anger.

"What's wrong?" He looks over at me.

"A lot of things." I continue to face forward, although the feel of his gaze tempts me to turn toward him.

"Want to talk about it?"

No, but what choice do I have? It's not like I can ignore Cal forever, and now that Dreamland is no longer an issue, I'd rather get everything off my chest so he can leave once and for all.

"Why are you selling the house?" I come out and ask the question I already know the answer to. It might be stupid, but I hope he comes clean and admits to his plan, even if it means risking what fragile thing we have built together.

Maybe then I could learn to forgive him.

Out of the corner of my eye, I can make out the rare frown line cutting across his forehead.

"We've already gone over this."

My heart pounds in my chest, the pace growing more rapid with each pump. "Then repeat it."

Tell me the truth. Give me a reason to give you another chance.

He releases a heavy exhale. "I want us to be able to move forward without the house holding us back."

His roundabout answer does nothing to stop my chest from caving in on itself. Each breath becomes impossible, the tightness in my lungs making them burn with every inhale.

I carry on, my face a mask of cool indifference despite the constant throb of my heart. "What if I want to keep it?"

His fingers tense against his thighs. "Lana…" He whispers my name as if I'm hurting him on some fundamental level, when I know that isn't the case.

I'm the one who is hurting.

I'm the one who gets to be mad.

And *I'm* the one who is going to walk away this time. Not because of his addiction, but rather because of who he is regardless of the drinking. Selfish. Self-centered. Self-destructive.

My fingers press into my thighs. "What if it makes me happy to keep the house? After all, I always dreamed of raising a family there. I wanted to enjoy summers by the lake, baking and building ships and swimming with the kids until their limbs cramp up."

I can see the future so clearly, it takes the pain in my chest and multiplies it by a hundred. Because even after all the lies, I want that future with Cal.

You wanted *that future with Cal. There's a past tense for a reason, so start using it.*

God. I'm so stupid.

"Why that house?" His voice cracks.

"Because it's *ours*. You might want to forget about all the history there, but I don't. And in the end, you running from a house won't solve anything when the real thing you're running from is yourself."

"Where is all this coming from?" He looks over at me with wild eyes reflecting exactly how he feels about the inheritance.

Desperate.

For once, we're on the same page. Because I feel desperate too. Desperate for him to tell the truth. Desperate for me to stay strong despite the urge to crumble beside him. Desperate for us not to lose everything we have built, even if it was built on a lie.

"Did your grandfather leave you an inheritance?" I ask point-blank.

"Yes." Cal does a good job keeping his expression flat, although the twitch of his fingers gives him away.

"He asked you to sell the house," I say with certainty.

One single nod makes my heart explode. Like a bomb, it detonates, blowing up any chance of me ever trusting another word that comes out of his mouth.

I already knew the truth, but having it confirmed destroys whatever bit of calm I had left.

"I see." My tongue scrapes against the roof of my mouth.

"How did you find out?" he rasps.

"I overheard your conversation after dinner. Someone left the window open…" A bitter laugh crawls up my throat, making my ears ache from the shrill sound.

"Whatever you heard, it's not what you think." He stumbles over the words.

"Of course it's not," I reply sarcastically. "Either way, I contacted the real estate agent and told him to lower the listing price. He said it's only a matter of time before someone puts an offer in."

"You did *what?*" His voice comes out low, his anger dripping from each syllable.

I stand and brush the dirt off my leggings. "Congratulations, Cal. Hope the twenty-five billion keeps you company at night, because I sure as hell won't." When I turn to walk away, Cal bolts to his feet and latches on to my hand, preventing me from leaving.

"Let me explain."

"What for? It's not like I trust a single thing that comes out of your mouth." I rip my hand from his grasp, nearly yanking my arm out of its socket in the process.

His fingers curl into a fist. "I couldn't tell you about the will."

"Why not?"

His head drops. "Because Grandpa told me not to."

"Since when do you listen to what people tell you to do? The Cal I knew and fell in love with would have told me about the will. Regardless of who said what, he would have been honest. Forthcoming. *Sincere*. He would have reasoned with me rather than gone behind my back, using my love for my daughter to work in his favor."

He flinches.

There isn't a single thing I wouldn't have done for Cal if he had asked me rather than lied, including selling the house.

He takes a deep breath. "There was a lot riding on my secrecy."

"Not nearly as much as what was riding on your honesty." In an act of betrayal, the tears I have fought appear, turning my vision blurry.

He pulls me into an embrace. "I'm so fucking sorry, Lana. I swear I wanted to tell you, but the decision wasn't up to me." His voice shakes, matching the trembling of his arms locked around me.

If this is the last hug I am going to get from him, then I might as well enjoy it. I lean into his touch, taking a deep breath of his scent, memorizing the notes of citrus and something distinctly him.

My ear presses against his chest. I listen to the sound of his erratic heartbeat and allow the steady thump to ground me.

I trace over the spot above his heart with my index finger. "Did you even want to get sober or were you also just doing that as part of the will?"

"What did you say?" His grasp slips before he corrects himself, securing me to his chest like he is afraid I might run off if he doesn't.

My fingers dig into his shirt, clasping on to the fabric. "Was this all some intricate plan to get me to let my guard down and sell the house faster?"

"What? *No.* Why would you even…" His brows tug together before they rise to his hairline. "The conversation outside. Shit—" He pulls back.

"Forget I asked. I don't care."

"*I* care."

My eyes shut from the pain slicing through my heart. I want to believe him. I really do. Yet I'm not sure I will ever be able to again. He has too much at stake that is contingent on my compliance. With the kind of pressure he is under, I'm sure he might say anything to make sure I don't back out of the plan to sell the house.

I won't. Whatever dreams I had about the home aren't worth the heartache attached to the man who owns half of it.

I push against his chest. It's a weak shove, but he releases me regardless.

"I want you gone from the guesthouse before I wake up in the morning." My voice cracks toward the end.

His frown deepens. "We can work this out together. Just let me get help and we—"

"There is no *we*. You made sure of that the moment you decided to lie to my face repeatedly, making me believe in some fantasy that wasn't even real."

To his credit, he takes my blow without blinking. "What we

have is real."

"Yeah, a real mistake. And one I don't plan on repeating with you ever again."

He recoils as if I physically hit him.

I turn and leave before I lose my nerve. Cal remains at the end of the dock, his eyes burning a hole into my back as I walk away. Each step feels as if I am traveling through quicksand. My legs barely cooperate as I leave behind the only man I ever truly loved.

I give him one last glance over my shoulder. "And when you leave Lake Wisteria this time, don't bother returning. It's not like you have any reason to come back anyway."

His face crumples like a crushed soda can, matching how my heart feels.

I turn away and take the long way back to the guesthouse. Despite every cell in my body begging me to stop, I hold my head high and march into the house like a soldier, ignoring the ache in my chest from where Cal ripped my heart out.

It's not until I crawl into bed that I give in to the tears. I cover my face with a pillow that smells like Cal, which only makes me sob harder. For Cami. For me. And for everything and everyone who has taken advantage of us and the love we are so willing to share.

The only person I can count on to make our dreams come true is myself, and it's time I learned that lesson once and for all.

CHAPTER FORTY-EIGHT

Cal

I fight everything in me not to take off after Lana. My hands twitch and my legs shake with the urge to grab her and force her to hear me out. To prove that I love her enough to fight for us and our happy ending.

Unfortunately, I know our situation can't be fixed with words when she thinks I'm a liar.

That's because you are.

No. I never lied outright, although weaving a story of half-truths doesn't make me any better. If anything, I feel shittier, knowing regardless of my intentions, the result is still the same.

I hurt her.

When you leave Lake Wisteria this time, don't bother returning. It's not like you have any reason to come back anyway. Her voice, strong and fearless despite the tremble of her chin, replays in my head.

Lana couldn't be more wrong, even if she has every reason to believe she is right. So long as she and Cami are here, I have every reason to return and fight for the people I love. There isn't anything I wouldn't do to prove to her that my inheritance has nothing to do with the way I feel about her and my reason for getting sober.

But how?

I run my hands through my hair, tugging at the strands to center myself. The bite of pain grounds me for a moment and eases the panic building in my chest. However, the relief is temporary as I come to grips with one of the last things she said.

I want you gone from the guesthouse before I wake up in the morning.

I don't want to go, but sticking around and upsetting Lana any more isn't an option. It will kill me to leave, knowing she most likely thinks the worst of me, but I can't think of a better punishment for hurting her.

It's what you deserve.

I sleep like absolute shit. My mind doesn't stop running, and I end up tossing and turning for a majority of the evening. By the time five a.m. rolls around, I call it a night and wake up. My head pounds, so I swallow a few pain relievers and get to work packing up my belongings before Lana wakes up. I focus on the task until it is complete, and my luggage looks about ready to pop.

My room appears the same way it did when I first arrived— empty and lacking any life. The only thing that sticks out is the photo I left behind on the bed.

Before I exit the bedroom, I check the drawers and closet for anything I might have missed. I nearly forgot the folded piece of yellow construction paper that I kept on top of my nightstand. With a shaky hand, I open Cami's card one more time.

Get better, Cow-L.

I trace the curve of the wonky heart before tucking it away in my backpack. The door across from mine remains closed, so I shut mine softly behind me and take off toward Cami's room on the other side of the house. There is no way I can't say goodbye to her.

Lana might not like it, but I can't go off to rehab letting her kid think I abandoned her. The thought of her thinking I disappeared without caring enough to say goodbye is a punishment I can't bear taking.

Cami is curled into a ball underneath her covers, clutching her stuffed lamb to her chest. She looks so at peace compared to her usual wild self when she is awake.

The ache in my chest that hasn't gone away since yesterday returns, stronger than ever before. Missing Cami will be inevitable. The kid has grown on me, and it feels like I'm leaving a piece of my heart behind with her.

You'll be back.

I swallow past the thick lump in my throat and shake Cami awake. Merlin jumps off the bed with a hiss before darting underneath it.

"Cow-l?" she rasps. Her hair resembles an eighties' hairspray commercial with the strands forming a helmet around her head.

"Hey." My smile is weak at best, but I try my hardest to stay strong for her.

She blinks a few more times to rid the sleep from her eyes. "What's wrong?"

"I wanted to say bye."

Her frown is instant. "Bye? Why?"

"I'm going away for a bit."

"Where?"

I reach for my backpack and pull out the card. "Remember when I told you I was sick?"

She nods.

"I'm going to go see a doctor so that way I'm not sick anymore."

Her small lips form a small *O*.

I take her small hand in mine and give it a squeeze. "When I'm feeling better, I'll come back for you and your mom."

"How long will you be gone?" Her glassy eyes shred whatever last bit of dignity I have.

You can't help hurting everyone you love.

It's a curse I plan on breaking, but a curse nonetheless.

"I'm not sure how long I'll be away." It depends on a lot of different things, all of which have to do with me.

She shocks me as she launches herself into my arms and wraps hers around my neck with a tight squeeze. "I don't want you to go."

Between her and Lana, I'm not sure if my heart will make it through this week without being ripped to shreds.

I rub her back. "I know."

She sniffles, making my chest tighten.

"I'm going to miss you." Her voice shakes.

God, if I don't get out of here soon, I'm going to end up not leaving at all. "I'm going to miss you too."

"You promise to come back?" She peeks up at me with tear-soaked lashes.

I swipe away the tears, erasing the evidence of her sadness. "I promise."

She releases a heavy sigh, and the tension in her shoulders deflates.

"I have a favor to ask you though." I tuck her card back into my backpack before zipping it up.

Her eyes widen. "Me?"

"Yup."

"What is it?"

I put on a serious face, like my very life depends on her. "Will you take care of Merlin for me?"

She gasps. "You're leaving him here?"

My throat feels all scratchy. "Yup. I can't take him with me, so I need you to be in charge." And that way, I have a valid reason to return, whether Lana wants me to or not.

Am I using my cat to convince Lana to see me again? Absolutely.

Do I feel bad about it? Not in the slightest, although I'll be sure to have food and supplies delivered to the house while I'm gone so she doesn't have to pay for a thing.

She stands tall and salutes me. "I'll take cares of him."

"And be sure to take care of your mom for me too."

Her head tilts, the tiny frown lines in her face making her look older than six years old. "Do you love *love* Mommy?"

"I love *love* your mommy more than anything. That's why I'm going to go get help."

Her whole face lights up from whatever idea is brewing

within that busy head of hers. "What if we go with you?"

Shit. All it takes is one shake of my head to have her smile falling.

"No. I wish you could, but this is something I've got to do on my own." I give her one last hug before rising.

"But you'll be back," she states.

"I'll be back—for you and your mommy."

"Pinky promise?" She holds out her pinky with a wobbly smile.

I lock our pinkies together and shake on it. "Pinky promise."

I give her one last kiss on the top of her head before turning around. My step falters as I take in Lana leaning against the doorframe, her eyes dark and her scowl unwavering.

"Hi, Mommy!"

She looks over at Cami. "You're up early." Her voice doesn't sound accusatory, but the glare she sends my way is.

"Cow-l woke me up." Cami throws me under the bus.

Love you too, kiddo.

"Why don't you try to sleep for a little bit longer? You have a long day today." Lana doesn't say anything else as she walks away, leaving me to be the one to shut the door. The heaviness pressing against my shoulders only worsens with each step I take toward the front door.

"Key." Lana holds out her hand. There is a slight tremble to her fingers that fucks me up inside.

"Lana…"

"Don't." Her voice wavers as if she is on the verge of crying.

Fuck.

I pull out my keyring and get to work removing the house key from it. Once I place it in Lana's hand, she tucks it into her back pocket.

"Good luck in rehab." Her voice sounds distant. Kind of like I'm underwater, fighting the current threatening to take me away from her.

"I'm coming back."

She reaches around me to unlock the door. "It won't change anything between us."

"Then what will?"

"Nothing. You got what you wanted. By the time you're out of rehab, I'm sure we will have a buyer ready to go."

"I'm not talking about the fucking house," I snap.

She blinks.

"I know you think the worst of me. That's fine. It's not like I don't deserve it. But just know that I didn't choose to go to rehab for the inheritance."

She scoffs as she crosses her arms. "You sure didn't choose it for me."

"No. I chose to get help for *me*."

Her mouth drops open.

"If I only wanted the inheritance, then I would have stuck around here for thirty more days and met the requirement asked of me. But instead, I'm going to rehab because I want to love myself as much as you love me."

She sucks in a breath but stays quiet.

"I want to be the man you and Cami deserve. Whether you believe me or not, that's the reason why I'm going to rehab. I've been through the process enough times to know it's thirty days of absolute hell, no matter which way someone cuts it. But every day I spend suffering in the prison of my mind is worth a thousand happy ones with you." I lean forward and press a kiss on the top of her head. She doesn't melt into me with a sigh like usual, but her shoulders drop a fraction.

I run my knuckles across her cheek. "I'm sorry about the house. I wanted to tell you every single time the subject came up, but I couldn't risk my brothers losing their inheritances after all the sacrifices they made. They would have never forgiven me, and I couldn't live with myself knowing I destroyed everyone's lives around me. I already hate myself enough as it is."

She looks away and swipes at her cheek with her sleeve.

I clasp on to her chin and force her to look me in the eyes. "I'll find a way to fix this."

Her eyes shut. "You can't."

"Is that a dare?" I half-heartedly tease.

Her bottom lip wobbles. "No. It's a reality."

The invisible talons wrapped around my heart squeeze until I'm left breathless and achy.

I step back before I end up kissing away the sad look on her face. "I'll return for you. Consider this your one and only warning."

Her lips press together. I offer her a half-assed smile before I walk to my car without looking back.

I *can't* look back and risk seeing the mistrust written all over her face.

I can only hope that whatever I said will hold her over until I can come back and prove that there is nothing in this world I want more than her and the family we can have.

Even if it kills me in the process.

The only thing saving me from collapsing face-first into my bed after Cal leaves is Cami needing to get to camp. After her spending a week away from all her friends, she is beyond excited to go back, which motivates me to get moving.

It's not until I finally drop her off that I am able to process everything. At least, that is what I had planned before my friends showed up at my front door, each of them carrying a bunch of grocery bags.

"What are you two doing here?" I gawk at Violet and Delilah as they shuffle into the guesthouse.

"We were summoned." Violet drops her set of plastic bags on the counter.

"By whom?"

Delilah begins unpacking the bags. "Cal."

I rear back. "*Cal* asked you to come here? Why?"

"Because he might be an idiot, but at least he's a thoughtful idiot who knew you would wallow in your misery for a few days before giving us a call."

I drop on to the couch and cradle my head in my hands. "Oh my God." My chest tightens to the point of pain.

He called your best friends because he knew you would avoid everyone until you could face them.

The way he can predict my every move… It makes me both happy and sick at the same time. Happy because I found someone who understands me on a cellular level, and sick because that person has all the power to abuse it.

And abuse it he did.

My eyes itch.

Don't you dare cry.

I rub at them until the tears disappear, although the heaviness pressing against my shoulders remains.

"Did he tell you about…" My voice drifts off as I think better of revealing the inheritance.

"The will?" Violet finishes for me. "Yeah, after he swore us to secrecy."

"He told you?"

"He didn't want you to feel obligated to keep a secret like that from us."

Oh, God. My shoulders slump. Why would he risk the consequence of losing his inheritance for me?

Because he cares.

I shake my head. "I can't believe he told you about the will."

"He did emphasize how we couldn't tell anyone or else his brothers will most likely ruin our lives." Delilah's lips press together.

"Either way, I still can't believe he said anything."

"He was a bit nervous, but I think only because he didn't like the idea of leaving you behind."

My chin trembles.

Delilah drops on to the couch on the other side of me and pulls me into a hug. "It'll be okay."

Violet also throws her arms around me. "You will get through this."

I hope so, because right now the idea of moving on from Cal feels impossible.

Especially when he plans on coming back.

It's been a rather quiet dinner. I've spent a majority of the meal stuck in my head, only speaking to ask Cami questions that get her going off on a tangent, her mouth running faster than an airplane engine.

"Can we watch a movie tonight?" Cami asks in the middle of dinner.

"Sure," I say absentmindedly as I twirl my pasta around my fork with no intention of actually eating it. My appetite dwindles with every reminder of Cal.

The empty placemat beside me.

The sink full of dishes that he would have volunteered to clean without me asking while I helped Cami wash her hair.

Merlin curled up underneath the table, right beside my feet, keeping me constant company.

"I miss Cal." Cami sighs.

My heart tears in two. "You do?"

She nods. "He told me he would be back."

My fork clatters against the plate. "He did?" The words come out like a wheeze. I only heard Cami asking him for a pinky promise, so I have no idea what Cal said to Cami while he was in her room.

She perks up. "Yup. After he gets better."

The tightness in my throat doesn't ease no matter how many deep breaths I take. "What else did he say?"

"He asked me to take care of Merlin for him." Her eyes brighten. "And you."

My lips press together to suppress the sob threatening to escape.

"Do you think he will come back soon, Mommy?"

"I'm not too sure." I crack at the end of my sentence.

"Do you love *love* him?"

My brows tug together. "Why are you asking?"

"Because he told me he love *loves* you."

A sharp stab of pain shoots through my chest. "I know."

"Will he be my new daddy?"

"I don't know." The air whooshes out of me like a balloon losing all its helium.

Her smile wobbles. "I told him I wished he was."

I blink. "You did? When?"

"On my birthday."

Oh, Camila. I pull her into a tight hug. "Is that what you want?"

She nods against my chest.

I knew Cami would love Cal. It's impossible not to, but hearing her admit she wanted him to be her dad cuts through me, especially when I'm not sure that will ever happen.

Cal might return, but how long will it take for him to fall back into destructive patterns? I refuse to let Cami be affected by him—no matter how much I wish the three of us could be together. If he chose to get sober for an inheritance, it will never stick. That much I know.

And I'm not going to wait around this time and watch the person I love most hurt himself again, even if I lose a bit of myself in the process once I let him go forever.

It's not until Cami goes to sleep for the night that Cal leaving truly hits me. His memory lingers in every corner of the house, reminding me of the happiness we shared together before he blew it all up.

Even Merlin seems sad about his owner's absence. He sits on the couch in the same spot Cal always occupied during movie nights. I try to relax on the other side and watch something, but my mind continues to drift back to everything about Cal.

Is he feeling bad about everything that happened?

Did he mean what he said about going to rehab because he wanted to rather than doing it for his inheritance?

Will he come back sober and willing to do whatever it takes to get me back or will he give up the moment I show a bit of resistance?

Questions run through my head, making it impossible to concentrate on anything happening on the screen in front of me.

With a groan, I shut the TV off and abandon my spot on the couch. Walking toward my room, I pause outside the door and turn toward the closed one across the hall.

Don't even think about it.

Except I'm not thinking as I enter the empty room Cal once occupied. He went out of his way to make the bed, which is something he never did unless I asked him.

I'm so quick to move on from the bed, I nearly miss the white rectangle that doesn't quite match the eggshell-colored comforter. The dull discomfort in my chest morphs into a sharp ache as I pick it up and read the message written across the back in Cal's messy handwriting.

> I dare you to wait for me.
> The <u>real</u> me.
> The <u>sober</u> me.
> The <u>best</u> me who wants to spend the rest of his days getting drunk on life with you.

He draws out a scoreboard that matches the plank we had, except there is an added tally to my side that wasn't there before.

I flip the photo. My vision blurs as I take in the three of us at Dreamland. Cami and I face the camera with beaming smiles, but it's Cal who steals the show with his smile. He looks sober. Alive. *Happy.*

I lose the battle with gravity and fall against the mattress, holding the photo to my chest like a life raft in the middle of an ocean. One edge creases from my carelessness, so I'm quick to place it on the nightstand.

Everything smells like him. The bed. The sheets. The pillow I end up cradling against my chest as I curl into a ball.

I dare you to wait for me.

Seven words steal my breath and fuel my tears. They fall down my cheeks before soaking the pillow beneath me. I'm not sure why I'm crying. Is it out of sadness? Hope? Fear that what he says might not be true?

Maybe a mix of all three if I'm being honest.

I make a promise to myself to leave in a minute. Except a minute comes and goes, and I still find myself unable to move from his bed.

At some point, Merlin curls up against me. The fact that Cal left him here tells me one thing.

He really does plan on coming back whether I want him to or not.

And a part of me wants him to do just that.

CHAPTER FIFTY

Cal

The trip from Lake Wisteria was a blur. I don't stop driving until I park outside Iris and Declan's house on the edge of the suburbs.

"Cal?" Iris blinks up at me. "What are you doing here?"

"I fly out tomorrow," I blurt out.

"I thought you were leaving Friday?" Her brows furrow.

I shake my head. "I moved up my flight."

"Why?"

"Because Lana kicked me out of the guesthouse."

"Oh, shit. Come inside." Iris shuffles me into the house before shutting the door behind me. I follow her into the barren living room.

I look around. "Where is everything?"

"We're moving into the new house next week."

"Already?"

She laughs. "It's been months already."

"Wow." A sigh slips out of me as I settle on to the airbed Iris has set up in front of the TV as a makeshift couch.

"What happened?" She sits on the other side of the air mattress.

"Lana knows about the will."

Iris's brows rise. "How?"

"She overheard Rowan, Declan, and me talking about it."

Her wide eyes only add to the growing anxiety building inside of me. "Shit. That's explains why she looked like a deer caught in headlights."

"I fucked up."

"What did you say exactly?"

I explain what Lana overheard.

Iris frowns. "Did she at least hear you out?"

"For the most part, but that doesn't change anything. She was already on thin ice with trusting me, and now…"

"She has no reason to trust you at all," Iris finishes for me.

My eyes drop. "No." She might not trust me, but I'll find a way to earn it back and not risk my inheritance.

Iris asks me for more information, so I share everything that happened over the last few days ever since the dinner.

"I could talk to her," Iris offers after hearing me out.

I rear back. "How would that help?"

"I could help her understand why you would keep a secret like that in the first place?"

My head shakes. "As much as I love you for wanting to help, I don't think Lana would go for it, so I'd rather you not unless she reaches out first."

"Are you sure?"

"Yeah. I've done enough damage as it is. Sending you there… I'd rather not risk upsetting her."

Iris lifts a shoulder. "You're the one who knows her best."

Which is exactly why I'm worried.

"What if she doesn't forgive me?" I voice my fear aloud.

She throws her arms around me. "I doubt you'll stop until she does."

I return her hug with one of my own. Despite my life blowing up around me, I always know Iris will have my back.

"I just want you to know that I'm so proud of you for taking initiative and getting help yourself."

I swallow past the thick lump in my throat. "I haven't even gone to rehab yet."

"No, but your willingness to go in the first place shows so much progress."

I lift my chin. "I'm doing it for myself this time."

"That's why it will work. You're going to get better, and I'll be rooting for you every step of the way." Her genuine smile battles against the constant chill that has been present in my veins ever since I left the lake house behind.

With Iris's help and Lana's friends keeping an eye on her, there is only one last thing getting in the way of me confidently going to rehab and getting my life in order once and for all.

I never thought I would spend my thirty-fourth birthday

voluntarily enrolling myself into rehab. It seems fitting with the way my life is going lately to spend it all alone, with nothing to keep me company but my endless thoughts about Lana and a bunch of fellow alcoholics going through various stages of withdrawal along with me.

No one at the facility acknowledges my birthday, which is fine by me. I honestly prefer it that way because I'm not the most pleasant company at the moment. Not having a single coping mechanism to distract me from my thoughts makes me anxious and uncharacteristically agitated with everyone I come into contact with.

No Candy Crush. No alcohol. No Lana and Cami to keep me company as I battle through therapy, group sessions, enough arts and crafts to drive me mad.

Despite being given my approved amount of Adderall, my brain doesn't stop running, long after I am supposed to be asleep every night. I'm plagued by the decisions I made and how Lana might be reeling from them.

I didn't mean to leave her alone with the fallout of my choices, but I didn't have an option. Sticking around would have only hurt her more. Leaving was the best option, even if it screws me up inside to be apart from her and Cami.

It'll be worth it.

The pain. The lack of alcohol to cope. The constant reminders of how I failed everyone around me because of my addiction.

Not anymore.

I make the same wish I did back at Dreamland, although I have no candle or cake to make it official.

I wish to kick my addiction for good.

CHAPTER FIFTY-ONE
Alana

The dull throb in my chest hasn't eased since Cal left two weeks ago. If anything, it only gets worse as the days go on. My attempts to keep myself busy only last for so long. With Cami at her friend's house and Violet and Delilah busy with work, I have no one left to distract me.

Even the realtor and the general contractor have been quiet about the house. When I voiced my concern about a lack of interested buyers, both assured me that everything was going according to plan.

The silence in the guesthouse quickly becomes unbearable, leaving me to my own thoughts. My head is a pathetic place to be these days. A sad, miserable place that reminds me of a fact I hate admitting to myself.

I miss Cal.

It's impossible not to when everything reminds me of him. Grocery shopping. Driving around town with my tires squealing. Spending thirty minutes scrolling for something new to watch only to settle on watching a competitive baking show we both have seen a hundred times.

Each day drags on at a snail's pace. With me not working, my days mainly consist of taking Cami to camp and sitting around the house in case Ryder and the crew need anything from me.

Part of me wishes Cal would show back up, if only for me to be angry at him again. It's a selfish thought that I dismiss in a matter of seconds, knowing that he is exactly where he needs to be. Yet still, I consider what it must be like to go through the process.

Is he struggling with any withdrawal symptoms?

Is he wishing he never went in the first place?

Is he talking through his issues and figuring out why he has difficulty staying sober?

The longer I think about everything he said before he left, the more I wonder if he was telling the truth. Calling the lawyer to find out would put the inheritance at risk, so I settle for the next best thing: Iris and Zahra.

We exchanged numbers before I left the night of Cal's birthday dinner, but I hadn't taken advantage of it until now.

Before I chicken out, I text them.

> Hey.

Their replies come in at the same time.

Iris
> What's up?

Zahra
> Hi!

I release a shaky breath as I hit send on my next message, which I spent ten minutes mulling over.

> I was wondering if one of you could help clarify a few things for me about the will.

Iris's reply is instant.

Iris
> I can be there in forty minutes.

Forty minutes? How is that even possible from her house in Chicago?

Zahra
> Ugh. Wish I could be there!

I busy myself with cleaning up the already-spotless house while I wait for Iris. The loud thrum of propellers interrupts me in the middle of scrubbing down the stovetop, and I rush outside to watch a helicopter land in my backyard.

"What the fuck?" I shut the door behind me.

I didn't know it was legal to land in someone's backyard.

Are you really surprised? This is Lake Wisteria. Anyone can be bought with the right price.

The moment the blades stop spinning, Iris dashes out of the helicopter. She rushes to the nearest set of bushes while clutching a hand to her mouth.

"Oh my God. Are you okay?"

She heaves once in a godawful reply. I wince as I help gather her braids in my hand to prevent them from falling in front of her face.

She throws up twice before being able to stand upright.

"Well, that went a lot worse than I expected."

"I have 7 Up and Alka-Seltzer inside."

"Sounds lovely." She wipes at her mouth with a frown.

I shuffle her into the house and find her a spare toothbrush. While she cleans her teeth, I pull out some snacks that my mom always said helped a sour stomach.

"You're a lifesaver." Iris drops onto the stool and pops a saltine cracker into her mouth.

"Are you feeling better?"

"Much. I wanted to drive, but Declan insisted on having me fly."

"Why did he?"

She lifts a shoulder. "He thought it was safer."

"More than driving?"

Her eyes roll. "I know. He's a bit overbearing these days."

I shoot her a look. "Hate to break it to you, but that's how he's always been."

She cackles. "I see why Cal loves you."

I tense.

Her eyes narrow. "He does love you, you know."

I become fascinated by my manicure. "I know."

"But you don't trust him," she states.

"He hasn't given me many reasons to."

Her soft smile reaches her eyes. "Although I was in a different position than you with the will, I can see where you're coming from."

"You were?"

"Did you really think Declan and I got married because we loved each other?"

My brows raise so high, I'm afraid they might be permanently stuck that way.

She snorts. "I married Declan because of the will. Falling in love with him was a convenient outcome I hadn't anticipated happening."

My mouth drops open. "You married him because of the inheritance?"

"Amongst other things." She runs a hand over her stomach absentmindedly with a small smile.

Is she…

Don't you dare ask that.

I bite down on my cheek to stop myself from blurting out the question burning in the back of my mind.

She looks up at me, as if remembering I'm still standing here. "I know it sounds crazy…"

"Because it is!"

She laughs. "Well, I married Declan because I cared about him and didn't want to see him lose to his asshole father."

"What does his father have to do with any of this?"

"Well, that's where everything gets a little complicated. If the brothers don't complete their individual tasks, their father gets their shares of the company."

"What? Why?"

She shrugs. "Their grandfather made it that way."

Shit. "So if Cal doesn't sell the house…"

"His father would earn eighteen percent of the company, plus the six percent that still remains unclaimed."

"You think his father owns six percent?"

"Not yet at least. Whatever Brady asked him to do isn't

complete yet."

"And what about Declan?"

A small smile teases at her lips. "He's close to getting his, but whatever happens with Cal and his task puts Declan's shares at risk."

My eyes screw shut. "Cal never mentioned that."

Probably because you didn't give him a chance to explain himself.

Guilt replaces some of the anger I've held on to ever since I found out about the inheritance.

"He didn't have an option before. But now that everything is out in the open…"

"I haven't told anyone."

She laughs. "I didn't expect you to. You care just as much about Cal as he does about you—no matter how angry you are at him."

"Am I that predictable?" There is a harsh bite to my question.

She holds up her hands in mock surrender. "Love makes people do selfless things."

I pull out a stool beside her and sit before my legs give out. "Like selling my home?"

She nudges her shoulder with mine. "Cal will figure it out."

My hands quit their fidgeting. "How do you know?"

"Because if you want it, he will stop at nothing to make it happen."

"Just like that?"

She snaps her fingers. "Just like that."

"What do you think, Ms. Castillo?"

I look up from the wood floor that looks brand new after Ryder restored it. The memory of Cami taking her first steps near the stairs fades away as I'm hit with the news that the house will be ready in a couple of weeks to be shown to potential buyers.

I'm sure Cal would be impressed by how the remodel is turning out. The interior designer Ryder hired is doing a phenomenal job making the house look exactly like our Pinterest boards. Although there are still some last-minute finishes that need to be added, everything is looking just like I wanted.

"Ms. Castillo?" the real estate agent repeats while looking at me as if I have lost my mind.

Maybe I have. The lack of sleep, worrying about Cal, and the looming open house have done a splendid job of keeping me up late at night to the point of delirium.

"Yes?" I shake my head.

"Did you hear anything I said?"

Heat rushes to my cheeks. "No. Sorry about that. Do you mind repeating it?"

He huffs as he pushes his thick-rimmed glasses up the bridge of his nose. "I just was mentioning that we have plenty of people interested in the property, and we haven't even had an open house yet."

"Wow. That's great." My voice could not sound more wooden if I tried.

The real estate agent lifts a fuzzy brow. "So you're aware, when we have multiple offers, that usually drives up the price."

"Fantastic." I rock back on my sneakers.

He frowns. "Is everything all right?"

"Sure. Why wouldn't it be?"

He shuts his folder. "If you're having second thoughts about selling the house…"

"No!" I raise my hand. "I'm just overwhelmed that we have so many people interested in the property."

Yeah, overwhelmed with nausea.

His tense smile doesn't settle my churning stomach. "If things go according to plan, Mr. Kane and you will have the property sold to the highest bidder during the open house."

"Great." The hollow pit in my stomach widens at the idea.

"I thought so. No way this house will last until the end of the open house."

I suck in a breath. "Let's start with the open house and take it from there."

The realtor goes over the details he has planned, all while I drift in and out of the conversation with a confirmatory nod here and there.

"Would you like to be present when the buyers come check out the property?"

I give my head a hard shake. "No."

I'd rather jump off the dock in a pair of concrete sneakers than sit through hours of people gawking at the home I love while I idly sit by, letting my heart get shredded to pieces knowing one of them will buy it from me.

Screw that.

Just because I'm selling the house to help Cal and his family doesn't mean I have to like it.

The shrill sound of my ringtone wakes me up. I thought sleeping in Cal's bed might help cure my insomnia, but Rowan's call shattered my theory before I had a chance to try it.

I lie back down and answer my phone. "Hello?"

"Alana." Rowan's gruff voice fills my ear. "How are you?"

"Wonderful, especially now that you woke me up."

He releases a huff of air. "Sorry about that. I didn't think you would be asleep at nine p.m."

Nine p.m.?!

Shit. I probably knocked out as soon as Cami did.

I grab the pillow that no longer smells as strongly of Cal and tuck it under my head. "I haven't been getting the best sleep lately."

"How are you doing?"

"About as good as one would expect after finding out your grandfather was hell-bent on making me suffer for some reason, although I'm not sure why. I was good to him. I even listened to his stories about Ireland like I hadn't heard the same ones a hundred times before."

His laugh is soft and quiet, drawing a smile from me. "He was a manipulative bastard, wasn't he?"

"Ugh. The worst. What did he make you do?"

"Run and renovate Dreamland for six months."

I scoff. "And here I thought we were on an even playing field."

"It wasn't as easy as it sounds, especially for someone like me."

"What's that supposed to mean?"

"That I was an idiot who needed a good ass-kicking."

My grin widens. "Zahra mentioned she helped knock a little sense into you."

"She did a lot more than that."

I can practically hear the smile in his voice. Bitterness rises, ready to exploit my insecurities regarding my own relationship, but I shove it down.

"I assume you didn't call me to gush about your girlfriend."

"No, but who says I needed a reason to call?"

"You're a Kane. You don't do phone calls unless there is something you want."

He laughs harder this time, making me grin. "I was hoping to speak to you about the tres leches recipe."

"Seriously?" I thought he would call to check in on the house sale or to ask me a question about Cal.

"*Seriously*," he repeats back in my tone, which makes me clamp down on my tongue to stop myself from laughing. "I was hoping we could come to a reasonable agreement."

"Why do you want it so badly?"

"Because I know talent when I see it, and you're the real deal."

Heat crawls up my neck before spreading all the way to my cheeks. "Really?"

"Yes. Cal mentioned you're interested in opening your own bakery, and I respect that kind of ambition. I'm sure you'll go far with your skills."

My phone slips from my grasp from how clammy my hand becomes. I don't breathe, let alone interrupt him as he continues.

"But I'm interested in developing a new land that features

Princess Marianna and a few other characters that I can't share a lot about yet unless you agree to help."

"Do any of these characters happen to be from Colombia?"

"Would that convince you to say yes?"

"Depends. Are you still offering me a million bucks for the recipe?"

"Let's make it five."

"*Five million?*"

"Cal was right when he called me out on only offering a mil. I just wanted to see if he pays more attention than he lets on, and he proved me right."

My mouth drops open. "You did that on purpose?"

He laughs. "Yeah."

"What is wrong with you?"

"Zahra's still trying to figure that one out, although compared to Declan, I'm the nice one."

I shut my eyes to center myself. "This is a lot to wrap my head around."

"Should I not mention the job then?"

"What job?"

"I'd like to bring you on as a baking consultant of sorts."

"A baking consultant?" I squeak.

"I see you and Zahra share the fond habit of repeating everything I say."

"That says more about you than us."

His deep chuckle makes the speaker on my phone crackle. "Are you open to the job?"

"Do I have to work at Dreamland?"

"Only for a minority of the time. We can fly you out on the

jet one weekend every month if that works."

Nope. Not going to comment on the private jet, no matter how much I want to.

Once a month sounds doable, especially if it is only a part-time job.

"How much are you offering?" I ask with a serious tone.

"Give me a few more recipes and you'll be retiring tomorrow."

Screw retirement. I could open my own bakery and travel around the world, getting the best of both worlds.

My answer is easy. "You know what? Sure. Why not?"

"I was hoping you would be up for the challenge."

I grin. "When do I start?"

"Does next month work?"

When faced with the option to sit at home all weekend or go to Dreamland, I make the same reasonable choice anyone else would make in my position.

"Sure, so long as Cami can come with me."

"Of course. My assistant will send you all the details and travel info."

I stare at the ceiling long after Rowan hung up the call and process what just happened. Working for the Kanes might not be what I expected for myself, but an experience like this would help me grow while giving me an opportunity to learn from other people. I can turn it into the adventure I always wanted.

And you achieved it all on your own.

Maybe dreams do come true after all.

CHAPTER FIFTY-TWO

Cal

I've had thirty days to stew in my decisions, dating back to the first time I ever took my first sip of alcohol. I wasn't like most kids who have their first drink at a party, under the influence of too many friends and not enough brain cells.

No one was around to peer pressure me into drinking. In fact, no one was around to care at all. My brothers were always busy doing their own things and my father was rarely home before nine o'clock., which meant no one was there to intervene.

That first night, I drank because I was angry at myself for missing a goal and losing the game for my team.

The next week, I drank because my father called me a stupid fuck for failing a test.

The time after that, it was the anniversary of my mom's death.

Slowly, drinking became a way to numb the problems. To

drown out the noise until I was better able to cope with the stressors around me. Except the time to cope never came. When I was presented with adversity, I ran and repeated the same habits that got me into trouble in the first place.

I never learned from my mistakes. I was too lost in my sickness to care much beyond stopping the pain, and everyone around me, especially myself, paid the price.

Not anymore though. I will do whatever it takes to stay sober, not only for myself, but for the people I love too.

My grandpa was right. Sobriety *is* a journey, except to get to the final destination, I needed to suffer through a month-long turbulent plane ride with no landing strip in sight.

That's what rehab felt like. But unlike the last time, I gave it a hundred percent because *I* deserved my all. I wanted to get better for myself and the future I will have once I do.

When I land in Chicago, I head straight to the AA meeting Leo recommended because I don't have time to waste. All the chairs are positioned in a circle, exposing us to one another. I take one of the last open seats, leaving the one beside me empty.

The chairperson begins, and one by one everyone introduces themselves. It's an intimate group made up of high-profile lawyers, executives, and professionals. I recognize a few from crossing paths at events, but no one comments on it. Because in this room, we are all the same.

Recovering alcoholics.

I've been through this process twice already, so I know exactly what to say when everyone turns to me.

I rise and take a deep breath. "Hi, my name is Callahan, although I prefer to go by Cal, and I'm an alcoholic."

"Hi, Cal," different tones and voices reply.

I ignore the urge to clench my fists. "Today is the first official day where I choose to be sober." Rehab might have helped me start off on the right foot, but not having access to alcohol isn't the same as choosing to be sober. At least not to me.

I want to be tempted by alcohol and resist.

I want to experience pain and overcome without a single drop of vodka.

I want to prove to myself that I can make it in the world as a sober man rather than one driven by the need to drown my emotions and insecurities with a temporary fix.

People clap like I just won the Stanley Cup.

A few more individuals introduce themselves. While one man is sharing how he is officially one-year sober, the door behind me opens. Everyone turns toward the sound.

The one person I never thought I would see at one of these meetings walks in, shaking an umbrella in one hand while juggling a briefcase in his other.

My father's eyes connect with mine. He doesn't look the least bit surprised to see me here, but me on the other hand?

I'm floored.

"Look who finally decided to show up," the chairperson calls out.

I think he introduced himself as Jeff? Jim? I don't remember much except that his job is to defend the worst criminals in all of Chicago.

No wonder the asshole drank.

"Sorry I'm late."

Sorry I'm late? My father doesn't apologize for shit.

Because he is faking it.

Since fate couldn't be any more of a bitch lately, he takes the only empty seat available—right next to me. I'm grateful that I look more like my mother because I'd hate for people to connect the two of us as anything more than strangers.

After all, that's all we will ever be.

The group turns to look over at my father, and he stands with a sigh. "Hi, my name is Seth, and I'm an alcoholic. I've been sober for 640 days."

What. The. Fuck.

I must have said the words aloud because everyone turns toward me with a range of expressions. My father's soulless gaze lands on me, making my skin crawl.

"Have something to say?" His low tone is a warning similar to that of a rattlesnake.

"Plenty, starting with why?"

"For the same reason you're probably here." He takes a seat and unbuttons the front of his sports coat.

Brady motherfucking Kane.

If my grandfather weren't dead already, I would have made sure he didn't live to see tomorrow.

I spend the rest of the meeting processing his reason for being here. Grandpa must have wanted him to get sober in exchange for something, but what? Six percent of the company? Twenty-five billion dollars?

Yet he didn't ask you to get sober. Just him.

I can't fathom why my grandfather would go through all that trouble of emphasizing the importance of sobriety being a journey, only to force my father into attending AA.

It doesn't matter. If I earn my shares, then the math will never be in his favor regardless if he earns six percent or not.

I mull over every detail, searching for clues over the last two years, only to be drawn back into the meeting by the chip person slapping a chip into my hand.

"Congratulations on being sober for twenty-four hours." The person in charge of passing out chips based on everyone's level of sobriety continues on to the next person.

I spend the rest of the meeting flipping the chip between my fingers. It's not until the metal legs of chairs scrape against the floor that I look up to find a majority of the members have already left.

My father rises from his seat, completely ignoring me.

"Did you ever want to get sober before the will?" I ask the question that has been festering in the back of my brain.

His beady eyes drill a hole into my head. "I never had a reason to."

The piercing sensation in my chest intensifies. "Not a single one?"

"No," he says in a flat tone.

"What about your kids?"

"What about them?"

To think you actually believed you were similar to this man.

In reality, the only thing my father and I have in common is an addiction. Because where he finds his family expendable, I find mine irreplaceable. There is nothing I wouldn't do to ensure I make them happy, which is something he couldn't even begin to understand, let alone reciprocate.

"Why did you drink?" I blurt out before I have a chance to

filter my question.

"Because I didn't know how to stop."

"And now you do?"

"I was heavily motivated to learn."

"Because of money." I don't bother tampering down the disgust in my voice.

"Who are you to judge? It's not like you're any better than me." He gives me a once-over glance that would make anyone else feel two inches tall.

"I'm here because I want to be."

"Because of money." He repeats my same words back to me.

I shake my head and stand. "Because I'm worth the effort."

His quick glance couldn't be more dismissive if he tried. "Are you sure about that?"

A bitter laugh explodes out of me. "You have always found me to be lacking, but I have something you never will have."

"A heart?" His mocking smirk deserves to be punched.

"A life worth living." I walk away. The heaviness pressing against my chest lessens with each step in the opposite direction.

"I have a life worth living," he calls out with an air of desperation bleeding into his voice.

"Then enjoy it while it lasts."

Once Declan becomes CEO and we all earn our shares of the company, my father will become the one thing he spent his entire life making sure I felt.

Insignificant.

I wait until I get in my car to call Lana. I'm not optimistic about her answering, but I hold my breath.

The pit in my stomach only stretches with each ring. My finger hovers over the red end call button, but I stop myself at the sound of her voice.

"Cal?" Lana's slight rasp tugs at my chest.

God. I missed the sound of her voice.

"Lana."

"You're out," she says before a door shuts on her end of the call.

"Yeah. Just left this morning."

"How was it?"

"The closest I ever hope to get to jail."

Her laugh is soft yet eases the tension in my shoulders better than any massage.

"How are you?" I ask before thinking against it.

"Fine."

"And how's our girl?"

The silence following my question is unbearable, but I refrain from filling it. There is nothing I won't do to show her that I want her and Cami, even if it means reminding her every chance I get.

Lana releases a heavy breath. "She misses you."

My chest tightens. "How about you?" It's a stupid question, yet I can't stop myself from asking it.

"I've missed you too." She whispers it like a dirty confession.

I didn't realize how much I needed to hear those words from her until she said them.

"I plan on coming home."

"When?" Her voice has a certain edge to it.

"I'm not sure." I bite down on my tongue. Until I have my shit sorted out, I don't want to return because Lana deserves better than that. She deserves the best I have to offer, and a twenty-four-hour sobriety chip isn't going to cut it.

"Then why call?"

"Because I wanted to let you know that I'm going to find a way to make everything right." Post-rehab me is motivated by a single goal: show Lana and Cami that I will spend the rest of my life proving how much I love them.

"That's all?"

"And that I love you," I add.

She sighs.

My grip on the phone tightens. "Just give me time to fix this, okay?"

Her steady breathing fills the silence.

"Okay," she says before the line goes dead.

"You're back!" Iris throws her arms around my neck and cries.

The moment I texted the family chat saying I was back in Chicago, Iris replied that she was on her way with Declan.

I peel her off me and take a good look at her face. "Are you crying?"

"Yes. I can't help it." She wipes at her face with frustration. "It just happens."

I shoot Declan a *what the fuck* look. He only shrugs as if this happens all the time.

Wait a minute… Declan would never brush off Iris's tears like that without a good reason—

"You're pregnant." The words fly out of my mouth.

She nods with a few tears streaming down her face.

"Holy shit. Congratulations!" I pull her back into a hug.

"Since when?" I look over Iris's head at my brother.

"We found out a week after you left."

"I wanted to tell you, but you weren't here." Iris's tears soak through my shirt.

"She was very upset about that. Cried for what felt like a day," Declan mutters.

"This is doing wonders for my ego."

Iris slaps my chest with a laugh. "I'm emotional."

"Yeah, an emotional wreck," I finish for her.

She pushes against my chest, and I release her.

Her nose wrinkles. "You smell like an airplane."

"Probably because I just landed a few hours ago and haven't had a chance to shower yet."

Declan pulls Iris away from me and into his embrace. "How was rehab?"

"Like a party, except no one wants to be there."

"Sounds like a typical Friday for me." Declan's lips twitch.

Iris's eyes roll.

"Did you get the chip?" Declan asks.

I pull it out of my pocket to show him. "That and a nice conversation with our father."

Declan's brows tug together. "Our father?"

"Turns out whatever inheritance he has is contingent on him attending AA meetings too."

My brother drops on to the leather sofa. "Shit."

"Yup. My thought exactly."

"Isn't that…triggering?" Iris sits down next to Declan and clasps his hand.

I shrug. "I spent thirty days getting over my daddy issues."

"And?"

"Turns out the only person I was hurting is myself, and safe to say masochism isn't my kink anymore."

Declan's smile is small but powerful. "Teach me your ways."

"Oh, you can plan on it once I get Lana back." Until then, nothing else matters.

"What do you think your grandpa offered him?" Iris asks.

"There's still six percent of the company left uncontested."

"I knew Grandpa wouldn't let him walk away with nothing. He always had a soft spot for that piece of shit." Declan rubs at his stubble while staring off into the distance.

"We'll figure it out." I pull out my phone. "Are either of you hungry? I was thinking about ordering delivery."

"Wait. You're staying?" Iris frowns.

"I still have a few things to sort out before I head back to Lake Wisteria."

"Like what?"

"How the hell I'm going to get to keep the lake house." I already spoke with the real estate agent and told him to hold off on accepting any offers, so it's only a matter of time before I figure out a solution.

Declan's frown deepens. "You can't keep it."

"I have a meeting with Leo tomorrow to see otherwise."

His chest falls from his heavy exhale. "And if he tells you that it's impossible?"

"Then I'll find a way to prove him wrong."

"Cal…"

"What?"

Declan leans forward on his elbows. "You don't need to come up with a solution on your own. We're here for you."

The pressure in my chest releases like a popped balloon. "Don't go all soft on me now that I'm sober."

His lips twitch. "Asshole."

"That's more I like it."

Iris's glassy eyes make me laugh.

"Seriously? You're crying again?"

She sniffles. "I'm sorry, okay? It's just so sweet to see you two getting along and being all brotherly."

I fake heave while Declan glowers, restoring the balance between us once more.

Iris and Declan keep me company during my first night back from rehab. Unlike before, I'm not plagued with heavy loneliness I want to drown with alcohol. Instead, I enjoy my time with them, all while reminding myself that I too can have what they have.

So long as I put in the work.

CHAPTER FIFTY-THREE

Cal

"Callahan." Leo claps me on the shoulder. "How are you doing?"

"Better."

He motions for me to have a seat before doing the same. "How was rehab?"

"You want the polite or honest answer?" I chew on the inside of my cheek.

"Shoot it to me straight, son."

"It was fucking hell. I can't believe I paid tens of thousands of dollars to go through that kind of pain."

The wrinkled skin around his eyes tightens. "Sorry to hear that, but I'm also very proud of you, and I'm sure your grandpa would say the same if he were here with us."

"I'd like to think so, since this was all part of his master plan."

Leo's raspy chuckle makes my lips curve upward. "All he wanted was for you to be happy."

I blink twice. "Really?" With all the shit he put me through with the inheritance and his will, it's laughable to hear. He knew what kind of position I would be put in with Lana. The least he could have done was give me a second option, especially if he cared about her as much as he made it seem.

Leo makes his chair creak as he leans back. "Is that so hard to believe?"

"After everything he required of me this summer, yes."

Leo chuckles. "I know his way of going about things seems… unconventional."

"That's because it is." Everything about my grandfather's will is far from the status quo. Like he couldn't bear the thought of being considered anything but unique, so he decided to have his legacy live on long after he did. Rowan's task to work at Dreamland. Declan's requirement to get married and have a child. Me having to spend the summer at the lake house before selling it despite my grandpa knowing how much Lana loves it.

"Whatever the case, he only wanted the best for you. That much I can guarantee."

"Even if it means selling the house despite Lana's and my wishes?"

He leans forward on his elbows. "Do you mind if I offer a piece of advice?"

My muscles turn to stone beneath my shirt. "What?"

He twirls the tip of his mustache. "There are multiple ways to buy a house."

My eyebrows inch up my forehead. "Who said anything

about me buying a house? Selling one is hard enough as it is."

"It doesn't have to be." His lips curve upward for a second before dropping back into their flat line.

I lean forward. "What do you mean by that?"

"I'm sure you'll figure it out." His fingers interlock. "What other questions do you have for me?"

My brain can't keep up with the emotional ping-pong match this man is putting me through.

I pull out the chip I earned and show him. "I plan on returning to the AA group tonight."

"That's good. I'm sure you'll get me that green chip in no time."

"About that...I wanted to ask if I'm able to split my time between this AA group and one being held in Lake Wisteria."

His head tilts. "I don't see why not."

My shoulders drop. "Great."

The landline on his desk rings.

Leo's gaze slides from the phone to my face. "Do you have any other questions?"

"Regarding the house—"

"All I can say is to follow your gut."

"What gut? I've just been winging it because I have no idea what I'm doing."

"Every choice you have made up until this point proves otherwise." He lifts the phone off the receiver. "Now if you don't mind, this client is being read his last rites…"

Jesus.

"I'll see myself out." I take a few steps toward the door.

"And Callahan?"

I glance at Leo from over my shoulder. "Yes?"

"I trust you'll find a way to sort all this out." He returns to his call, and I shut the door behind me.

I trust you'll find a way to sort all this out?

"What a load of shit."

After going through another dreadful run-in with my father at the AA meeting, all I want to do is call Lana and hear her voice. So, instead of keeping away, I do just that.

"Hey." I balance my phone between my ear and shoulder as I climb into bed.

Lana releases a heavy breath before speaking. "Cal."

"How are you doing?"

"Fine."

I see we are sticking to one-word answers now.

"And how's Cami?"

"Good." Her tone is as flat as her response.

My heart pounds harder against my rib cage. "Is everything okay?"

She lets out a loud sigh. "Not really."

I'll count her two-worded reply as a win. "What's wrong?" I sit up in bed.

"Someone put an offer on the house."

"Oh." My stomach sinks.

"Yeah. *Oh.*"

"I'm going to fix this." I'm not sure how yet, but I will find a way.

"So you say." Sheets rustle on her side of the call.

"I'm working on it."

"Iris and I talked."

I swallow hard. "And?"

"You and I both know there is no other option regarding your grandfather's will. And as much as I love that house, there is no way I'll let you screw over everyone to keep it."

My chest tightens. "Lana—"

"I need to go to sleep. Tomorrow is going to be a long day with back-to-school night."

"You're starting back up already?"

"Yup. And Cami starts at her new school next Monday."

"Can I go with you?" The question rushes out of me.

"To take her to school?"

My racing pulse isn't doing me any favors. "Yeah."

"I don't think that's a good idea."

"Why not?"

"Because I don't want you hanging around her."

My chest feels like she cracked it in half with a crowbar. "Okay. I understand."

"I don't want to hurt you—"

I stop her. "I know."

"It's just that—"

I don't let her finish. "You don't trust me."

"No, I don't."

"Then I won't stop until I give you every reason to." This time, I'm the one to hang up the phone. Prolonging that kind of conversation won't help either one of us, and I'd much rather spend my time finding ways to prove her wrong.

Instead of going to sleep like I had planned, I pull out my laptop and get to researching different ways to buy a house.

Turns out Leo wasn't just spouting shit after all.

He *was* right. There are multiple ways to buy a house—both legal and illegal.

I trust you'll find a way to sort all this out.

Leo wasn't trying to fill me with false confidence, but rather offer me a clue. It turns out my grandfather wasn't the only tricky bastard.

Leo is too.

I last one whole week before giving up on my idea to stay away from Lana. Even if she hates me for it, I can't go another night without seeing her. Now that I have a solid plan for the house, there isn't much else keeping me from her.

At least nothing but her.

Before I stop by the guesthouse, I make a quick detour for Wyatt and Delilah's place.

Delilah throws the door open. "What are you doing here?"

"Is your husband around?" I try to peek over her head, but she snaps her fingers in my face.

"Why?"

"I need to speak to him about something."

She crosses her arms against her chest. "If the reason you came back here is because you want to stir up trouble—"

"He's not." Wyatt pulls Delilah away from the door and tucks her underneath his arm.

His chin tips in my direction. "You're back."

"Yup." I pop the *p*.

His left brow rises. "Permanently?"

"So long as Lana wants me to be."

Delilah frowns. "Are you sober?"

I flash my chip in front of her. Wyatt's eyes narrow at the chip before he looks down at Delilah. "Can you give us a minute?"

She rises on the tips of her toes and gives him a kiss on the cheek. "Fine."

Wyatt smacks her ass as she walks away, earning himself a half-hearted glare from over her shoulder.

"Want to take a walk?" He motions outside.

"Sure." I tuck my hands into my pockets and step off the porch.

"How was rehab?"

"About as good as I remember."

He snorts a laugh. "Liar."

"It was torture, but I'm glad I did it."

He claps me on the shoulder. "Hopefully it sticks this time."

"I was hoping…" My voice drifts off, the courage I had from earlier evaporating.

"I'd be your sponsor?"

"If the offer still stands, that is."

He looks at me out of the corner of his eye. "Depends if you tell me why Lana is upset with you for leaving."

My brows rise. "Did she say something?"

Not that I would blame her if she did.

"No, and Dee has been tight-lipped about it any time I ask."

Damn. "She has?"

"Yes. And since I didn't want to put Dee in a position to choose between me or her friends, I didn't bug her about it."

I suck in a breath. "It's complicated."

"Complicated enough to drive you to drink?"

I shake my head. "No. I'm finding other ways to cope."

"Like?"

"Well, I wasn't allowed to build a boat in rehab because they were afraid I would get high off the glue or something, so I read. *A lot.*"

He rears back. "Wait. You can read?"

I give him a shove with my shoulder, which knocks him off-balance. He laughs, which only makes me break out into a chuckle too.

"What book did you like most?"

"Catcher in the Rye."

His rubs his jaw. "I don't feel like I appreciated that book as much as I should have when I read it in high school. Maybe I should give it a reread now that I'm an adult with more life experience."

"Definitely. I think it's a new favorite of mine."

"What did you relate to most?"

"It's hard to pick a particular theme, but maybe that I need to care about myself before prioritizing others."

He nods. "And how's that going?"

"Falling in love with yourself is ten times harder than falling in love with someone else, especially when I don't like myself very much."

"You'll get there."

"Did you used to feel that way?" I ask.

His gaze flickers across my face. "All the time."

"How did you get past it?"

"By becoming someone I was proud of."

We continue walking in silence. Delilah and Wyatt don't live on the lake like we do, but their neighborhood is quaint and quiet, which makes it easy for me to get lost in my thoughts.

I'm not sure how long we walk for, but my calves are burning by the time we arrive back at their house. I've never had a sponsor before, so I'm not sure what to expect of the process, but a quiet walk wasn't the first idea I had in mind.

Yet I feel more at peace than ever.

"See you tomorrow at AA?" Wyatt tucks his hands into his athletic shorts.

"Absolutely."

A knock on the door pulls me away from the show I was watching. I rise on to the tips of my toes and look through the peephole.

Oh God.

My hand trembles as I go to open the door. Cal doesn't give me a chance to take him in as he lifts me off my feet, knocking the air out of my lungs.

"Fuck, I've missed you." His arms wrapped around me tremble.

My heart clenches. I push against his chest, needing space to think.

"Just give me one more second."

"One." I tap on his shoulder.

He sighs as he puts me down on my feet, making sure to take his sweet time. "Sorry for that. I just got ahead of myself after spending the last thirty-seven days dreaming of coming home."

Home.

Whatever control I had over my emotions unravels like a flimsy bow. I place a shaky hand against his cheek, and he leans into it.

"I'm proud of you for getting sober. Even if it was just for—"

He cuts me off. "*Me*. It was for *me*."

I release a shaky breath. It's not that I don't want to believe what he says, but I've been burned too many times by him to do anything but doubt him.

He pulls something out of his pocket. "I wanted to bring you this." He holds out a single chip. The slight tremor of his palm makes my chest tighten. "I know it's not much, but I plan on earning every single one for the three of us."

The three of us.

Warmth floods my chest like a broken dam, spreading from my chest to my toes. There is nothing I want more than for him to prove me wrong, but a big part of me is worried to believe him. Worried to hope. To dream. To trust that he is finally getting the help he needs.

Cal places the chip in my palm and closes my fist around it. "I will be at the motel if you need me."

"I thought you hated that place."

"Not nearly as much as I hate being far away from you."

I reach out for the doorframe to stop myself from falling over. His lips tug into a small smile, although he walks away before I have a chance to truly enjoy it.

I peek behind him at the bright yellow SUV in the driveway. It looks like something straight out of a comic book, with all the sharp lines and chrome. "Is that a Lamborghini?"

He throws me a smile from over his shoulder. "Yeah."

"What happened to your old car?"

He rubs the back of his neck and looks away. "Someone told me my other one isn't safe for a kid."

I blink.

He got a new car because you didn't think his other one was safe enough?!

My grip on the doorframe tightens because I really do think my legs might give out.

"See you around?" His smile is hesitant.

I can only nod.

He drives off in his brand-new SUV he got for us while I remain staring at the space he previously occupied. I expected to feel relief at him leaving, but instead, disappointment presses against my shoulders.

Isn't this what you wanted? Him gone?

That might have been the case, but what if he is telling the truth? What if he really is getting sober because he wants to better himself?

Only time will tell.

I'm driving back to the house after dropping Cami off at her dance class when I get distracted by the bright yellow Lamborghini SUV outside of the shop I've spent the last month ignoring.

Is that Cal?

My suspicions are confirmed as I catch him standing outside the shop, staring up at the building. I pull over and put my car hazards on. With shaky legs, I walk over to the man standing outside the store I always dreamed of opening my bakery in.

"What are you doing here?" I ask.

He looks over at me with eyes concealed by sunglasses. "Checking out the building."

I turn to look at the shop. The red *Coming Soon* sign from before is no longer displayed across the windows.

"They left?" I walk up to the window and peek inside. The space is completely empty besides a few abandoned paint cans and a plastic sheet protecting the floor.

"I guess so," Cal says from behind me.

I peek over my shoulder at him. "Why?"

"I overheard someone at the bookshop mentioning that the new landlord hiked up the rental prices."

Shit! How will I ever afford this place now?

"What happened to Vinny?" Vinny's family made a small fortune off renting out their tiny strip of Main Street for generations, so I'm surprised they parted with it.

"I heard he got bought out."

My shoulders slump. "I wonder how much the new landlord is charging now if it ran them out of business before ever opening."

"You could call their office and ask for a price." He slides his sunglasses over his head.

I bite down on the inside of my cheek. Truth is, I'm tempted to give them a call. With all the money I'm getting from the deal I made with Rowan, I could probably afford the rent.

But still, something stops me—good old self-doubt, always popping up when I least expect it.

How many shops have tried to be successful here only to fizzle out? What makes my idea so different from the last bakery that opened here? Or the store before that?

"I'll give them a call tomorrow," I say.

Tomorrow sounds good. *Safe.*

He points at the sign taped to the door. "I dare you to give them a call now and ask."

My eyes widen. "What?"

"You heard me." His smile expands.

I shake my head hard enough to make my ponytail slap me in the face. "No."

"Don't tell me you're scared," he taunts.

"I'm not scared. I'm just…"

Damn it. I *am* scared.

Screw him for calling me out on it though.

His cocky smirk has me whipping my phone out of my pocket and dialing the number.

"You know what? I will call them just to prove I'm not." I stab at the screen like it offended me. My finger shakes so hard, I misdial the number twice before getting it right.

A woman answers the phone. "Hello?"

"Hi, I'm calling to inquire about unit number seven on Main Street."

"Ahh, yes. The rental unit. Is that the corner one?"

"Yes."

Cal leans in closer, but I step away, not wanting him to overhear me receive crushing news.

"The property is available."

"For how much a month?"

"Five hundred dollars."

"Five hundred dollars?" I rub my eyes. "How is that possible?"

"According to the landlord, the property has a whole family of mice living inside. As you can imagine, that's not exactly a selling point."

"A whole family of—" Everything clicks into place.

Vinny selling the property after it had been in the family for years. Cal standing outside the building, daring me to call the number and ask about the rent.

"Excuse me, something just came up." I hang up and turn to face the new landlord. "You bought the building."

He doesn't even blink. "I've always been interested in real estate."

"Monopoly doesn't count."

He fights a smile and fails.

My eyes narrow. "Are you the new landlord?"

"Technically speaking, yes."

"Why would you do that?"

"Because turning your dreams into realities makes me happy."

"It makes you happy." I repeat his words, processing them.

He frowns. "Is that so hard to believe?"

"I don't even know what to believe right now." The sobriety chip. His new car. The empty shop ready to be leased if I want it. It feels like too much all at once, and I'm not sure how to handle it all.

"I just want you to know if you want the shop, it's yours. No strings attached."

I grimace. "I hate being bought with gifts."

"It's not a gift if I plan on charging you rent."

I snort a laugh. "Five hundred dollars a month is nothing for a spot like this and you know it."

His gaze burns as he follows the curves of my body. "Well, if sex is on the table, then I'll take that as well."

I jab him in the ribs with my elbow before taking a few steps toward my car.

"Where are you going?" A hint of desperation bleeds into his voice.

"Far away from you." I need to think, and I can't do that with him smiling at me and talking about sex.

"But what about the shop?"

"Ehh. It's a cute gesture, but maybe I want to explore my options beyond Lake Wisteria."

Who am I kidding? Him buying the whole building to save the shop I want is something straight out of a Dreamland fairy tale.

He takes a step forward. "Where?"

I smile at Cal for the first time in weeks. "I'm not sure yet."

"Don't make me go buy up all the properties you're interested in."

"You'd go bankrupt."

"Not even close, but it would put a nice dent in my bank account." His eyes draw me in like a lighthouse in the middle of a storm.

I shake my head in disbelief. "You're insane."

"No, Lana, I'm in love. There's a big difference."

"What's he doing here?" Violet's head snaps toward the front door of Last Call.

Delilah and I follow her gaze. I lock eyes on Cal, who hasn't noticed us sitting in our usual spot by the back.

The pit in my stomach becomes a canyon as Cal waves down one of the bartenders and orders his usual vodka tonic. He takes a seat by himself on the other side of the bar, giving everyone his back. I can't make out if he is drinking yet or not, but my stomach rolls all the same.

"He shouldn't be here." My fingers press into the leather booth, leaving indentations behind.

"I'm sure he has a good explanation." Delilah stares at her drink.

I stare at her like she grew a second head. "A good explanation?"

She doesn't answer.

Violet scoffs. "What happened to getting sober?"

"He promised me he was." I reach for the chip I keep on me at all times.

So much for that.

"Just hear me out—" Delilah tries to get my attention, but I'm too far gone.

My frustration boils over, and before I have a chance to stop myself, I charge over to his table.

"Alana!" Delilah calls after me, but I can't hear her over the pounding of blood in my ears.

Cal looks up at the sound of my name, and his eyes widen as he catches me stomping over to his table. A few people turn to look over at us, the unwanted eyes making my cheeks heat.

"Here, asshole. You can have this back now." I throw his sobriety chip on the table. It spins a few times before landing beside his drink.

The muscles of his back turn rigid underneath his shirt. "I gave it to you."

"I don't want it."

"Why?"

"Because it doesn't mean anything." I motion toward his drink.

He pushes the chip back toward me. "I'm not drinking."

"Then explain this shit."

"Have a seat and I will." Besides his clenched jaw and rough voice, he does a good job at tempering his anger.

It only pisses me off even more. The only reason I take a seat is because I feel like my legs might give out at any moment.

The hardness in his expression softens as he takes a good look at me. "It's not what you think."

A bitter laugh escapes me. "Of course it isn't."

"Give me a little more credit than this. I'm not risking everything with you for bottom-shelf vodka and flat soda."

I stare into his eyes. "Then why order a drink in the first place?"

"Because I want to prove to myself that I'm stronger than my biggest weakness." He stares at the glass in between us like it's the enemy.

My mouth drops open.

The fight leaves him with a single deep exhale. "How can I expect you to trust me if I don't trust myself?" His voice cracks. There is a slight tremor in his hand, and I grab on to it instinctively, wanting to ease some of his pain.

Our fingers interlock. Warmth spreads up my arm like

wildfire, sparks shooting off my skin like embers off a flame.

I push the drink away from both of us. "You're doing this because you don't trust yourself?"

"Learning to trust myself again is a process."

"Then find a different one because this is torture."

His gaze lifts. "It's not nearly as bad as knowing you still don't believe anything I say."

My chest caves in on itself.

"What do you expect? You hid a pretty big secret from me."

"I'm going to fix it."

"How?"

"It might take you a few years, but I'm pretty sure I can wear you down."

My eyes widen. *"Years?"*

"All I have is time."

"You plan on living at the motel for years?"

He recoils. "God, no."

"Then what?"

He lifts my hand to his lips and kisses the scar on top of my knuckle before letting my hand go. "You'll see." He stands.

"Where are you going?"

"I'm going to go hang out with Wyatt."

My brows hike. "You and Wyatt are friends?"

"He's my sponsor."

I blink. That explains why Delilah tried to stop me from making an ass of myself.

If only you had waited to hear her out.

"Will you be at the open house tomorrow?" His question comes out of left field.

"The open house? Why would I do that?"

"Because I plan on checking out the house and seeing what Ryder did with the place."

I stand up on shaky legs. "Well, I won't be. I have plans."

His smile is a weak one that doesn't sit right on his face. "Oh. That's a shame."

"Why?"

"Don't worry." He kisses my cheek before walking out of the bar, leaving his full vodka tonic and his sobriety chip behind. His absence only causes the chasm in my chest to widen even more.

Go after him, the hopeless romantic whispers.

I ignore the voice that has done nothing but get me in trouble and swipe the chip off the table before returning to my friends. The evening goes on, but my thoughts remain trapped in time, replaying Cal's words over and over to the point of obsession. The only thing that strikes me as odd about our conversation was him asking if I would attend the open house.

The question came out of nowhere, and he seemed disappointed by my answer.

If only I knew why.

CHAPTER FIFTY-FIVE
Alana

The real estate agent sends me updates every thirty minutes about the house. According to him, we have three buyers who are currently engaging in a bidding war over the property. I knew that might happen if I set the price low enough to entice buyers, but hearing it from the real estate agent's mouth makes the whole process of selling the house very real.

I resist the temptation to head over there and check if Cal showed up. Instead, Violet, Delilah, Wyatt, and I decide to stick to the guesthouse and our private dock out back. I want to take advantage of the last few times I'll get to enjoy the lake with my friends before the summer is over and the house is sold.

No one has brought up Cal since last night's trip to the bar.

Cami and Wyatt play in the water while Delilah, Violet, and I sit on the dock, soaking up the sun.

"Aren't you a little curious about the bidding war?" Delilah nudges me with her shoulder.

"Not really." I tuck my phone away. In the end, whoever buys the house will be inconsequential.

"I would be." Violet reapplies sunscreen on her face.

My phone vibrates with a new text. I expect it to be the real estate agent with another update, but Cal's name flashes across the screen.

> Do you still want to check out the buyer interested in purchasing the house and see if they're legit?

I consider it. When I told Cal I wanted to find someone who loved the house as much as me, I thought I could bear the idea of speaking with them. But the more I think about it, the less I feel capable of doing that.

> No. You can handle it.

A text from the real estate agent pops up before I lock my phone, letting me know that he has asked everyone to give him their best offers.

Already? How is that possible?

I call him right away.

"Alana! You won't believe it."

"What?"

"We had someone put in an offer for two million dollars."

"Two?" I reach out for Violet's shoulder to stabilize myself. When I lowered the price to a million, I expected to barely receive anything over asking price, but to have someone offer double?

I might faint.

I can feel the real estate agent's excitement through the phone. "Yes! I've asked the other buyers who are interested in the property to put in their final offers within the next hour."

"But—"

"This is the best-case scenario."

For him or me? Based on how much he is charging, the agent will walk away with a pretty penny once all the paperwork is done, especially if the buyers are driving up the price.

My phone vibrates with a new message from Cal.

> I just heard one of the buyers mentioning how they plan on bringing the house down to the foundation and completely rebuilding it because they prefer a modern open-floor plan. Are you sure you don't want to meet with them?

I jump up.

Hell no. I refuse to let anyone who wants to buy the house tear it down.

Violet peeks up at me. "What's wrong?"

"Can you all watch Cami for a little bit? I need to handle something back at the house with a buyer."

Wyatt waves me away like it's no big deal. "We're going to do an ice cream run in a little bit if that's fine with you."

"Yeah, sure. She has a set of clean clothes laid out on her bed," I reply over my shoulder before stomping toward the main house.

Over my dead body will someone purchase the house only to tear it down. Cal and I did not go through the process of renovating the whole thing for someone to erase all the history and charm we worked so damn hard to keep.

I'd rather pick the person with the cheapest offer who might actually love the place than give it away to someone who won't appreciate the property.

I walk into the house with every expectation of finding people roaming the property. Except when I arrive through the back door, the only person around is the real estate agent, who stands at the kitchen counter with his phone pressed against his ear and a folder with sheets spread out in front of him.

"What's going on?" I stop to catch my breath after powerwalking over here.

He hangs up the phone with a smile. "We just received another offer."

"Really?"

"Yes."

Ugh. "So, there are four in total?"

"Correct." His gleeful clapping grates on my nerves.

"Where are they?"

"Two had to go check out another house having a showing at the same time, but the other two are waiting in the living room for our final decision."

"Perfect." I walk past the real estate agent, ignoring his shouts.

I follow the long hallway toward the low murmurs of two people talking, although I can't make out what they're saying.

I enter the living room. "Cal? Where did the other buyer go?"

He turns at the sound of my voice. "You came."

"Of course I came. No way am I going to let some asshole tear down the house."

A tall man almost the same height as Cal walks around him. He wears an expensive-looking suit with an equally fancy watch, looking out of place compared to Cal's relaxed look of jeans and a linen shirt.

"And who are you?"

"The asshole who wants to tear down the house." He holds out his hand. His fingers are long like that of a pianist, lacking any kind of calluses that would suggest hard work. "I prefer to go by Lorenzo Vittori, though."

Lorenzo Vittori. The name sounds familiar, but I can't place it. He doesn't look like someone I know, but there is something about his dark gaze and eye shape that sparks recognition.

"Vittori?" I grip his hand and give it a quick shake.

"Yes."

"Was your mother the one who used to work at the Hawthorns' house by chance?"

His jaw ticks. "She was."

"You two know each other?" Cal's head tilts.

"Our mothers were friends before my family had to move away," Lorenzo replies.

"How is she?" I ask out of politeness.

"Dead." His voice is flat and void of any emotion.

Cal's eyes widen as he looks over at me.

"I'm sorry to hear that," I offer.

Lorenzo doesn't even blink. "Have you considered my offer, Ms. Castillo?"

Okay then. Safe to assume Lorenzo likes to get to the point.

"Not really, seeing as you want to destroy my house."

"I prefer to describe it as tapping into a property's true potential." He smirks in a way that seems well-practiced, as if he trained himself to charm others. If it weren't for his lifeless eyes,

I would have believed it.

"I'm going to have to pass."

His brows crinkle for a second before smoothing out. "What if I match the highest offer?"

"Which is?"

"Three million." Cal tucks his hands into his pockets.

Wait. What? Last time I spoke to the agent, he said two million.

Lorenzo blinks twice in the most human display of emotion I've seen. "You're joking."

Cal grins. "Unless you want to counter, it looks like mine is the best and final offer."

Mine is the best and final offer?

Mine?

Mine?!

Cal made an offer on his own house? Why would he do that?

The room spins around me as I try to wrap my head around what the hell is going on.

Lorenzo's eye twitches. "You're insane to pay that much on a place like this."

Cal lifts a shoulder. "We do crazy things for the people we love."

Lorenzo's upper lip curls. "Let's pray I never find out." He tips his head in my direction. "Good day, Ms. Castillo. Wish you two the best of luck with this endeavor because you're going to need it."

He waltzes out of the room, taking his air of superiority with him.

"Asshole," I say.

"Couldn't agree more," Cal grumbles. "I never thought he would leave."

I turn to face him. "What the hell is going on, and why are you putting an offer on a house you own?"

Cal's smile wavers. "Because I'm not the one buying the house."

"What?"

"I'm speaking on behalf of a trust."

"What trust?"

"The one I made for our future kids."

The air whooshes out of me. "You opened a trust for our *future kids*?" I choke on the last two words.

"Yes."

I reach out for the fireplace mantle to stop myself from keeling over. "But why?"

"Because I wanted to prove to you that the inheritance means nothing to me personally."

Oh. My. God.

"How much is in the trust, Cal?"

He hesitates. "Does it matter?"

I shoot him a look.

He doesn't hesitate as he says, "Twenty-six billion once we sell the house."

"To Cami and whatever hypothetical children you think we are having one day."

"To their *trust*. It's a whole complicated legal loophole, but it works. Grandpa's lawyer and I sorted it all out."

My knees give out, but Cal wraps an arm around me before I crash to the floor.

"Twenty. Six. Billion. Dollars." I pinch my arm, wince at the pain, before repeating the same move again.

Cal swats my hand away and rubs at the red spot. "They won't have access to the whole thing all at once."

"Well, that's a relief. I was worried what might happen if the kids had the urge to blow through twenty-six billion dollars on a whim."

His eyes narrow. "I can't get a good read on how you feel about all of this."

"I'm not even sure myself."

"Are you happy?"

"Yes." My eyes mist.

So damn happy. Not because of the money—there is no way I would let Cal give up his entire inheritance—but because we get to keep the house.

His arms tighten around me. "Then it was worth it."

"How is this even possible?"

"You wanted the house, so I found a way to keep it."

"Iris *was* right."

His head tilts. "About what?"

"She said if I wanted something, you would find a way to make it happen."

He grins. "You should know by now I'd do anything for you."

My heart squeezes. "Anything?"

He clasps onto my chin. "Absolutely anything. Although I can't take all the credit for this plan. Without my grandpa's lawyer dropping a cryptic hint, I would have never thought about opening a trust."

"I'm still wrapping my head around that."

"What about it?"

"Why you would give anyone that kind of money in the first place."

"It's not anyone. It's our *family.*" His smile reaches his eyes.

My legs threaten to buckle, but Cal holds me up.

Shit. I never stood a chance against him once he got sober. Hell, I barely stood a chance when he was still drinking, which only proves how screwed I was from the very beginning.

He brushes his knuckles across my cheek. "I told you selling the house never had anything to do with an inheritance."

"So, you decided to give it all up to prove a point?"

"Without you agreeing to sell the house, there would be no inheritance to give in the first place."

"We really get to keep the house?" I ask again to confirm.

His smile grows. "Only if you accept my final offer."

I look around the room. "Where are the other buyers?"

"I scared them away."

"*You?*" A laugh explodes out of me, making Cal's grin widen.

"Did you bribe them?"

He shakes his head.

"Threaten them?" I probe.

"No. I'm not Declan."

I bite back my laugh. "Then what?"

"I explained my situation and how I was trying to win back the woman I love."

A warmth blooms in my chest, right above my heart. "Then what happened with Lorenzo?"

"Asshole refused to back down. Said he didn't know what was more disappointing: me making poor life choices for something as fickle as love, or everyone else walking away after I confessed I was hopelessly in love with you and desperately needed to buy the house."

"Hopelessly in love with me, you say?"

The butterflies in my stomach flutter as he cups my chin. "I've always loved you, although at first it was platonic and innocent. But the love grew as we did, morphing into something more mature. Something strong enough to stand the test of time and distance every single year. A love built on memories of the past and a hope for the future." He tucks a wave of hair behind my head. "A future I can't see with anyone but you."

My heart pounds furiously against my chest as if it wants to be heard.

He keeps going while clasping on to my trembling chin. "Purchasing the house isn't about buying your love or trust or anything like that. I know that will only come with hard work and proving to you that I'm committed to being the best version of myself for both of us. The only reason I want to buy the house is because I want to buy into the future you want, whether it's with me or someone else." His voice cracks.

"Although I desperately hope you want that future with me. The one with the kids and the dock and all those model ships you want to build every summer. I want to spend my life daring you to do shit you're afraid of, while having you push me to do the same. Just like I want to become the man you always dreamed I could be once I got my life together."

My heart swells at his words. "I thought you hated this place."

He shakes his head. "I hated being reminded of the person I could have been had I gotten better sooner."

I reach up and cup his cheek. "And now?"

"I see it through your eyes, and now I can't imagine being anywhere else but at your side—whether you are at the lake or on the other side of the world. Wherever you go, I want to follow. Whatever you accomplish, I want to be there to congratulate you. And whenever you struggle, I want to be there to pick up the pieces and hold you together until you're strong enough to stand on your own."

A tear slips down my cheek. "What changed?"

"I did." He grips on to the back of my neck and pulls me forward. "Staying sober is going to be a process. Thirty days in rehab is a good start, but it's not an instant cure for a lifelong addiction. I'll have to put in the work and commit to bettering myself every single day. I only hope you're willing to share the journey with me, because God, I want you to. I know I don't deserve another chance, but I'm begging you to give me one anyway. Just give me one last chance to show you that I can be the man you want to spend the rest of your life with. That I can be the one to turn your dreams into realities."

I take in the man I've loved since before I even understood what the word meant. "One last chance?"

He nods.

I cradle his face and press my lips against his. "Break my heart again and I'll put a bullet in you for real this time."

He smiles against my mouth. "Be sure to aim for the heart then, because that's the only way you'll keep me away."

I wrap my arms around the back of his neck and rise on the tips of my toes, so our lips are only a few inches apart. "Deal."

CHAPTER FIFTY-SIX

Cal

oud banging has Merlin jumping off my lap with a hiss and taking off toward the stairs. Lana doesn't have a chance to reach for the knob before the front door bangs against the wall and Cami comes barreling inside.

"Cow-l! You're back!" Cami throws her backpack on the floor and sprints toward me.

I kneel and open my arms. "Hey there, kiddo."

Cami throws her arms around my neck. "I missed you."

My heart lodges itself somewhere in my throat as I tighten my grip. "I missed you more." My voice quakes, the slight tremble making Lana's eyes water. She gets down on the floor beside me and joins our hug. Wyatt tips his head before shutting the door to the lake house behind him.

"Are you all better now?" Cami peeks up at me.

My smile wobbles. "Yes."

"Really?" Her blue eyes turn impossibly brighter.

"Yup. Did you take care of Merlin for me while I was away?"

Her grin stretches wider. "Yes! I fed him. A lot."

"I saw that. I'm going to have to get the guy a little treadmill with how much food you gave him."

Cami giggles, making my chest flood with warmth.

"And I gave him water. I tried to sleep with him, but Mommy hogged him."

"Did she now?" I spare Lana a look.

She gives me a little shove with her shoulder.

Cami pouts. "She didn't like to share."

I fake gasp. "What? How dare she."

Lana sticks out her tongue. "I do too like to share. I just needed a cuddle buddy."

"I'll be your cuddle buddy." I wink.

Cami presses her palm against my cheek. "Are you staying?"

My throat tightens as I wrap my arm around Lana and tug her against me. "Of course."

"Forever?" Cami asks.

"Yup."

"And *ever?*"

I laugh. "That's the plan, so long as you want me."

She squeals as she wraps each arm around us and squeezes. A feeling of weightlessness takes over me, replacing the heavy feeling in my chest that has been present ever since I left Lake Wisteria for rehab.

Cami breaks away with a smile. "Are you and Mommy going to get married now?"

The blood drains from Lana's face. *"Camila."*

"What?"

Lana shoots her a look. "You shouldn't ask people that."

"Why not?" She crosses her small arms against her chest.

"Because it's rude."

I drag Lana's left hand toward my lips. "One day I plan on it."

Cami cheers while Lana blinks. I smile against her skin, my lips brushing across the goose bumps. Even Merlin comes back down to rub his body against us with a purr.

"Do you love my mommy?" Cami bats her dark blond lashes up at me.

"I love her more than anything." I answer while staring into Lana's deep brown eyes.

"What about you, Mommy? Do you love Cal?" Cami clasps her hands to her chest.

"I loved him long before I even understand what love really was."

Cami cheers as I place a soft peck against Lana's lips.

Having a family of my own makes me feel complete in a way I never dreamed was possible. It took me a long time to realize that no amount of alcohol, drugs, or money will compare to the high I get when surrounded by those I love.

And I will stop at nothing to make sure I never lose them again.

Walking down Main Street with Cami and Lana is a completely different experience this time around. Usually, the locals stick to either ignoring me or shooting daggers in my direction whenever I make my way through town.

Today is everything I hoped for but never thought was possible. People actually take time to stop and speak with us, treating me like I'm not a social pariah. I'm so shocked, I find myself speechless on more than one occasion, including when Meg stops me outside of her bookstore to tell me she saved a copy of a new sci-fi release she thought I might like.

It's almost as if I entered an alternate reality where people in Lake Wisteria no longer hate me for the mistakes I made six years ago.

Cami, Lana, and I walk into Holy Smokes BBQ with every intention of grabbing a quick bite to eat. Our plan is immediately hijacked by the townspeople sliding their tables against ours and creating one long table fit for a medieval feast.

"So Cal's finally back." Isabelle drops onto the bench beside me.

I look at her with narrowed eyes. "So you *do* remember my name."

She taps her water glass against mine with a wink. "Don't let it get to your head."

"Too late. I can feel it inflating already."

Isabelle's son, Ernie, places a tray full of meats at the center of the table before heading back toward the counter for another round.

"What's the special occasion?" Lana asks.

"You no longer moping about while waiting for this one to return." Isabelle beams.

Lana frowns. "I wasn't moping."

"You totally were." Isabelle turns toward me. "Everyone in town gained weight this month while trying to keep up with how many baked goods came out of this woman's kitchen. My butt now has its own zip code thanks to her and those darn Nutella pies."

"And cookies!" Cami raises her fist clutching a crayon in the air.

"Isabelle!" Lana throws her hands in the air.

I crack a smile. "No need to get embarrassed on my account."

Her eyes narrow. "I'm not embarrassed."

"Should I not tell him about how you wore his hoodie for a whole week?"

"You know what? I'm going to go take a walk off a very short dock now, thank you very much." Lana moves to rise from the bench, but I snatch her hand first.

"I think it's cute that you missed me."

Her lips flatten into a thin line. "Cute? Because Isabelle isn't the only one whose butt needs a new zip code."

I wink. "Just how I like it."

More people come to sit at our table, and the attention quickly shifts away from Lana. Similar to the dinner with my family, I am content with staying in the background and listening to everyone else speak. The stories they share range from two schoolteachers and an ongoing prank war, to how annoyed people are with Julian Lopez and his company buying up properties around the lake.

I feel like I'm no longer an outsider looking in but rather someone who belongs. It provides a sense of fullness I didn't know I needed. In Chicago, I'm the Kane brother who lacked drive, ambition, and any goal besides being the family fuck-up.

But here at Lake Wisteria, I'm just Cal, a somewhat normal guy who likes reading books, tipping people well, and spending time with his family.

I might be a billionaire, but no one around here treats me as such. They poke fun at my family's company, my fancy car, and tease me endlessly about how in love I am with Lana.

I don't mind it one bit as I spend most of our dinner laughing until my stomach aches. It's not until Cami yawns and Lana calls it a night that I realize something.

Coming back to Lake Wisteria wasn't just about finding myself, but about finding a family. A massive, three-hundred-person family who would drop everything to help one of their own, including my girls.

And hopefully me one day.

CHAPTER FIFTY-SEVEN

Cal

I flip the green chip, studying the writing engraved into the curved edge. After spending three months in AA, I feel stronger than ever. Everything seems to be going right for me. Once I show Leo the chip, I'm all set to move on with my life and leave the will in the past.

"Still committed to staying sober?" My father stands up beside me. The last few stragglers find their way out of the meeting room, leaving me alone with him.

"Why do you care?"

"I don't."

I release a soft laugh as I stand. My head clears his by a couple of inches. "You know what I find interesting?"

His dark gaze peers into me. "What?"

"I spent the better part of my life always making excuses for you. I thought that if you got sober, you would be better. *Kinder*. But it turns out, you're just the same miserable person with or without alcohol. And you know why?"

His eyes narrow. "I'm sure you'll tell me whether I care or not."

"You hate yourself, and no amount of alcohol is going to change that. You're a pathetic person with equally pathetic wishes who will never find happiness, whether you search for it at the bottom of a bottle or with an inheritance you don't deserve." With one final look at my father, I walk away, leaving him burning a hole into my back.

It wasn't until I confronted my self-hatred that I realized my father and I shared the same issue. That he and I were two sides of the same coin, turning our hatred of ourselves into a weapon—him against the world and me against myself.

But unlike him, I'm here because I refuse to give up on myself.

Not today. Not tomorrow. Not ever again.

Since I'm already in Chicago for the AA meeting, I decide to stay the night and attend the board meeting the following day. As much as I want to head back to Lake Wisteria, there are a few things I need to do before I can.

Declan sits at the head of the table, occupying my father's usual spot.

"Where's Seth?" the Head of Product Development asks.

"I will be standing in as CEO for the time being." Declan

doesn't look up from his phone.

"And how long is that?" someone else asks.

"Indefinitely." Declan doesn't blink.

Rowan shoots me a puzzled look. I press my lips together to stop myself from smiling. Declan wanted to surprise Rowan about the pregnancy after today's meeting while Iris has brunch with Zahra now to share the news.

The meeting is short. Business is good and everything is running as it should, minus Seth no longer sitting at the head of the table.

When Arnold, the Head of Acquisitions and Sales for the DreamStream Division, stands and gives his monthly report, I keep my mouth clamped shut. Rowan nudges me once, but I ignore him. I've spent the last three months speaking with Arnold privately, not that my brother is aware.

Turns out the solution wasn't trying to fit myself into a company role but rather developing a role that fits me, my needs, and my interests. While I want to help the streaming company be the best version of itself, I don't want to be in charge of the whole damn thing. Leadership isn't my style. Becoming a consultant or something less obligatory is more my speed, all while giving me the ability to actually speak on behalf of the company and acquire new projects.

Once the meeting is adjourned, I pull Arnold aside to schedule our next meeting with his team. I don't have an assistant or anything fancy, so I coordinate everything myself.

My brothers stick around, whispering behind my back. It's not until the room clears out that I finally face them.

I turn around and cross my arms. "Are you two done talking

about me?"

"What was that?" Declan motions toward the spot Arnold just occupied.

"Don't worry about it."

His eyes light up. "Keeping secrets from your new CEO already?"

Rowan's jaw drops open. "Is it official?"

Declan spares him a glance. "Not until the lawyer draws up the final paperwork."

I grin. "Congratulations, Daddy."

Rowan chokes on his inhale.

Declan's eyes narrow. "Call me that again and I won't hesitate to rip your tongue out and mount it behind my new desk like artwork."

Rowan's eyes bounce between us two. "Does anyone want to fill me in on what's happening?"

Declan pulls out his wallet and hands Rowan a photo of the sonogram. "Here."

"Holy shit. You're going to be a dad." Rowan traces the circle. "It looks like a jellybean."

"Say hello to your nephew." Declan preens like a peacock showing off its feathers. It's the most un-Declan-like behavior I have seen, which only makes me laugh.

"Could be a girl," I tease.

Declan taps his chest. "I have a good intuition, and my gut tells me it's a boy."

Rowan's eyes roll. "And if it *is* a girl?"

"I already have a heart doctor on speed dial and every police captain in Chicago under my payroll to arrest anyone who steps within six feet of her."

"You can't arrest every guy or girl they're interested in," I say.

He swipes the photo out of Rowan's hands while glaring at me. "Watch me."

My car is packed and I'm ready to head back to Lake Wisteria when I receive a call from Leo asking me to come to his office for an emergency meeting. Before taking off in the direction of Leo's office across town, I text Lana to let her know that something came up and I'm not sure if I will make it home tonight.

I spend the entire drive fidgeting from anxiety. When I enter his office, my nervousness is only amplified as I find my brothers staring my father down from opposite sides of the sitting area.

Leo sits behind his desk with a neutral expression. "Callahan. Please take a seat."

He motions to the only empty spot available beside my father. I sit down, practically hugging the edge of the leather couch to avoid him.

"I'm glad you all were available tonight to meet with me." Leo opens a file.

Like we had any other option.

"What is all this about?" My father's voice hints at his building temper.

"I was asked to read one last letter from Brady."

"Another letter?" Rowan sits up.

Leo tips his head in confirmation. "This one was addressed to the four of you."

Declan remains quiet, his gaze glued to Leo pulling out the letter from an envelope.

"*To my family,*" Leo begins. "*A man's legacy shouldn't be determined by how much money he made or how successful he was, but rather by the memory he left behind and the way he made people feel.*" Leo pauses to look up from the letter.

"What?" Declan grunts.

"Sorry. Your grandfather noted that I should pause for dramatic effect."

I explode with laughter. Rowan and Declan follow, the three of us filling the whole room with the sounds of our amusement. My father remains rigid beside me, completely emotionless.

Leo continues, his lips tugging upward. "*My way of going about you four earning your inheritance was unusual. Leo warned me as much when I called him at two a.m. after a crazy dream, letting him know I needed to revise the will.*" He pauses again to look up. "I did. Just for the record."

"Cut the useless chitchat and read the damn letter," our father barks.

Leo doesn't balk or snap, although a small tic in his jaw appears. He refuses to give my father any attention as he returns to his reading. "*Each of you were given a task that I chose based on your strengths and weaknesses. Given that Leo is reading this letter rather than the other one I wrote, I assume the four of you met the requirements asked of you to receive your inheritances.*"

Leo pulls out a second sheet of paper from the envelope. "*To my son, Seth. I gave you two choices regarding your inheritance. While I had hoped you would rise to the challenge and pick the more difficult path, you went with the easier option of the two.*"

What two choices? Were they like mine and based on contingencies, or was he given two clear paths from the beginning and it was up to him to choose?

My father's foot shakes, his only nervous tell.

"I understand why you chose to get sober in order to receive your shares of the company. I really do get it. Just like I understand that I cannot with good conscious hand them over, knowing you made that choice to benefit yourself."

What. The. Actual. Fuck? Are parts of our inheritance revokable now?

The blood drains from Declan's face. We lock eyes for a moment before returning our attention back to Leo, who continues reading off the page.

"If you truly have changed, then your sons will make the appropriate choice that reflects that transformation. If you have not made amends for the mistakes you've made and the hurt you've caused, then you never truly learned anything despite my letters and pleas, and therefore are unworthy of receiving your inheritance."

"Motherfucker," my father whispers under his breath. "Well played, Pop."

Leo ignores his comment. *"To my three grandsons. In addition to you receiving your percentages of the company and your inheritance, I grant you one last thing that I denied you before. A choice. You can choose to deny your father his six percent of the company shares and have them redistributed amongst the investors, or you can choose to give him the shares."*

Holy shit.

Holy. Fucking. Shit.

My gaze snaps to Rowan and Declan. Both of them sit with

their elbows on their knees and their chins cradled over their clasped hands.

"Regardless of what you three decide, I hope you learn from your father's example. What can be given can easily be taken away. Fortunes. Lovers. Family. Don't make the same selfish mistakes we made because I can guarantee it leads to nothing but an empty life and an equally empty heart."

"And to my son, I hope you change out of the goodness of your heart before it is too late for you."

Leo folds the letter and returns it to the envelope.

"Can I have the other letter he wrote?" my father asks, shocking us all with his question.

Leo raises a brow. "It doesn't have any legal standing."

"I know that."

Leo pulls out a third folded sheet of paper and hands it over to my father. He doesn't read it in our presence, instead choosing to tuck it inside of his suit with a shaky hand.

Leo clasps his hands together. "Each of you will vote yes or no regarding your father's inheritance. We will start with the eldest grandson."

Declan rises and buttons his suit. Instead of sharing his feelings aloud, my brother leans over to whisper something into my father's ear. The color drains from my father's face. I'm not sure what Declan says, but my father looks as if he saw a ghost.

Declan returns to his full height. "I vote no." He walks out of the room, leaving us behind to make our own decisions.

My father turns a fraction of an inch in my direction.

I'm not ready to say my truth yet, so I stumble over my words. "Can Rowan go next?"

Leo glances over at my brother.

Rowan shrugs before rising to his feet. "I'm honestly disappointed you didn't choose the more difficult path. After abusing us for years and using our weaknesses against us, turns out you're the weakest one of us all." Rowan shakes his head at Leo. "I vote no." He exits the room and shuts the door behind him.

My father rises from his seat and leans over to pick up his suitcase.

I'm not shocked by his dismissal of me. I spent the last thirty-four years of my life being subjected to the same treatment, although I'm better equipped to handle it now. "What about my vote?"

He stands tall. "It doesn't matter."

My blood heats beneath my skin, fueling the rage building inside me. I step into his space and stare him in the eyes. "Despite your attempts to treat me like I don't exist, I matter just as much as the other two."

"It's nothing personal."

"Maybe that's your issue. If you actually acted like a human being, maybe things could have been different."

His jaw clenches. "Vote or get out of my way."

"I will once you tell me what the first option was."

His right eye twitches. "Why?"

"Because I want to know, and you owe me that much."

He looks away, his jaw working as he considers my request. His resigned sigh fills the silence, barely heard over the strong beat of my racing heart.

"He asked me to seek forgiveness from each of you and put

my shares up to a family vote like today." My father takes a step toward the door, but I reach out to stop him.

"Why didn't you choose that option?"

"I didn't want to risk the shares for something I knew was impossible after everything I had done."

"Trying and failing is better than not trying at all." I'd rather fail time and time again than limit my options and fail anyway.

It took me a long time to think that way, but I'm done choosing the easy route. Just look at my father and what that got him.

Nothing but misery.

He will have to spend the rest of his life wondering what would have happened had he sought to get help and earn our forgiveness. While we live the rest of our lives happy with our families, he will sulk in his misery and failure, knowing deep down there was a small chance we could have learned to forgive him had he put in the work.

But I guess none of us will ever know.

I look over at Leo. "I vote yes."

Leo's brows jump, and my father's eyes widen. I know my vote is a toss away, but I would rather fuck with my father one last time, making him wonder what he could have done to earn that one other yes.

Kill them with kindness, Mom always said.

I hope my father drops dead because of it.

CHAPTER FIFTY-EIGHT

Cal

My father walks out of Leo's office with his head held high despite his monumental loss. My brothers scowl at him until he foregoes the elevator and disappears down the emergency stairs exit, the banging of the door echoing across the waiting room.

"I'll be in touch with the paperwork for the house." Leo gives me a pat on the shoulder before shutting the door behind me.

My brothers turn to face me.

Rowan's eyes brighten despite the flat line of his lips. "We were thinking about grabbing dinner if you're down."

"Sure. I'm starving." I take a step toward the elevator, only to pause at Declan staring at the door my father left through.

"It's really over," he mutters under his breath.

Rowan claps him on the shoulder. "Don't tell me you're sad."

"I'm just…" His lips press together.

"Disappointed?" I offer.

Both of my brothers turn to look at me.

"Exactly." Declan looks away. "It feels stupid to be after we got everything we wanted…"

"I feel the same way, especially after he told me Grandpa gave him a choice to make amends with us and still picked himself."

"Not surprised." Rowan's lip curls.

Declan's shoulders tense. "Even after all this time and everything we've been through, it's hard to accept your father is a selfish piece of shit."

"Tell me about it. I'm the one who spent half of my life in therapy trying to." My smile doesn't reach my eyes.

Rowan snorts a laugh. "At least one of us got help for our daddy issues."

"Consider that two." Declan shakes Rowan's hand off his shoulder and heads toward the elevator.

Rowan's mouth drops open. "*You're* going to therapy?"

"Don't tell me you haven't considered it." Declan shoots him a look.

Rowan shakes his head. "I'll stick to living vicariously through you."

"Coward."

Declan shares all the baby facts he has learned over the last few weeks during the drive over to an Italian spot he loves. Never in my life did I think I would hear my brother gushing about having a kid, but I'm happy for him and Iris. After all the shit Declan has been through, he deserves a chance at being the kind of father we wished for.

So do you.

The reminder has me calling Lana from the bathroom so I can wish her and Cami a goodnight.

Once our waitress drops off our waters and takes our orders, Rowan starts talking about the upcoming Dreamland renovation and the land he and Zahra worked on together with the Creators team.

I ask Rowan more questions than usual, earning a bright smile from him.

Declan turns to me. "I'm proud of you."

"Of me? What for?"

His brown eyes lighten. "For so many different things, but most of all for how far you've come in such a short amount of time. It makes me happy to see you happy and…free."

My throat tightens. "Who knew you were such a sap?"

"What can I say? Iris's pregnancy hormones must be rubbing off on me."

Rowan snorts. "I don't think that's how it works."

"Fuck off. This is exactly why I never say anything nice." Declan throws his balled-up paper straw wrapper at Rowan's face.

"Fine. My turn." Rowan lifts his water in the air. "I'd like to make a toast to us finally achieving our dreams."

I tap my glass against his. "And the women who helped us along the way."

After dinner with my brothers, I don't stop driving until I reach the lake house at midnight. I'm careful not to make much noise as I disarm the alarm and walk up the stairs. Lana and I claimed the newly configured master as our bedroom, which happens to be on the opposite side of the second floor, far from Cami's room.

Lana lies in the middle of the bed, curled up with a pillow tucked between her arms. Moonlight pours through the curtain she left open, illuminating the curves of her face. I lean down to kiss the top of her head. She doesn't stir, so I take the opportunity to shower prior to getting in bed.

The mattress dips under my weight as I crawl underneath the covers.

"Hey," she rasps as she turns around to face me. "What time is it?"

I wrap my arms around her and tuck her against me. "Late."

"I thought you were going to stay in Chicago." She snuggles into my chest.

"I didn't want to wait." I spent a good chunk of my life away from Lana, so the last thing I want to do is waste any more time.

Plus, I promised Cami chocolate chip pancakes in the morning, and I really don't want to let her down.

"Did everything go okay with the lawyer?" She blinks up at me, clearing the sleep from her eyes.

"It was…interesting."

She frowns. "What happened?"

"Turns out Grandpa had one last plot twist in him."

Her eyes widen. "What do you mean?"

"Grandpa gave us the option to vote on whether our father should receive his shares or not."

"Oh my God." Her mouth remains hanging open.

"I know. We were surprised to say the least."

"So that's it? You're free of him?"

I nod. "Declan just ran his first board meeting today."

"That's amazing." She smiles up at me. "And how did the conversation with Arnold go?"

"He wants me to meet him and the team next week to go over some ideas I have."

Her smile widens. "I'm so proud of you."

I look away. "I haven't even done much yet."

"What do you mean? You're the reason the Kane Company has one app instead of four now. I'm pretty sure you're half of America's hero right about now."

Heat floods my cheeks. "Only because you helped."

She cups my cheek. "I barely did anything. You're the one who has spent weeks combing over data and meeting with teams to go over acquiring more content."

"It's a work in progress."

"Kind of like us." She grins.

I can't resist kissing her in that moment. Lana melts into me, deepening the kiss until we are both breathlessly ripping at each other's clothes. I tease her, and she does the same back, driving me mad with the desire to fuck her.

She licks. I nip. She sucks. I bite. She teases me with her tongue. I fuck her pussy with mine.

It doesn't take me long to find myself between her legs. She guides my cock toward her center, and we both groan as I sink inside of her. With how hard she grips my ass, I wonder if she will leave permanent marks against my skin similar to the ones she left on my heart.

Every time we have sex, it always feels desperate. As if we

both are trying to make up for lost time. Like I want to bury myself inside her and never leave.

I torture her for what feels like an hour, driving her to the brink of an orgasm before retreating back.

At one point, she flips us over and takes control, spinning around until her ass and curved back is all I see as she bounces up and down my cock. The position feels like heaven, and Lana seems to agree based on the moans coming from her.

With a few flicks and pinches of her clit at my command, she comes, taking me over the edge with her. I don't stop driving her up and down my cock until my body no longer trembles from coming hard enough to see stars.

Lana slides off me, making us both sticky from our release. Her nose wrinkles at the mess.

"Shower or towel?"

She yawns. "Towel. I'm too tired to do anything else."

"Hold on." I come back with a wet towel to clean us both up the best I can before collapsing into bed.

Lana cuddles up against me and tucks her head between the crook of my neck. "I love you."

My chest tightens. It took me a while to feel worthy of those words from her, but I'm slowly getting used to them.

"I love you too." My lips brush against the top of her head. There is nothing I won't do to make sure Lana spends the rest of her life being cherished like the gift she is.

She changed my life and proved to me that loving myself matters just as much as loving others. Because in order to show up for everyone else, I need to show up for myself first.

The future won't be easy. I'm not foolish enough to think I

won't be tested and tempted into falling back into hurtful patterns. But with Lana, Cami, and our family by my side, anything feels possible. Even the failures.

And I think that's what my grandpa was trying to teach me all along.

EPILOGUE
Alana

ONE YEAR LATER

Y ou'll close up for me tonight?" I tug my apron over my head.

Gabby, my amazing employee, pauses her sweeping to look up. "No problem, boss. I got it."

I have three people working for me, all of whom are incredible in their own ways. Besides their love for baking, they are passionate about testing out new recipes to see who can make the next best Dreamland dessert. Turns out my tres leches recipe was a hit, and Rowan is already pressuring me for more sweets.

He is the reason I have been working later than usual this week. If it weren't for him asking me for a new holiday recipe, I would have been the one to pick up Cami from school. Instead, Cal has been the one to take care of her while I've been obsessing over what holiday treat I plan on presenting to Rowan this weekend when we go visit the family at Dreamland.

My phone rings in my hand. "Shit. Bye, Gabby!"

"Where are you?" Cal asks when I answer.

"On my way." I flip the switch for the neon sign before walking out the front door. The *Sweets and Treats Bake Shop* sign lights up above me.

It was the same name my mom and I came up with together one day while standing in the same spot. I'm sure my mom would be proud, knowing I finally achieved the dream of opening my own bakery.

"You're still at the shop, aren't you?" Cal's question drags me away from my thoughts.

"I'm leaving now, I swear!" I juggle my phone between my shoulder and cheek while digging around my purse for my car keys.

Someone groans in the background.

"What was that?" I ask.

"The television. See you soon. Love you. Bye." He hangs up.

Huh. That was weird.

The stars are already out by the time I pull into the driveway of our lake house. I expect to find Cami and Cal in the living room working on the new boat he bought, but the place is pitch black. I reach for the light switch near the sliding door, only to stop myself as something outside catches my eye.

The dock is lined with candlelit glass lanterns illuminating a path toward the end.

"Oh my God." My hand shakes as I open the sliding door and step out onto the wraparound deck. I walk down the steps and across the massive lawn, straight toward the shadow standing at the end of the dock. Grass crunches underneath my feet, breaking the silence.

Cal looks over his shoulder. The moon shines above, illuminating his entire face. "Hey," he calls out loud enough to be heard from a distance.

"What's all this about?" I say with a loud voice. I think I have a good idea what is going on, but only because Cal picked a terrible spot to hide an engagement ring. I've been waiting weeks to see when he would pop the question. He even teased me twice, with him making a big deal out of tying his shoe on two separate occasions.

I swear he knows I know.

He turns to face me. Something long and wide is cradled against his chest, but I can't make it out from here. The dock creaks beneath my sneakers as I close the gap between us. My heart pounds so hard that I'm afraid it might break a rib in its attempt to bust free from my chest.

"What's that?" I stop in front of him and point to the piece of wood in his hands.

He flips the piece of wood.

My eyes widen. *No way.*

"Is that…" I reach out with a trembling hand and trace the *L* etched into the wood beside the *C.*

"You didn't think I would really let the construction crew throw it out, did you?"

My tongue feels heavy. "Why didn't you say anything?"

"I had big plans for it, and I didn't want to risk you burning it or something."

I look up at him with watery eyes. "What kind of plans?"

"The forever kind." Cal holds the plank in one palm while

he reaches into his back pocket and pulls out...*his Swiss Army knife?!*

"Cal..." I press my palm against my gaping mouth.

He kneels and props the plank on his thigh. The sharp blade glints as he presses the tip beneath the *L* column, right below my other strikes.

"I dare you to spend the rest of your life with me." He drags the tip of the knife down, making a solid line. "I dare you to let me love and protect you and Cami and every other kid we have with my whole heart." He adds a second strike. "I dare you to take a risk on me, knowing that things won't always be the easiest and that I will struggle, although I have every intention of being the man you will always deserve." A third slash is added. "I dare you to trust me to be your companion, your lover, and your best friend. To let me be your biggest cheerleader and the shoulder you cry on when things get hard, trusting that I will be the one to wipe your tears and fix whatever hurt you." His fingers tighten around the knife as he draws the fourth slash.

"I dare you to marry me."

Tears spill down my cheeks as he adds a diagonal line across the other four.

He places the plank on the dock before grabbing a ring from his pocket. It looks even better than I remember, the brilliant diamond sparkling more than the surface of the lake at noon. The jewel is a tasteful size—big enough to spot from a long distance but small enough to not risk getting robbed.

It's absolutely perfect and everything I wanted for myself.

"What do you say, Lana?" He grins. "Are you crazy enough to accept the challenge?"

My chin trembles. "Like I ever stood a chance at saying no to you." I hold out my hand.

Cal slides the ring up my finger before standing and pulling me into his arms. I cradle his head between my hands and kiss him with every ounce of love and adoration I feel. His fingers dig into my hair, fusing our mouths together and drawing a sigh from me.

He breaks away all too soon. "I love you."

"I love you too—always have and always will, so long as I live."

He steals another kiss before pulling back again. "She said yes!" he calls out to the dark.

My mouth drops open as people pop out from their hiding places. The whole town, plus Cal's family and my friends, step on to the lawn and make their way toward us. Music pours from the speakers and a party gets started around our pool.

My eyes narrow at the man with a massive grin on his face. "You were that confident I would say yes, huh?"

He winks. "I caught you trying on the ring with the goofiest smile on your face while practicing your surprised face."

Oh my God. My cheeks heat.

"Why didn't you do anything sooner?" My eyes widen.

"I had fun seeing you get all worked up every time you thought I was about to propose."

I slap his shoulder with a laugh.

He traps my hand within his and kisses my knuckle above the ring. "It was cute."

"Cute? I probably looked crazy trying on that ring."

"No. You looked like mine."

My stomach dips at the hungry look in his eyes.

"Mommy!" Cami dashes down the dock, clutching her stuffed lamb to her chest. She launches herself at us, and Cal lifts her into his arms before wrapping his other one around me.

I smile up at them. Cal was right. There was no way I would ever say no to marriage because there's nothing I want more in life than to spend the rest of it with them.

Our forever family.

EXTENDED EPILOGUE

Cal

THREE YEARS LATER

Every single July, Lana and I invite the family out to join us at Lake Wisteria. Besides the holidays, it's one of the few times we are able to get everyone in the same place together. Now that my brothers have their own families, life is busier.

Slowly, the Kane family has expanded. Rowan married Zahra pretty soon after Iris gave birth to baby Ilona and Declan became CEO. It didn't take long for Rowan and Zahra to have their first kid, Ailey. The little kid is a riot, taking after her mother in personality and her father in looks.

Lana and I took a little longer to have a kid. We both wanted a baby, but the process wasn't the easiest. It tore me up inside to see my wife struggle with the loss of one and the continuous letdowns every month after. There was nothing I could do to help, and it tested our relationship, along with my commitment to staying sober.

Without Wyatt, I'm not sure I would have been strong enough to resist the pull toward drinking. He and Lana assured me I would have been, but who knows.

Sobriety truly is a journey, but I wouldn't want anyone else in the passenger seat but Lana. With her by my side, I know I can make it through anything.

I'm glad I didn't fall off the wagon, because then we had Esmeralda. Sweet baby Esme with her toothless smile, dark blue eyes, and full head of brown hair. Cami was beyond thrilled to have the baby sister she always dreamed of, and Lana and I were content to be a family of four forever, especially after the hardships we went through to have Esme.

So, imagine our surprise when only two months after Esme came into this world, Lana got pregnant again.

We traced back the conception date to our trip to Ireland when we visited the town where my grandpa was born. The odds of having Irish twins conceived in Ireland almost seemed too good to be true. Like a divine intervention of some sort. Or better yet, a Brady intervention.

I honestly wouldn't put it past Brady Kane to make a deal with some higher power in the afterlife, making Lana's dream to have a big family come true.

Lana places my birthday cake in front of me before leaning over my chair to whisper in my ear, "What are you wishing for this year?"

I shoot her a look. "Like I'd tell you."

She grins. Even after traveling the globe and visiting the most beautiful places, nothing compares to Lana's smile. It lights up her whole face, making her skin glow and her eyes shine.

Esme might give Lana a run for her money though. Our little girl doesn't have any teeth yet, but it only makes her smiles that much cuter.

Lana peeks over at me with narrowed eyes. "You're wishing for a boy this time, aren't you?"

"Am I that predictable?" I ask.

"Yes," Declan and Rowan reply at the same time.

I roll my eyes. "I swear, I send a couple of photos of little kids in hockey gear…"

"And boys hitting golf balls." Rowan places Esme into Lana's open arms.

"Don't forget about the boy driving around on a mini dirt bike." Zahra buckles Ailey into her highchair. The kid claps her hands together at the sight of the cake.

I raise my hands in mock surrender. "It's not a crime to manifest."

"Girls can play hockey, hit golf balls, and ride dirt bikes too, you know?" Lana raises Esme's tiny fist in the air for emphasis.

"Does that mean I can buy Cami a dirt bike for Christmas?" Rowan smirks like the instigator he loves to be.

"*No*," Lana and I both answer at the same time.

She laughs as she begins lighting the first of thirty-eight candles. I grab on to the lit one and help her tackle the rest of the unlit candles while she rocks Esme.

Ilona comes running into the room with Iris on her heels. Based on the guava icing covering Ilona's mouth and hands, it's safe to assume she already had a taste of my birthday cake. One quick glance to the side confirms my suspicions.

"Sorry." Iris winces.

"Don't worry about it. I always like my food to be checked for poison before I eat it."

"Lana loves us too much for that." Zahra beams.

Declan points at me. "You on the other hand…questionable."

Iris tries to wipe Ilona's face with a cloth napkin, but she darts off in the opposite direction. Declan snags his kid before she can bolt from the room and places her on his lap. Ilona shakes her head to resist, making the beads at the ends of her braids clink together, but Iris ignores her as she clears the remnants of icing from her face.

"I found it!" Cami dashes inside the dining room and places a crown on my head.

"Perfect. Just what I needed." I drop a kiss on her cheek.

She wrinkles her nose as she wipes at her face. "Dad," she whines. "Gross."

Despite how many times I hear the name from Cami's mouth, my chest still tightens sometimes at the sound of it. Cami started calling me her dad a year after Lana and I got together and never stopped.

I hope she never does.

I tickle her. "I miss the days when you didn't think boys have cooties."

"Ugh. Stay away from all boys. They have flesh-eating bacteria that will make your skin fall off," Declan says with a serious face.

One of these days I'm going to kill him.

Cami's eyes widen. "What?" She wipes at her cheek harder.

I wrap an arm around her and pull her against me. "He's just joking."

"Am I?" Declan waggles his brows at Cami, making her laugh. It's strange to see my brother let his guard down around the kids. It makes him seem human.

Lana laughs as she hands me Esme before snapping a photo of me, the kids, and my cake. Half the candles are already melted, so Lana urges everyone to begin singing the happy birthday song. My brothers can't hold a tune to save their lives, but the girls save the day with their cheery tone and sense of rhythm.

"Make a wish." Cami grins at me.

I shut my eyes and blow out the candles.

I wish for a healthy baby and healthy wife.

No matter how much I joke about having a boy, I don't give a damn what the gender is, so long as Lana and the kid are safe.

Everyone claps and hoots. Lana begins cutting the cake for everyone.

"Psst." Cami grabs my hand. "I want to show you something."

I shoot Lana a look as Iris grabs Esme from my arms. My wife only offers me a small smile before returning to her task.

"What's up, kiddo?" I allow Cami to lead me out of the dining room.

"I have a present for you."

"What is it?"

Her eyes roll so hard, I'm afraid they might get lodged into the back of her head. I laugh as she leads me into the kitchen and passes me a manila envelope.

"What's this?"

"Open it." She gestures toward the envelope.

There is a slight tremble to my hands as I pull out a sheet of paper. My vision turns cloudy as I read the first line.

"You want me to adopt you?" I double-check the adoption papers to be sure.

She nods, her eyes looking as misty as mine probably do.

I ditch the papers and lift her into my arms. She might be getting a little too old for me to carry her, but I can't help it. I still remember the days when she begged me to.

"Will you be my daddy? For real?" Cami blinks up at me.

I repeat the same words I told her three years ago. "There is nothing I'd like more."

Lana pops out from the hallway where she was secretly recording the whole thing while holding Esme. Tears stream down her face, ruining her makeup.

I pull the three of them into a hug.

I thought I could never be happier than I was with Cami and Lana, but I was partially wrong. There is no way I could ever be happier than I am in this moment with the family I always dreamed of and the future I always wanted.

Author's Note

Saying goodbye to the Dreamland Billionaires is bittersweet. While I'm so proud of each of the Kane brothers for their personal growth, I am also sad to let the Kanes and their heroines go. This Dreamland world has changed my life in so many ways. It brought me new readers I care so much about and publishers who wanted to take a chance on me. But also, this series kept me company during some very difficult times in my life. It brought me comfort when I felt alone and provided me with an outlet to share a piece of my heart.

I hope you enjoyed this world. Like me, I hope it can bring you comfort when you need it and an escape whenever the real world gets a little too hectic to cope with.

Thank you for being a part of this journey and being part of the reason I pushed through when I doubted myself. Thanks for reading, sharing, and supporting me. And from the bottom of my heart, thank you for believing in me.

Until the next world!

Lauren

Also by Lauren Asher

Throttled

Dive into my Formula 1 world with Noah and Maya, a brother's rival forbidden romance.

Collided

A story about two friends who complete a naughty bucket list together.

Wrecked

An enemies-to-lovers forced proximity romance featuring a Formula 1 bad boy and his PR agent.

Redeemed

If you like fake relationship romances with a grumpy hero, check out Redeemed.

The Fine Print

A grumpy-sunshine office romance featuring a fairy tale theme park.

Terms and Conditions

A marriage of convenience between a grumpy boss and his assistant.

Scan the code to read the books

Acknowledgements

It truly takes a team of incredible people to help me pull off writing a book.

Mom—Writing about a dedicated mother came easy because you have always been the best role model and cheerleader for us. Thanks for helping me get through my writer's block and inspiring me to write about something different.

Mr. FOF—Thanks for reminding me that the little romantic gestures are just as important as the big ones.

To Christa, Pam, and the rest of the team at Bloom Books—Thank you for making this release such a special one for me. Not only did you help me bring my story to the next level, but you also helped share with all of the United States and Canada. Seeing my books in physical stores was an experience I will cherish forever.

Anna and the team at Piatkus—Thank you for helping me share my stories not only with the UK and the British Commonwealth, but also the world. It truly has been the coolest experience to catch Piatkus editions of the Dreamland Billionaires all over the world.

Kimberly, Joy, and everyone at Brower Literary & Management—I appreciate your commitment to helping my books find new readers and guiding me through this wild publishing world.

Nina, Kim, and everyone at Valentine PR—You've made the process of releasing a book a complete breeze. I can always count on you to not only make me feel like family but help organize everything for me.

Becca—Calling you when I was 75% into my TFP draft and unsure about the product was one of the best decisions I have made. I'm so grateful that Erica saved the day for me and connected us because I value not only your incredible editing feedback, but also your heart. I'm happy to have you in my corner, pushing me in all the best ways.

Erica—I can't believe we are closing out another series together. This one brought me a ton of laughs with you, from Henry Ford to Pizza Cal (and Matt's voice notes about *those scenes*). I am grateful to not only have you as an editor, but also a friend.

Sarah—Working with you on my books has been the best experience. You're someone I always look forward to emailing once I'm ready with a draft, knowing I can always count on you to give my manuscript and my characters your all.

Mary—To the day one, thank you. FOF calls you the goat for a reason, and it's not only because of your graphic design skills, but also your commitment to bringing my stories to life.

Jos—I can always count on you to be a text or call away. You never blinked at my chaotic thoughts, and I appreciate your friendship and constant support throughout this process.

Nura—I appreciate you for so many things. Your enthusiasm about my couples and reading every single draft of my books keeps me motivated to keep going, so thank you!

To my sensitivity readers—I appreciate you taking a chance on an early copy of my book and giving me feedback on how to improve the character's stories and backgrounds. Your recommendations really helped elevate the story.

Final Offer

To my beta readers—Thanks for being part of the process since the very first draft. This story came a long way all thanks to you and your incredible attention to details.

About the Author

Plagued with an overactive imagination, Lauren spends her free time reading and writing. Her dream is to travel to all the places she writes about. She enjoys writing about flawed yet relatable characters you can't help loving. She likes sharing fast-paced stories with angst, steam, and the emotional spectrum.

Her extra-curricular activities include watching YouTube, binging old episodes of *Parks and Rec*, and searching Yelp for new restaurants before choosing her trusted favorite. She works best after her morning coffee and will never deny a nap.